DELUCA

DELUCA

The Porn Star Brothers Series

L.J. DIVA

★ Royal Star Publishing ★

Chances is an imprint of Royal Star Publishing
www.royalstarpublishing.com.au

First edition paperback published in 2019
All Rights Reserved, Copyright ©L.J. Diva 2019

Trade Paperback ISBN: 978-0-6484864-0-4
Dust Jacket Hardcover ISBN: 978-1-922307-35-4
E-book ISBN: 978-1-925683-35-6
A catalogue record for this book is available from the National Library of
Australia.

Cover design: Royal Star Publishing and Odyssey Books
Cover photos: ManuelHurtado/Shutterstock.com
Typesetting in Minion Pro by Royal Star Publishing

Dedications

In 2014 a vague idea to write a book about a porn star came to me. In 2015 the idea brewed and grew and when my idol, Jackie Collins, passed away, the idea flourished with a vengeance.

Jackie Collins is the only inspiration in my life when it comes to writing. She had the passion, the brains, the ballsy rollicking attitude, and the kind of life that made me want to *be* her.

Without her, these books would not exist, for I would not have had the inspiration to follow in the same 'write whatever you want' league. Without her, I will continue trying to write the kind of books she wrote. Real, ballsy, and bonkbustingly good.

Jackie,

the Porn Star Brothers book series is dedicated to you as so many of my other books are. I thank you for the inspiration you have given me and hope you continue giving me, to go on and write more. I hope that you are well and having a good laugh wherever you are. I miss you and will continue doing so. Sometimes I think I feel you egging me on with my writing. Maybe that's true, and maybe it's just my rampant imagination; the same imagination that has given me the books I have written so far in my life. And sometimes, I really wished I could be you. You will forever be my idol and inspiration and I thank you.

RIP, Miss Jackie C.

And to the three Stefanovic brothers, Carlos, Pedro, and Tomas, without whom I would not have had names for my porn stars.

2008

"So, what do you think?" Tony asked the Stephanopouloses as he sat in their living room. "Will you come to Spain and help me clear out the family home?"

Carlos Stephanopoulos, world-famous film writer, director, and producer, sighed. "I'm not sure I want to visit that memory." Carlos had known Tony's father and grandmother in the '70s, and last saw him at his wedding to Vivian, but they'd never seen him, or his mother Connie, again. And thirty years after seeing Antonio at their wedding, his son, Tony, had walked into their lives as their son Cabot's date. Smack bang on the day of their thirtieth wedding anniversary. It brought back memories for Carlos that he didn't want, but he made the decision to tell Tony about his father's and grandparents' deaths. Tony hadn't taken it well, but then he *was* finding out the truth after thirty years.

Carlos glanced at his wife who was gently moving back and forth to calm their first grandson, Adam. Their daughter, Diana, had given birth barely a month earlier and Viv was in her glory. He saw the glow that holding a newborn had given her as she softly smiled down at her grandson. Her finger gently stroked his cheek, and he gurgled and cooed in her arms. "Viv?"

"Mmm?" She looked up dreamily, her peaches and cream complexion made dewy by the glow of grandmotherhood.

"Tony's asking us to go to Spain to see the family home," Carlos said.

"Oh, that's nice. Didn't you mention something about that last year?" She went back to staring at her grandson. At seventy-one, she had finally become a grandmother, and didn't know how long she had left to enjoy it. She'd been a late mother, having Diana at forty-one, and the boys at forty-five, and now, finally, she was a grandmother.

"Yes, I did, Mrs S," Tony said. "It's time to get the house done up for the summer rental period, but now that I know the truth about my father and grandparents, I want to go back and find their graves and finally take care of things properly. I've left everything in the vault. The lawyers may be looking after the estate, but I have to fix things first before the renters start coming."

Tony glanced at his boyfriend, Cabot. They'd met in October 2007 when he'd come to Mykonos searching for the man who'd sexually assaulted him, but instead found Cabot going by the name Darren Holbrook which was an experiment set up by his therapist. Cabot had been experiencing his own assault and had contracted HIV from it, as he'd done, and they found out it was the same guy who had assaulted them both. Cabot came clean about the experiment to him and who his family was. Apparently, Xanthe Metlos, the therapist, thought Cabot's fame and family name was getting in the way of him finding his true self, so she gave him a new identity. Not that Tony minded, his own therapist had suggested something similar with him to deal with his assault.

On the day of Cabot's parents' anniversary, he'd found out about his father and grandparents, finally knowing the truth about their deaths. Everything made sense. How the house he'd inherited was beautiful, but felt haunted, how the office was cold and forbidding. It was where his father had shot himself to death. The house felt weird to him, and he hadn't been back since the one and only time he'd visited when he'd inherited the entire DeLuca estate on his twenty-fifth birthday five years ago.

After finding Cabot and falling in love, he knew his life was with him, whether that was in Mykonos, New York, or London. Cabot and his twin brother Antonio, bizarrely named after his father too as the twins were named after dead friends of their parents, were models that travelled the world and spent many years in New York, but after contracting HIV, Cabot changed on his journey to finding himself and had decided to model part-time only, which suited his brother as they were a package deal. They still modelled for *Haus of Stefan*, their sister and cousin's fashion house. Diana, being a model and Alena, a mega-famous singer, had turned their love of fashion into a brand and all of them modelled for it. But Cabot wanted more out of life, and had taken up his uncles' cause of talking about HIV and AIDS and being a campaigner.

Tony had agreed wholeheartedly and was by his side one hundred percent. He also had no problems with Cabot wanting to help out at Tomas and Roger's AIDS care home in Miami. And this year, Cabot was talking about following in Tomas and Roger's footsteps even more, by having them become trained dieticians and nutritionists, so they could keep their health in check. And he vaguely remembered something about becoming personal trainers. All of that was on top of Cabot's half share in *The Mykonos Assault and HIV/AIDS Support Centre* he'd set up with his cousin Alexis the year before, after she too had been assaulted.

Six foot, blue-eyed, golden-brown Cabot was gorgeous, in *and* out of clothes. They hadn't been intimate until Christmas after a long stern talking to from Xanthe and AIDS specialists and honorary family members, doctors Dan Ardent and Derek Blaine. They had come clean about the number of partners they'd had, what STDs they'd dealt with, and what inhibitors they were taking. Dan and Derek gave them the all-clear physically, Xanthe mentally, and at Christmas, they had made love for the first time and hadn't stopped since. Staying with Tomas and Roger was a bit awkward, but since they were all gay, it didn't really impact on anyone. They were definitely going to have to find themselves their own place now since he'd decided to stay on Mykonos permanently.

"Fix things how?" Cabot asked from beside his father on the couch in his childhood home. He gazed lovingly at Tony, his lover of six months.

Tony smiled softly, and wrapped his legs around his boyfriend's from the easy chair beside the couch and played footsies. "I want to find their graves. Find where they're buried. Maybe put a headstone on. But I don't know." He cast his greeny-hazel eyes down. "I don't want to live there, ever, so I'm not sure about leaving them there. No one will want the place with their graves on the property, and since I don't want to be there, then I don't have them with me, and that's not fair either."

"Have you thought about cremation?" Viv asked. "If you don't want the house, then find them, cremate them, and sell the place off. But clearly, Antonio wanted you to inherit the estate. He set everything up for you."

"But what's the point in that?" Tony asked. "That's *their* life. I never grew up there, Dad came to England to be with us, then went back to Spain when his father died. He never came back. Next thing I know, Mum's crying and looking at paperwork, and telling me Dada's never coming back." He saddened at the memories, the pain twanging in his heart. "He never came back, I never saw him again. I was two years old and I never saw my father again."

"Naw, Tony," Cabot murmured softly, realising just how lucky he was to still have two parents who loved him. "I'm sorry."

Tony's lips turned up a little at the corners. "Thanks, Cabot. So am I. I'll never know my father, and my mother's passed, so I only have half-siblings and they don't care except for what they can get out of me. All of my immediate blood family is gone." Sighing deeply, he released himself of the pain. "So…what do I do about it?"

"I didn't know your mother had passed," Cabot said. "You've never mentioned it." His hand slid over the couch arm and onto Tony's, squeezing gently.

Tony shrugged. "It happened a few years back. I'm okay with it, but I don't talk about it because it makes everything too final. Too…" He struggled for the words. "Finished, over. My family's gone. That's how come I stayed for Christmas and New Year. Because I had nothing immediate to go back for."

"I could go back with you," Cabot said, weaving his fingers in and out of Tony's. "We could holiday there this summer. After Spain maybe? I don't think Antonio and I have *a lot* of jobs on, so we might have a couple of months."

Tony's lush lips moved up into a smile. "That would be nice. I can show you where I grew up."

Cabot matched the smile. "That *would* be nice. So, back to the matter of your house. What do you want to do?"

Another sigh. "I don't know. I don't want to live in it. I don't know if I want to keep it. I have no children to hand it down to. So…there's no one after me for it to go to. I guess Dad figured he and Mum would have more kids, or that *I'd* grow up to have kids, but he probably never figured I'd turn out gay like his father."

"Not that that's a bad thing." Viv smiled at her potential son-in-law. "If you weren't gay, you wouldn't have met Cabot and made him a better person."

Tony's smile brightened and Cabot blushed. "You're right, Mrs S, but still, I won't be having kids of my own, and I doubt I'll be able to adopt any unless they were HIV positive too. That's a long way off at this time, and I'm already thirty this year. I've had the estate almost five years now, and after everything that's happened in the last two, it's made me realise that life is precious and I have no family in England, except for my grandparents who are awesome, and some aunts and cousins, and I definitely don't have family in Spain. So, except for a holiday home, I have nothing. There's nothing to make me go there. Nothing to make me stay. I can pack up what's in the vault and keep that, but everything else is of no consequence."

"What's left in the vault compared to the house?" Carlos asked.

"Well, the house is full of antiques and furniture that I have no real need for. All old-fashioned and heavy, and tonnes of my grandfather's memorabilia. The vault contained photos, certain prints, family heirlooms, money, jewellery, collections. I left most of it there, just kept a few photos. I couldn't take it, didn't want to. Too much heartache to deal with. I haven't been there in five years, but now that I'm turning thirty this year, and have Cabot and your family, it makes me want to do something about mine. So…" Thoughts slid through his mind. "I think it's time to deal with it and get it over and done with."

"And you want us to come with you," Viv said. "I know you mentioned it before, but now that Adam is here I'm not sure I want to leave." Bending down, she left a soft kiss on his forehead and got a gurgle in return.

"He's fine, Viv," Carlos said. "He's a healthy one month old, and Diana has everything under control. And then there's Angie and Mama if need be."

"But Diana's a new mother and needs me," Viv replied. "Just as your mother helped out Angie and me thirty years ago, I want to be here for Diana now."

"And Diana's doing fine," Carlos soothed. "It's only for a week or two, and we never did send off Connie and Antonio. We didn't know for a month they had passed away. We owe it to them."

Frowning, she gazed at him. "Don't guilt me into this. I was heartbroken as much as you were, but they've been gone for twenty-seven years."

"It doesn't mean we can't pop over to Spain for a week or two, just to pay tribute to them," Carlos told her. He was just as guilt-ridden as he had been in 1981 when he'd found out they'd killed themselves. He could have warned Connie that Stephano had male lovers and multiple STDs, plus the potentially fatal gay plague. But his family had warned him off calling, and so Connie ended up with STDs and HIV. She killed herself because of the heartbreak and shame of having a gay husband who was full of STDs. Antonio killed himself from the shame of all of it and left his son behind. And that cut Carlos to the core every goddamn day since, and Viv knew it.

She saw his forlorn expression and felt the burden he did. "You really want to go?"

"Yes." His eyes pleaded.

Feeling the emotional pull from her husband's pain compete with the emotional pull of her new grandson, she asked, "How long would we be gone for?"

"A week, two tops," Tony said. "I want to find their graves and clear out the vault. That shouldn't take long. I can have it packed up and sent here to sort out later. But I want to do something about their graves, give them headstones, or cremate them. I don't know. I'm hoping that I'll know what to do when the time comes. When I find them and see where they've been buried, I'm hoping I'll know whether to leave them, or remove them. Maybe if I cremate them, I'll sprinkle half of the ashes, and keep the other half. They'll always be there, but I'll have them too. Then if I ever sell the place, their souls will still be there."

"Their souls are there anyway," Viv murmured. "Connie and Antonio have been there for twenty-seven years. They'll stay there regardless."

"Maybe," Tony replied. "Or maybe they're waiting for me to return and do something. Maybe they want me to take charge and clear the air. Maybe I should get some sort of exorcist in to exorcise the air and grounds, to make it not feel so haunted."

"Maybe," Cabot said. "It could only help. If it feels haunted, then maybe it's time for their spirits to be set free."

*****

They discussed it further over dinner that night as they all sat around the tables in Jenny Stephanopoulos's home. The whole family always gathered for dinners and Sunday lunch with the matriarch and patriarch of the Stephanopoulos family. If it weren't for Australian born Jenny, and her Greek-born husband Spiros, the family would not be as close as they were, nor have the family businesses and careers they had.

"I think it's a wonderful idea," Jenny said as she sliced through her lamb cutlet. "Maybe you can finally put it all to rest." She knew full well the guilt Carlos carried around with him and felt partially responsible for it. She had convinced him to say nothing, because it was none of the family's business, and upon finding out about Connie and Antonio's deaths, had not only felt her son's burden, but her own. And it was the one thing she continually convinced Carlos not to tell Tony; that Carlos had not warned Connie about her husband's diseases. After all, what good would it do, especially all these years later?

"So do I, Mrs S," Tony agreed. "I'd like to take Cabot there anyway, but since Mr and Mrs S knew my father and grandmother, I thought they'd like to come along. Antonio, too."

"Me!?" Antonio looked up in surprise from across the kids' table. He was sitting opposite Tony who had Cabot to his left. "Why would you need me to come? You've got Cabot." He watched Tony's twinkling exotic green eyes. He'd never been sure about the whole relationship between Tony and his brother. He'd been with his brother for twenty-five years, living, working, breathing the same air together. It had just been them. The Stefan twins, Steele and Phoenix, taking on the world. But after Cabot contracted HIV and tried to kill himself, and Antonio had saved him from jumping off the Brooklyn Bridge in New York last year, Cabot had been a changed person since coming home to Mykonos in August to deal with it.

And Antonio finally had the space to breathe on his own. But when Cabot met Tony, his jealousy arose and suddenly he'd felt like an outcast in his brother's life. Once Cabot made decisions about his career and talked things over with him and Tony, it all settled down. They were still brothers, still twins, and would still work together. Just not as frequently. He had nothing to fear from Tony. Especially since he'd decided to stay on Mykonos.

"Because you're his brother," Tony replied. "Since being with him, *his* family has become *my* family, and you'll be my brother-in-law one day. So, why shouldn't you come?"

Cabot heard the words brother-in-law and choked on his lamb. His blue eyes widened, taking in the wide-eyed surprised faces of his cousins around him, and his aunt, uncles and parents at the other table. He swallowed and looked at everyone in a panic. Tony had never mentioned anything about getting married.

The rest of the house was quiet as they all stopped eating and talking to stare in their direction.

Antonio eyed Cabot's expressions and smirked over his beer glass. "Clearly, you haven't discussed *that* with Cabot yet."

Tony smiled brightly. "No, but I'll get around to it one day." He glanced at a very red Cabot. "It *will* happen."

Cabot folded in on himself, unable to look at anyone, embarrassed and excited, and quickly shoved food into his mouth for something to do, so he didn't have to say anything.

Jenny smiled; things were finally happening for Cabot, and she was glad he had found someone outside of Antonio to be in his life. And glad that Antonio finally had the freedom to get a life.

Tomas and Roger had looked over their shoulders at the boys. Now they smiled at each other and Roger slid an arm around his husband and kissed him on the cheek. Tomas smiled and went back to eating.

Carlos glanced at Viv and she raised her brows back. He was unsure of what to say. While he had accepted Tony in Cabot's life, and hence the family's life, he wasn't sure marriage was the next best thing for either of them. Diana was busy with Adam, Antonio was still reserved, and so was he. And he knew Viv adored Tony, but... He swigged back his beer and glanced from Tony and Cabot to his wife. She was smiling brightly, happy that Cabot was back to normal and in love with one person instead of the whole male population of the entire planet.

Jenny glanced at the adults at the dining table. Pedro and Angie were to her right with Carlos, Viv, Diana and baby Adam beside them. With Diana giving birth in April, fortunately, they had finished the house she lived in before the next generation came into the world. She *had* shared the house below Carlos and Viv's with Alena, but Alena had to move out so Charles could move in. They redecorated, did up a nursery, and had Charles's belongings packed up and shipped in from New York. And he was back to being fit and well after the traumatic experience he'd suffered last year.

Charles was opposite Diana, with Simon and Deidre Dencott, Roger's long lost son and daughter-in-law, next to him. They had only come into the family last Thanksgiving after a DNA test proved Simon *was indeed* Roger's son by an old co-star Roger had done pornos with in the mid-'70s. Roger and Tomas were next to them on Jenny's left. All were smiling at Tony's declaration.

"So, looks like you'll all be going then," Jenny continued.

"It's also your birthday and anniversary this month, Mama. We don't want to be away for that," Carlos reminded her.

"Neither do we," Antonio added from the second table. Looking over his shoulder, he added, "We missed everyone's last year and don't want to miss anyone's again."

"We can go and be back by then," Tony pushed on, desperately wanting his new family to go with him. "It will only be a week or two, if that. We can be back for the next celebration. When is it?"

"The twenty-second of May," Antonio told him. "We celebrate Grandma's birthday, and her and Grandpa's anniversary, on the day between the dates. Then Alena and Diana are thirty in June, Grandpa's eighty-three in July, and Cabot and I are twenty-six in July."

"And I'm thirty in August," Tony added.

"Most of us are in the first half of the year," Dom said from beside Antonio. "It gets awful busy with parties and presents." He'd had his birthday a month earlier in April and turned twenty-five, and was in the process of coming up with a business to use his trust fund for.

"Yes, so it's all over by July with us." Cabot finally spoke up. "Then the anniversaries are in November, with Thanksgiving, and it all starts again." He noticed Alexis and Alena still trading glances at each other and then glancing at him. He pulled a face at them and finished off the last of his lamb.

"I'd better write them all down in my diary so I can keep up," Tony said. "But getting back to Spain. We can leave in a few days, and if we're there too long then you guys can fly home for the parties then fly back. I don't want you missing out on things on my account. But I would like you to see it since you knew my family. And if I end up selling it, or something, at least you can say you've been there to say goodbye."

Viv heard his words and glanced at Carlos who stared back. The adults knew the story, and watched them trade silent remarks back and forth with their eyes and facial expressions.

"I *would* like to go," Viv finally said. "But I don't want to leave Diana and Adam. He's barely a month old."

"Oh, Mama, don't be silly," Diana said. Diana Villiers Stephanopolous

Kensington was the eldest grandchild, and at twenty-nine had finally given birth to her first child. She and Charles had quietly married at Christmas in a small ceremony, making it all legal before their son had come. She'd been on a break from modelling since November, and planned to move her life in a new direction once she turned thirty. Now that she had a husband and child, she was able to sit at the adults' table when there was room. "We'll be just fine for a couple of weeks. We've got Grandma and Aunt Angie to help, along with his cousins, and I'm not working yet, so you can take time out and go to Spain. We'll be fine. In fact, I wish *we* could go to Spain. It's been quite some time since I visited."

"Are you sure?" Viv fretted. "I don't want to miss a single minute with Adam. Everything's come too late for me. I'm seventy-one for goodness sakes, and just become a grandmother. I want to live and see and breathe every moment with you both."

Diana smiled, mildly amused. "We'll be here when you get back. You can't stop living your life because your grandchildren start coming along."

"I know, I know," Viv told her. "But I've had a full life and lived so much. I'm old, and I don't know how long I have left, and I want to spend every moment with my grandbaby while I can."

"Mama," Diana chastised. "You *are not* old, and Adam will be here when you get back. It's only a week or two."

"I know, but even a week seems too long," Viv replied. "It just seems like yesterday I was having you, and you were in my arms and I didn't let you go." Smiling at the memories, she lovingly looked at her daughter, the spitting image of her when she was that age. "You were such an amazing baby. Vocal like your father, but a beautiful, amazing baby, and I was so proud and happy to have you."

"Aw, Mama, that's so sweet, but really, go to Spain and put your burdens to rest," Diana told her, squeezing her hand. "Go. To. Spain!"

Viv sighed. "I want to…I do, but—"

"Go. To. Spain," Diana repeated.

"Oh." Blushing, Viv gazed down at her grandson and knew he'd be fine with all of the family to look after him and Diana. "All right."

*****

Tony and the Stephanopouloses stepped off the family's private jet into the beautiful spring air of Madrid. It was the first week of May, and only two days after they'd decided to come. In a flurry of packing, getting their passports and legal papers together, they had flown in for a one to two-week stay. After booking two cars at the airport rental depot, and consulting maps, they were on their way north-west. They could take the highway straight to the town where Stephano had built his luxury escape. Because Madrid was inland and not near the beach, he'd wanted a water view, and found it in Manzanares el Real.

An hour later they made their way up the winding driveway of the estate and pulled to a stop in the circular driveway. Tony didn't want to pull up to the door because he knew his grandmother had thrown herself from the turret on the left and landed in the driveway. He didn't want to drive over her. Parking under shady trees, Tony and Cabot alighted and stood staring while Carlos, Viv and Antonio pulled in behind, shaded from the midday sun.

"Oh," Viv murmured. "Just as I remember it." Her eyes took in every detail of the palatial three storey home. A beautiful marble statue of a bull and bullfighter surrounded by a fountain stood proudly in front of the home surrounded by the circular drive. It represented Stephano at the height of his bullfighting career. The home was a light terracotta colour with dark wood beams holding up the front entrance way and each floor's balconies. The turret, which was an old bell tower, was to their left on the corner. That was where Connie had thrown herself from to land on the cobblestone steps and driveway. The trees were thick and lush and surrounded them and the house, with its terraces along each side. It was imposing, beautiful, forbidding...and haunted.

"Tony," Cabot muttered standing by his lover's side. He saw the pain etched on his face as well as his parents', and his heart went out to all of them.

"She died here," Tony barely said. "She died here." He was trying to figure out exactly where his grandmother would have landed after throwing herself from the turret. Slowly moving towards the spot, he stood where he thought she would have fallen, and felt an icy chill move up his spine. "Grandma?" he whispered and closed his eyes for a moment.

The others had wandered after him and stood silently by. Viv made the cross symbol even though she wasn't religious, and Carlos squeezed his eyes shut at the pain he'd caused by not telling Connie about her husband.

Antonio stood back, having his own weird feelings. The man who'd shot himself in the office was the man he was named after. As if *that* didn't have its own burdens.

Tony shuddered. "Is…this where…?" He let it trail off.

"Possibly," Carlos replied quietly. "We never saw photos, never knew exactly where." His breath was being forced out of him by his chest constricting, and his chest was constricting because of his guilt.

A long whoosh of air left Tony. "Well, we'll have to do something. A small ceremony, light some candles, throw flowers. Something."

"We will," Cabot murmured, standing beside him and rubbing his back. "We will."

"But for now," Tony breathed in and let out a sigh, "Let me show you my family's villa; one only the wealthy, or hard working, could afford. It's called *Mi Amor Mi Corazon*. That's Spanish for *my love my heart*." He flashed a small smile at Cabot, who blushed, then led them to the shaded front entrance and pulled the key from his pocket. "My grandfather clearly wanted the best his money could afford, and he found this place and restored it. It brought a lot of money to the community when he did that. He used the companies from the local town so everyone could make money. The estate agent told me it took exactly one year to do." He opened the door and ushered them into the cool darkness.

"Oh…it's just how I remember it," Viv said, eagerly looking around. "Beautiful, cool, very Spanish."

"Well, I've only been here once." Tony shoved his hands into his jeans pockets, and stood beside them as they all looked at the imposing dark wood accents and furniture, and deep terracotta floor tiles. The staircase moved up the centre of the house across all three floors, making the entrance way huge. Hallways on either side led to the back of the house, and there were rooms off the entrance and hallways.

"It looks exactly the same as when I visited in the '70s," Viv replied. "Nothing has changed, and I like that. But it's also…a little creepy. As if I've been transported back in time." She gazed around and smiled at the melancholic memories. "Connie would come waltzing down the stairs and welcome you into her home and party. And her parties were extravagant. Lots of models, TV stars, movie stars, directors, producers, musicians, other bullfighters. The parties would take up the whole house, and only those of us who were their best friends got to stay in a guest room on the first floor. Connie and Stephano, along with Antonio, had the second floor. Their bedroom had the bell tower attached." She breathed in shakily and looked at her future son-in-law with tear-filled eyes. "I am so sorry."

He smiled sadly. "Thank you, Mrs S. I think your stories will help fill a hole in me. I have no idea about their life before me. I had never been here until five years ago. I never grew up here, never visited, so I have nothing of them. Have heard nothing *about* them. So your stories will be most helpful. Let me show you around." He led them to the left side of the house that contained an impressive formal lounge room which moved into an even more impressive dining room followed by a kitchen. Stairs led down to an open and spacious living/lounge/party area that ran across the whole length of the house, with several seating and eating areas, and floor-to-ceiling windows and bi-fold doors leading to a terrace covered in vines for shade. A huge barbeque and eating area was to the right, and a lounge area to the left. Marble statues and railings ran around the terrace which led down another level to the pool, which had an image of a bull and bullfighter on the bottom in coloured tiles. Down below that was another level of lawn, and in the near distance, the picturesque lake that Manzanares el Real sat on. Trees surrounded the estate all burgeoning with green leafy branches. Olive, lemon, and orange trees grew off to the right, with several buildings way behind them on the level of the pool and lawn. A forest grew to the left.

"Wow." Cabot stared open-mouthed. "This is…"

"Beautiful," Antonio finished, gobsmacked by what he saw.

"And it's still as breathtaking as ever," Viv added, and more memories came flooding back. "The times we partied out here, it's still exactly the same."

"I…*am* impressed," Carlos muttered as his eyes took everything in. "Antonio never mentioned growing up in a place like this. He used to talk more about his parents' separation than anything, except for how many girls he could get."

"I guess my grandparents' separation had an effect on him," Tony said and gazed over the view. "But this place *is* beautiful."

Viv felt the rumblings inside her and her body started to collapse. She grasped the marble railing in front as they stood overlooking the pool and its stunning picture inlay.

"Viv." Carlos quickly grabbed her. "You okay?"

"Mama." The twins dashed forward.

"No," she barely whispered, choking back the tears. "Too many memories."

Carlos picked her up as she fully collapsed and carried her to a lounge on the terrace.

"I'll get some water." Tony ran inside and found the fridge fully stocked, so he brought out a glass of chilled juice instead, and saw the family crowding around in worry. "The fridge is full of food. Maybe you need to eat something. It's quite warm today."

Sipping the chilled juice, she felt better. "Maybe. It's just…" Her mind wandered off. "So many memories…"

Carlos was beside her, a protective arm around her shaking shoulders, a hand on the glass that she couldn't keep a hold of. "It's too much of a shock."

"Yes," she murmured, seeing the concerned expressions on her sons' and husband's faces. The boys were kneeling before her, rubbing her wrists to get her blood going. "The house, the grounds, it's all exactly the same, as if I'm still in the '70s. The furnishings, the furniture placement. *Nothing* has changed in thirty years."

"Probably how my family wanted it," Tony said from a nearby chair. Leaning forward, he looked on in concern. "The house had been shut up except for an occasional cleaner, gardener and maintenance crew that kept it from falling apart until I inherited it. It sat with no one in it until then, when it started being rented out. Their graves are never mentioned for fear of graverobbers. I'm surprised it hasn't been broken into in all these years."

"Maybe people are too scared to," Antonio said as his eyes darted around. "There's a feeling." Seeing his mother was better, he got to his feet and sat on the couch arm.

"Yes, there is," Tony agreed. "I felt it the last time I was here; I feel it now. Spirits at unrest. Waiting…" His eyes flicked over to the forest, dense and lush and green. It was calling to him…

"I think we should eat because I'm starving," Cabot said, trying to lighten the mood. "We can have a nice lunch, and then empty out the vault this afternoon to get that over and done with."

"The vault's in the office," Tony told him, dread creeping into his stomach. "Where Dad…"

"We'll be there with you, Tony," Viv said, feeling much better. "You have us here to help you. We can air the office out, and get some fresh air in there. That might help. And I'm sure that if Antonio *is* still here, he'd want you to get the things from the vault, so you have to go in. The boys can carry everything out and put it in the back living area, and once it's cleared out, you can lock it up and never set foot back in that room."

Tony sighed. "Yeah, I guess…it's just…that room feels cold. Like… he's…"

"Still there," Carlos finished, his heart on the verge of breaking for the billionth time in twenty-seven years.

"Yeah." Tony shook his head. "I can't think about it now. Why don't us boys get our luggage and put the cars away, and maybe, if you don't mind, Mrs S, you and Mr S could whip up some lunch."

Viv smiled indulgently. "Of course we can. It's the least we can do since you've let us stay here." While she and Carlos went to prepare lunch, the boys gathered the luggage and Tony gave them a room each on the first floor. They put the cars in the garage on the pool level, and walked up through the back of the house, just as Carlos set a huge tray of food on the terrace table.

"I thought we'd eat out here." Viv carried out a jug of icy drink and glasses and set them on the table. "Antonio, can you run in for the plates? They're on a tray in the kitchen."

Antonio retrieved the tray, and they sat down to filling sandwiches full of succulent meats, cheeses, and salad vegetables. Dessert was berry flavoured yoghurts and ice cream. Once they were sated, talk turned once more to the office.

"I really don't want to go in there," Tony said. "It's cold and creepy."

"Did anything happen when you went in with the estate agent?" Antonio asked, sipping his lemon drink.

"No." Tony shook his head as he thought back. "It just felt cold and weird. *He* certainly didn't tell me my father had shot himself in that room. He didn't even tell me how Grandma and Grandpa had died. I didn't find that out until your parents' anniversary last year." Looking at his future in-laws, he added, "No one had ever told me until that day. Mum didn't know, and the lawyer and estate agents either didn't know, *or* wouldn't tell me, but you'd think after all those years, *one of them* would have said something. But no, no one did. Until I met the two of you."

The guilt settled over Carlos like a thick smothering blanket. "I really wish I could have done something to prevent this, Tony. You don't deserve to lose all of your family within three months of each other. And through their own hand. That's not fair on you."

"What could *you* have done?" Tony asked. "From all account of things, they were headstrong people who did what they wanted and to hell with anyone else, regardless of who that person was. If me being alive couldn't stop my father killing himself, or my grandmother killing herself, then what could you have done?" The pain had eaten away at him since he'd heard the story.

"I don't know." Carlos resigned himself to it. "I could have called more. Wrote more. We had the odd letter from Connie about you. But we basically lost touch after the wedding. I didn't see your father again, and I didn't see your grandmother since just before that. I guess we all got busy. Us in New York, your father in England with your mother and you. At least you had that time. At least you have photos. I don't even have that except for the wedding video. Oh, God." Sighing, he sat back in his chair. "I really wish I could have done something."

"Unless you knew what my grandfather was up to and did nothing about it, I have no idea what you *could* have done," Tony told him. "So please, stop feeling guilty." Standing, he cleared the dishes, and only Cabot and Antonio saw the guilt-riddled look their parents gave each other.

"You two okay?" Cabot asked as he placed glasses on the drinks tray.

"We could have done something," Carlos whispered before shoving his chair back and taking off down the stairs that led to the pool and lawn.

"He really shouldn't feel guilty," Tony said to Viv as she stood to follow. "It's not his fault."

"That doesn't stop it, though," Viv tearily said and dashed after her husband.

With a sigh, Antonio got to his feet. "Guess we're on clean-up duty." He eyed his brother and gathered the plates and cutlery that was left, and each carried a tray into the kitchen and cleaned up.

"I need to freshen up," Cabot said as he hung the tea towel up. "Back in a minute." He walked out of the room and Tony followed. They went up to the bathroom and Cabot took a leak while Tony pulled the family album and a few photos from his bag. They were all he had of his father with him and his mother. And one photo had another couple, a dark curly-haired older woman, and a silver-grey distinguished man he knew to be his grandparents. It was taken on his second birthday.

"What'ch'ya lookin' at?" Cabot came up and slid his arms around Tony's waist. "Is that you?"

"Yeah. My second birthday. These are my grandparents, Connie and Stephano DeLuca. And this one," he shuffled the pack, "is my dad." He showed Cabot an old Polaroid of him, his father and mother.

"Wow, you look so much like him." Cabot gently took the photo and peered closely at it. "They looked happy."

"Yeah, Mum said they were," Tony said. "They met in Mykonos and he followed her, moving to London after your parents' wedding. They had nearly three years together. Mum said she was so happy. And then when he found out about his father, he told her he had to go home. She understood, but he…never came back. And *that* she didn't understand. The estate paid for child support and an allowance that she got, but it didn't make up for the fact he was dead and I didn't have my father."

"Oh, Tony, I'm so sorry." Cabot handed the photo back and wrapped his arms around his lover. He couldn't imagine losing his parents, let alone a partner or child. Not that he'd be having one now. Not being HIV positive. "I'm so sorry, Tony."

"So am I," Tony murmured, staring solemnly at the photo. "So am I."

"I'll leave you to freshen up," Cabot said, kissing him on the cheek. "Take your time if you need to. I'll go and find Antonio."

"Okay, see you in a bit." Tony watched the door close behind Cabot and burst into tears.

"Antonio," Cabot called as he wandered downstairs and back out to the terrace. He found his brother looking down over the balcony at something. "Hey, Tone, what'ch'ya lookin' at?" He got to the railing. "Hey, it's Mama and Papa. We should go—"

Antonio's hand snaked out and grabbed Cabot's arm. "Leave them, they need space." He pulled Cabot back beside him, his eyes never leaving his parents.

"What do you *mean* they need space?" Cabot frowned, puzzled by Antonio's words. He gazed down to the lawn, following Antonio's intense stare, and saw his father hunched over, head in hands, and his mother comforting him. They were sitting on a marble bench by the pool. "What's going on?"

"He's angry because he's full of guilt," Antonio muttered, his eyes boring into his parents' backs. "Did you see the way he was behaving before? The look he and Mama gave each other when Tony said that unless they knew what his grandfather was up to and did nothing. The guilt was all over Papa's face."

"But what *could* he have done?" Cabot asked, leaning close to his brother as they stared down at their parents.

"Called, written," Antonio said. "If they *knew* they could have done something."

"But if they weren't listened to, or believed?" Cabot went on. "If Tony's family were as headstrong as he said, why would they listen to what Papa had to say?"

"I don't know," Antonio replied. "I don't know, Cabot. Even if he knew something and called up, or wrote a letter, that would be no guarantee Connie, *or* Antonio, would have listened. But at least he would have tried."

"And then he'd feel guilty for not trying hard enough," Cabot said, watching his father wipe his face and his mother rub his back.

"He already feels that guilt. He didn't try hard enough. I wonder who stopped him?" Antonio muttered more to himself.

"Stopped him from what?" Cabot asked, curious as to why his brother was so fascinated by it all.

"Stopped him from telling Connie and Antonio," Antonio replied. It was weird talking about a man he was named after and had never met. And he was now in his house with his son of the same name.

"Who said anyone did?" Cabot murmured, glancing over his shoulder for Tony. "Who said anyone stopped him from telling them? But what *I* want to know is, how did *they* find out he was gay and had AIDS in the *first* place. I've seen the letter that Harry DeVille sent to Mama and Papa. Tony showed me. He told them Stephano had cancer and STDs and passed them on to Connie. And that he had been found up the ass of his male toy boy. But there was *nothing* about HIV or AIDS in that letter."

"Someone *had* to've stopped them." Antonio frowned at the question. "They *must* have found out in New York before 1980 when he died, and they were sent the letter. They *must* have known what he was doing to pass it on to his wife. Papa knew Connie intimately and took her money for it. Why didn't he call, or write? He should have told her if he knew, but he didn't, and that meant someone stopped him. And Mama knows all about it."

"All about what?" Tony asked from behind them. He'd seen them huddled together and staring over the balcony as he'd walked outside, and wondered what was so interesting.

The boys jumped and spun around. "Ah, Tony, you scared us." Cabot held a hand to his thumping chest.

"Sorry." Tony smiled at his lover. "Knows all about what?" he repeated, wondering what secrets they were keeping.

"The house and your family," Antonio covered for them. "Mama must know all about this house with the times she's been here. And can probably tell you a lot more about your grandmother."

"Yes, I hope so." Tony stepped over to the railing, stood between the twins to separate them as he still had a bit of jealousy at their closeness, slid his arm around Cabot's shoulders, and stared down at Carlos and Viv, watching them stand and stare across the view. "She must have some wonderful stories to tell."

"Oh, Viv, I don't know how much longer I can keep it in for," Carlos quietly wailed to his wife. "I feel so much guilt. Even now."

"Oh, Carlos," Viv murmured as she rubbed his back. "I feel guilty, too. I didn't expect Connie to ever kill herself. She and Harriet and I always had parties, and happy times, in the clubs and at their homes. I never saw any reason, or behaviour, to suspect she'd ever kill herself."

"Until she found out her dead husband was riddled with cancer and sexually transmitted diseases," Carlos muttered. "What in fuck's name would that have done to her?" Running a hand through his hair, he heaved a sigh from the pit of his stomach. "I *cannot* believe the guilt I still feel. It's just as powerful as the day Harry's letter arrived and we read it." Slumping onto the railing in front of him, he leaned heavily on his arms. "I can't believe how heavy it feels after all these years."

"If you told Tony, would that alleviate your guilt?" Viv asked. "Would telling him you knew about his grandfather and didn't warn Connie make you feel better?"

"I don't know." He stared down at the bushy land below them and followed it out to the lake. So calm, so peaceful. Unlike the guilt in his gut.

"If you had warned Connie, and she laughed in your face, would you feel better knowing you'd tried?"

"Yes." He looked at her. "That's my guilt, Viv. The fact that I knew and didn't even *try* to warn her."

"If Tony had never walked into our lives, how would your guilt feel?"

He thought a moment. "Not as heavy."

"Well, all I can say is, that we're here, and maybe it's time to alleviate your guilt."

"And how do I do that?"

"I don't know." She shrugged. "Talk to them, tell them you're sorry for never contacting them. Never telling them. If their spirits are still around, they may hear you."

"But at the end of the day, they're still dead, and Tony's without a father and grandmother because I said nothing," Carlos reminded her. Standing, he sighed. "I have no idea if my guilt will ever be alleviated unless I get it out in the open."

"Does that mean telling Tony?" she asked.

Carlos pondered for a moment. "Maybe."

After trudging back upstairs, they sat on the terrace and talked, deciding it was best to clean out the vault that afternoon to get it over and done with.

"I'll open the curtains and window to let light and air in," Viv said. "You open the vault, and then we'll pass it all out to the boys who can put it down in the living room for you to sort through. Once done, we'll lock it up again."

"I don't know, Mrs S." Tony breathed in and let it out slowly to calm himself. "Just knowing it's where he…" Choking, his hand flew to his mouth, and he glanced at the second floor. "The office is between their bedrooms on the second floor. I don't know if I can…"

"The estate agent, or lawyer, whoever it was that came here with you, had no problem taking you up there," Cabot said, warily eyeing the curtain covered windows. "Do visitors not use that room?"

"No one uses those rooms," Tony said. "That was the one thing I specifically requested. That those rooms are not used during rental season. The other was that everything be kept intact. That's why my grandfather's costumes and accolades are in glass cases in the entertainment room. It extends down the other side of the house off the hall and entrance. We haven't been in there yet."

"Well, why don't we start there?" Viv suggested. "We can work up to the top floor and you can show us the history of your family."

He nodded and swiped a hand over his face to remove his tears. "Okay, Mrs S, good idea." Leading them inside, he showed off glass case after glass case of his grandfather's matador costumes. There were ten in total, five down each side of the three-room entertainment suite. In between sat glass cases of photographs, awards, accolades, plaques, the key to the city, and newspaper clippings. It was a real archival room.

"Wow, Tony, all of this is awesome." Cabot's eyes were wide to take everything in. "It's like a museum."

"Yeah," Tony murmured, looking at one costume and reading the plaque at the bottom. "A real museum that I never grew up in. Never got to see. Never got to know. But my father did. Mum said he told her all about his life here, and planned on bringing me here one day so I could see it. But obviously, that didn't happen." Sadness washed over him, and a lone tear trickled down his cheek. "He could've chosen to come home to me and Mum. Be a family, raise me, maybe give me brothers and sisters. Brought us here to live and grow up like he did. But he didn't. He chose to leave us instead."

"Oh, Tony." Viv slid an arm around his shoulders. "I don't know how many times I can say I'm sorry until it makes it okay."

"It will never be okay, Mrs S," he replied, looking forlornly up from the plaque. "It will never be okay."

"No," she agreed. "I guess it never will be. Not for you." Taking a breath, she added, "Why don't we move on? This room is just as I remember it, always about Stephano DeLuca. A display of his prowess in the ring. Just like that bull fountain out the front, and the image in the bottom of the pool. It was *always* about him. Never about his wife or son. Just about him." She glanced around at the large portraits and advertising posters from his old fights. The room was all about

Stephano and Stephano alone. Back then it was magnificent. Now, it was just smothering.

"Let's move on, shall we?" Viv led the family out into the hall, and they walked upstairs where Tony showed her and Carlos their room for the duration of their stay.

"Oh, my goodness." She laughed lightly. "It's the same room Connie used to give me when I came and nothing has changed." The huge four-poster bed sat in the middle of the room against the wall opposite the door, with an armoire on either side. A small bathroom was through the door on the left, and the windows sat to the right, overlooking the terrace, pool, and lake views. "She always wanted me to have the room right below hers. And it still looks the same." Running her fingers along the cupboard beside the door, she wandered over to the window. "The view was always beautiful. Especially in summer and spring. The breeze wafted across the water and up the hill to the house. It was magnificent. You know there's fountain spouts in the pool?" Viv turned to her family. "At least there used to be in the '70s. Connie and I went skinny dipping one night when Stephano and Antonio weren't home. We put the fountains on, drank champagne, and swam naked."

"Viv!" Carlos raised a brow. "You saucy minx."

"Ew, Mama, no." Cabot screwed up his face and covered his ears.

Antonio stood by looking mildly amused, used to the dramatics of the family.

"Way to go, Mrs S." Tony grinned, then it slipped away. "They'd all be alive today. My father and grandmother if she didn't contract…"

"Antonio would be a few years older than me," Carlos reminisced. "Your grandmother would be in her eighties."

"And probably still skinny dipping," Viv said. "That was Connie. Colombian through and through. Loved to party, loved to love, loved to have it all." The burning anger slowly rose from the pit of her stomach. "She loved to do so much, why she would be bothered killing herself over that lecherous asshole, Stephano…" The anger made its way up her insides. "Why would she throw away her life on that no good son of a bitch?" The anger rose to her heart. "You stupid bloody woman! Have you got the keys, Tony?" The anger seethed within her and needed to come out.

"Ah, yes, Mrs S." He pulled a keyring from his pocket and displayed the three old-fashioned keys with big initials on top. "S for Stephano, A for Antonio, and O for office. There are others, but they're of no consequence."

"Give them to me. We're going up." Viv snatched the keys and stormed upstairs. "Connie, you bloody idiot. Are you here?" she yelled and inserted the key, cranking it to the left, and pushing open the huge wooden door to their bedroom.

"Viv?" Carlos asked from behind her. "What are you doing?"

"Connie," Viv screamed, fists clenched by her side, her anger spewing forth. "You bitch! *Where are you?* How *dare* you do this to us." Storming around the room, she flung open the curtains and windows to reveal a massive bedroom with an equally massive four-poster bed, and a bathtub under the window overlooking the front courtyard. She flung her arms out. "Connie, you come out here now and explain to us how you could do this to us. I'm waiting, Connie." Frenetically moving around the room, she saw everything was pristine. "How dare you leave your grandson. How dare you leave me." Her fist pummelled pillows on the bed and small spots of dust danced in the daylight filtering into the room. "And you were so goddamn gutless you had to throw yourself out of the fucking bell tower, you selfish, self-centred woman. You killed yourself over your stupid ass husband and left your only son and grandson alone. All because of Stephano fucking DeLuca." Pointing her finger, she stabbed it at an imaginary Connie. "You took your life for a sorry ass asshole like him. You stupid bloody woman." Twirling, she hurried past four stunned faces and across the dark wood landing to Antonio's door. Opening it, she did the same as his mother's room. Flung open the curtains and windows. "You selfish gutless coward, Antonio Stephano DeLuca. You selfish gutless coward. You left your son and wife to be with your dead mother and father. How stupid, idiotic, moronic, gutless, selfish could you fucking be?"

Once more, four stunned faces watched her storm around the

room, and Tony was in tears with Cabot comforting him.

Carlos's own anger was seething, and he wished he could do what Viv was doing. But something held him back. His guilt, maybe.

"Look what you've done, Antonio," Viv yelled at him. "You left your son alone and without his father, you selfish prick." Racing past the others, she unlocked the office and opened the curtains and windows. Spying the desk, she pummelled the thick chair behind it with her fists.

"This was your father's room, Tony," Cabot whispered after Carlos and Antonio had followed his mother. The two of them stood in the quiet solitude. "It was where he grew up."

Tony's watery eyes took everything in. The bed, the cupboards, the furnishings. He hadn't been in those rooms five years earlier, just the office. And he could feel him there. "He's here," he whispered.

"Yes, I guess he would be," Cabot continued in hushed tones. He spied something on one of the bedside cupboards. "Oh, look. Your family."

Tony slowly moved over to it and picked up the frame. "I saw the same one in Grandma's room. They're the only photos of them in the house. Except for what's left in the vault."

"Then maybe we'd better go and see what's in the vault," Cabot suggested.

Tony gently set the photo back in its place, and followed Cabot out of the bedroom to the office. He stayed in the doorway listening to Vivian take her anger out on his father. Pummelling the chair with her fists, kicking the desk with her espadrilles, and screaming at Connie for being so stupid.

Finally, Viv calmed down enough to see the four of them standing there. "Okay," she huffed, and flicked loose strands of hair out of the way. "Let's get the stuff out and we'll be done."

"You okay?" Carlos asked from the other side of the desk, knowing his wife had been holding in this pain for too damn long, just as he had.

She thought a moment and gazed around the room. "Better, but *not* okay because what *they* did was *not okay.*" Spying Tony over her husband's shoulder, she added, "Let's get this done, Tony. You ready?"

Reluctantly, he stepped into the room, and felt that the mood had changed slightly. Pushing on the hidden door in the wall to the side of the desk, it popped open, and he pulled it back to reveal a huge vault door. After quickly dialling the combination, he pulled it open with a creak. "It runs the length of the room, so it's a long one."

"Fine." Viv moved to his side. "Start getting everything out. Boys, you can take it out to the landing, you've got the tables and chairs to put it all on, or start using the floor. We'll take it downstairs later." She watched Tony carry out print after artwork after box for about half an hour before it was empty. "Make sure there's nothing left because if you aren't coming back here, it will be a waste."

He quickly searched each shelf and the floor and found nothing. "Finished." Walking into the office, he closed the vault door and locked it, then set the fake wall over it. Turning, he saw the desk and chair where his father had sat while writing out all of the papers for him, getting his lists in order, writing wills and trust fund papers. It was the desk where he found his father's old gun, pulled it out, put it to his head, and shot himself. The sob came from his gut.

"Tell him." Viv pointed to the chair. "Get your anger out on him whether he's here or not. That's where he sat. That's where he did the deed. That's where they found his body. Tell him what a horrible life you've had without him and Connie. Kick the shit out of him. Go on."

All the years of grief rose to the surface of never knowing his father and grandmother. It didn't matter if Stephano was dead, he was the cause of all this anyway. The reason he'd lost his father, the reason he'd lost his grandmother. "That bastard's the reason I lost you," he screamed, spit coming from his mouth. "I hate him. I hate Stephano fucking DeLuca for taking my family away from me. That bastard took my family." He swiftly kicked the side of the desk in a succession of rugby-style manoeuvres before slamming his hands down on the desk.

Viv heard a faint click, and looked down to see the very bottom of the desk had popped out a couple of inches. "Oh, a secret drawer." Bending down, she pulled it out and removed the papers. Feeling around inside, she found nothing else, and closed it back up.

Everyone gathered around the desk.

"How did that happen?" Cabot asked, excited by the mysterious events.

"I must have hit something when I kicked it," Tony replied, wiping his eyes with his t-shirt sleeve so he could look at the papers Viv had laid out on the desk. "What are they?"

"Blueprints for the estate, and this." Viv handed a long white envelope to Tony. On the front, in large looping handwriting, it said, *DeLuca Burial Plans.*

"Oh, my God, it can't be," Tony whispered, staring at the writing. "It can't be."

"Can't be what?" Antonio asked. "Come on, open it." With his hands on his hips, he was over the theatrics from Tony and his mother.

Tony opened the envelope and read the note aloud. *'Follow the long white hall to the disco ball, and where the tree is, bury us there, side by side, underneath, remove everything, and allow nature to overtake it all. Remove the ball, remove the hall, remove all trace of us'.*"

"What?" Carlos arched a brow. "That makes no sense."

"Why would he want to remove all trace of them?" Cabot asked. "That's not fair to you, Tony. It means you were never going to find them. Never see them again."

"The hell it does," Viv fumed. "I bet they didn't expect their heir to ever meet with people who knew them. I doubt Connie expected *her* grandson would meet *my* son and that we'd be here. That *I'd* be here again after '75." Sifting through the papers, she came across the architectural plans for an outdoor terrace. "Say hello to long white hall and disco ball. They were the nicknames Connie gave the white marble path that led into the woods to the white round marble dancing pavilion. We had such lovely summer dances there." Her eyes glazed over as she remembered. "The path led off the back terrace and through the woods until you came to a lovely round clearing, surrounded by marble statues and benches. It was beautiful in summer. Stephano or Connie would hire orchestras to play, and we'd drink champagne. But I didn't see the pathway." Spinning around to the window, she leaned out.

"Whoa, careful." Carlos rushed to her side to hold onto her.

"It's not there," she cried, looking off to her left. "The path is gone and the trees have grown."

"Where?" Tony was beside her, peering out of the window to the left.

"There." She pointed. "The path started between those two bull statues on the terrace railing. It led off between those two massive trees."

Tony pulled himself back in. "At least we have an idea where they're buried. The next step will be finding the place and getting professionals out here to clean it up. It's probably covered in ten feet of vines and debris. I'll have to check for a phone book, or ask the agent, or lawyer."

"They should be able to help," Cabot said. "But in the meantime, can we get out of this room? It's creepy with him watching us." He stared in disdain at all of the photographs on the wall of Tony's grandfather.

They gathered all the paperwork and walked out. It was another room dedicated to Stephano DeLuca and his prowess in the ring, and Tony didn't want anything from it. They made several trips to get everything downstairs and into the back living space.

Viv stood examining the artworks and paintings, and pointed to one. "You know, I've taken note of what's in the house, and none of that's as valuable as these paintings you've got. One like that cost a fortune at auction. And these statuettes." She picked up a one-foot high marble statue. "Go for a good million, or two. Your father knew his stuff to put all of this away for you. I'm surprised no one's stolen it all in twenty-seven years."

"So am I," Tony replied, looking over the lists of items. "Especially after my first visit when the lawyer saw everything. And you're right about those ten paintings. It says here they are the only paintings in the family worth anything. An investment by my grandparents. There's also the gold coin collection, a stamp collection, family jewellery, legal papers, the artworks, and several rare books. The note says all belonging to Stephano and Constance DeLuca." He flipped the page over. "Here's the first of my father's belongings. One signet ring, one ID bracelet, one necklace, one watch. A variety of family photos, but nothing else." Flipping to another page he read. "The personal family items include the house, land, and all within and on it. The bank account in trust, and personal items such as jewellery, pens, writing sets, etc." He scanned the list. "The house in London... What?" He quickly read the note about the home he grew up in belonging to the estate, and hence being his. It had been his since he inherited five years ago.

"You own your home in London?" Cabot asked. "The one you grew up in?"

Tony's eyes scanned the address for the house. "Yes. Bloody hell, it was bought for my parents, but was owned by the estate to be handed down." Stunned, he looked up at his lover. "I own my home in London." A gurgling laugh came out of him. "I own the house I grew up in."

"Is it a nice home?" Cabot was happy for his lover, but also knew that his ex-stepfather still lived there.

"Lovely," Tony replied. "At least, it was when I left. God knows what my ex-stepfather and his brats have done to it." He finished reading the list. "And there are photo albums which I already have."

"I don't think you have this one," Viv remarked and picked up a white album. "I found it buried under the books." Flipping it open, she gasped. "Oh, Tony, you don't have this one?" Handing it over, she prepared for tears.

Looking at the album, he saw the marriage certificate for his parents. His eyes homed in on the date. "May 1978... Jesus... May fourteen. That's thirty years ago." He looked at his in-laws. "Thirty years ago they got married, and now thirty years later they're both dead and I'm without either of them." Wiping away tears, he looked at the first photo. An 8x10 of his parents on their wedding day. "Oh, my God, I remember now. I used to see Mum looking through an album all the time after he was gone. I would take a peek and see these photos. She has the same ones." His finger gently touched his parents' faces. "But, I was young, saw the ring on her finger, knew I had a father, but once he never came home, things all changed. She cried a lot, twirled her ring a lot, looked at the album a lot." He flipped through the pages, smiling softly at each photo. "They looked happy, and there's Mum's sisters, and parents, and their friends. Mum's family isn't big, but they're lovely people." Coming to the last page he saw an 8x10 of his parents with both grandparents. "They're all so happy. Who'd have thought? I never knew what year they married." Swallowing the lump in his throat, he closed the album and glanced teary-eyed at the cover. "Mum would cry in May, and one day, in particular, she would cry all day and look at a white book. I think it's an album like this one, but I was never allowed to see it after that. I have no idea where it went, or if it's still at home. My ex-stepfather probably chucked it out along with the rest of her stuff when she died."

"Oh, that's horrible," Viv said. "You mean you have nothing of her?"

"Just the photos I have from the vault. She didn't really care about taking photos until my siblings came along ten years later. But my aunts and grandma did. I've never seen these." Looking at the album, he smiled. "My stepfather thinks he owns the place. Won't he get a shock when he finds out the house is in my name as a part of the DeLuca estate."

"What will you do?" Carlos asked.

Tony shrugged. "Go home when we're in London and raid the house for the albums, see if Mum's stuff is there. If he calls the cops, I'll have proof I own the house and have every right to be there. I'll find out what he's done with them." Sighing, he fell onto one of the sofas that wasn't burdened by family heirlooms, and looked at all they'd found. "I have no need for paintings and artwork, or coins and stamps. And I'm not sure about the books. Quite frankly, I don't care for their belongings, I just want my father's, *and* my father."

"I'm sure you can auction off everything you don't want," Viv told him. "The paintings will bring tens of millions...each."

"Where would I auction them off to?" Tony asked dazedly. "I'd have no idea how to go about that."

"Well, there's Christie's, Sotheby's, Bonhams, all have showrooms

33

in New York, or London," Viv replied. "I could contact them for you."

"Thanks, Mrs S. I guess I just have to figure out what I'm going to do with it all. I don't have kids to hand it down to."

"You might have, one day," Cabot wistfully said from beside him. "We might be able to adopt, or have a surrogate."

"We're positive, Cabot," Tony said. "I doubt they'd let us adopt kids."

With a nonchalant shrug of his shoulder, Cabot replied, "You don't know that. So think about it. What would you want to hand down to our children one day?" Sliding an arm through Tony's, he smiled encouragingly.

Tony smiled back. "Well, the artwork and paintings definitely don't matter. And I'm not sure about the coins, stamps and books. I'm not into those things. I doubt I need to keep them for the kids." Glancing over the boxes before him, he added, "The photos are important, and personal items, especially from my father."

"Like these?" Carlos asked as he held the open velvet box in his hand. He hadn't meant to, he was compelled to, as if something, or someone, was making him reach for it and open it. He rose from his seat and sat next to Tony to show him. "These are your father's. He used to tell me all about them when we met." Picking up a white gold signet ring with a bullhead insignia, green emerald eyes and a thick band, he lifted Tony's right hand and slid it on his ring finger. "Your father received this for his twenty-first birthday. He received it last because his fingers had finished growing. It has the DeLuca family symbol on it. The bull. Because of what Stephano was and did. Antonio joked that he could leave an imprint if he punched anybody, and it was a great knuckle duster. He often threatened to imprint my face because it was too pretty for him."

"Oh, please," Cabot grunted and rolled his eyes.

"Hey," Carlos jokingly snapped. "This pretty face helped make *that* pretty face of yours that Tony's fallen in love with. If it weren't for mine, *you* wouldn't have yours."

Cabot blushed and a small smile came to his lips. He nudged Tony, who smiled back and snuggled into his side.

"And this..." Carlos lifted the ID bracelet in white gold. "He received for his sixteenth birthday and wore it on his right wrist." He secured it around Tony's wrist and straightened it.

Tony traced his father's name with his finger, a soft smile coming to his lips, for it was also his name. His heart ached, his stomach clenched. This was his father's.

"And this necklace has the bull symbol. Antonio received it for his eighteenth birthday. He always complained about bulls being on everything, but realised it was his father's life and what had afforded him a luxurious upbringing." He clasped the chain around Tony's neck and adjusted the pendant. "It's the right length. The bracelet and ring are the right sizes. As though they were made for you."

"Or my father," Tony murmured, staring down at the pendant.

"Yes." A whisper of a smile crossed Carlos's lips. "And lucky last." He lifted the black leather banded white gold Cartier watch. "He got this for his twenty-fifth, not long before I met him. He'd been travelling since he was twenty-one, working in resorts on Ibiza, Italy, Crete, Greece. He only wore it on special occasions, like our wedding." The smile grew soft with remembrance and he buckled it on Tony's left wrist. "Your father would want you to have these. Even if you don't wear them, he did. He hated the symbol, but knowing they were from his parents made him proud to wear them. And he treasured them." He cupped Tony's face with his left hand. "He would have loved you so much. And the fact he did all of this showed that, regardless of the fact he knew he couldn't survive without his mother, he loved you. It just wasn't enough. So, he did what he could before he did what he did. I know it's hard. It's hard for us, too, but you have what you have of him, and we have a few memories of him and Connie."

"Well, *you* certainly have memories," Cabot muttered, glancing from his mother to his brother, thinking he would get a smile, or laugh in response.

"Not the time, Cabot," Antonio replied.

Cabot blushed and folded in on himself in embarrassment, seeing his mother's frown and his father's scowl.

Tony raised a brow and smiled. "Yes. I have all of this. But I want my father. I wanted him there to hold me and read to me, teach me football, take me to school." He deflated. "I didn't have that."

"And I'm so sorry that you didn't, Tony." Carlos pulled him into his arms. "None of this makes up for the loss you've had. But that's something you'll have to deal with inside yourself. You'll have to come to a decision about what you'll do that will suit your heart and your soul. None of us can tell you how to deal with it. It's something you'll just have to learn to do yourself. You'll have to deal with it in your own way, so that you can move on with your life. Antonio hasn't been here for twenty-seven years, and he's missed out on you, and you on him. It's not fair."

"No," Tony sobbed. "It's not."

"No," Carlos agreed, gently stroking his hair. "It's not."

After a few minutes of silent sobbing, they got up and started sorting the inheritance into piles. What to sell, what to keep, and what to donate to libraries, or museums. They sorted out papers and photographs. They raided the phone books for names of gardeners and masonry companies, but at the end of the day realised the lawyer and estate agent could probably help most. After organising for them to come the next day, they ate dinner on the terrace to watch the sunset and the twinkling lights of the town come on.

Retiring early, Tony and Cabot lay in bed, and with the bedside lamp on low, Tony shuffled through the photos of his father, studying his features as he had done a million times before. But it was different now. Now, he was back in the house, had been in his father's bedroom, the office, and found where they might be buried. With jetlag overtaking him, he placed the photos on the side cupboard, turned the lamp down, and settled back with Cabot in his arms. They kissed, fondled, and kissed some more before wrapping themselves around each other for sleep. They drifted off, but for Tony, it was anything *but* peaceful, with words and images of his father and grandparents floating through his mind.

1949

Stephano Antonopoulos DeLuca narrowed his eagle eyes and stared down his long pointed nose at the snarling beast before him. He held steady while the beast stomped a hoof, lowered its head, and aimed its horns right at him. He knew the slightest twitch, the slightest loss of concentration could make it the end of his career.

Staring the beast in the eye, he waited, his muscles tiring just as the beast's would be. But he couldn't flag, he couldn't relax. He had to be awake and on top of his game. And the game was nearly over.

The beast snorted and charged, aiming his horns for the creature provoking him, but the creature was good and deftly swung the cape away as he sidestepped him with a flourish. The beast stopped and shook his head. He was tired and dazed, confused as to why all the creatures around the ring were screaming at them. The noise altered his concentration and he heaved a sigh. This wasn't fun anymore. When he'd started, it had been, but now, he just felt old and worn out. Turning, he came face to face with the creature. He was young and good-looking, and dressed in a beautiful regal outfit. He did not know the colours, and would have loved to have seen them, but being colour blind, he had no comprehension of what colour was. Wearily, he pawed the ground and walked towards the creature. It was time. Time for this show to be over so he could get back to his pen for a rest and food.

Backing away slowly, Stephano's eyes never left the beast. He knew it had had enough and so had he. Watching the magnificent animal slowly lumber towards him, he held himself steady. The end was nigh, and it wouldn't be long.

The beast pawed the ground and snorted. He was done with this and wasn't interested anymore. So, with a sideways stare at the two-legged creature, he heaved his body to the ground and admitted defeat. The creatures around the ring screamed, clapped and cheered. If that was what he got for lying down on the job, he should have been doing it more often. He just wanted food and water and a good lie down.

Surprised by the bull's defeat, Stephano flung his arms into the air to claim victory, then flung his cape around in a few fancy manoeuvres to make the crowd scream more. With renewed energy, he pranced around the bull waving his cape before making a lap of honour around the ring. Kissing fans' hands, accepting roses that were flung at him, he waved and blew kisses, smiling like the prized matador he was. Stephano DeLuca was the champion bullfighter of Madrid. Of Spain. Of the world. And no one came close to him.

At twenty-eight, he was on top of the world *and* his game as the master bullfighter of the country. He'd come into this world in 1941 at the age of twenty, and just a short eight years later, had made his way, *all the way*, up the ladder to the prime position of matador, earning one million dollars a year for his talent. And the last year had been worth every cent. He'd taken out every fight, bought and renovated a Spanish estate outside of the city, maintained an apartment in Madrid, and lived the lavish lifestyle to which he'd grown *very* accustomed.

Moving around the ring, he was grabbed and kissed by men and women until he was stopped by one woman in particular. She grabbed his face with both hands and planted a kiss on his lips. There was an explosion in his pants as well as his chest, and his tongue delved into her mouth for an instant before he pulled back. She was beautiful, vivacious, and well bosomed. Her feisty expression dared him to kiss her again, her bosoms dared him the same. Black curls rioted on top of her head, and her brown eyes sparkled excitedly. Dressed in a red and black señorita dress, she slipped a piece of paper into his costume and melted back into the crowd.

Stunned, he tried to find her by hurrying around the ring, but could not. Taking a quick bow, he slipped out of the ring and down the long corridor back to his room. He dumped his cape on a chair, pulled his costume off and stood naked for all to see if they'd walked in. Spying the paper on the floor amidst the clothes, he picked it up and read off a phone number. *Mmm, could it be her?*

Weary after a long session, he showered, dressed, and went back to his apartment where he called the number on the paper he held in his hand.

"Hello?"

"Yes, hello. This is Stephano DeLuca. I was given this number to call."

"Yes, Señor, you were," Constance Philomena Stephanova Constinopolous purred down the line. "I slipped it into your costume."

"So, *you* were the one who kissed me?" Stephano smiled, remembering the explosiveness of it.

"Yes, Señor. I am. And I want more. Are you up for it?" Connie wound the phone cord around her finger as she remembered her ovaries exploding at the mere touch of Stephano DeLuca.

"Oh, I'm *definitely* up for it," Stephano told her. "Your place or mine?"

"Yours. That a problem?"

"Not at all." The sly grin spread across his face as he gave her his address. Fifteen minutes later he answered the door to her stark naked.

Still in her señorita dress, Constance was boldly staring at the beautiful naked man before her, already standing to attention. Stepping inside, she lifted her dress to show she wasn't wearing undergarments, and in one fell swoop, he slammed the door, pushed her against it, and planted himself inside her, ramming home like the bullfighter he was.

"Oh God, oh God, oh God," she screamed as the magnificent beast rode her hard. She had never had a man as magnificent as him, and he filled her completely. "Ah, fuck me, fuck me." She yanked open the bodice of her dress for her bouncing bosoms to be free, and he devoured them as they squashed against him.

Carrying her to his bed, they rolled around for three days almost non-stop. Him on top, her on top, him coming in behind, her coming on backwards.

His hands never left her breasts, his mouth never left her pussy, unless his penis was doing the job. The riot of black curls extended to between her legs, and he loved to bury his face in all of it.

On the fourth day, they lay back, smoking expensive cigarettes, consuming bottles of rich champagne, and eating exotic fruits and cheeses off silver platters.

"I must leave tomorrow for Seville. I have bullfights scheduled in a couple of weeks and will need to be there early to prepare." Blowing smoke rings, Stephano aimed them at Connie's breasts, and flicked a thumb over the velvety nipple that was enlarged and delicious.

She snuggled closer to him, purposefully thrusting her breasts at him, and he willingly obliged her, sucking the large bud into a mountain peak. "Will you be gone long?" she asked, her hand expertly manipulating his erection, making him come in her hand. She wiped it on the sheet and kept on manipulating until he shoved it inside her, pinning her to the bed, thrusting with the might of a bull. And she accommodated his every need. "Will you be gone long?" she repeated after he'd exploded.

"A week or so," he huffed and rolled off. Food was all over the bed and squashed in orifices, champagne dripped from upended glasses and bottles. But he had a maid to pick it up, so he didn't care.

"And how many women will you have while you're away?" Connie arched a brow and shoved her breasts in his face.

"I don't while I'm working. I wait until after. Like now. Otherwise, my mind is on other things and I cannot concentrate." He eyed the luscious globes in front of him.

"And is it like that all the time?" Connie took a long drag on her cigarette and accepted another glass of champagne. "How many women have you bedded, Matador DeLuca?"

Stephano grinned. "At least one after every fight."

"And how many fights have you had?"

"Hundreds," he exaggerated.

Connie's brows rose, in amusement or disdain, she wasn't sure. "So, how many little Stephano DeLucas are out there if you've slept with hundreds?"

"None, that I know of." Stephano finished off his champagne. "I use protection, and no woman has come forward yet to claim it. So... none."

"And what about the future?" Connie asked. Her goal had been to get her claws into Stephano DeLuca right from the beginning. "Plans to get married, have children, pass on the DeLuca name?"

"One day," Stephano told her, stretching out the stiff muscles in his back and glancing around at the mess in his apartment. "I'll need a good strong woman to give me many children. The DeLuca genes must go on." His eyes roamed Connie's body, seeing just how full and voluptuous it was. *Definitely ripe for children,* he thought.

"But until then?" Connie persisted.

"Until then I will have any woman I want," he said. "Until I have found the one to have children with."

"And what if you've already found her?" Connie slid her foot up and down his leg. Her knee rubbing softly against his thigh and side.

He cocked a brow, looked from her leg to her and asked, "And you think you are the one, do you?"

Running her well-manicured blood-red fingernails across his chest, she gave him her best Cheshire cat grin. "Why not. Did we not just spend three days together? How many other women have you spent three days with? How many women have satisfied you the way I have?"

"Well..." He contemplated while watching her tongue slide over her lips. "You are the first I've spent more than one night with, so yes... there must be something special about you. If I've spent three days with you already, there *must* be something that's making me keep you here."

"And what could that possibly be?" Connie asked innocently. "The curls on my head, my big luscious lips?" Fluttering her lashes, she went on. "My big bouncing bosoms, the curls between my legs, or the way I can satisfy you in bed?" She rubbed her leg against him and Stephano rose to the occasion.

His hand slid between her legs and entangled itself in her curls before sliding inside. "Is this what you want?"

Arching against him, she purred. "I want more than a quick fuck. I want a man who can satisfy me all the time." Sitting on top of him, she slid down his penis and proceeded to bounce away.

Her bosoms were mesmerising to him and he buried his face in them knowing that no other woman had breasts so delightful, or a pussy so accommodating. He didn't know what it was about her, but he definitely wanted more.

*****

Eight days later, after successful fights in Seville, Stephano was back in Madrid and screwing Connie in his apartment. "Oh, I have missed this." He groaned as she clenched her vaginal walls around his cock. "I have missed this so much."

"Then you should have it permanently." Connie breathed heavily. "You could have it all day and all night at your beck and call."

"Yes," he huffed. "Yes, yes, I should put you up here permanently." Gripping her hips, he hung on, having barely survived the time without her. Trying hard to keep her off his mind while preparing for his fights, he had almost lost concentration and been gored, but fortunately, his last eight years had trained him well and his body had reacted instinctively, stepping out of the way at the last second. He'd come through and pulled it off, winning the crowd's love and cheers. But, oh, how he'd missed Connie and the warmth of her entrance. "Connie," he breathed. "Let's get married."

She stopped bouncing, surprise all over her face. "What?"

He was surprised too, for marriage had not been on his mind two seconds ago. But he liked the idea of this woman being his wife. To be there when he came home from fights to screw him all he wanted and give him what he needed. She could be the partner he needed. And at his age, people had been asking if he'd marry soon. Thinking nothing of it, he hadn't worried about it. But now that he'd found a Colombian firecracker in bed, he *did* think about it, and it had come to him in that instant only, and popped right out of his mouth.

"You want me to marry you?" Connie asked, secretly thrilled that it had taken only a week and a half to get what she wanted. At thirty, she had already been called an old maid for nearly ten years by her family back home. They married girls young, but she wasn't interested and forged her own path through life. With a passion for Spain, bullfighting, and dancing, she'd hopped on a plane and hightailed it over to Madrid just to meet the most famous matador around, setting her sights on Stephano, and planning exactly what she'd do and how to go about it. He was a powerful man in more ways than one. Physically, he was tall, broad and muscular, with jet-black hair and piercing black eyes. And she matched him perfectly with her own black hair and sparkling eyes. Between them, they would make beautiful babies and be a fiery couple. Between her Colombian genes and his Spanish ones, they were bound to make fireworks as long as they lived. And the fact he was the country's best-known matador meant fame and fortune, so she would be well looked after. "Are you...sure?"

"Why not?" He laughed and rolled her over so he was on top. "Marriage never interested me before, but I have found you, Connie." Breathing hard, he plunged in and took her as deftly as he took the bulls in the ring. "What do you say? Will you marry me?"

Briefly closing her eyes against the orgasm, she thought, *how could I say no to this?* "Oh, God yes," she cried.

*****

One month later, the wedding of Stephano DeLuca and Constance Constinopolous occurred at the newly renovated DeLuca estate *Mi Amor Mi Corazon*, outside Manzanares el Real an hour out of Madrid. It was a magnificent three level home with terraces, a pool, lawns, and different levels as the property climbed down the hillside toward the beautiful reservoir lake. It boasted a bull motif on the iron gates, a long driveway that curved around the bull and bullfighter fountain, and many bull statues dotted through the gardens as they led down to the bull and bullfighter tile inlay in the pool.

It was a beautiful summer day, and Stephano wore a simple tux while Connie went all out in a frilly multi-layered white frothy wedding dress with her hair piled high on her head and covered in a veil. Her feet were swathed in white satin slippers, and bountiful jewels hung from her neck to hang between her bountiful bosoms. She was the picture of happiness. She was marrying one of the most famous men in Spain, across the bullfighting world, and she was marrying him today, in front of family and friends. They were in a beautiful white marble pavilion in the forested area to the left of the house. He'd had it specially built for parties, and what better way to christen it than with his wedding?

They toasted with bottles of the finest champagne, caviar and salmon, duck, deer and chicken. It was a fine feast held only by the rich and famous who could afford it, and *they* could afford it.

For their honeymoon, they travelled across Europe for a month before settling back in Madrid, where Stephano went back to work, and eight months later, Antonio Stephano DeLuca was born, wailing down the hospital with his screams.

Stephano was extremely proud that his firstborn was a male. "He will carry the DeLuca genes well," he told Connie in the hospital as he held his son. "Look at the fine cheekbones, the piercing black eyes, and what a healthy head of black hair. Look at it." He was amazed that their child had come out with such a full head of hair, but considering how endowed they both were in that area, it wasn't hard to see the resemblance. Holding his son up, he stared into his black eyes. "Hello, my boy, Antonio Stephano DeLuca. Yes, that's right. I'm your father and you have my genes running through you." He gently bounced Antonio. "Yes, my son, you are mine."

"He's also mine." Connie laughed lightly from her position in bed. Her curls, as usual, were piled high on her head. She glowed with happiness at being married and with a newborn child.

Her child. Hers and Stephano's.

Their son. Antonio DeLuca.

The love of her life.

1956

Stephano was carried aloft the shoulders of his picadors and paraded around the arena. In his sixteen year career, it was his two-hundredth bullfight and he would be celebrating, and Connie and Antonio were in the crowd to help him with those celebrations. He spied them and waved. His beautiful boy Antonio excitedly jumped up and down with his six-year-old exuberance, and Stephano indicated to his picadors to take him over to the crowd. Reaching the barrier, he deftly picked up Antonio and swung him into his arms and they continued their way around the ring. Roses were thrown, screams were heard, the cheering grew incredibly.

Waving and blowing kisses, Stephano and Antonio were carried out of the ring and set down in the corridor that led to the dressing room.

"Well, my little Antonio, what did you think of Papa's two-hundredth bullfight?" He touched his finger to his son's chin.

"It was good, Papa." Antonio bounced from one foot to the other. "But I would have taken that bull down in ten minutes flat."

Stephano's laugh belted out of him, rising from his gut and coming out loud and hearty. "Oh, you would, would you, my little bullfighter." Seeing his son's black hair and dark eyes frame his wide cheeky grin, he beamed. He was so proud of his son. Even though he was six years old, Antonio was already proving to be quite an expert on bullfights. Dressed in his blue shorts, and a tucked-in blue and white striped short sleeved shirt with a bow tie to match, Antonio was the love of his life, even above Connie who came rustling down the corridor in her Spanish dress. "Ah, my love." Stephano held out his arms to her and enveloped her beautiful bosoms in his embrace. "What did you think?"

After kissing him on both cheeks, she said, "You're getting better with every fight. Precision, perfection, superb."

"Thank you, my love. This one here," he nodded at Antonio, "thinks he could have taken the bull down in ten minutes."

"Yes, Papa, I could have," Antonio gushed. "I would have got him into the left side of the ring, done a fancy spin, waved my cape and pow, he's down. I would have, wouldn't I, Mama?" He gazed expectantly up at his adoring mother. For regardless of the strict hand she had in raising him, she always did it with love and lots of hugs and kisses. Plus, she was his biggest champion.

"Yes, my darling, you would have." Reaching down, she touched his cheek. "You are a much better bullfighter than your father," she added cheekily.

"Oh, is that so?" Stephano noticed the arched brow and amused smile. Picking Antonio up, he added, "You are a better bullfighter than I, Stephano DeLuca, are you?"

"Yes, Papa." Antonio nodded. "I am."

Stephano's hearty laugh was back. "Well, in that case, you can perform the rest of my fights for me. Come, let's get changed and go out to lunch. What time must you leave?" They headed for his change room.

"Four at the latest," Connie told him. "We must get back to Madrid to get Antonio ready for school on Monday."

"Ah, back to school." Stephano nodded. "Yes, schooling is important."

"But I want to fight bulls like you, Papa," Antonio said. "I do not want to go to school."

"But you must, Mi Amor, you must. Education is important. You need to learn mathematics and physics, so you can learn how to outmanoeuvre the beasts."

"Did you go to school, Papa?" Antonio asked as he was set down on the lounge in his father's change room.

"Yes, my son. I did. And graduated with honours, so you must too." Stephano gently tapped his son's button nose. "Go to school and make Mama and Papa proud. You are the only DeLuca heir and you must do as we say. I will get changed."

Connie heard his words and inwardly flinched. After Antonio, she'd had several miscarriages, the last resulting in a hysterectomy. There would be no more DeLuca children. No siblings for Antonio, no more sons for Stephano. And while she desperately hated everything that had happened to her, losing her babies *and* her uterus, she desperately loved Antonio in return and made up for her losses by loving him and providing him with everything he needed. Watching him try to fling one of his father's capes around, though it was way too long and bulky and smothered him like a tent, she smiled. Besides the fact he had incredible genes, he was her beautiful baby boy with his long black lashes framing his beautiful black eyes. He peeked out from under the cape and grinned, her smile growing larger in return. Yes, he was her baby. Her only baby. And he always would be.

That night, Stephano celebrated his fight at *Casablanca*, Seville's fanciest restaurant, with his assistants, the bullfighting community, and hangers-on. They drank, they ate, they watched flamenco dancers flounce around the room. The music was loud and lively, and Stephano was thoroughly enjoying himself as the centre of attention from all the ladies and some men. During the course of the evening, he asked where the bathroom was.

"Out back on the right, and make sure you go right because you do not want to go left," Miguel, his long-time banderillero, told him.

"Why do I not want to go left?" Stephano asked drunkenly.

"Because left is for men only." Miguel winked.

"I am man," Stephano replied. "So why can I not go there?"

"Because it is for men who want men," Miguel said. "Where men dance for men. Where men please men."

Stephano frowned. "I do not understand, Miguel. I will see for myself."

"Not unless you are into men on men." Miguel giggled, drunk on a couple of litres of alcohol.

Stephano wandered out the back of the restaurant and into the toilet where he relieved himself. Once done, he freshened up, checked himself in the mirror, and wandered back. But curiosity got the better of him, and he made his way to the room on the left.

A spotlight was on a man at the back of the room. Dressed as a flamenco dancer, he made slow, precise movements as he built up to the crescendo, and then slowed again. Stephano stood against the wall and watched, fascinated. The man was the most beautiful he had ever seen. Tall, lean, elegant. His black hair was slicked back, his dark eyes framed by darker lashes, framed in turn by dark brows on a strong brow bone. Fine cheekbones and jaw complimented his full lips. His skin was the colour of cream, and his long elegant fingers held and played the castanets with finesse. Long lean legs stomped boot-enclosed feet on the floor as he danced and slid his way through the song. The small band in the corner played enthusiastically, and the men standing around the room, or sitting at small tables, were enthralled by the performer and the dramatic way he told his story through dance.

The dancer looked up under his lashes and spied Stephano against the wall beside the door. In elegant smooth movements, he made his way over and danced for him.

Stephano stood mesmerised by the man, by his beauty, his body, his movements. It was intoxicating and thrilling, and he was getting high and drunk on it. The attention the man showed him, the sensuous way the dancer watched him, danced *for* him, moved in front of him, made his member engorge, and he couldn't take his eyes off him. For Stephano, it was the first time he was seeing same on same. His penis strained for release, pushing against the fabric of his shorts and pants, an antenna searching for the signal that was attracting it, rising, moving in the direction of the waves rolling off the dancer in droves.

When the song and dance were over, the man was back in the centre of the dance floor. He bowed, and accepted roses from several men in the room, who went back to their companions for attention.

Watching the room for a few moments more, Stephano left, and standing in the hallway, he breathed hard. That was the most exquisite thing he'd just seen, and what a turn-on it was.

"I've never seen you here before."

Stephano's head whipped to his right. The dancer stood beside him. His mouth went dry, his penis strained. "I've never been here before."

"You look as though you could do with some air. Come." The dancer led the way out the back door into a small courtyard, carrying a bottle of champagne which he cracked open and drank from. "Want some?"

"Yes." Stephano breathed in and accepted the bottle. He drank willingly, and watched as the dancer removed his jacket.

"You are Stephano DeLuca, prize bullfighter, no?" the dancer asked, watching Stephano intently.

"Yes, yes I am." Stephano slowly backed up against the wall as the dancer advanced on him. "And you?"

"Rolfonso," the dancer replied. "I am Rolfonso, great flamenco dancer of Spain. And *your* future lover." He stepped closer and came toe to toe with Stephano against the wall. "We will make beautiful love together, Stephano." He laid his hands flat against Stephano's chest. "Beautiful love," came out in a whisper before his lips touched themselves to Stephano's.

Stephano moved his head away. "What are you doing? I am not into men. I am married."

"Ah, but your erection proves otherwise." Rolfonso's hands slid down to rub Stephano's crotch before he unzipped, pushed the pants down, and took Stephano's penis into his hands. He went to his knees and took Stephano into his mouth.

"Oh, God," Stephano blurted out at the warmth around him. "Oh, God." The champagne bottle fell from his hands and he arched against the wall. Everything left him. His energy, his will, his brain. All he felt and wanted was this beautiful man around him. "Oh, God." He came and Rolfonso took it.

Rolfonso stood and ripped at Stephano's clothes, and then his own, so he could feel the bullfighter's naked flesh against his. Passionate kissing led to passionate touching, and hands encased around balls and penis. Fingers gripped buttocks, mouths mashed, tongues tasted, and they came once more.

"Oh, God." Stephano collapsed against the wall, having never felt such explosive orgasms before. "Oh, God. What are you doing to me?" he puffed as his chest expanded and released quickly. "What are you doing?"

"Making you mine." Rolfonso turned Stephano around and bent him into the wall. "I am making you mine," he breathed in his ear. "We will be so beautiful together, Stephano DeLuca. You are mine and I am yours from now and always. Forever." With his hands gripping Stephano's chest and penis, Rolfonso entered from behind.

"Argh." Stephano gurgled in shock and constricted his muscles.

"Relax," Rolfonso told him, and pumped away on his penis. "Relax."

Stephano relaxed and rode Rolfonso to the peak of insanity.

That night, they became lovers, and saw each other every time Stephano was in Seville. They made a beautiful pair; the dark-haired matador and the dark-haired flamenco dancer. And they made beautiful love when they did. It was Stephano's first affair, having never cheated on Connie before, but not quite his first dalliance with men, having been attracted to a couple in his youthful days of puberty. Of course, he kept it from Connie. Men always kept their affairs from their wives, and besides, she didn't need to know about it. She'd only try and take Antonio away from him and a public divorce would be messy. So no, she didn't need to know. Besides, he still enjoyed making love to Connie, and they had a great relationship. But Rolfonso provided something Connie could not, and even he didn't know what that was.

They were lovers for five years until Rolfonso was killed in a plane crash on his way to meet him. To ease his grief, Stephano took another flamenco dancer as his second lover to remind him of Rolfonso and keep the fires burning.

1961

"Oh, Stephano, oh, Stephano. You are such a man for your age. You are as fit as ever." The young man lay face down and grasped the side of the bed. He was getting a pounding from the great matador, Stephano DeLuca, and loved it. At twenty-eight, Mickelangelo Herreras was an up and coming flamenco dancer and had come across Stephano by accident. He had been waiting tables at the local café in Ronda, Spain when Stephano had come in. The attraction was instant, and after a lot of drinks that night at the local bar, they became lovers. Mickelangelo knew Stephano could keep him in comfortable quarters, so he didn't need his job at the café anymore. Everything was paid for and taken care of, and he could focus on his dancing, which Stephano made him do naked every time he was in town, which was three times a year. But sometimes, he flew to Seville or Pamplona to see him, or because Stephano called him to come. And come he did. In Stephano's hand, mouth and anus. Stephano was an amazing lover, strong, virile, masculine, manly, gorgeous, filthy rich, and powerful in bed. His thrusts showed he had the prowess to please and manipulate, and manipulate he did. Stephano manipulated Mickelangelo all he liked, and Mickelangelo loved every minute of it. "Oh, God, oh, God," Mickelangelo screamed and dug his nails into the sheets.

If it was one thing Stephano knew how to do, it was to make a man scream in pleasure as they came. Rolfonso had taught him much and made him the lover he was today. Stephano released and collapsed onto his lover, thinking about his poor deceased Rolfonso and the amazing nights they had spent together. They had holidayed in Mykonos and Ibiza as a couple several times each year, loving the gay scene each island offered them. No one knew who they were. But Rolfonso was dead and Mickelangelo had taken his place.

It pained Stephano to lose Rolfonso, and he had drowned his sorrows in alcohol, finding a new lover at the same time. His son, Antonio, would always be the love of his life, but his Rolfonso came a close second, with Connie way back at third. Not that he and Connie were separated, they weren't, they were still very much a married couple who lived happily outside of Madrid with their eleven-year-old son. Antonio was his pride and joy and he would always love and adore him, but they didn't need to know about this hidden side of him that he kept from the world; a side he had only discovered the night he met Rolfonso. And he'd loved every minute of it. While still grieving for his beloved Rolfonso, he'd found solace in Mickelangelo's arms. Not even Connie could console him, not that she knew about it. Just that a close friend had died and it pained him so.

Stephano pulled out and rolled onto his back to stare at the ceiling in the Ronda apartment he kept his lover in. It was a cool fall Saturday afternoon, but he was hot.

"Oh, Stephano." Mickelangelo slid a hand over Stephano's body and licked his way across his lover's chest to his mouth. "You are fabulous." Lying full out on top of him, he laid his head against his lover's breast to hear his heartbeat.

"I know." Stephano sighed, glad that at forty he could still get it up with no problem. Even with Connie. The warmth and soft silkiness of his lover's body seeped through to his. He found it relaxing, but his lover's manhood against his own was stirring that fire in the pit of his stomach as it always did. Sliding his hands through Mickelangelo's hair, he expertly guided him down his body to his manhood where Mickelangelo proceeded to make him very happy.

Stephano was a very considerate lover. He'd kept his two lovers in apartments that he paid for, given them money to live on, and taken them on holidays. So, when Mickelangelo left him five years later for a richer, older man, he vowed to never pay for another lover. He stuck by that for three months until he met Constantine Manzo at a bullfight in Pamplona.

1966

Stephano flounced through the door of the manager's office at *Plaza de Toros de Pamplona* and demanded to know why he was sharing the ring with a new fighter. "He is not as experienced as me. He has not done this for as many years as me. He lacks...*everything*," Stephano roared, waving his fist in the air. "Why does the great Stephano DeLuca have to share with this...this arrogant, pompous infidel?"

"I'm sure he thinks the same about you," Alfonso Rivero told him. As the bullring manager, he was used to hearing from fighters whinge and whine about each other, and demand top billing and their own air time. It was boring and a waste of his energy. "Stephano, Barbero Scorsosa wanted Manzo in this fight. He knows you don't do doubles, but *he* wanted Manzo in the ring with you. Now, you're being paid a hell of a lot of money here, Stephano. Don't whine about it." He got up from behind his desk and moved around to Stephano. "You, my friend, are being paid two million dollars for tomorrow, double your usual pay, and if you want that money, you will do the job you are being paid for."

"And if *he* doesn't do his job and someone gets hurt?" Stephano asked, burning at the pompous routine he had to endure.

"Make sure it's not you," Alfonso told him.

Refusing to speak to Constantine, Stephano had also refused to prepare with him, waiting until they were nearly ready to enter the ring the next day before even bothering to speak to him.

"We really should have rehearsed our act for today," tall, dark and gorgeous Constantine said as he limbered up for what was to come.

"*I did rehearse*," Stephano coolly proclaimed. "I rehearsed my performance as I always do. I practised for exactly one week, and *I* know what I am doing. What I do *not* care for is what *you* are doing."

"Well, you should since we are in the ring together." Constantine bounced up and down lightly to get the blood flowing in his legs.

"Get yourself gored by the bull, *I do not care*," Stephano spat and his eyes narrowed. "*I* am Stephano DeLuca, *matador* of Spain. *You* are a nobody. I have been doing this for twenty-five years and did not get to be a matador by using other people to get me there. I work alone. I will not help you, nor save you, in the ring. So, if you need it, do not ask."

"Wasn't planning on it." Constantine wondered what was going through the great matador's head. All he'd ever heard about Stephano DeLuca was good. He was a professional who worked hard and got the jobs done. And he'd seen him as nothing other than a mentor, looking up to him his whole life. Stephano made him want to be a bullfighter, and at twenty-eight, he'd worked his way up the ladder just as Stephano had done. But looking at him, he saw nothing but a Spanish temper and downward brows. The frown did nothing for his beautiful features, and the light dusting of grey at the temples made him look devastatingly distinguished. In all of Stephano's career, he'd never been gored, and that was one thing Constantine wanted to achieve in his own career.

"Get ready, you are on." Alfonso stood between them, putting an arm around each one's shoulder. "Go out there and earn your money. And *try not* to get gored."

Constantine was announced first as the newcomer. He did a circuit of the ring to cheers and screams, and then it was Stephano's turn.

He casually walked from the corridor into the ring, stood to screams and cheers from the crowd giving him a standing ovation, and gave a dramatic twirl of his cape before bending into a deep bow. He took his time walking the ring, reaching out to the crowd, waving, blowing kisses. He wanted Constantine to know exactly who was in charge. Taking his spot in the centre, he posed and waited for the bull to enter.

The beast came storming into the ring, eyeing him off, but Constantine quickly jumped between them to gain the crowd's attention. *And* the bull's.

Constantine drew the bull to the other side of the ring and proceeded through a series of twists and turns, showing off for the crowd.

But the bull saw through the façade, and when Constantine's back was turned because he was too busy showing off, the bull shoved a horn right up his...

Stephano watched the whole thing and kept his laughter under his breath. Not that anyone would have heard over the noise of the crowd screaming out. He knew show-offs like Constantine, and they didn't learn until they had a horn up the ass. Watching Constantine run away to be checked over, he took his stance. Arms out, cape ready, he stared down his nose at the bull and the bull stared back.

After stomping a foot, the beast charged the remaining matador who swiftly stepped out of his way. He was a creature he'd dealt with before, and knew how tiring it could be. Turning, the bull threw all of his energy into a series of moves in the vain hope the creature would wear out more, but the first creature he'd had to deal with had worn *him* out and now he just wanted it to be over. Finding extra strength from the pit of his stomach, the bull charged at Stephano over and over, circling, moving, twirling in a frenzied dance around the ring. But it wasn't enough. The two-legged creature had all the power, and he had no energy left. Admitting defeat, the bull collapsed and watched as the creature was hoisted upon the shoulders of others and carried around the stadium.

Stephano was carried into the corridor under the stadium and let down. He spied Constantine nearby and smirked. "Still alive?"

"Not as dead as you might have hoped," Constantine replied, arms crossed, a scowl on his face. But underneath he was nothing *but* impressed over the way Stephano had handled the bull with such fine precision and finesse. He just tried not to show it.

"Stephano." Barbero Scorsosa came up to him. "You are worth every penny of the two million I'm paying you." Grabbing Stephano's face, he kissed both cheeks. "*Every* penny."

"Two million!" Constantine exclaimed, his arms falling to his sides in shock. *"How the hell does he get two million?"*

"Because *he* is worth it," Barbero told him with a dirty look. "And *he* is not stupid enough to get gored because *he* was showing off. *You're* lucky you're getting the money I'm giving you since you weren't out there long enough."

Constantine winced and blushed furiously, embarrassed by his inability to show Stephano what he was made of. He'd humiliated himself and it was a lesson learnt. *Don't fool around in the ring with a twelve-hundred-and-fifty-pound beast.* He watched the smiling matador being whisked back to his change room, and shamefaced, went back to his.

That night, everyone was celebrating at *Victoria*, a heavily influenced Colombian bar and restaurant for men only. Stephano had been there before, but had never sampled anyone. He hadn't needed to as he'd had Mickelangelo. But he was celebrating his win over Constantine, showing that years of practice and prowess succeeds over stupidity and recklessness. They dined on bull meat finely covered in ground herbs, vegetables topped with rich sauces, and succulent berries and cheeses for dessert.

They watched the entertainers perform native dances, and sing Colombian songs until Stephano decided to sample someone from the back room, and found his way there to watch two men make out in front of a crowd of horny men.

Standing in the dark at the back, he noticed other men getting it on in the room, completely ignorant of the voyeurs. He spotted Constantine watching from the opposite side of the room and saw a man on his knees performing oral sex on him. Surprised, even though he shouldn't have been, Stephano watched on in interest.

Constantine's hands were in the man's hair, yet his eyes were focussed on the entertainment, so no one would notice he was getting his cock sucked.

But Stephano noticed, and wanted in on the action. He hadn't had a lover in months and missed the warmth of a mouth around his cock. Scanning the crowd, he saw a few eligible men and gave one the eye. Motioning for him to follow, he made his way outside to the back courtyard and unzipped his pants. The young Colombian boy followed dutifully and got to his knees and did the job right up until the crescendo, leaving Stephano satisfied…for now.

The Colombian went back inside and Stephano sighed, leaving his manhood free to air out for a few minutes.

"So…that's what the great DeLuca cock looks like."

Stephano whirled around, but saw no one until the person emerged from the shadows. The anger rose. "Constantine… What do you want?"

"That." Constantine nodded to his role model's cock. "And so much more."

Stephano eyed the twenty-eight-year-old with renewed interest. Tall, good-looking, prime beef. "And what would you know about what I want?"

"I know that, even though you're married to a woman, you have needs that clearly only a man can satisfy." Constantine moved closer. "You just got your cock sucked as I did. Clearly, you like *men* to do that job."

"So? What is it to do with you?" Stephano pushed himself back into his pants.

"I want in on that cock." Constantine stood in front of him. "I have looked up to you since I was a child. You were who I wanted to be when I grew up. I wanted to wear the costume and fight the bulls, and get all of the adoration and love. You are my role model, Stephano." He moved closer. "You are who I wanted to be. Now, I get to meet you and work with you."

Stephano snorted. "For what it was. You are an idiotic, pompous ass who lacks the skills required to be a matador. You will *never* be me. You will *never* learn to *be me* as long as you have that arrogant, *I am better than you,* show-off rubbish. Because *that*," he pointed a finger in Constantine's face, "is what got you gored up the ass today."

"Well…" A small smile lit up Constantine's lips. "Not quite. He hooked his horn between my legs and lifted me, ripping my pants and scraping my flesh. But I'll be okay. One thing *I do know*," he said as he slid his hands into Stephano's pants and grasped his cock, "is it's not a bull's horn I want up my ass."

Stephano stared into his eyes under the dim back light. Constantine was just like him. A bullfighter with a love of power and what it could do. He'd had two flamenco dancers, and was now presented with a younger version of himself, and at the root core of his pompousness, he liked what he saw. Grabbing Constantine, he shoved him against the wall and helped pull his pants down. "Is this what you want?" he breathed on Constantine's cheek. "Me up your ass."

"Yes." Constantine could feel the burgeoning cock and balls against him. "Oh, God, yes. I want the power of Stephano DeLuca inside me."

"You want the power?" Stephano thrust inside. "You want the power of Stephano DeLuca inside of you." Another thrust.

"Yes, oh, God, yes!" Constantine ejaculated. "Give it to me. I want the great Stephano DeLuca inside me. Oh, God!" he cried.

And so, Stephano DeLuca found lover number three.

1971

The twenty-first birthday of Antonio Stephano DeLuca was a huge affair. Hundreds of people came from near and far to celebrate at the DeLuca estate. Stephano and Connie spared no expense for their son, hiring his favourite rock band, inviting all of his friends, and their friends, and people they didn't really know. It was a matter of getting as many well-known Spanish and Colombian celebrities as possible so it would be reported on the news. Antonio had spent the day by the pool with friends, going down to the lake for a few hours at one stage, and getting out of the way while caterers and party planners did their thing, and by seven-thirty that night, it was in full swing at the dance pavilion for the kids, while the adults and friends stayed on the back terrace. Champagne and wine were flowing, and food was ready to be served. And at nine, the band took a break and everyone converged on the terrace.

"Oh, Antonio, my darling, are you having fun?" Connie asked as she swished past in a bright taffeta concoction and bearing a plate of food.

"Yes, Mama," he replied, and dug into mini hamburgers and fries from the barbeque.

"Good, good. Nothing's too much for my baby," Connie told everyone. "Whatever he wants, he gets."

"That's because he's a DeLuca," Stephano said to the crowd of hangers-on who were after a piece of him. "As only son and heir of the great DeLuca fortune and estate, he is entitled to it all upon my death. Meantime, Antonio, my son, I have your present. Everyone gather round, gather round, gather round." He walked over to his son and put an arm around his shoulders. Antonio was two inches taller than him, but had his dark Spanish features, topped with a big toothy grin and black slicked back hair. "Now, my son. For your sixteenth, we gave you your ID bracelet. And for your eighteenth, we gave you your bull pendant necklace to signify your DeLuca heritage." Noting the sparkling white gold pendant around his son's neck, highlighted against the tanned skin and dark chest hair being shown off by the open black shirt Antonio wore, he smiled in a fatherly manner. "I am proud that you wear this, my son, it means so much to me that you honour your heritage and your parents." He teared up and dabbed his eyes with an expensive silk burgundy handkerchief.

"Of course, Papa, of course," Antonio told him. "I am proud to be a DeLuca." He gave his old man a hug and pat on the back.

"Okay, okay," Stephano said. "To finish off the significant birthday presents, I want to present you with this last one for your twenty-first birthday." Pulling a small velvet box from his blazer pocket, he handed it over to his son. "Happy birthday, my little Antonio. You have finished growing now, and it will fit."

Antonio took the box and opened it. "Oh, Papa." The crowd gathered with eager eyes as Antonio removed the ring and slid it on the ring finger of his right hand. "It's magnificent." The square cut white gold ring had the bull insignia on it, with emeralds for eyes. The wide band fitted him perfectly.

"Happy birthday, my son," Stephano said and hugged his one and only offspring fiercely.

"Thanks, Papa," Antonio murmured into his father's shoulder, over which he spied his mother. "Mama."

"Oh, my baby." Connie gave him a kiss and a hug and didn't want to let go. "You're a man today."

"Mama." Antonio blushed at the thousand-strong crowd watching them. "Not in front of everyone."

"Why not?" she gently chastised. "You are my baby. You are a man today."

"Speech, speech," his friends cheered him on.

"Um, okay." He let go of his adoring mother and faced the crowd around him. "Thank you to everyone for coming tonight. I'm so glad you were able to. My friends, family, everyone else, thank you for being a part of this momentous occasion. I want to thank my parents," he glanced their way, "for this awesome party and for raising me the way you have for the last twenty-one years. I've had everything I needed, everything I wanted, and yet I have a straight head on my shoulders, and it is thanks to that, that I now go out into the world and start working." He looked over the excited crowd. "From now on, I am working my way across Europe and having a blast while I'm at it. Mama, Papa and I have talked about this moment for the last ten years. Papa is sad that I did not follow him into the business as I said I wanted to at six years of age."

Everyone laughed and Stephano grinned. "Ah yes, when you told me you were a better bullfighter than me," his father reminded him, much to everyone's amusement.

Antonio reddened. "Yes, Papa, but I grew up, and now want to do my own thing. I want to travel and see the world, and I'll be doing that from now on. So, thank you to Mama and Papa for this party, and the presents, and thank you to everyone for coming." He hugged and kissed his way through the crowd, as his friends gathered for a look at his ring. Besides that, Connie had bought him a new luggage set and wardrobe of clothes, and Stephano had set up a trust fund for him in case of emergencies. He was going to be leaving in a week for Ibiza to work through the summer.

Going back to the party, they danced until dawn when everyone watched the day start with a magnificent sunrise over the hills and lake of Manzanares el Real.

*****

A week later, they saw Antonio off for his adventure with Connie crying the whole time.

"Connie." Stephano patted her arm as he held her. "He's only going across the water to Ibiza. You can see him anytime you want."

"I know." Connie dried her eyes. "But this is the first time he'll be away from home in twenty-one years. He's never been away from my side for one night, let alone months."

"I know, but we must let him go. He is an adult now. A man. He must make his own decisions and do his own thing."

"You hate it that he didn't follow you into bullfighting," Connie reminded him. "You wanted him to follow in your footsteps."

"Yes, yes I did." Stephano nodded absentmindedly. "But..." He remembered back to Antonio's party and the last five years with Constantine who was all set up to take his place when he retired in a few months. He'd not only been his lover, but his mentor, his tutor. He'd worked him hard to perfect his strategies in the ring, as well as the bed, and Constantine had excelled at everything, including their lovemaking.

"But..." Connie prompted, knowing he was thinking about his retirement.

"But..." He came out of his dreamland, remembering the stolen kisses he'd shared with Constantine at Antonio's party. "I have a protégé in Constantine, and he will be the new matador for Spain."

"Yes," Connie murmured, recalling the looks of longing she'd seen between her husband and his student. "Constantine is a very good-looking young man. He could almost have been *you*, many a year ago." She kept her tone casual.

"Yes, yes," Stephano muttered as they wandered back to their car. "That's what I see in him. Me. He's me many a decade ago. And with all the work I have put into him, he is set to be my replacement."

"Do you want to retire?" Connie asked, climbing into the car.

"No." Stephano slid in beside her. "But I am old now, and not as young and spry as I used to be."

"Old," Connie snorted. "Fifty is hardly old."

"Yes, that is true," Stephano agreed. "But my body feels it. Preparation time takes longer, I don't move as I once did, and because of that, I could be gored by a bull. I do not want to risk that. I want to go out on a high. A thirty-year career with no casualties, no war wounds. That is a record that will stand the test of time."

"So…what will you do with all of your things?" Connie fanned herself with a delicate lace handkerchief. "All of those costumes and ephemera?"

"I am already having glass cabinets made, so the costumes can be on display in the entertainment room, and I'll be putting all of my personal collection on display as well."

"The entertainment room will become the Stephano DeLuca memorial room," she remarked snidely. "So, I not only have to live *with you*, but with *all of that* as well."

Stephano arched a brow. "Yes, Constance, you do." He wondered what the tone was all about, but figured it was some sort of mid-life crisis thing with Antonio leaving. Putting it out of his head, he drove them home, talking about his plans all the way.

*****

Stephano took to the famous Spanish bullring, *Plaza de Toros de Las Ventas* in Madrid, for one last time. It was his fiftieth birthday, thirty years to the day since he entered the profession, since he first stepped into a ring. And here he was one last time to give the crowd what they wanted. He made the circuit, waved to friends and family, including Antonio who was back for the weekend, and took his place in the centre.

Taking his stance, he prepared himself for the beast. It came snorting, stomping, pawing, and shaking into the arena and came to a weary stop just metres from him. The next few hours were going to be an energy zapper and he needed to keep his wits about him. He pranced, he twirled, he spun away from the beast time after time, coming within millimetres of being gored, much to the crowd's delight and horror. But he wasn't, for his reflexes held true and got him out of the way in time.

After an exhausting three hours and twenty-nine minutes, the bull gave up. And as per tradition, and it being his final performance, Stephano spared the beast, pardoning him so he could live his final years in a grassy green field somewhere.

The crowd screamed, cheered and applauded.

Stephano's cuadrilla came to carry him away amidst roses and confetti, and left the ring. His family met him in the corridor under the stadium.

"Oh, Papa, you won, how exciting." Antonio was applauding his father as he came up. "Well done, Papa." Hugging tightly, he kissed both of his father's cheeks. "Well done."

"Thank you, my son. It means a lot to me that you are here to see me leave the sport I love."

"Why wouldn't I be?" Antonio smiled brightly. "I grew up here."

"Yes, yes you did." Connie ushered them along. "And it's where your father and I met, but he must be tired, and we need to get home for the party."

"Yes, we cannot forget the party," Stephano said. "My farewell to the ring."

Later that night at their lavish estate, the festivities were in full swing. Everyone from the bullfighting community was there to bid him farewell from their regal sport.

Connie played hostess, and Stephano regaled the crowd with stories and anecdotes from the last thirty years.

"I want to thank everyone for coming," he said after hushing the one-thousand-strong crowd. "When I came home this afternoon, I needed a nap." A few twitters were heard. "I never used to, so that tells me it is time to go. Time to hang up my cape and do other things. I'm the big five-oh today, and that makes it the big three-oh that I've been in this business. I hold the record for having never been gored. And I have made it through five hundred fights in my illustrious career." Wild cheering and applauding lasted for a few minutes until he calmed them. "Thank you, thank you. A few months back, my son turned twenty-one. Today, I turn fifty. I have been in this business for thirty years, and now, it is time to start a new chapter. I am retiring to travel and see more of the world. Have more parties, celebrate life, celebrate my *fabulous* life, and to finally take the time to spend on myself. What else would I like to do? Maybe I'll take up a hobby," he joked. "But for now, just enjoy this party because the food and drink is on me."

Antonio exchanged a glance with his mother. The last section of the speech made it sound as though he was off on his own to live the good life without his mother, and he didn't like that one little bit. Waiting for his father to come over to him, he said, "So, what are you and Mama planning to do now? A holiday in Ibiza, maybe?"

"Maybe, my son, maybe." Stephano slapped him on the back. "We will come and see you do what you do, shall we? What is that?"

Antonio inwardly rolled his eyes. "I'm a bartender, Papa. I get to make everyone's drinks and serve celebrities."

"Mmm." Stephano's expression was sour. "A servant? You are better than that, Antonio. You are a DeLuca."

"I know, Papa. But it's what I want to do. I want to be in the clubs, so I'll do any job I can get. I feel alive with the music, and it's awesome during the day out on the beaches."

"Ah, the youth of today," Stephano complained to those around him. "They are too obsessed with this rock music and these clubs." Small laughter went through the older people standing nearby.

"Well, you did just call yourself old, Papa. Clearly, you're still living in the dark ages." Antonio broke free from his father's grasp and headed for the house.

But Stephano saw red at the disrespect. "Antonio, get back here at once and apologise to me," he roared.

But Antonio ignored him and kept walking.

"For what?" Connie stared at her husband's red face. "Reminding you of what you just said, or telling you you live in the dark ages? Either way, he was right." Following her son's footsteps, she found him in his bedroom packing. "Are you leaving?" she panicked. "Please don't leave yet."

"Mama," Antonio complained. "Did you hear the way he spoke? Like a single man about to set off on an adventure by himself."

"I know, darling, but that's just your father. He'll be lost without bullfighting." Giving him a big hug, she didn't let go. "I have missed you. Please stay the weekend." Staring adoringly up at him, she saw his resolve melt away.

"Mama." He gave in. "I can stay until the morning, and then I have to get back tomorrow night."

"Good. Maybe I will take a holiday and come and see you," she suggested.

Downstairs, Stephano was still seething, but the partygoers were trying their hardest to ignore the temper tantrum and continue with the party.

"The little brat," he hissed as Constantine was trying to console him. "How could he say that to me?"

"In the grand scheme of things, he's right," Constantine told him. After five years together, he knew how to deal with Stephano's temper and fears over growing old and irrelevant. "You *did* say you were old, and *you do* live in the dark ages. Times have moved on; many people have many menial tasks and jobs. That's how stuff gets done. How do you think this party is running?" He waved a hand at the waiters. "By people doing menial jobs like serving food and drink. You've known for a good decade he didn't want to follow you into bullfighting. So, why the big deal now?" He rubbed Stephano's shoulders to calm him, but tried to keep it casual.

"Because I have retired," Stephano told him. "And things are different now."

"How so?" Constantine sipped his champagne and noted how resplendent his lover looked in his charcoal grey Italian silk suit.

"Well," Stephano took a second to think. "Now I am going to have to fill my days with something else."

"You could always train future bullfighters," Constantine suggested. "Stay in the business, teach your methods and prowess. You've certainly taught me these last few years." He sidled closer and got a sexually charged glance in return.

"Yes, you could be right. I could teach for a few years and write a book. Tell of all I know. I am still young, I still have much to give. Yes, Constantine, that is a very good idea. And one I will start doing something about tomorrow."

"So, do I get you tomorrow?" Constantine asked under his breath, his fingers playing with his lover's collar while his eyes darted around to see who was watching. "Or can I have you tonight?"

Stephano eyed the good-looking flesh beside him. "I'm sure I could fit you in sometime tonight."

From Antonio's bedroom window, Connie eyed her husband and his protégé hiding off to the side under the vine-covered terrace, hoping no one would notice. But *she* noticed. Noticed the touching, the longing looks. Had noticed at her son's party, noticed it tonight at her husband's party. The way Constantine gazed at her husband niggled at her. And the way Stephano gazed at Constantine made her blood boil. But what could she do? She was just the wife.

*****

For the next year, Stephano concentrated on writing his book on the aspects of bullfighting, how to become the world's best matador, and teaching classes at the *Plaza de Toros Las Ventas*. It was very fortuitous for him and he thrived on the attention. Soon, every country involved in bullfighting wanted him to teach a class and he took it on. It was a challenge that excited him. He and Constantine had broken up after his retirement, and his relationship with Connie was flagging. But he was having the best time of his life, passing down his tips and tricks to the one common denominator that all of those countries shared, and he was just as loved as he was when he was fighting. Just not by Connie. And he came to the realisation on his fifty-first birthday.

"Constance, Mi Amor, come, sit down." He led her to the couch in the entertainment room. "There is something I want to discuss."

She had an inkling of what was coming. Had dreaded it for a year, and now it was finally coming out. "What is it, Stephano?"

"Are you happy with us, Constance?" Stephano held her hands gently.

"I guess," she murmured, fearing the worst.

"Well, I think that the time has come," he paused, "for us to pursue our dreams. And I don't think you have done that. Looking after me and Antonio for twenty-three years, you have left yourself behind. It is time for you to find *you* again and be free."

"Do you want a divorce, Stephano?" she cried out in alarm.

"No, no, not unless you do." He patted her hand. "What I was thinking, was a separation. Then we are free to do whatever we like without pressure to please each other, or to make each other happy. You can do whatever you want, go wherever you want. If you want to go and stay with Antonio you can, and you don't have to worry about me."

"Do you have a lover?" she asked point blank, knowing her suspicions were about to come true.

"I..." He blinked and glanced away. "...Have had some."

Connie pulled her hands away from him. "I knew it!"

"But I *do not* at the moment, and this is not about that. I am fifty-one, and retired from the career I had for thirty years. My life needs to change, and I know you're not happy, Constance, surely you want to go and live your life now? Travel the world, see family and friends, party."

"Yes, but *I* am married...*to you*. And what will *you* be doing?" she asked furiously. "Is this just a reason for you to go and screw around more?"

A deep sigh left him. "Connie, I am not happy in this relationship. I love you, I do, but I am not *in love* with you anymore. I would like us to stay married, so Antonio has his parents together, and so you are financially stable for the rest of your life. You gave me a son, I will take care of you for the rest of your life. But I think our life has become stale with each other, and we both need to get out and spread our wings. With other work, other ventures, and yes...other people. But we will *always* have each other, *and* Antonio, *and* this place. We can use this as our home base in Spain, and there's the apartment in Madrid. It is for the best, Connie. A separation is for the best."

"For you, maybe," she spat. "What will Antonio think when you tell him you've left me?"

Stephano looked away in dread. His son was the love of his life, and he knew he would never be forgiven by him for cheating on his mother, or leaving her to live the life of a single man. But it was a chance he had to take to make himself happy once more.

They both sighed.

Her life was over.

His was just beginning.

1977

"Ugh, I absolutely hate it," Antonio told his co-worker, Carlos Stephanopoulos, the good-looking half Greek half Australian he worked the beach bar with in the mornings at the *Mykonos Desert Resort* on Mykonos. "They're still married, but have been separated for five years or so. Both have other lovers, but I find it gross. You don't stay married to someone, but screw other people."

Carlos flung his shoulder-length golden-brown hair back and grinned. "Your parents are what, in their fifties? For some people, being married to the same person can get boring."

"That's what Papa said five years ago. That he still loved Mama, but wasn't *in love* with her. That it was time to explore other things *and* other people." Antonio popped open a bottle of wine.

"And have they?" Carlos asked before serving beers to a group of tourists.

"Yes." Antonio shuddered. "Mama definitely has, which is gross, but as for Papa, well, I'm guessing he has, but none of us really knows."

"How come?" Carlos smiled brightly at three pretty young girls and they giggled in return.

"For the first five years after his retirement, he travelled and worked as a teacher, passing on his bullfighting skills to up and coming protégés. He wrote several books and kept working, but the past year he's just kind of disappeared."

"What? He's missing?" Carlos asked, and rinsed out a beer jug in the sink.

"Well…not exactly." Antonio paused to take a breath while there was no one to serve. "He said he was going travelling because he was finished with his work and not to worry. Since they're separated, they have no need to check in with each other, *or me*, apparently."

"You have *no* idea where he is?" Carlos took a swig of beer while there was a lull in the crowd.

"Not at this moment." Antonio raised his brows and served a customer.

"So…he could be dead in a ditch for all you know?" Carlos pulled out two margarita glasses and started making the drink.

"Could be," Antonio replied. "The first five years they'd call me once a month to see how I was. But this last year, Papa hasn't done that."

"You *really* don't know if he's dead or alive?" Carlos frowned. He'd hate it if his parents disappeared and didn't contact him or his younger brothers. In fact, his mama tried hard to keep the family together.

"Nope." Antonio had a quick drink of water. "Right now, at this very moment, I have no idea *where* my father is, or *what* he's doing."

More like *who* he was doing…

*****

Stephano DeLuca just so happened to be doing an Italian stud in his private cabana on the island of Corfu. He'd been holidaying there for the last month to take in the summer warmth for his weary old bones. But he wasn't weary at that moment as he hammered away at the stud beneath him. The man was tall, lean, and dark. Everything Stephano liked. As well as being twenty-five years of age, because at *his* age, he liked them young and impressionable. Finishing up, he grasped the stud's hands and their fingers entwined, gripping at the bed sheets.

"Ugh," the stud, Marco Montier, groaned. A model and aspiring singer, he had taken a shine to Stephano's dark good looks. And older men always thrilled him. They had the maturity he wanted and the expertise he craved. He came as Stephano plunged into him. "Oh…"

He sighed and collapsed onto the bed. "Oh, God that was so good. So good. You are definitely a stud, Stephano DeLuca."

"So I'm told." Stephano kissed Marco's shoulder and rolled off. Stretching out on the bed, he released all breath and smiled to himself. Life was good. Life was oh so good these days, and they had been for the last six years of his life. A five-year career as a teacher and author had been very fruitful, money and men-wise, and he'd had many lovers, choosing to sample the world instead of just sticking with one for five years at a time. This last year he'd retired from teaching to travel and be on permanent holiday. And he'd loved every minute of it. The freedom to go where he wanted and not tell anyone. The freedom to do what he wanted and no one knew. He hadn't kept in contact with his son as he once had, and maybe it was time to call Antonio again. Maybe he would go to Mykonos and stay a month or two there to spend time with him and reconnect. Show him he was okay. Of course, he would have to keep his sex life a secret. Antonio couldn't know it was men he was having affairs with, because if he did, he'd tell Connie. And he and Connie still got together on the odd occasion because the passion was still there. In fact, other lovers and time apart had brought the passion back to their lives, so when they met up in Spain, or ran into each other overseas, they'd hook up. Connie was happier after five years of travelling, and spending time with Antonio, and Stephano was happier being free to pursue his passions. With one passion, in particular, that was sucking on his cock at that moment.

Oh, yes, he was very happy indeed.

*****

That night, Antonio met up with his mother for dinner. He'd been bartending in the Greek islands for three years, and every summer Connie would spend her holiday there to see him even though her base was currently in Hollywood.

"Mama." He kissed both cheeks and held out her chair.

"Thank you, my darling." Connie gently touched a hand to his face before sitting. Fluffing her napkin and laying it over her lap, she looked at her son. "You look healthy and happy today."

"I am, Mama," he replied. "But I'm worried."

"About what, darling?" Connie looked into his dark troubled eyes.

"Papa." Antonio stared back. "I haven't heard a word from him since my birthday. Christmas before that, and months before that. Where is he? What is he doing? Is he okay? Why have we not seen him, or heard from him?" He waited for the waiter to deliver the drinks and menus before continuing. "Is he alive? Dead? Does he care that we worry?" They quickly scanned the menu and ordered, waiting until the waiter had left to continue their conversation.

Connie adjusted the sequined shawl around her shoulders, making sure her breasts were on full display for any man who tried to capture her attention. The restaurant was full, from local men to tourists, marrieds to singles, and many were eyeing off her ample display. "I'm sure he does on some lower lever, my darling, but he's your father. Our whole marriage has been about him and what *he* wanted. Our separation has been about the same thing. He wanted it because he thought our love life and life together was stale. You know how upset I was at the beginning, but you made me see how it meant I could now go out and pursue other things. And I have. I'm having the time of my life. I party like there's no tomorrow, I work with charities and organise balls and fundraisers. I holiday with you regularly, spending the summer months wherever you are." She smiled up at the waiter who set a plate of food in front of her.

"But are you happy without Papa?" Antonio had never liked the concept of their open marriage.

"I am very happy, darling." She patted his hand. "I went after your father on purpose, and I put up with everything he did. As much as I didn't like the concept of us living apart with separate lives while still married, I can thank him for it now because he cared enough to support me and let me live the life I had been accustomed to. That was a very kind thing to do, and I appreciate it. It's meant I can afford all I do and still reap the benefits of being married to a famous matador."

Antonio sighed and lowered his voice. "But, Mama. I don't like it. I don't like knowing you're both screwing who you want. You're my parents, you should be together." He glanced around the restaurant to see if anyone was listening in on their conversation.

"Oh, my darling, that's not how every relationship, or marriage, works. People grow apart. They stop loving each other, they divorce or separate like your father and me. You'd know all of this if you settled down and had a relationship, or got married and provided us with grandchildren."

"Mama." He frowned. "When I find the right girl, I will. But it's not as though I haven't had relationships. I've had girlfriends since high school. I know about relationships, and breaking up is hard. But not as hard as separating after twenty-three years of marriage. Even though you're *still* legally married."

"No, it isn't." Sipping her wine, she saw how healthy he looked. "But as your father pointed out to me five years ago, he loved me, but wasn't *in love* with me, and after some heavy thinking, I realised the same. I had been suffocated by *him*, *his* career, *his* home, *his* life, *his* status, and all I'd done was support him and raise you. I didn't have a life of my own anymore. But now I do."

"In Hollywood of all places." Antonio grinned and speared a piece of fish.

Her grin matched his. "Yes, I've been there for three years now and it's *fabulous.* No one knew who I was, so I got a completely fresh start. You have to come and visit, darling, you'd love it. I bet I could get you into acting. A movie or two. With your dark good looks, you would make a million girls swoon."

His laughter was light. "Mama, I already make the girls swoon."

"But no one special yet?"

Smiling indulgently, he sipped his water. "No, Mama. No one special yet."

"Well, I hope one comes along so you can make DeLuca grandbabies before I die."

"Mama," Antonio complained and then changed the subject. "And what will you be doing tomorrow?"

"The same thing I do every day, darling." A mischievous twinkle slid into Connie's eyes. "Having a spray tan and lying on the beach."

*****

"Oh, Carlos," Connie called the next day as she stepped onto the mat ready for an oil spray. It was something she had been doing on this holiday, purely so the hot half Greek half Australian golden-haired stud, Carlos Stephanopoulos, could see her in full bloom. "Will you save a special massage for me later?" She stood straight with her shoulders back so her large breasts were front and centre, and remembered back two night previously when she'd gone for a massage at the masseur tent on the grounds of her hotel, and *definitely* received more than she bargained for.

As masseur, Carlos had been showing a penchant for massaging women in all the right places. And, after hearing a secretive whisper or two from other ladies at the resort, she'd booked herself in and showed him exactly where and how he should massage her. And he'd massaged her all the way to an orgasm for which she'd paid extra.

"Connie, my luv." His Australian accent was strong and his bright blue eyes twinkled. "Do you want me to take you to heaven tonight?" Carlos sprayed her down with coconut oil as she turned. It was his third job with the resort, where he tended the beach bar in the morning for tourists, the coconut beach spray tent in the afternoon for sunbathers, and the masseur tent for hotel residents by night.

"Oh, yes, Carlos." Her accent came thick and fast as black tendrils of hair gently hung down from the riot of curls captured on top of her head. "I want you to *come* and massage me tonight. I pay well." She handed over the two dollars. "For golden stud like you, I pay very well." She wandered off leaving him blushing furiously.

*****

After a restful afternoon on the lounges by the water, and dinner with Antonio, Connie headed to the massage tent that night and stopped at the closed curtains. "Oh, Carlos," she sang.

"I'm not open yet, Connie, you'll have to wait a few minutes." He spread out a new sheet on the massage bed.

"Well, *I am* open Carlos and ready to be massaged by your long, strong…fingers…"

Carlos frowned and grinned at the same time. "You'll just have to wait, Connie." He scattered rose petals on the bed, lit candles, and made sure the thick curtains were tightly closed. Checking his watch, he let Connie in, marking her off the booking sheet. Every massage had to be booked in so they knew how long for each, and so customers weren't just waiting at the curtain ready to come in. That's why the cabana was in a private area of the resort, only frequented by guests when they were let in.

He closed the curtains after checking to see if anyone was around, and found Connie naked on the bed. "Connie," he admonished. "You know we start off slow and build up to the crescendo."

"Oh, I know." She bent her knees and spread her legs. "But I've been waiting for you all day."

He stood between her legs and closed them. "On your stomach first."

She groaned. "Do I have to?" Being older hadn't stopped her from living as though she was still in her twenties, and her body was the same. Still full in every sense, from her voluptuous bosoms to her voluptuous thatch, curved hips, strong thighs, and even stronger vagina.

"On yer stomach," Carlos said and crossed his arms. "Time's money and you're wasting precious moments."

Connie quickly rolled over, and Carlos mounted the table, sitting on her buttocks to massage her shoulders.

"Oh…Carlos…" She groaned, gripping the sides of the table.

He slowly ran his fingers up her spine and across her shoulders to loosen the muscles, doing this for several minutes before making his way down her legs until he was standing at the end of the table, massaging her calves, her ankles, her feet, hitting the pressure spots of pleasure.

"Oh, God, Carlos, take me, fuck me."

Carlos knew she was ready, and so was he. Pushing down his shorts, he set his erection free and allowed it solace in the one spot it awaited. After snapping on a condom, he grabbed Connie by the ankles, yanked her down the table until her lower half was barely hanging off the bed, and proceeded to fill her aching soul.

"Oh, Carlos, oh, God, yes," she groaned, burying her head in the bed and grasping the sides of it until her knuckles went white.

His hands continued their massage, his penis joined in. Up her spine his fingers went while he matched the movement inside her. Down his fingers came to her backside as he withdrew. Up her spine again, and down her spine again. Over and over.

"Oh, God, Carlos, now, now, oh, God, now," Connie panted.

His thrusts became fast and furious, grunting into her until he was done and she was screaming his name.

They collapsed on the table, still entwined, but Carlos soon pulled out and cleaned up. Sweat trickled down his face and he pushed his hair back.

"Oh, Carlos…"

He turned to see Connie sitting on the end of the bed.

"Come, my darling." Her arms were outstretched and her bosoms inviting. Carlos was enveloped into her embrace as she pushed his tank top over his head and let it fall to the floor. His shorts followed. She pulled him close and rubbed herself over him. The feel of his hot Adonis body against her no longer youthful one felt refreshing. Her breasts remained hardened against his chest, and his hard-on came back. "Carlos, oh, Carlos," she whispered. "Take me, take me again."

He took her on the edge of the table, with hard grunting thrusts until he was done and she was on her back, remaining inside as she grabbed his hands and placed them on her breasts.

"Squeeze," she commanded. He squeezed. So did she, and he hardened again. "Squeeze."

They played the game until they both came and both stopped squeezing.

"No more." Carlos stumbled back, panting. He was done, and she was only his first customer. Checking his watch, he saw her time was up and quickly dressed, saying, "Time to go, Connie," before brushing his hair back.

"Go, Carlos? Oh, no, I'm not going anywhere. I've booked you out for the whole night. Come to me, Carlos, let's see if you have the stamina to please Constance DeLuca all night. If you can, there is big money in it for you."

Looking at her open arms and open legs he cocked a brow. "Big money?"

"*Very* big money."

He stripped off. "All right then."

*****

"Oh, darling, I have found the perfect stud. He is pleasing all of my needs and does it to me almost every night," Connie said down the phone line to her friend Harriet DeVille in L.A. the next day.

Harriet was the wife of bigwig porno producer Harry DeVille, and everyone always joked about them being Harry and Harriet. "How big is he?" she asked.

"Big enough to fill me ten times over," Connie replied.

"But how...*big...is he*?"

"Oh, you mean cock size? About ten inches."

Harriet drew a breath. "And what does the rest of him look like?"

"Five-foot-ten, long golden-brown hair, blue eyes, golden-brown tan, muscles from here to there..."

"Would he be good enough for us?"

"Oh, darling, he'd be good enough for everyone."

"Well, maybe I should fly out there and take a look?"

Connie bristled. No one was taking her man while she was in town. "No, no, darling, he is much too busy. You stay and deal with your business, but if he's ever out your way, I'll recommend you."

There was silence.

"Are you trying to keep him all to yourself, Connie?"

"He's hardly all mine," Connie replied. "I don't think I'm the only one he services."

"Is he using protection?"

"Of course."

"At least he has the brains to do that."

"And the head!"

They laughed.

*****

Antonio spied Carlos walking funny as he turned up for bartending duties the next day. "Whoa, dude, what happened to you?" He finished making the drink and handed it over to the sexy young thing at the bar.

She winked and waved her fingers at Antonio, and then saw Carlos. Her eyes went wide and she stopped sipping her drink, which was just as well since she wasn't looking where she was going due to her attention being diverted to the hot bartender that had just arrived. She tripped, her face went into shock, and she fell face first into the sand.

"Oops." Antonio raced around the bar to help her to her feet. "Are you all right, miss?" Antonio picked up the glass once she was standing.

"Oh," she cried in a British accent and brushed herself off. "I feel so stupid."

"No, no," Antonio soothed. "Women lose their mind when they see Carlos. I'll get you another drink." He helped her to a bar stool and quickly made another margarita. And instead of handing it over the counter, he took it around to her to see her eyeing Carlos off. "Here you go…ma'am."

She finally noticed he was there and blushed. "Oh, I'm sorry. I didn't see you…" Accepting the drink her gaze travelled up and down his muscular frame and finally registered what a hot hunk of man meat he actually was.

"Most women don't," Antonio replied dryly, feeling the heady Greek heat rise between them.

"How much?" she asked.

He raised a jaunty brow. "For what? Carlos?"

She blushed harder. "The drink."

"Oh." Now it was Antonio's turn to blush. "It's on the house. Since you had an accident and all."

"Oh." The redness deepened and her eyes became hooded. "Thank you."

"Welcome." He stared into her pale green eyes and felt the tingles.

"I'll just…" She moved and pointed to her friends who all stood wide-eyed and giggling.

"Right." Antonio smiled and waved at her friends whose eyes grew wider and they all blushed.

"Um, thanks."

"No problems."

"Um, bye."

"Bye."

"I'll just…" She backed away from him only to nearly trip again.

"Whoa, careful." Antonio grabbed her by both arms before she could fall.

"Oh, um, thanks…" Gazing up at him, knowing she was beet red, she felt dizzy. Dizzy over this manly man touching her. Holding her by her arms, his face so near, the heat so…

Antonio felt that heat and nearly rose to the occasion. Keeping himself in check, he stared down at her. "That's okay. Don't forget sunscreen."

"What?"

"You're red." He waved a finger at her wavy hair. "You don't want to burn in this hot, heady Greek sun." If he played his cards right, he might score with this girl by the end of the day. It's not as though Carlos should have all the fun. Right?

"Um, thanks, I'll put it on." She reluctantly slid from his grasp and turned, and with a wave, walked over to her friends who all started teasing her about the hot bartender helping her.

Antonio smiled and waved to all of them and got back to work. It was not as if he wasn't good-looking. He was full of brooding dark good looks and hot and spicy personality. He'd had no complaints in the bed department either, but when Carlos was around, he got fewer women perving at him and more women asking for Carlos's phone number. He felt like a dud next to the Greek god even though he had been the stud in his high school and college. Growing up half Spanish, half Colombian, and being raised in Spain, he'd been celebrated for being his father's son and for being so damned gorgeous. But here, he seemed to be a nobody. Even though his father was a big time bullfighter, name dropping him got him nowhere. Especially on the Greek islands every summer.

He made it back to the bar. "Did you see that little hottie? I think she's into me," he said to Carlos and picked up a towel to wipe down the bar, gazing in the direction of the girls who he noticed occasionally looked back.

"Could be, man." Carlos served up two beers and three margaritas. "She certainly noticed you *after* she fell over."

Antonio smirked. "Are you saying she didn't notice me before that?"

Carlos grinned back. "You did see her looking at me, right?"

"Nah, man. She wasn't looking at you at all," Antonio joked. There was an edge to his voice, because quite frankly, he was sick of not getting any attention when Carlos was around. It was if he was suddenly invisible and the only man on the planet was Carlos. "So, what's with the weird walk this morning? Hard night was it?"

"Yeah, man, I was hard all night. Got worked real hard." Carlos cracked open a bottle of champagne and poured five glasses.

"By some hot young thing?" Antonio didn't particularly care for Carlos's exploits, but a part of him always wanted to know the gritty details just to see whether he was missing out on any pussy that was in town.

"Nah, man, your mother!" Carlos joked and pulled out more glasses from under the counter.

Antonio blinked. "You screwed my mother?"

Carlos glanced over at him and saw his expression. "Joke, dude!"

Antonio blinked again. "Oh, right. Coz you know, my mother actually *is* in town."

Carlos stopped what he was doing. *"Your mother's in town?"*

"Yeah." Antonio served up a wine. "Constance Philomena Stephanova Constinopolous DeLuca. I'd be surprised if you haven't met her already."

"Connie?" Carlos stopped dead. *"Connie's your mother?"*

Antonio looked at his surprise. "Yeah, that's what people call her, why?" He didn't like what his gut was telling him.

Carlos tried not to let his panic show. "Uh, there's a Connie that comes for a spray every afternoon…oil spray…average height, black curls piled on her head, accent, big…" He held his hands in front of his chest. "Ah…" He lowered his hands.

Antonio raised a brow. "Yeah, *that's* my mother." He stepped towards Carlos and poked his chest. "And *you* stay away from her."

Carlos put his hands up in defeat and backed away. "I've not gone near her," he lied, which he'd got quite good at doing after all the years of being a lothario. "Just oil spray, man, nothing else." He watched Antonio back away and turned around, breathing deeply to calm his nerves.

Antonio's gut niggled him, and he wondered why Carlos had reacted the way he had about his mother being in town. Had Carlos been near her? Touched her? Done something other than spray her down with oil every afternoon? He'd noticed how tanned his mother was becoming, more so than on other holidays. *Was* she up to something with Carlos? Oh, God, how gross!

*****

Later that day after work, Antonio spied the same redhead and her friends hanging around the hotel when he left for dinner. They'd come back to the bar for more drinks throughout the day, and now they seemed to be waiting for him.

"Girls." He was headed to a local restaurant since his mother was busy. They'd had lunch together, but she was meeting friends for dinner and an evening of adult fun. Which he hoped *wasn't* Carlos.

"Hello," the group chorused and casually followed him along the beachfront to the restaurant, pretending to figure out where they would be dining that night.

He was aware of them and grinned. Maybe he would score with the redhead by the end of the night after all.

The casual atmosphere of the restaurant he'd chosen allowed you to sit outside, or inside in the open plan dining room. Tonight, the bi-fold doors were pushed back to allow the sea breeze to waft in, and the aromas and spices were already thick in the air.

Ducking into the restaurant, he hid against the wall until the girls were upon him. "Hello again, hoping to have dinner with me?" he asked the blushing redhead.

Her friends giggled and pushed her forward. "Yes, yes she is," one said.

"Rachael," the redhead chastised and blushed harder, head down, eyes averted from the hot hunk of man meat before her.

"What's your name?" Antonio asked her, noticing how pretty she actually was. Her wavy hair framed her pale features. Green eyeliner and pale shadow perfectly highlighted her eyes. Her cheeks had a rosy glow, and her lips were coated in gloss that he wanted to kiss off.

"Her name's Cynthia, Cynthia York," another girl said.

"Well, Cynthia York." Antonio held out his hand for her to take. "Will you have dinner with me?"

With a flaming red face, she looked from her giggling friends back to him and slowly reached out her hand to take his. "Yes."

"Then say goodbye to your friends, Cynthia York." He glanced at them and grinned. "She'll tell you all about it tomorrow."

They giggled and watched him lead Cynthia into the restaurant.

After settling at a table and ordering, small talk got underway. "So, Cynthia York, what do you do?" He placed his elbows on the table and rested his chin on his hand.

"Um." She tucked a wayward strand of hair behind her ear. "I'm a receptionist for a big music company."

"Really? Cool." Antonio smiled, showing off his pearly whites. "Here on holidays?"

"Yes. I have two weeks off." Butterflies were wreaking havoc in her stomach because he was gorgeous and turning her bones to jelly.

"And is this the very beginning of your holiday? Because if it's the end, I'm sad that I've missed out on it...*and* you..." He let the sentence linger in the heady air between them.

"Oh." Glancing around, she saw her friends had disappeared.

"*Is it* nearly over?" he asked sensuously, staring deeply into her eyes. He'd never seen pale green eyes before and loved what he saw. They made her exotic to him as he'd grown up surrounded by dark-eyed, dark-haired people. That's why Caucasian people intrigued him. The difference in hair and eye colour was astounding and always made him curious about other races, cultures, and ethnicities. And working across the Mediterranean, he'd seen all of them come together in the holiday meccas he'd worked at. But this one intrigued him most of all.

"Um, no," she replied breathlessly, unable to tear her eyes away any longer. "We flew in last Saturday."

"So, I have you all to myself for…twelve days." Antonio nodded at the waiter who brought their food.

"Umm…" Her breath came in short gasps as the exotic masculine man before her devoured her with his eyes. "My friends…"

"You can share me if you like, but I'd prefer to just be for you." He seductively slid a piece of asparagus into his mouth and bit down.

"Oh…" Her rosebud lips moved into an o shape and her eyes grew wide. She hadn't had a Mediterranean lover before. Hell, she'd only had sex with two men. One was at twenty-one after her birthday and she didn't do it with him again. And the second was a guy she'd dated for a year. Both were British, both were pasty white, and nowhere near the hunk of manly flesh before her. She imagined his arms around her, his lips on hers. Oh, how she wanted him, but God, she was on holiday and couldn't risk anything serious. "I don't even know your name, or anything about you," she finally said.

He smiled. "Antonio Stephano DeLuca. At your service."

"And…your name and features…where are they from?" Cynthia bit into a carrot stick and watched the way his hands expertly moved to cut up his food. Oh, what those hands could do.

"Spain. My father's a Spaniard, my mother's Colombian. I have their dark good looks. I grew up in Spain, but left at twenty-one to travel and work across Europe. I've been working here in Mykonos for three years now over summer, and in winter I work in London in the clubs.

"You've been travelling since you were twenty-one? How old are you now?" The more she learned the more she liked.

"Twenty-seven. And you?" He hoped she was older, but she looked younger.

"I'm twenty-seven, too," she gushed. "I've been working at the record company since I was twenty-one. This is only my second overseas holiday. I went to Ibiza three years ago."

"Don't get to travel much?" Antonio finished off his meal and waited until she did.

"No, unfortunately. I work in London and live in London, so it's quite expensive. I'm only able to save up for a holiday over three years. But I make sure it's enough so I have plenty to spend just in case." She really was gushing now, but once she'd started, it all seemed too easy to talk to him.

"I know what you mean." He nodded and called the waiter over to order coffee and dessert. "I guess I'm lucky. As an only child, my parents helped me out by setting up a trust fund for me at twenty-one. So if I got stuck for money, I could rely on it. I've chosen not to. I've worked hard for what I have to prove to my parents I could do it without their help. Fortunately, when you're a bartender in an island resort, you get free staff accommodation."

"What do your parents do if they set up a trust fund for you?" She could hardly believe her luck. Gorgeous and well off.

His smile was soft as he thought about his parents. "My mother was a wife and mother for twenty-two years, and then became a woman of the world when she and Dad separated. She flits around the world on permanent holiday, and organises balls for charities. My father retired from bullfighting six years ago and spent five years teaching it and writing books about it. He's spent the last year who knows where with who knows who."

"Your father's famous then?" Cynthia finished off her baklava and sipped the strong black coffee.

"He's the most famous matador in all of Spain, in all of the bullfighting world." Antonio arched a dissatisfied brow and drained his cup. "But less about them and more about you. Your place or mine? Remembering that I'm staying at the hotel's staff rooms."

"And I'm sharing with one of the girls." Cynthia blushed.

"Any way you can let her know to stay with your other friends?" Antonio slid his hand over the table and placed it gently on hers.

"I…um…guess…" she murmured, her fingertips brushing his skin.

Antonio stood and paid the tab, then led her back to the hotel. *The Windmill* was situated on the hill and was a fair walk, but that just heightened the sexual frenzy bubbling up inside of them before the door to her room had finished opening. He had her in a lip lock, and then hands were all over each other in a mad dash to get clothes off.

Her pale skin shimmered in the moonlight streaming through the window, and they fell onto the bed. "Mmm, mmm, wait." She pulled her mouth away.

"What?" Antonio's chest heaved with gasping breaths.

"Do you have…protection?"

"You want me to wear a condom?"

"Yes, please."

He tried to remember if he had any and scurried off the bed to dig into his jeans pocket. He found one, and rolled it on, then rolled back onto Cynthia. "Ready to feel the passion of a Colombian Spaniard between your legs?"

Breathing in sharply as he entered, she managed, "Oh, God yes."

*****

The next day, Antonio had lunch with his mother.

"How come you couldn't have breakfast with me this morning, my darling?" She sliced through her bacon and egg omelette and piled up her fork.

"Because I have work, Mama, you know that. We don't all get to be ladies of leisure." He eyed her lunch. "Do you not have bacon and eggs for breakfast?"

"Don't change the subject," she chastised with a laugh. "I only eat fruit for breakfast and make up for it at lunch. Personally, I think it's because you were with a girl last night. Get lucky did we?"

"Mama." He rolled his eyes and knocked back his coffee. "God."

"Is she someone special, or just a hookup?" Connie watched his face flame up in embarrassment.

"What? Like yours and Papa's hookups?" He cocked a lip and looked away. "Gross, Mama."

"No, it isn't. It's sex, and it's incredible. It nourishes the soul," she told him gaily, knowing it annoyed him when she talked about it. "What's her name?"

Thoughts of last night flashed through his mind and he opened his mouth. "Cynthia."

"And where's she from?"

"London."

"Caucasian?"

"Redhead with green eyes and she's beautiful," he blurted, unable to stop himself.

Connie smiled and finished her food. "Stolen your heart, has she?"

He thought about it. "Yeah, I think she has."

"Oooh!" Connie exclaimed. "A girl's taken my baby's heart. How old?"

"My age."

"And what does she do?"

"Receptionist for a record company in London."

"Boyfriend? Husband?"

Antonio looked up in alarm. "Not that I know of, and not that she said."

"When do you see her again?"

"Dinner."

"And tonight?"

"Of course."

"And when will I meet her?"

"Mama." He groaned and leaned back in his seat. "We've only just met and hooked up. I don't even know if this will go anywhere."

"But I'm sure it will." Connie called for the check. "You spend your nights with her and your lunches with me. If I get to meet her, I meet her." She shrugged. "It's no big deal. I'm planning on staying all summer before I go home to L.A. Why don't you follow her to London?"

"If it works out, I might," Antonio said. "I work there most winters anyway."

"Good. You can take her to the estate in Spain, and I could fly in and see you, and we could show her the place, or maybe spend time together in London. If she's my future daughter-in-law, I want to get to know her."

"*Mama. Jesus.* Things haven't gone *that* far. I only met her yesterday." He quickly stood and pulled out her chair. "Enough, already."

"Oh, my baby, don't be embarrassed." She linked her arm through his and they walked out into the sunshine. "It's not often I get to see you gush over a woman who has captured your heart."

"Well, I don't know about that." Antonio slid his glasses over his eyes. "But let's see how the next eleven days go, and who knows."

*****

On Friday night, Connie found herself smack bang in the middle of a murder and rape investigation. She heard a ruckus and what sounded like a gunshot outside of her room. Sticking her head out of her private ground floor retreat, she saw Carlos speed up to her.

"Quick, I need to hide."

She ushered him in and locked the door while he dressed. "Was that a gunshot I heard?"

"Yep," Carlos panted. "Some crazy guy pointed a gun at me while I was um…" He shrugged. There was no time for politeness. "Fucking a client, and shot at us. I ran, but I think he got her. I think she's dead. I gotta get outta here."

"Wait just a minute, you should go now. I'll get you to the ferry."

"No, I have to go home." He pushed his hair back and he moved for the door. "I have to get my bags, my money, my passport. I need to go home."

"You need to leave the island," Connie said and came up with a plan. "You go and get your things then find me at the wharf. I'll get you to Athens and the airport. Go, go get your things."

With a nod, he sped off home, and Connie quickly looked around, formulating a plan. Grabbing her carry-on bag, she filled it with the necessary items she would need to fly out of Greece, and anything else she couldn't do without in the next two days, and quickly rang for the bellboy. Telling the person at the front desk she needed to leave on the ferry and to take her trunks to the wharf, she asked for the rest of her things to be packed and sent to her Hollywood home.

The bellboy arrived with the trolley and packed the empty trunks onto it, then followed her to the lobby where she booked out and made the necessary arrangements.

She turned up at the wharf with two trunks and a large bag.

"I need the ferry to Athens. I'm going shopping tomorrow," she said.

"Of course." The purser rang up her ticket and carried the trunks over to the waiting area which just happened to be in shadows.

Connie spied Carlos sneaking over to her and quickly unlocked the trunks. "Get in. You can hide until the airport."

Carlos frowned. "I have to hide in your trunk?"

"Do you want people to find you?" she fiercely whispered. "It was all over the hotel by the time I left. The cops have been called and are on their way to your house. I saw the big brute of a guy and that girl. She was screaming bloody murder that you had tried to rape her, and were raping her friend when they came upon you. They said you shot the girl."

"What!" Carlos exploded, but quickly quietened down, slinking back into the shadows. "*I did no such thing.* She was my client. I thought she was there for sex."

"Apparently, she shouldn't have been there at all. She's set to marry some Greek bigwig, but had sneaked out just a week before the wedding while he was out of town."

"Look, I know nothing about that, but some thug tried to shoot me, so I need to get out of here." He eyed the trunk. "Even if this is the only way."

They heard footsteps and saw supermodel Vivian Villiers approaching. "Darling, what have you got yourself into?" She held her arms open for him. Viv was an old friend of Connie's who'd been holidaying on Santorini when Harriet DeVille had called her and relayed what Connie had told *her* about Carlos. She'd hopped the ferry over to find out about their latest stud and had spent the last few days with Carlos in bed.

Carlos embraced her. "I have no idea, Viv, but I need to get the hell out of town."

"Well, isn't it a good thing I decided to come along. I know the perfect way to get you out," Viv said, eyeing their surroundings for anything suspicious.

"How?"

"Just get in the trunk, darling," Connie told him.

Carlos frowned again, but resigned his fate to an expensive Louis Vuitton trunk. He managed to fold his frame into the trunk and use his bag as a pillow.

"I'll put your case in the other one," Connie said and quickly packed it *and* Carlos up as the ferry approached.

Vivian went off to score herself a ticket, and within half an hour they were aboard the ferry to Athens where they arrived within the hour.

The trunk was lifted and dropped.

"Careful," Connie cried out. "That is a very expensive Louis Vuitton, and if you damage it, you pay for another one."

There were some mumblings and then they were moving, finally making it onto the private jet belonging to a friend of Vivian's. The trunks were set down in one of the luxurious bedrooms and then the attendants left.

Connie and Viv waited until they had left the plane and went into the room where they opened the trunk with the body.

"Bucket," was the first word out of Carlos's mouth and Viv managed to grab a champagne bucket just as he vomited.

"Ugh." She grimaced.

Carlos looked up as she gave him a towel to wipe his mouth. "You try getting around in a trunk and see if you can keep it all down. Where are we?"

"On a private jet owned by a very good friend of mine." Viv sat on the bed and watched Carlos stumble out of the trunk. He hefted his bag out with him. "We don't need to show our passports, we can just go."

"You managed that?" Connie asked. "I was going to put him on a public plane."

Viv smiled mischievously. "Private is better, and the friend owed me a favour. No one knows we're on here, but I will have to let the pilot know. Let's take a seat." She went to tell the pilot, and he filed the flight plan. Ten minutes later they were winging their way to Hollywood.

"What am I going to do?" Carlos paced back and forth down the aisle. "I have no idea who those people were, what they wanted, or who they were after. Were they after me or the girl?"

"Nobody really knows," Viv told him. "All I heard was a bunch of screaming as I walked through the lobby. The girl was screaming that you had raped her and were attacking her friend. And her fiancé had tried to save them both."

"That's basically what I heard," Connie said, nodding and glancing at her friend and stud lover, knowing full well Viv had been with Carlos too.

"I've never raped anyone in my life," Carlos spat angrily and ran a hand through his hair. "What am I gonna do?" Slumping into his seat, he repeated, "What am I gonna do?"

Viv and Connie were sitting side by side, dressed to the nines in their finery, having left the rest of their belongings on the island. They looked at each other, a plan formulating in their minds.

"Well, darling, it looks as though you'll have to go on the run. Change your name, live in another country," Viv said.

"Away from my parents, my brothers, my job?" He didn't like saying it, let alone thinking it.

"I don't think you'll have that anymore, darling," Connie said. "You're wanted for rape and murder. You wouldn't keep your job."

Carlos sighed. "My life has just gone to shit."

"Not necessarily. Have you thought about pursuing that career I talked to you about?" Viv asked.

His brain was so fogged he didn't comprehend what she was saying. "What career?"

The women shared a glance. "Your porn star career."

Carlos tilted his head. "You expect me to take on a public career knowing full well someone's just tried to kill me and has accused me of rape? I'm an escapee!" he reminded them. "They get one look at me in a movie and they'll know exactly where I am and come and get me."

"Not necessarily," Connie said. "We change your name, maybe your hair…"

He frowned. "How much am I supposed to change in order to stay out of the fuzz's way? How long am I supposed to keep running?"

"Well," Viv replied. "Maybe you don't have to." She exchanged another glance with Connie. "A certain producer we know happens to be good friends with certain people in certain places. If you make money for him, he will make things disappear."

"Things?"

"Problems."

"Like murder and rape charges?" Carlos raised a brow. "He can't be that good."

"Oh, he's very good," Connie said. She'd met Harry and Harriet DeVille when she'd first moved to Hollywood and they'd instantly become friends. Seeing what Harry did for a living, she reached out to him to find men for her, and he obtained more than enough to entertain her.

"You'd be amazed at what he can do," Viv added, remembering back to what Harry had done for her in her early modelling years.

Carlos shook his head. "I don't think anyone can save me. Hell, I don't even know what the hell is going on." He was tired. All of his energy had been sucked out of him in the last ten hours, and now he was spent.

"Why don't you go and lie down in one of the bedrooms," Viv said. "We could all do with a rest."

"Mmm." His eyes were already half closed. "Okay." He slowly made his way back to the bedroom where Connie's trunks were, grabbed a pillow, and was out like a light.

They landed in L.A. fifteen hours later and woke him up. "Time to leave darling," Connie said.

He yawned. "Where are we?"

"We're in L.A.," Viv said, coming into the room. "I've made some calls, and our passports will be checked on board, but we should be free to go after that."

"Our passports? But they'll know where I'm from." Carlos felt panic start to rise, but squelched it down.

"That's what one of my calls was about," Viv said, collecting her things. "The person doing the checking is a big fan of mine and will see to it personally we are let through. And as far as I know, nothing has hit the newspapers over here yet, so it's probably been contained on Mykonos."

Carlos thought about his family. *What the hell must they be thinking? Have they read the letter? Or have the cops got to them?*

"Don't worry; we'll lie low at my place for a few days while we get some things sorted out. Then we'll help you start your future," Connie said.

"Will it be a future where I'm not arrested and charged with murder and rape?" Carlos asked.

The women shrugged. "Who knows?"

"Great. So you can't even guarantee it."

"Hello, Miss Vivian, it is Marco," a voice called out.

They stopped.

How much had he heard?

Vivian left the room to greet him. "Of course, Marco, how are you, darling?"

"Oh, very good, Miss Vivian, I am here to look at your passports."

"Of course. Here's mine, and the others are just getting theirs."

Connie and Carlos retrieved theirs and walked into the aisle.

"Ah, oh, my God." Marco's eyes lingered upon Carlos, and Carlos panicked. "You are gorgeous," Marco went on, so clearly gay. "And what is *your* name?" He held out his hand.

"Carlos," he said simply and handed over his papers.

Next, Marco checked Connie's and handed them back. "And you are here in L.A. for?"

"Work," Viv said. "Boring!"

"Play," Connie said smugly.

Carlos said nothing.

"Well, everything is in order," Marco said, handing back passports. "Enjoy your stay, ladies." He eyed the gorgeous Adonis before him. "Carlos," he purred and turned on his heel.

Once he was gone, Viv laughed. "You certainly got off to a good gay start. One fan down, five million to go."

"Yes, and speaking of going, is the limo ready?" Connie asked, peering through a window.

"Ready and waiting," Viv said.

"Good, let's go."

They carried out bags and trunks and settled into the back of the limo. The ride took half an hour to wind their way through Laurel Canyon and pull up at the high metal gates which buzzed open. The chauffeur drove them up to the front door.

Climbing out, Carlos saw a huge one level home spreading left and right with thick greenery, bushes and trees, large windows, and a high brick wall.

Connie showed Carlos to a bedroom with a view of the pool out back. "This is for you, darling. The whole wing is yours. I'm at the other end."

Carlos cocked a brow. "You mean you don't want me staying with you?"

Connie's wicked laugh echoed around the room. "I wish. But you're not on the job while you're here, you're my guest, so I will leave you alone. Come outside when you've freshened up."

He put his things in the huge walk-in closet and took a shower in the large tiled bathroom. Dressed in the clothes he'd left out, he met Connie, who'd also changed, and Viv by the pool. Huge serving platters of food were on the table and jugs filled with juice, coffee and water sat next to them.

"Help yourself, darling, you must be famished." Connie shoved a forkful of omelette into her mouth.

He wasn't, but the smell made his stomach grumble, and he piled a plate high with food.

Viv got off the phone as he put the first spoonful into his mouth. "I just spoke to Harry about your problem. At first, he didn't want to help sight unseen, but Connie and I convinced him you're worth it, so he's helping you. He's getting his private investigators to Mykonos today to find out what's going on and to track down those two people. We're going to find out who they are and what they're up to."

Carlos swallowed and took a gulp of juice. "Is it wise to tell people?"

"Harry runs a porn studio; privacy is his middle name. If the secrets about his actors got out he'd be in deep financial trouble, so keeping secrets and personal issues out of the press is his speciality."

"So, if I work for Harry, he'll cover up my past?"

"As much as he can," Viv said. "He covered up *my* porn movies."

Carlos looked up in surprise. "*You? You* were in pornos?"

"When I was a wee lass," Viv said, blushing in embarrassment. "I hated the fact I'd done them and regretted it badly, but I needed the money and didn't do any more. Harry covered them up."

"Wait, *you* did porn movies, and hate that you did, but you want to push *me* into doing them instead?" Carlos was confused by the weird contradiction.

Viv shrugged. "It wasn't for me. But it is for you, and I think with your talent…" She squeezed his hand. "You'll go a long way and be a big, big star. Big…huge!" She held her hands about two feet apart.

"I'm not that big." Despite his love of sex, it was still embarrassing for him to hear women talk like that.

"It's true," Viv replied. "And Harry wants to meet you tomorrow."

"That soon?"

"That soon."

He nodded. "Okay. Is it safe for me to get around? How will I get there and where am I going?"

"For a start, Connie and I will be taking you in her limo, so you don't need to worry about getting there or being seen. And second, we'll be going to their house, so it will be a private setting."

"And what will I need to do? Do I need to perform?" He raised a brow jauntily. "With one of you?"

Connie tittered.

"Oh, you've already performed." Viv blushed. "Probably not, no, you will need to show him your goods, so wear something you can slip out of easily."

"Like every other day of my life then," Carlos joked despite the seriousness of the situation.

"Pretty much," Connie said.

"And then what?"

"Then you have a career as an actor," Viv replied. "You'll be famous."

He pulled a face. "Great."

"You just relax for the rest of today and catch up on your beauty sleep. You still look tired. I'll be back tomorrow," Viv said, getting up.

Carlos rose and hugged her. "Thank you, for everything." They kissed.

"Anything for you, darling." She wiped his mouth free from her lipstick. "See you tomorrow. Connie." She waved and disappeared into the house.

*****

At Saturday lunchtime, Stephano waltzed into the *Mykonos Desert Resort* and booked into his room. He'd been lucky to get one as the hotel was booked out normally, but after some kerfuffle with the police, a number of guests had left, leaving rooms free for the picking.

"Ah, yes, Mr DeLuca, your room is ready now. Our guest left in a hurry last night, and we needed to pack belongings this morning to send on. But it is fresh and clean. Mono." The concierge clicked his fingers at the bellboy. "Room number 69 on the ground floor, private suite. We hope you enjoy your stay, Mr DeLuca. It will be an honour having such a famous bullfighter in our midst."

"Please, please…" Stephano held up a hand. "I am just here to see my son and have a holiday. So I'd like my presence to be kept quiet while I'm here, please. I believe my son is actually working here."

"Your son?" the concierge repeated. *DeLuca, DeLuca*, he thought. "Oh, Antonio DeLuca. He's your son? Of course. I hope you enjoy your stay, Mr DeLuca."

"Thank you, I will." Stephano nodded at the man and followed the bell boy to the private room.

Opening the door, the bellboy let Stephano past before pushing in the cart. "Sir, towels and robe are in the bathroom. We have a supply of Greek island toiletries, as well as a basket of Greek island delicacies for you. Our turndown service is at seven-thirty every night, and there is a walk-in closet for your convenience." He finished setting the luggage by the closet. "Anything else, sir?"

Stephano had been sniffing the air and recognised a faint scent. "Was the previous tenant a woman?"

"Not sure, sir, but I think so," the bell boy replied. "If there's anything you need, the concierge will accommodate you." He took the ten dollars Stephano offered as a tip. "Thank you kindly, sir." Pushing the cart out the door, he closed it behind him and pocketed the money.

Stephano wandered around the room and peered out the French doors to the private garden attached to it. It was a lovely room, no ocean view, but it had the privacy he was after. Setting his overnight case on the bed, he unpacked his toiletries and placed his shaving and personal grooming kits in the bathroom. His case was double-sided, so he flipped it over and removed a personal writing set, diary, a couple of books to read, and his pills and sleeping mask.

The scent of the room kept wafting into his nostrils and he was surprised by it. It smelt like Connie's perfume, and while he knew she holidayed in Mykonos every year to be with Antonio, he didn't know if he'd bump into her. Maybe the scent was a premonition of what was to come. And since he was there to see Antonio, of course, they would be more than likely to run into each other. Not that *that* was a problem. They got along better now than they did five and six years ago when he'd retired and gone into teaching. Life had changed in many ways. Antonio had left home, he'd retired after thirty years *and* turned fifty. It was time for him and Connie to be happy emotionally, and if that meant living apart and only coming together on the odd occasion, then that's what it meant. She had come around eventually, and from all reports, was thriving.

After closing his cases, he called the front desk to find out where his son was, and was told he would still be at the beach bar. He asked directions, freshened up, and took a leisurely stroll down to the beach to find his son and co-worker swamped. When it was his turn, he asked for a glass of chardonnay.

Antonio barely glanced at the man. "Coming right up." Cracking open a fresh bottle, he poured it and handed it to the man who'd taken his sunglasses off. "Papa!" he cried, and dumped the glass on the counter, champagne spilling over the rim.

"Antonio." Stephano held his arms out. "Come, my son. Give your old man a hug."

Antonio moved out from behind the bar to hug his father. "When did you get here?"

"A short time ago," Stephano told him. "I thought I'd come and see my son for the summer."

"Where have you been? I haven't heard from you since my birthday and Christmas before that," Antonio admonished him. "I didn't even know if you were dead."

"Well, I'm not." Stephano chuckled. "I'm very much alive, and very much happy."

"So? Where have you been?" Antonio demanded, crossing his arms.

"Well, I've spent the last two months in Corfu, Italy before that. Not to worry, Antonio, I'm all right. How's your mother?"

"Antonio, I need help here," the new bartender yelled out.

Antonio's head whipped around. "Yeah, coming."

"Get back to work," Stephano said. "I'll sit and wait." He drank his champagne while Antonio served drinks until there was a lull.

"Mama's fine." Antonio wiped his brow with the back of his arm. "She's been here since May, but I got a note this morning saying she had to go home to deal with some things."

"To Spain?" Stephano held his glass out for a refill.

"No, L.A. She said she'd call. I also have to deal with a bartender leaving, so I'm training a new one." Antonio poured the drink and served another customer.

"So…she's good then?" Stephano sipped the chilled golden fluid.

"Yeah, she's really good. Really happy. I probably won't see her again until later in the year."

"Why's that?" Stephano casually took in the beach vibe and the golden studs lingering nearby, eyeing them off with interest.

"My job here goes until the end of October, then I head for London."

"To work in clubs again?" Stephano arched a brow in distaste.

Sighing, Antonio served beers before turning to his father. "You know that's what I do. I love it and it pays well."

"But you have your trust fund, so you don't need to work," Stephano argued.

"Oh, really?" Antonio put his hands on his hips. "When did *you* decide that? Certainly not when I was a kid, or a teenager, or twenty-one. You always told me I was to work hard for what *I* wanted and not leech off my parents."

"I know, I know." Stephano waved a dismissive hand. "But now that I am free to travel and do what I want, it is a life of luxury and one that I enjoy very much. And since your mother has the same lifestyle, why shouldn't our son?"

"Which sounds good in theory, but goes against everything you taught me," Antonio reminded him. "Am I suddenly supposed to give up my work ethic that you ingrained in me just because you've found relaxation in your retirement?" Shaking his head, he made a jug of margaritas.

"I understand that, I'm just suggesting it," Stephano said. "I worked hard for my fortune, and your mother has reaped the benefits of it because she gave me you, and looked after us and supported my career. You are our only heir, so it will all go to you one day."

"Not for a good few decades," Antonio said. "You're only in your fifties; you could live until you're a hundred."

Stephano's laugh was hearty. "Yes, that is true. But I could also be killed next week. So, I have updated my will and paperwork with the lawyer. It will all go to you if something happens to me. You may as well start reaping the benefits. But I see now is not the time to talk about this, as you're busy. What are you doing for dinner?"

"I'm busy every night. How about lunch tomorrow?" Antonio asked. "I have an hour between twelve and one every day."

"Okay. I will see you tomorrow. I'm staying here at the hotel."

"So was Mama," Antonio mentioned, handing over three glasses of wine to a customer.

"Yes, it's funny. I smelt her perfume in my room and wondered about it." Stephano downed the last of his champagne and paid the bill, then set up a tab for free drinks for the rest of the day. "I will see you tomorrow at lunch, my son. We will meet here."

"Okay, Papa, see you then." A hug and a kiss and they went their separate ways.

*****

Over the next week and a half, Antonio spent every night with Cynthia and every lunch with his father.

Stephano spent every night with a different bronzed-bodied lover. He did not want his son to know what he was up to, so spent the night somewhere else. He tried to convince Antonio to take a life of leisure and follow his dreams, but his arguments couldn't really stand up against all the years he'd taught him work ethics. So, eventually, he gave up and allowed Antonio to do what Antonio wanted. Just as he did.

*****

At the end of her holiday, Cynthia bade farewell to her lover. Sad to be leaving, she didn't want to let him go and begged him to come to London now instead of later.

"Please, please come to London with me." She clung to his hands, not wanting to let go. "It's still only June, and November is so far away. I don't know how I'll live without you until then."

"Cynthia," he chided gently. "You know I can't come until my work here is finished, and that won't be until the end of October. I'll be there in November as promised. But I'll ring every night to see how you are. How's that?"

"I guess it will have to do," she sulked with pouting lips. "And I promise I'll answer and we'll talk all night."

"It's a promise." Antonio kissed her goodbye and let her go.

With Cynthia and Connie gone, Antonio and his father lunched together every day for another month before Stephano moved on to Europe. He promised to call more and asked his son to join him on more than one occasion. Antonio reminded him every time that he had a job to do and couldn't leave. So, Stephano promised to be in London in November to see his son.

He bade him farewell, and left Mykonos.

*****

In October, after months of Hollywood life watching Carlos become a huge porn star, but no longer reaping the benefits of that life, Connie was called to Harry DeVille's office along with Vivian.

Storming around his office while Harriet, Connie, and Viv sat on the sofa, Harry told them all the sordid details of Carlos's life and the mess he'd got himself and famed African American photographer, Aneeka Ne Masta, into in the last few months and the lengths he was now going to fix the problem. "How long does it take to find someone, God in blazes?" The phone rang and he grabbed it in a second. "Yes."

"He's heading to Vegas at this stage," Tony Vega, the company bodyguard Harry had put on Carlos's detail, said. "No word on Aneeka or Carlos, but one of the men has been identified."

"Okay, keep me informed." Harry replaced the phone and resumed his pacing. "He's been taken to Vegas."

Harriet fluttered her handkerchief. "What is going on, Harry? Why would someone do this?"

"I don't know, but I won't rest until I find out."

Hours later, Harry got off the phone with his investigators.

"Well?" Harriet asked, running her pearls through her hand.

"They're on the trail. They've checked back in Mykonos, nothing there. They've checked back in all the places the cops have been, nothing, but..." He waved a finger. "They have found out something very interesting. There is a private plane registered to a Greek company out of Athens that flew into O'Hare Airport three days ago."

"Is that important?" Connie asked. She had camped out at Harry's since this started. It was the most exciting thing to happen to her in years, if not decades. Not that Carlos's misfortunes were something to be excited over, but after meeting him and having her way with him, and then the kidnapping, she was having more fun than she had in years, although her anxiety levels *were* rising. She prayed every few minutes for God to keep him safe.

"Well..." Harry paced. "It may or may not be. But, since it's from Athens, and Carlos is from Mykonos, I wonder. Of course, the CEOs could just be here on business, but there's a name that's popped up that we know from Carlos's last lot of trouble."

"And who's that?" Viv asked, clutching her handkerchief to her mouth.

"Gustoff Dropopolous."

"And who's he?" Harriett asked.

"The man at the resort that claimed Carlos raped two women and then shot one."

Connie's eyes widened. "Oh, my God. That means I could have seen him."

"Did you?" Harry asked.

She shook her head slowly. "I don't think so. I only opened my door at the sound of the gunshots and saw Carlos race up. I let him in, locked the door, and pulled the curtains tight."

"Did *he* see *you*?"

Another shake. "I don't think so, otherwise he might have attacked us at the pier and he didn't."

Harry stood in front of her. "Well, the fact that he's still around is highly suspicious, and my men are on it. I'll let Tony know the next time he calls in."

"What will he be able to do?"

"Pass it on to the cops," Harry said.

*****

Days later, with the whole ordeal at an end, they got the call to come to Athens right away. Taking the DeVille private jet, Harry, Harriet, Connie and Vivian flew over and booked into the *Elegance Hotel* and anxiously awaited Aneeka's call. When it came, they hastened to her suite.

"Jenny, this is Harry and Harriet DeVille, Connie DeLuca and Vivian Villiers." Aneeka introduced them as they came through the door. "Everyone, this is Jenny Stephanopoulos, Carlos's mother."

They all shook hands, and Jenny asked, "Which one of you got my son into porn?"

Viv and Connie flushed at their parts in it, but Harry guffawed. "Well, I'd like to think that he got *himself* into it. After his sexual endeavours on Mykonos, I'd say the boy was ripe for the picking."

Connie watched on, in amusement or horror, she wasn't sure which, as Jenny Stephanopoulos ripped into Harry and Harriet. She watched Harry go silent, and Harriet quake in her boots, seeing the timid side to the pair she'd known for three years, and never knew to back down from a confrontation. Especially Harry. But this was something new, and she found it somewhat amusing. Keeping her mouth shut at her role in all of it, she watched on as the ass whipping came to its natural conclusion.

"Good. Now go and sit in the corner and say nothing until you're spoken to," Jenny told them. "You *are not* the important ones here, *my boys are.*" They skulked away, and Connie followed, smirking at the dressing down she'd just seen.

Vivian jumped in nervously, wanting to know about Carlos. "How is he? I haven't spoken to him since before the kidnapping and I'm so worried."

Aneeka stopped grinning at the two Harries' discomfort to quickly fill her in without going into detail. "He's fine. They are off doing their man thing and will be back later. You'll see him then."

During that reunion, Connie sat quietly on the couch in the Stephanopoulos suite watching each scene in amusement, everyone huddled together on the sofas, crying and dabbing their eyes. She marvelled at the boys' good looks, and saw how they clearly got them from both parents. And the fiery temper she'd seen in Carlos, that definitely came from Jenny. She caught up on all the gossip with Bette Olander, Bertha St John, and Willow Bertram who had turned up for Tomas, discussing the differences between the three boys and their appendages. Bertha told them all about Luiz and Tomas's affair with him, and Connie regaled them with stories of how Carlos had her night after night, and what his magic wand could do before it was owned by Viv.

Unfortunately, it was those stories that finally got them kicked out of the suite when Spiros Stephanopoulos overheard after they'd become boisterous with their recollections.

Connie waved goodbye to her chatty companions, arrived back at Harry's suite, and went to her room. Deciding to call Antonio to see if he was still working, she made the call.

"Hello."

"Hello, my darling, it's me. I'm just over in Athens and was wondering if you were still working. I thought I might pop over for a couple of days to see you and find out what your plans are."

"Hey, Mama. Yeah, I'm still working, but only have a couple of days to go. A week at the most." Antonio wearily sat on his bed in his room and sighed. It had been a long six month work period, and while he loved being in Mykonos in the summer, he was definitely worn out by fall.

"Good, good. I'll hop over tonight. Can you pick me up at the airport? We can have dinner together."

"Of course. Just call me back with the details."

*****

A few days later, he received a message from the hotel clerk that Carlos had called and left a number where he could be reached, and was now calling back. "Hey, Carlos, how are you, my man? Long-time no hear," Antonio said down the line to Athens. "What the hell have you been up to?"

"You wouldn't believe it even if I told you, man," Carlos joked.

"Try me," Antonio said, and went on to listen to the most incredible story he'd ever heard. If it weren't for growing up in Spain and meeting powerful men who expected favours, he wouldn't have believed it. "You *are* kidding?"

"Nah, man, I'm not. All of that happened, but the most important thing is I'm getting married next week and wonder if you can come."

"When next week, and to who?"

"Friday the fourth of November, and to model Vivian Villiers."

"Get out, you lucky bastard!" Antonio exclaimed. "You scored Vivian Villiers. Wait, have you two been together since that day at the beach bar?"

"Yep, we pretty much have. And I proposed the other day and she said yes. Figured I'd call and see if you could make it."

"Ah, yeah, sure. I can stay back a couple of days; my job ends on the thirty-first. I was going to fly out for London, but I'll stay back. I'll just change my plans. Besides, Mama's here for a quick visit, but says it's too cold, so she'll be gone in a day or two, then I'll catch up with her in London or Madrid."

"Oh." Carlos hadn't realised Connie had left Athens after their reunion the other day. "Okay, well, I'll see you on Friday the fourth. The wedding's at the church and the reception at *The Windmill*, so I'll see you then."

"Sure, man, see you then." After hanging up, Antonio called Cynthia. "Babe, I'm gonna be a few days late. I have a wedding to attend on the fourth, so I'll fly out on Saturday instead."

"Oh…okay." The disappointment in her voice was evident. "Anyone I know?"

"Remember that hot bartender you tripped over…" He grinned.

"Oh…" She blushed. "You're kidding?"

"Nope. He's marrying supermodel Vivian Villiers and I got an invitation. I'll change my flight to Saturday and see you then."

A soft sigh escaped her. "I can't wait. I miss you so much I ache for you."

The tense feeling in his stomach tightened. "I ache for you too, and can't wait to be with you again. I love you, see you next week."

"I love you too. See you soon."

*****

Monday, the thirty-first of October, was Antonio's last day as a bartender and hotel employee. He spent the next three days doing paperwork, finding a suit, and doing some shopping for Cynthia.

*****

On Friday, he attended the wedding of Carlos Stephanopoulos and Vivian Villiers, a massive one-hundred-people-plus affair with wild dancing, music, and much fun and laughter. He sat with Carlos's cousins and lamented over how the hell Carlos had scored such a hot woman for a wife, and met Roger and Angelina, and Jenny and Spiros when Carlos introduced members of the family to him.

At one point, he noticed Carlos talking to a video camera and sneaked up behind him, flinging his right arm around his friend's shoulders while his left hand waved his beer bottle around. "My name is Antonio DeLuca, and I've known this guy here," he pointed to Carlos, "Carlos Stephanopoulos, for three years. We've bartended together during the day, and now I'm at his wedding to the incredibly gorgeous Vivian Villiers." He grinned. "After three years of getting his rejects and sloppy seconds, he goes ahead and marries the woman I would have loved to have had."

"Hey," Carlos protested. "She's mine and you're lucky to be here."

"Yeah, yeah. Congratulations man, who'd have thought you'd get married at twenty-four and settle down before I did? And with a supermodel sixteen years older than you. You suck, and I'm jealous.

But seriously, congratulations, man."

"Thanks, man," Carlos said and the camera turned away.

After celebratory festivities went into the wee hours of the morning, Antonio finally managed to get back to his hotel room for eight hours of sleep before finalising his leave. His plane left at three that afternoon and he arrived in London that night into the open arms of Cynthia; a place he knew he never wanted to leave.

1978

It was a beautiful May spring day, and the wedding of Cynthia York and Antonio DeLuca was a small affair. She invited her small family and the friends who had been with her in Mykonos when they met, and he invited his parents and three best friends. Carlos and Viv couldn't make it because Viv was heavily pregnant, but both wished them well.

They stood facing each other in the dance pavilion, holding hands and grinning like two idiots about to take the plunge.

"Do you, Antonio Stephano DeLuca, take Cynthia Suzanne York, to be your lawfully wedded wife?"

"I do." His grin grew wider and he squeezed her hands.

She looked radiant in her simple white cotton dress that wafted around her ankles, with long frilly sleeves and a frilly neck. And she'd wound flowers through her brilliant red hair. Being six months pregnant had given her a glow, and Antonio was more than ecstatic at becoming a father. They certainly hadn't planned on it so soon, but since it happened almost the moment he'd arrived in London, they decided to run with it and see where it took them, with Antonio suggesting they get married when she'd announced she was pregnant.

"And do you, Cynthia Suzanne York, take Antonio Stephano DeLuca to be your lawfully wedded husband?"

"I do." She gazed adoringly at her new husband. The baby moved inside of her as if giving consent to the union.

"Then, by the power vested in me, I now pronounce you, husband and wife. You may kiss the bride."

Antonio gently took Cynthia's face in his hands and softly laid his lips on hers. They were as sweet as she was.

The small crowd cheered loudly, clapping and throwing rose petals instead of confetti. The happy couple laughingly made their way down the marble path to the back terrace where the food was being served and champagne was flowing. They partied and danced into the wee hours before leaving for their honeymoon.

They weren't going far, just to the family apartment in Madrid, as Cynthia had never been to Spain before and wanted to see the city. Antonio showed her around, and took her to a bullfight. Constantine Manzo was Madrid's current favourite matador thanks to his father. Cynthia hated it, and Antonio admitted he did too, even though he'd loved it as a child, when he'd told his father that he would be a better bullfighter than he was.

When their two weeks were up, they flew back to London for Cynthia to go back to work. She would be training a replacement over the next few months, before quitting to be a full-time mother, and they would live off Antonio's trust fund which Stephano had topped up as a wedding present. They moved into their new home in a suburb of London, a present from Connie and Stephano, bought and paid for so their son and grandson would have a place to live. With four bedrooms, three baths, and a guest bedroom on the ground floor, Cynthia and Antonio had a ball decorating with new furniture and homewares, and by the time the baby arrived, it was perfect for their little family.

*****

On August the 18th, Antonio Stephano DeLuca II was born. A healthy eight pounds eight ounces, he screamed the house down and made Stephano laugh with joy. There was finally another DeLuca heir in the family and he loved it.

Connie was just as ecstatic, doting on him from the moment he was born. It had taken her back to when Antonio came into the world, and she was loving every minute, taking over from Cynthia when she was too tired to deal with it. Both Connie and Stephano stayed in London through summer, Connie in the house with them, Stephano at one of the city's poshest, but private, hotels, so he could still have his dalliances.

"Oh, hello, little Antonio," Antonio cooed as he gently bounced his healthy baby boy. "Look at you. You are alive and in this world and screaming down the house. Yes, you are." He gazed lovingly into his son's eyes. They were an exotic mix of brown with green, making them almost a minty milk chocolate. The baby's hair was a chestnut colour, as if someone had run red-dye-covered hands through his black hair giving it a red glow. His chubby little hands were clasped together in front of his chubby little face and he yawned, tired after screaming for hours non-stop.

Antonio smiled. The love radiating out of him was overwhelming. It was nothing like he'd ever felt before, not for his mother, not for Cynthia. The love he was feeling for his son was the most powerful thing that took over his body. How a tiny little human being could have such an effect on him, make him feel so completely in love, and *full* of love like he'd never known, astonished him.

Cynthia came into the room and handed him a bottle of heated milk, and tiredly leaned against the door jamb, watching with love and happiness flowing from her every pore.

Antonio slowly walked around, feeding Tony. "Yes, you're hungry, aren't you, my little one. Yes, yes, you are. Very hungry. No wonder you were crying, coz your tummy was empty, yes, it was. You were hungry."

Cynthia smiled at her husband and the joy he radiated. They had been home from the hospital for a week and she was exhausted, but Antonio was loving being a father, and with her mother's and Connie's help, she was able to get settled into being a new parent. It helped that Antonio did all the work. He was such a doting father, it was incredible, and she was incredibly lucky to have found such an amazing man to be with. Her heart was overflowing with love for him and it would never stop. Not even in death. He was it for her, her forever, and if they were lucky enough, they would have more children to bring home to their little house.

Antonio glanced up and caught her smile, then smiled himself. His life was perfect. A beautiful wife, a brand-new baby boy. It was all he'd ever wanted and now it was his.

Forever.

1979

Stephano walked into *Studio 69*, the hottest club in New York. He'd heard about it on the gay grapevine and wanted to give it a try, especially since Pedro Stefan was the DJ there. He knew about the Stefan/Stephanopoulos family, having found out that Carlos was Antonio's ex-bartender co-worker who had absconded two years ago, and that Connie had played a part in it. That was something he'd found out by accident, overhearing a conversation Connie was having on the phone when he was visiting Antonio and Cynthia last Christmas. He didn't know who she was talking to, just what she was talking about.

Carlos and Vivian, and, oh, how she missed what Carlos could do to her and how she hadn't found a man who could do that since.

He'd known Connie had lovers, as he did, but how could he be angry at her for having them. It was the fact she had *paid* Carlos with *his* money. But, since an argument about it would have more than likely revealed his gay tendencies in a fit of anger, he kept the information to himself and didn't begrudge her.

The music brought him out of his memories and his gaze roamed around the club. A hot sexy heat wafted around him, carrying scents of man and woman, mixed with alcohol, drugs and sex. And he wanted in. It exhilarated him down to his toes, made his gut throb with the anticipation of sex and men, and made his erection strain for release in multiple directions at once. It wanted in on the scene before him. The hot lusty sweat of man on man pulsated it with urgency and made it move in the direction of the hot black roller-skating waiter that rolled past.

Leon had worked at *69* since it started, and had sampled all of the men who were interested, except he desperately wanted the ones who weren't. Like Carlos Stephanopoulos, Pedro's brother. He'd seen Carlos's movies ten times each, the same with the other brother, Tomas, and his films. But it was Carlos he wanted most. All ten inches of him. In his mouth, up his ass. But Carlos wasn't interested, so he kept it in his pants. Except when he was fucking every man who wanted him. And the hot looking stud that had just walked in was eyeing him off right now. He served the drinks and rolled over to the man, slowly circling him as he went. "Can I get you a drink, big boy? You're lookin' mighty thirsty."

Stephano eyed the man and took in the details. Strong, athletic, African American, which he'd never had before, big mouth, long tongue that could do wonders, he was sure. He liked what he saw and ordered a drink. "Champagne, your finest. Is there a table I can sit at to enjoy it...*and* the view?" He gave Leon the once over and Leon responded in kind.

"We have booths on the side if you don't mind sitting with other people." Leon came to a halt in front of Stephano and slid a finger down his lapel. Sidling closer and flicking his tongue at Stephano, he added, "And I can get you anything else you like. Drugs, drink, men. I'm off at six tomorrow morning, but I take a break in half an hour." He was desperately hoping he could sample the man before him. The dark exotic features intrigued him, and he wondered what race, or ethnicity, he was.

Stephano reached out his right hand and grasped Leon's crotch, finding it standing to its fullest attention. "Then I will be expecting *you* served to me on a platter in half an hour."

Leon ground against the hand, enjoying the manly embrace. Oh, yes, he definitely wanted this man. "Then I will get your drink and show you to a table." His eyes rolled back and his head fell, he choked for air as he orgasmed in his tiny gold shorts and breathed on the exhale. "Oh...I will definitely be ready for you in half an hour."

Stephano let him go, and he slowly rolled backwards toward the bar to get the champagne. Turning, he stopped at the bar and gave the order. "Finest champagne to the hot stud who just arrived," he told Mike Gatos, the bartender.

Mike grinned at Leon's dazed expression. "I take it you just got off."

"Whoo, did I ever!" Leon gripped the bar as his body swayed. "All he did was give me a rub and I was his. I should go change my shorts."

Mike screwed up his face and handed the champagne over. "You might want to deliver this first."

"Oh, *I will* deliver." Leon flashed a cheeky grin and rolled off toward the Spaniard. "And here is your champagne, sir." He presented his tray with a flourish and waited until Stephano took the glass. "And I will take you to one of our private booths. You may have to share, unless you want one all to yourself to do anything you want in. Can't guarantee it, though." He linked his arm through Stephano's and escorted him over to the wall where the booths were set up. "Here we go. I think you're sharing this one with Stan. He's a regular. Banker by day, party animal gay by night. But don't give him everything you've got, because I want some later." Leon settled Stephano into the booth and asked if he wanted anything else.

"Yes…" Stephano stared into Leon's big brown eyes. "Bring me the whole bottle when you bring yourself in half an hour. And make sure we have somewhere to go that is private. I do not want to do it here."

"You sure 'bout that?" Leon asked, sliding his hand over Stephano's shoulders and slipping onto his lap. "To get off in the club is quite an experience. The music, the lights, the sexual tension, and musky smells make it all the more thrilling." He nuzzled Stephano's neck. "You can get off even more."

Stephano felt a hand on his crotch and left it there. "I'm sure you can, and who knows, in half an hour I may be up for it."

Leon expertly finished the job and slid off his lap. "I hope so, coz I can bring you up and take you down, and make you spin round and round." He spun around in circles, head back, arms up in the air, and then stopped, watching Stephano's eyes glitter with excitement. "I'll be back in half an hour." He rolled off and got back to work.

Stephano's eyes followed him, and then flitted from man to man to finally land on Pedro Stephanopoulos. He watched him dance around the stage and fling his arms in the air, and wondered if the brothers were there. He craned his neck to see if he recognised anyone, but couldn't find any other Stefan in the house, so his gaze moved on. The roller-skating staff were all buffed up bodies of pure testosterone, and he could see why *69* was the latest in hottest clubs for gay men. The music was a little too loud for him, but at least it covered any sounds being made by the sexual actions of fellow party goers. The fact it was a club did not stop sex from happening, if anything, it promoted it to the fullest and highest extreme, and encouraged it to happen on the dance floor itself, not to mention against the walls and bars, and who knew where else.

Stephano had never been in a club so vibrant and out there, and out for the gay population. There were no openly gay ones in Spain, it was all hidden in back rooms, and only the odd one here and there across Europe and the Mediterranean. Except for Mykonos, which was thriving in its own way. Part of him felt uneasy, the other part felt right at home. He didn't have to hide his sexuality there, as everyone else was the exact same way. He didn't have to worry about his wife or son finding out. Didn't have to worry about the bullfighting community back in Spain finding out. He had absolutely nothing to worry about within the four walls of that club.

And he loved it!

A man approached the booth and sat down. "Phew, sharing a booth tonight, I see. Hello, I'm Stan, Stan Kosnov. And you are?" He held out his hand to the striking Mediterranean man and couldn't wait to sample him.

"Stephano," he replied, shaking Stan's hand. "Stephano DeLuca."

"Well, more like Stephano DeLucky. Look at you, all hot and spicy." Stan sipped his cocktail and eyed Stephano over the brim. "Italian? Greek?"

"Spanish," Stephano replied, wondering if Stan was someone he could get into.

"Ooh, Spaniard. I've never had a Spaniard before." Stan slid around the booth. "I haven't seen you here before. First time, I take it?" He casually crossed his legs, leaned an elbow against the back of the booth, and swayed toward Stephano for a closer look.

Stephano smiled in return. "Yes, first time here. I have heard much about this place since I got here to New York, and thought I would try it out." He looked Stan up and down. "And see what I could find."

"Oh, you'll find all types here," Stan flirted. "Straight, gay, queer, we're all weird here. Except for the DJ, he's straight out straight and married to a pretty young thing who had his baby last year. She's a cute little bundle of joy, she is. And the family comes in sometimes to party, especially for their birthdays which just happens to all be on Valentine's day, and then sometimes over the Christmas New Year's period."

"Does he wear those shorts every time?" Stephano inquired, glancing around to other staff nearby.

"Oh, they all do. But Pedro's the only one with a twelve inch schlong." Stan tossed the dregs of his drink back. "But, being straight, his pretty little wife is the only one to get it on a regular basis. Although, he has done porn movies. Maybe you've seen them?" He clicked his fingers to get the attention of the passing waiter to order another drink, then turned to Stephano. "Anything for you?"

"Not yet, I'll get my next one in," he checked his watch, "ten minutes."

Stan watched him with interest and waved the waiter away. "And why ten minutes?"

"Because that's when my bottle arrives, and so does ejaculation!" Stephano toasted his glass to Stan and turned his gaze to Pedro. "Twelve inches, huh?"

"Oooh, I love ejaculation." Stan moved closer. "Can anyone join in?"

Stephano's lips slyly moved up at the edges. "Who knows. Maybe I will sample everyone here who is willing."

"And who are you sampling in ten minutes?" Stan asked, his finger trailing over Stephano's leg to his crotch.

Stephano caught it, making Stan look up in surprise. "The waiter. Have you had him?"

Stan slid closer still. "And which waiter would that be? There are so many gorgeous buff bodies in this place, it's hard not to keep it up when they're all dressed in those teeny tiny gold shorts." His soft grey eyes bored into Stephano's dark ones. "You tend to not remember, or even ask names here. It's all mysterious and secretive and under the covers." A chuckle left him. "Although, most of it's out in the open, and not undercover at all. As you can see." He waved a hand across the room. "It's all out in the open for all to see. Once we step inside these four walls, we leave our old life, our daytime life, and any issues we have at the door and let them all go. When we step in here, we let our true selves free, and be who and what we want to be." His hand slid over Stephano's leg to his crotch. "Are you up for that, Stephano DeLucky?"

"It's DeLuca," Stephano stated and looked from Stan to Leon as he rolled to a stop with his champagne. "And right now. I'm up for anything." Taking the bottle from Leon, he put it to his mouth and swallowed the chilled crystal fluid. "Shall we stay here, or have you found us a private place to share?"

Leon slid onto Stephano's lap and waved Stan away. "Except for downstairs, which no one gets into unless you get the gold deluxe invitation, the only other places are the offices, the toilets, or the back alley. And you can have your back alley serviced anywhere in this club." His right hand expertly undid Stephano's pants and moved inside. "So…how about I service you right here. There are curtains if you want them drawn. You can still hear the music and see the lights, but no one will see in. And everyone knows when the curtains are drawn to not enter, because an orgasm is in progress."

"Yes," Stephano slurred through champagne and sex hazed eyes. "Close the curtain."

Leon gestured to Stan who quickly got up and closed both curtains, making sure no one could see in before slipping back onto the couch next to Stephano. He knew he was about to get lucky. "And the sofa here is wide enough for a bed." He patted it and arranged the cushions so he was comfortable.

"Yes," Stephano murmured, his eyes closing as Leon went down on him. "I see…that…"

Stan wanted in on the action. He'd had Leon before, and knew what a big mouth could do to a man, especially when enclosed around a penis, so he pulled his own out and ran a hand through Leon's wild black afro while rubbing against Stephano. "Have you ever had an African before?"

"No," Stephano muttered, his hand joining Stan's on Leon's head. His eyes opened and he watched the scene. "Never had an American before."

Stan slid his right arm around Stephano, bringing him closer. "Well, you'll get two for the price of one tonight. And that price is free. Free for the taking, free for the fucking. We'll do whatever you want, Stephano DeLucky. Whatever you want."

Stephano came and briefly closed his eyes. It was a new thrill, getting sucked in a club, knowing full well that just on the other side of the curtains were hundreds of people all vying for a look, or a fuck of their own. It excited him and aroused him even more. "I want to see the two of you fuck."

Stan's penis hardened to full capacity and Leon moved his mouth from Stephano to Stan. Stan's head fell back in ecstasy as Leon slid between his legs and he wrapped them around Leon to hold him there.

Leon went at it. Sucking, blowing, giving it all he had.

Stephano watched on in amazement that neither man had any insecurities or hesitations at sucking in a club. He leaned back on the couch, took a swig of champagne and watched on as Leon finished up, slid up Stan's body, and then turned around and back ended him. He bounced up and down until Stan cried out.

"Fuck, me, oh, God, fuck me." He hung on to Leon as if riding a wild bull and flopped around the couch.

Stephano's brow rose in surprise. *These Americans certainly know how to let loose.*

Leon came to a grinding halt, dismounted, waited for Stan to roll over and lean over the back of the couch before he entered. Thrusting urgently, he gripped Stan's penis and gave it a good going over as he hammered home. When done, they both rolled onto their backs, cocks out, bodily juices flowing freely.

"Well…" Stephano took another drink. "You Americans know how to give it good, and have a good time. But do either of you know what we Spanish men are like…?"

1980

It was the weekend after Valentine's day and Stephano had finally celebrated with his new lover. A younger man, no different to any other he'd had. All were in their 20s or 30s these days so he could be the big man in charge with his maturity and knowledge in the bedroom. But over Christmas, he'd met Jamal Devron, a thirty-nine-year-old African American police officer with the NYPD.

Stephano had first seen Jamal when he'd gone into the precinct to file a complaint of theft. He'd had his wallet stolen, more than likely because his pocket had been picked, and had lost almost a thousand dollars. They'd spied each other across the room, and sparks had ignited. He'd casually managed to leave a business card on Jamal's desk with his name and number on it as he'd walked by, and thought nothing more of it until seeing Jamal at *Studio 69* that night when he stopped by to see what was happening. From his spacious bed in his luxurious room, he spied Jamal scowling at himself in the bathroom mirror.

Six feet of black man with a close-cropped hairdo and newly trimmed moustache looked back at Jamal as he stared at himself. He felt something scratchy in his throat and coughed. He'd been trying to kick a bug for weeks.

That was the problem with February; it may have been the end of winter, but the bugs just weren't disappearing. *At least it's not like the flu I had last year,* he thought.

Seeing the fifty-something Spaniard in incredible shape with a head of jet-black hair and blacker eyes walk into the bathroom, he thought long and hard about his new lover. He had a body to die for and a cock that could perform magic. And it performed magic on him. Normally he went for the younger men, hot Latin, Brazilian, Middle Eastern, all twenty-something so he could be the big man in charge with his badge and cuffs. But after seeing Stephano in the precinct that day, and finding his card on his desk, he'd somehow come across him later that night at *Studio 69*. There were fewer people there as the regular hot DJ slash porn star, Pedro Stefan, wasn't in, but he'd gone anyway as it was one of the best places to pick up. And pick up he did. Stephano had taken him home and hammered away until the sun came up, performing trick after trick with his magic dick, and his magic tongue, and his magic fingers.

And God how those fingers had Jamal in the palm of their hand. "Oh, God." He groaned as Stephano's hand moved back and forth on his cock. "I really have to get dressed for work," he breathed, his eyes closing against the rush of blood.

"Not just yet, not until I have my final fill for the morning," Stephano told him, taking him into his mouth and getting what he wanted before forcing Jamal onto his back on the floor and sitting on his face while shoving his own cock into Jamal's mouth. "Suck it," he commanded. His legs pinned Jamal's arms down as he leant forward to kneel and thrust his magic dick back and forth into Jamal. "Suck it, suck it. Oh, God, suck it. Yes, yes, yes, oh, God, I'm coming, I'm coming. Yes, oh, God, yes, yes, yes." Sitting back, he moved and mounted Jamal's hard cock, slowly going up and down while he got his breath back. "Oh, yes," he moaned, feeling the width of the man he was on. "Oh, yes."

Jamal let him do all the work and lay back, noticing the marks on his lover's body and the scratches from him. He coughed and tried to sit up, but he kept coughing, and the movement stirred Stephano further.

"Oh, God, yes," he groaned. "But stop coughing, you are ruining the moment."

"Can't help it," Jamal rasped. "Damn bug I picked up at Christmas."

He looked down, and that's when he saw the small spots on Stephano's dick. He'd seen them before on other lovers, especially in the last two years. Damn genital ulcers, no wonder he'd got them last year. It seemed to be a thing going around, but he'd gone to a doctor and had been treated. But, here they were again. "I gotta go, Stephano," he rasped, his throat worse than usual. "I gotta get to work."

"Just one more," Stephano said, bouncing along like the bullfighter he was. "Just…one…more…ah…" He stiffened, his eyes widened to the size of saucers and his jaw dropped open. "Ah…" The air slowly left his body and he stared at the ceiling.

"Stephano?" Jamal hadn't seen him act like this before and it worried him. "Stephano?" He poked his arm.

"Ah…" Stephano released and settled onto Jamal. "Sometimes you just need to hold it all in and let the release take its toll."

"Its effect, you mean." Jamal eyed his lover's face.

"Whatever." Stephano shrugged and got to his feet. "Now, you must not be late for work, and I must not be late for my flight." He eyed his abs in the bathroom mirror before stepping into the shower.

"Flight?" Jamal looked up sharply from his spot on the floor. "You didn't tell me you were going anywhere." He slowly clambered to his feet.

"I wasn't, but my wife is back in Spain after her long sojourn around the world, and we need to sort some paperwork out."

"Wife!" Jamal exclaimed. "You didn't tell me you had a wife."

"Well, I didn't tell my wife I was gay, and we have lived separate lives for many years. But we occasionally catch up for old times' sake." He turned off the faucets.

"So, am I the only man you've fucked?" Jamal stood in the middle of the bathroom watching as his lover towelled down.

"Of course not." Stephano shrugged. "There have been many men, especially these last years."

A noise came from Jamal as he stared in disbelief and understanding.

"What?" Stephano asked. "You didn't think you were the only one, did you? Just as I am not the only one for you."

Jamal finally got his act together. "No…no…I guess not. I just didn't expect a goddamn wife. At least have the decency to be free, especially from a woman."

"I am." Stephano walked into the bedroom of his spacious two-floor penthouse apartment. He'd bought it the year before when he'd discovered the joys of New York's gay sex scene and needed a private place to partake in it. "We are just bound by law, nothing else."

"That's bad enough," Jamal replied. "But you also got ulcers on your dick, and should get them seen to."

Stephano looked down and shrugged once more. "I've had those for ages. Everybody has."

"Yeah, well, I certainly don't have those blotches on my body." Jamal pointed to the reddish-purple spots on Stephano's feet.

Another shrug. "Ah, old man's disease. They can be covered."

"Really?" Jamal pulled on his pants. "Old man disease? So, you're old? You're so old that old man disease has spread to your torso?"

Stephano glanced down. "Dry skin, bruises, of no importance."

Jamal shook his head. What the hell had he got himself into? An older man who'd made no mention of a wife, an older man that had the same sexual diseases as every other man he'd been with had. *Jesus fucking Christ, is the whole gay community fuckin' disease ridden?* Fixing his cuffs and doing up his tie, he looked in the mirror. His uniform stared back, *glared* back, yet his eyes were haunted, dull, and the frown lines were deeper, more evident, and so were the spots, small, around his ears, one near his collar. He figured it was an African thing, having seen those on the continent with the same markings in books and on TV. But, after seeing similar ones on his lover's body, he was beginning to question what they actually were.

*****

Ten days later, after a quick dash to Spain to deal with some legal paperwork with Connie and have a quick fling, he was back and received a call. A surprising call at that.

Putting the phone down, he cut the conversation short, thinking about what he'd just been told. He'd been in Leon Talley's little black book, and Leon was dead, and a young man by the name of Pedro Stephanopoulos had wanted to know if he'd be attending the funeral on Saturday.

"What did he die of?" Stephano had asked.

"Many sexually transmitted diseases, cancer, pneumonia, a whole bunch of horrible icky stuff," Pedro had replied.

"My, that's horrible," Stephano said. "Thank you for telling me, young man. You wouldn't happen to be related to a Carlos Stephanopoulos, would you?"

Pedro had baulked. "Why?"

"My son once worked with a Stephanopoulos."

"Your son?"

"Antonio DeLuca, in Mykonos."

"Oh, right. He worked with my brother at the resort's summer bar. Why?"

"He fucked my wife for money. I won't be attending Leon's funeral, but thank you for calling."

He sat thinking about Leon and sexually transmitted diseases. He knew that he, Stephano DeLuca, had some of his own. What man didn't? But that was normal, right? He glanced down at his bare ankles and saw the blotches creeping up his legs. They appeared here and there on his torso, but disappeared after a week, or three. He hadn't seen a doctor for them, and knew that his father and grandfather had had them as well. He knew it was a Mediterranean thing that older men got, so there was no need to worry about it. Right?

He dashed off to the toilet where his bowel relieved itself, and he saw himself in the mirror. He'd dropped a few pounds from the diarrhea, and his skin was looking a bit grey. Thank God his quick fling with Connie happened before the diarrhea started. Otherwise, it would have been a mess.

She was always up for a good time. They'd been married long enough, but they'd gone their separate ways with separate lovers years ago. She had hers, he had his, but every now and then they came back together for a quickie, and they always enjoyed it.

After clearing up, he stood, only to be overcome with cramps and a shortness of breath. "Ugh. What is this? I must have caught Jamal's damn bug."

*****

It was now June, and Stephano was in London spending a couple of months with Antonio and Cynthia. He loved spending time with little Tony, and being a doting grandpa. And fortunately, his diarrhea had settled down, so he didn't have any emergencies in front of his family. He still stayed at a private hotel, though, and had his medical issues seen to by a doctor. But, outside of giving him medication, there wasn't much else they could do except suggest a thorough exam, which he refused. Stephano DeLuca had never needed an examination by any doctor in his entire life. He had been fit and healthy all his years, and wasn't stopping now.

He flicked open the *New York Times* the hotel had kindly got for him while he was in town and started reading. A bank robbery here, a spate of pickpocketing there. *No wonder I lost my wallet,* he mused. *Looks like it's become quite prevalent.* Thinking back to the time he'd reported his stolen wallet, his thoughts soon turned to Jamal and how they met. He generally went for exotic types like himself. Italian, Spanish, Greek, hell, he'd even had Colombian men to see if they were different to Connie. He'd only dipped his toe into the African pool of men a few times, even though their big mouths and even bigger dicks had pleased him plenty.

With his memories wandering, he turned the page and came across a half page burial notice for fallen NYPD officer Jamal Devron.

"What the fuck...?" he muttered, staring down at the paper. The black and white pictures did Jamal no justice, and the story that went with it offered no real clues except for Jamal having a cancer called Kaposi's sarcoma, which was prominent in African and Mediterranean men, and Pneumocystis pneumonia.

"Jesus...Christ..." The paper fell from Stephano's hands onto the table and lay there, like a blank accusation staring back at him. Telling him, over and over that something was wrong, something was happening, and it was affecting everyone. Not just his ex-lovers, but everyone in the world. And soon, it would affect him.

He had the same spots as Jamal. Was that the cancer? This... Kaposi's sarcoma? Were they the blotches he had on his body? He knew he had the odd genital herpes here and there, as most of his lovers did, and he received medication for them, but the cancer and pneumonia?

"No...no, it can't be...why would he die of such things?" Stephano was at a loss. *True, Jamal had a bug when I saw him just a few short months ago, but surely it could not have been this cancer, this pneumonia that's mentioned in the paper. I cannot catch this pneumonia, can I?*

He read the story again, gaining no new insight into the death of his ex; a man he'd only had a couple of flings with across December to February. Once he'd flown back from Spain, he hadn't seen Jamal again. Hadn't called, hadn't gone to his place, nothing.

And now...he was dead.

Just like Leon.

He remembered that call. The one from Pedro telling him he was in Leon's little black book of lovers, and had been asked if he wanted to attend the burial. Why would he? He'd had a fling with Leon a couple of times in 1979 while he was in town. It was his first foray into American *and* African men, and he'd liked it well enough to keep seeing American men when he was in town.

Turning his thoughts back to Jamal, he considered the rumours he'd heard when he'd been in New York. Gay men were getting ill, no one knew what it was, and no one knew how they got it, but they were starting to die off. Should he be worried? Maybe. But when two of his ex-lovers were dead, maybe it was something he should look into.

He thought about the men from *69* that he'd dabbled in. A regular called Stan, some of the other waiters, and downstairs in the private rooms, where he'd been specially invited by the owner, there were all kinds. Even male celebrities you wouldn't consider, or know, to be gay, were down there getting it on with other men. That was the point of the rooms downstairs. Only the very famous, or the very rich, got in. And, occasionally, some of the regulars did if they got the golden ticket.

He chuckled and stroked his chin in thought. "I should write another book about all of the things I know. That would really get the publishing world's pulse racing. But then, it would also out me to the world." His brain calculated a few things. "Maybe if I use a nom de plume. A woman's, perhaps. That would really get the blood pumping, the juices flowing. Outing all of the gay men in New York, especially the ones you see on the news every night, or the soaps during the day. Oh, yes, those little tidbits of information would set the world aflame."

His mind wandered back to the nightly newsreader, the star of the biggest rating soap in the world, the editor of the bestselling fashion magazine, the former athlete turned movie star, and the countless actors, singers, authors, and high-profiled celebrities he'd watched and encountered the few times he'd been downstairs at *Studio 69*. He'd sampled, how could he not, and partaken in many a moment with many a celebrity, knowing full well it would be kept as secret as their status.

"I wonder how all of them are?" he murmured and flicked through the paper to the obituaries. He scanned for names he knew, but didn't find any. So far, it was just Leon and Jamal he personally knew of, and he hoped everyone else was fine. Wondering if he should find out, he considered how to go about it.

Except, he didn't.

In fact, he couldn't have cared less.

Stephano spent the next four months travelling the globe as he always did, enjoying the sights, the sounds, and the men, as he always did. It was the way he lived his life now, travelling from country to country, city to city, island to island, sampling all the delights he could find.

But, did he once go to the doctor to find out what the spots on his body were?

Did he bother to find out how many more of his ex-lovers had died, or were sick?

No.

Because Stephano DeLuca did, what Stephano DeLuca wanted. And to hell with everyone else.

*****

In October, the weather had cooled off in London and New York, so Stephano travelled down to Mexico and the island of Cancún, to finish enjoying the late summer sun to keep his bones and body warm. That's the way it was with old age, he was finding. While he could still get his penis up, he couldn't necessarily get his body up. His bones ached on a regular basis, and his skin was thin and blotchy. His weight had dropped significantly in the last couple of months, and his muscle tone was no more.

Looking in the mirror, he saw a worn out old man staring back. His once thick jet-black hair had greyed through, more prominently at the temples, and it had thinned and receded too. His face was hollow and colourless, lifeless, as he turned this way and that, looking, staring at the changes in him. His flesh, his skin, his body.

He turned side on and studied his physique. Slouching, withering... limp.

"How in the hell did I get this way?" he asked his reflection, frowning at all he saw. "How did the great Stephano DeLuca get to look like this? This, this, *shell* of a man." His hand waved weakly at his reflection, taking it all in, and his head shook with dismay, embarrassment, and shame.

He had not gone to the doctors as he should have. He did not have the examinations that he should have. He had not checked up on his former lovers as he should have.

No. He had denied it all and gone on living life as if there was no tomorrow. No end to his lavish, extravagant, unrestrained, debauched lifestyle. He had fucked all the men he wanted, never used protection, never worried about the end of his life. He was the great matador, Stephano DeLuca, bullfighter of Spain, bullfighter of the world. He would live on and on for all eternity...

Coughing, he quickly grabbed a tissue from the box on the sink, and wiping his mouth, saw the blood on it. He looked up into the mirror and saw the stain his blood had formed on his lips. Stained them bright blood-red. Blood, like all of the bulls' blood he had stained the great bullrings of the world with after almost every fight. Blood, like all of the times the toilet had been stained with it when he urinated. Blood, like all of the times he had bled after anal sex. Blood, the colour of all of his dreams that had been coming in droves for the last few months. Since reading about Jamal, and remembering about Leon, and wondering about all of his ex-lovers and whether he should check on them.

He hadn't, and now he was wondering if he was paying the price for not doing so.

There was a knock at the door and his ears pricked up. Glancing sharply over his shoulder, he debated on whether to answer it. He knew who it was. His Filipino houseboy-come-maid who had been treating him as if he were the king of Spain. Treating him to sensuous massages every day and night. To lavish meals and spa treatments, to the magic of his penis.

Ah, yes, being ill had not slowed Stephano DeLuca down. If anything, it had made him more rampant.

He yelled, "Come in," through the bathroom doorway and quickly cleaned his mouth with toothpaste and wash. With one last look in the mirror, he slid his hands over his hair to slick it back, sucked in his sagging gut, and walked out into the lounge room of his luxurious suite in the very private hotel cabana on the edge of the water. He'd wanted as private as possible, which he always got when he travelled the world. A man of his tastes and dalliances needed it, and every hotel concierge was more than happy to oblige.

"Ah, Jomar-Ko, there you are. I was wondering when you were going to turn up today." He stood proudly in the middle of the room and waited for his houseboy slash toy boy to compliment him on his physique.

"Ah, Mr Stephano, sir, you looking very fit and handsome today." Jomar-Ko gave Stephano what he wanted, even though he knew it was a lie. As with most men over fifty, they all thought they were still in shape and as manly as they used to be in their twenties. They weren't, and the great bullfighter, Stephano DeLuca, was no exception. So, Jomar-Ko lied. As he always did. "Are you ready for me today, Mr

Stephano?" He slid out of his clothes and let them fall to the floor. "I am very horny today, Mr Stephano. How would you like me?" At twenty-two, the very gay Jomar-Ko had travelled all the way from the Philippines to work in Cancún. It allowed him to be freely gay, without putting it out there too much. He was average height, lean and muscular, and while he worked as the housemaid, he serviced the men in many other ways, finding it to be very profitable. And in his spare time, he watched porn videos, like the ones with the great Stefan brothers, to learn a few lessons, and then he used them on his clients. And boy, were they left very happy indeed. He was making *a motza* out of it. His erection was long and strong, and Stephano greedily eyed it.

Walking over to Jomar-Ko, Stephano's right hand grasped it and pulled him closer.

"Ooh, Mr Stephano," Jomar-Ko squealed. "You are very feisty today." His hands slid over Stephano's body and his smile lit up his face. "You are very fit, today, Mr Stephano. Have you been working out?"

Stephano preened a little. "Why, yes, but only when you come, my dear Jomar-Ko. Only when you come…" He left the sentence hanging and led Jomar-Ko over to the bed by his penis. "Let's get to exercising, shall we?"

"Ooh, Mr Stephano, how do you want me?" Jomar-Ko bounced onto the bed and spread his legs. "Do you want to eat first, Mr Stephano?"

Stephano considered it a moment. "Yes, I think I might." Lying between Jomar-Ko's thighs, Stephano delighted in Asian cock. It was not something he had on a regular basis, in fact, he rarely went for Asians at all. But, he was finding in his old age he couldn't be picky when it came to who he could fuck.

"Ooh, Mr Stephano, you so good with your mouth," Jomar-Ko groaned, his hands in what was left of Stephano's hair, hanging on and keeping his head there. "You so good with your tongue too. Ugh, ugh, Mr Stephano," he gasped, as he lost all sense of control and came as the deed was finished. "Oh, Mr Stephano…"

Stephano looked up and saw Jomar-Ko's eyes closed in ecstasy, a light sweat on his face, and a dirty smile on his mouth. "Now it's your turn, my boy."

"Ugh, Mr Stephano." Jomar-Ko slowly opened his eyes to see Stephano making his way up his body. "Mr Stephano, you know you too big for me to take. But I will take you anyway."

Stephano rolled onto his back and Jomar-Ko got to work. Sucking Stephano's dick like it was the world's best lollipop. "Mmm, mmm, mmm." Jomar-Ko came up for air. "Oh, Mr Stephano. You so big I think I might choke on you." He went back to work and took Stephano as he came.

Stephano lay back in euphoria. Getting his cock sucked always did the trick to get him started. It got him up, and got the blood flowing. And always, *always* made him feel alive and young again.

"Mr Stephano, you no go to sleep on me are you?" Jomar-Ko kissed his way up Stephano's blotchy old body and laid his head on his chest. "What you want to do now, Mr Stephano?"

"I want to fuck you," Stephano murmured, hearing light wheezing coming from his chest. His breathing hadn't been easy lately, and he'd needed lots of steam baths and showers just to help keep his airways open. He'd even thought of going to the doctor for asthma medication in case that's what he was coming down with. And if not, then it might make him breathe easier anyway.

"Okay, Mr Stephano. How do you want me?" Jomar-Ko straddled him. "You want me on top like this? Or you want me underneath you so you come in behind?"

"Face down on the bed," Stephano told him and watched as Jomar-Ko prepared himself, face down, for the entrance of the great DeLuca cock. With a little more wheezing, and a few extra seconds to get going, Stephano rolled onto the back of his toy boy and gained entrance.

"Oh, Mr Stephano," Jomar-Ko groaned, his eyes rolling to the back of his head. "You so big and so good. Harder." He gripped the bed sheets and put it between his teeth for something to bite down on. As much as he was gay, anal sex didn't really do it for him, especially when he had a man up his. And right now, it just wasn't happening right.

"Oh, that's good," Stephano breathed out and in, air becoming harder to suck in. "I...oh..." breath, "can't..." Dizziness overcame him, his heart pounded in his chest, his muscles convulsed, and while death was nowhere near Stephano's mind, he knew what was coming. Knew his breath, his heart, his body were about to give out. Knew that all of his lovers, all of his one night stands, all the times he never wore protection because that's not what gay men did, all the times he told himself to go to the doctor and didn't when he should have, were now bringing his life to an end as the air was leaving his body.

"Ooh, Mr Stephano, you good today." Jomar-Ko felt the jerky movements of the spasms, but didn't realise there was anything wrong with the man in his anus. "You go, Mr Stephano."

Slowly jerking to a stop, the last thing the mighty bullfighter of Spain, Stephano DeLuca, thought of before his breath came out of him and his heart stopped was, *this is how I will be remembered...*

No moments about his beloved wife Connie, or his beloved son Antonio, or grandson Tony, and what this would do to them. No, Stephano Antonopoulos DeLuca was just as selfish in death as he had been in life. All he was worried about was himself.

"Mr Stephano?" Jomar-Ko perked his head up at the silence. "Mr Stephano? You okay? You didn't fall asleep on me, did you? Mr Stephano?"

Receiving no reply, and hearing no snores, Jomar-Ko glanced over his shoulder and saw Stephano staring, unblinking at the bed. "Mr Stephano? You okay?" Grabbing Stephano's wrist, he checked for a pulse. It wouldn't be the first time he'd had a client die on him. But die *up* him?

Feeling no pulse, he tried to turn. "Mr Stephano, wake up. Mr Stephano." Using his hands, he pushed at Stephano, trying to either wake him, or move him. He was unsuccessful at both, and all it did was dislodge the blood in Stephano's throat to come dripping out onto Jomar-Ko's back and slide onto the bed. "Mr Stephano," he shrieked. "Mr Stephano. Ah, help, me, somebody, ah." His shrieks reached the highest decibel level as his panic wreaked havoc on his own body. He still had a client's penis up his ass and he couldn't move him. He was stuck. So he shrieked more. More so when the door came crashing in and the hotel security burst through the door.

"Freeze, stay where you are."

The armed guards aimed their guns at Jomar-Ko and he screeched louder. Flapping his arms and legs, he tried to get out from under Stephano, but with the guards just standing there scratching their heads at what to do, he couldn't do much.

The hotel concierge came through the door. "Stop that...oh..." He stopped mid-sentence when he saw the scene and quickly spun around to shut the door. "Stop that damn screeching," he snapped at Jomar-Ko. "You got yourself into this, and now we need to fix it. The police are on their way. I called them when we heard the screams."

Jomar-Ko finally ran out of breath and collapsed onto the bed. He didn't know what was to become of him now, but there was no way he could get out of it, no matter which way he tried.

The police arrived within minutes and surveyed the scene. "So, what do we have here?"

"A hotel guest seems to have passed on." The concierge told them Stephano's name and who he was, mentioned the screaming, and the scene as they saw it.

"Well, looks like you'd better call the doctor in then. First the hotel doctor, and then the medical examiner," the chief constable said.

The concierge called in the doctor who promptly proclaimed Stephano DeLuca to be dead, and he helped roll Stephano from the housemaid whom the police promptly arrested.

"But I not do anything," Jomar-Ko whined as he was sat up on the bed, his cock flopping around for all to see, and was placed in handcuffs. "Mr Stephano hotel guest. I just do as he says."

"Except you do this with every other gay man in the hotel, Jomar-Ko." The concierge was exasperated, but still placed a towel over the maid's lap so no one had to look at him. He knew full well who Stephano DeLuca was and what he did, and this was going to be an absolute bitch to explain to the police chief of Spain.

*****

"Mama, calm down, what's going on?" Antonio asked down the line to Spain.

"Your father, oh, your father. He is dead, Antonio, dead," Connie shrieked back. "They are sending the body home for burial. I don't know what to do, Antonio. I don't feel well. I feel sick all the time, and I can't deal with this."

"Dead! Jesus…" Antonio slipped into shock and crossed himself. He hadn't seen his father since just before last Christmas and New Year. "Okay, Mama, calm down. I'm coming. I can be there in a few hours. Calm down. I'm on my way."

"Okay, my baby. Please come, please come."

"I'm on my way." He hung up and breathed deeply. "Oh, my God."

"What is it?" Cynthia asked, coming up behind him and sliding her arms around him. "What's wrong?"

"My father." Antonio slumped against the wall next to the phone table in the hall. "He's dead."

"What!" Cynthia's hands flew to her mouth. "Oh, my God, Antonio. When…? How…?"

"Mama didn't say." He shook his head at the madness and took a breath. "She didn't say, but his body's being sent home. I have to go. I have to go to Spain to be with Mama. She said she's sick and can't deal with it. I have to go home."

"Of course," Cynthia murmured. "Do you want us to come with you?"

"No, no, you stay here with Tony. I don't want you having to deal with Papa's funeral, or Mama's illness. Tony shouldn't be around her if she's sick."

"Of course. Call me if you need me." Rubbing his arms, she added, "Come, I'll help you pack."

*****

Antonio arrived in Spain and drove to the estate, finding his mother in a state of confusion and illness in her bed. "Mama, have you seen a doctor?" He went to her, into her arms, and held her tight.

"I have, but they say there is nothing wrong with me, just a cold or flu. But all they do is take my temperature and blood pressure. Meanwhile, I'm on my deathbed." Realising what she'd said, she burst into tears and cried in his arms all night.

*****

The next day, the body of Stephano Antonopoulos DeLuca was flown into Madrid and taken to the morgue. Antonio and Connie met it there and identified it.

"What are those spots on his face? He had them months ago when he'd been home to do some paperwork concerning his will and estate," Connie said. They'd hooked up and she'd noticed them. And now something was niggling in her gut. "You need to do an autopsy, you must."

"We do not know," the morgue technician said. "But we will do an autopsy if you like."

"Yes, do one," Connie snapped, the niggling feeling growing in the pit of her stomach.

"Yes, please do," Antonio told him. "I want to know what my father died of." He led his mother back into the waiting room where they were met by the local authorities.

"Mr DeLuca, Mrs DeLuca, I am so very sorry for your loss." The chief of police removed his cap and looked downcast. "On behalf of Spain, and myself, we are very sorry at such a terrible thing. You have our condolences." He cast a small glance at a crying Connie and then moved his gaze to Antonio. "Ah…Mr DeLuca, may I have a word with you in private?"

"Of course." Antonio nodded and helped his grieving mother sit on a chair. "I'll be back in a moment, and then we'll go." Leaving her, he walked to the other side of the room to talk to the chief. "What is it?"

"Ah, Mr DeLuca. I do not know how to say this, but your father was found in a compromising position upon his death. So far we, and the Cancún police, have kept it quiet and will continue to do so, but just so you know, it could come out, about where and how he was found."

Antonio sighed and rested his hands on his hips. "I know my father had lovers, chief, it was nothing new." It may not have been new, but it was highly embarrassing that *other people* knew.

"Ah, yes, ah…" The chief paused and held out an envelope. "Here is a report from the officers involved. I think it best you read it when things are a little calmer, and you can deal with it. In the meantime, we will keep this quiet and take the utmost time and care with your father."

Antonio took the envelope, puzzled by the chief's words. "Thank you, for everything."

"You're welcome, Mr DeLuca. Safe journey home." The chief watched Antonio lead Connie out to their car and drive away. *Oh, the poor bastard. He has no idea about his father.*

*****

Antonio didn't get a chance to read the report because Connie found it instead. After ripping the envelope open, she found that her husband had died while in the throes of passion with a twenty-two-year-old Filipino housemaid in his cabana in Cancún. The toy boy had been arrested under suspicion of murder, but the police doctor ruled it a heart attack.

"Housemaid," she murmured. "Male…twenty-two-year-old male…" Her eyes studied the words over and over, and her brain tried hard to figure it out. Stephano had been having sex with a male. A man… No… He couldn't possibly…

Searching her memory for all clues to his lovers, she recalled how there were never any other DeLuca heirs. Illegitimate ones, anyway. There were never any close female companions, or co-workers. They were all men. *But it's a man's world,* she thought. *Of course, he'd have men around him.* She recalled the longing glances with Constantine Manzo at his retirement party, and remembered how he'd stayed outside until late, coming in rumpled and smelling of sex and cologne. Cologne that wasn't his. And when he'd declared he wanted to separate, he'd stated there had been lovers. But…male…lovers…? No… It couldn't possibly be.

"Antonio," she shrieked. "Antonio, where are you?"

"Mama?" He came running from the office upstairs. "What is it? Are you okay?"

"No, I am not," she almost screamed. "Look at this. What is that?" Waving the papers in his face, she waited while he took them.

Reading them, he realised they were from the chief. "I'd forgotten I had these, the chief of police gave them to me and he..." He re-read the last paragraph. "What! He what! A twenty-two-year-old *male* housemaid. Wait...no!" Looking into his mother's horrified face, his head shook mechanically. "What...? A man? What does this mean? Papa had sex with men?"

"No, no, I do not want to hear it," Connie spluttered and wiped her mouth with her handkerchief. There were spots of blood on it, but she hid it from Antonio's eyes. Even though she had her suspicions, she didn't want to hear it. She stumbled over to the window and slumped into a chair to stare out at the terrace. "It cannot be, he cannot have been with men."

"Oh, Mama, no." Antonio comforted her for the rest of the day, calling in specialists to see to her ailing condition. That night, he called Cynthia and Tony, telling them he wouldn't be coming home for a while, that he loved them, and he'd see them soon.

*****

After two long months of autopsies, phone calls, and deliberate stalling by the Spanish coroner's office, their ruling finally came through the week before Christmas. Stephano had Kaposi's sarcoma, Pneumocystis pneumonia, low blood cells, genital ulcers, and a variety of sexually transmitted diseases. They were told this in the morgue.

Neither Antonio or Connie could believe their ears, and Connie demanded another round of tests. "I do not care what you want," she shrieked at the coroner. "You have taken two months to give me my husband's body. You have not called us, or consulted with us, and have told us nothing. I want an independent report done so that you," she thrust her finger at the coroner and chief of police, "cannot lie and deceive me. I do not believe *any* of it. *Any of it.*" She viciously waved her hand. "And I will not rest until I have the truth. I want an independent coroner and morgue to do the testing, in an independent lab, so the results cannot be tampered with. I will take my husband's body." Scathingly casting an eye over them, she sat down to wait. "Antonio, call up another doctor and lab. I will wait here." She was frail, having lost a lot of weight in the last few months. Her illness had not gone, and she was still coughing up blood. Her thick black curls were no longer piled on her head, but hung thin and limp around her face. Her once exuberant eyes were dull and bland. Her skin had a slight yellow colour. Her health was all but gone.

Because they'd already looked up independent labs just in case, Antonio made the call, and within half an hour, they came to collect the body.

"Mrs DeLuca," the coroner was explaining as the body was wheeled out. "We took the utmost care with your husband, treading very lightly. And we tested the samples three times to make sure we had the right test results."

"I do not care. I do not believe any of it." Connie coughed into her hanky. "You kept my husband's body from me for two months, and now it is nearly Christmas. I cannot see my grandson because I am so ill."

"Maybe you should be tested," the coroner suggested, noting the yellow skin and dark under-eye circles. "He would have passed on many of those things to you if you'd had sex."

Enraged, Connie struggled to her feet and feebly left the office.

Later that night, she rang her good friends Harry and Harriet in L.A. and told them the whole sordid mess.

"Oh, Connie, darling, that's just horrible," Harriet consoled her. "What will you do?"

"I do not know. I do not know." Connie dabbed her wet face. The tears had not stopped falling all day, or for the last two months for that matter.

"Connie, listen up and listen good," Harry told her. "I want you to go and see another doctor and get yourself the full medical. If you've had sex with him then he could have passed the diseases on to you, and Connie, listen carefully. If Stephano *was* gay, which it's a safe bet he was, then you'd better be doubly careful because there's some weird thing going on with gay men over here. They're getting sick and dying off. And if that's happening to them, then it could've happened to him too, so I suggest you get tested immediately. There's a gay disease going around and I pray you don't get it. He's probably passed on the STDs."

"Oh, of course not, he wouldn't do that to me," Connie protested.

"You don't know that, Connie," Harry pointed out. "If he's been fucking men for decades, then God knows *what* he's passed on to you. Go and get yourself checked, Constance."

A day later, taking their advice, Connie went to the doctors performing the autopsy and asked for a physical. She gave blood, saliva, and urine samples, and a lady doctor performed an internal examination. She was promised the results at the same time as her husband's. It was Christmas, but she wouldn't be celebrating.

Antonio had been ringing Cynthia and baby Tony every day. "I'm sorry I can't be there for Christmas," he told her. "I feel awful that this has taken so much time, and we can't spend it together."

"So do I," Cynthia replied. "You should be here with us, or we should at least be there with you. Let us come over, Antonio." The last two months had given her a bad feeling that didn't go away."

"No, no, with Mama being sick I don't want Tony, or you, getting sick too."

"You *still* don't know what it is?"

"No, not yet. Every doctor seems so damn useless."

"We can stay in a local hotel, then you can see Tony and me every day."

"I don't want to risk it, my love. I need to bury my father and get my mother well. But I have a really bad feeling that she won't make it."

"Oh, Antonio, no. Is she that bad?"

"I think her grief over my father has made it worse. I think she's wasting away from the grief and heartache."

"I know how she feels. Tony's barely eaten since you've been gone.

He calls for his dada every day."

"You tell that son of mine we'll see each other soon. And that Dada loves him very much. And his mama too. I'll call every day to talk to you both, but I doubt I'll get back for New Year's either."

"We can come over, Antonio. You don't have to miss out. Neither do we." The cold hand of fear clenched itself around her heart and made her blood run cold. Something was telling her to pack up and go, not to take no for an answer.

"No, my love. We need to bury my father and get treatment for Mama. I don't know how long it will take, but we will be together soon. I love you."

"I love you too." As she hung up, that fist squeezed tight.

*****

A week later, all test results were in. Stephano did indeed have all of the diseases stated by the coroner, and he had passed the STDs onto Connie. Disbelieving, she went into denial, while Antonio organised for his father's body to be delivered to the funeral home in Manzanares el Real where the big black glossy coffin with the big gold initial S was waiting. He drove his mother home, not believing that she had caught sexually transmitted diseases from his father. The doctors had given her a bag of medication to treat each one, and Antonio promised to make sure she took them. The doctors were worried that they'd been left untreated for too long, and were causing ten times the problems, and would soon be untreatable. On top of that, she had the same low blood cell count that Stephano had. They didn't know what it was, just that it was bad, and they vowed to research the strange test results thoroughly, having never seen a virus like that before.

That night, Connie called Harry and Harriet, still in a state of shock. It was true, and she couldn't believe it. Her bastard husband had passed along every STD he had to her, and now she was dangerously ill from it. Distraught, and unable to deal with anything, she hung up.

1981

Antonio called Cynthia for New Year's and told her the whole story.

"Oh, my God, Antonio, how horrible for your mother."

"Yes. Now I'm glad you and Tony stayed away. If she passed any of it along to either of you…"

"Why don't you bury your father and bring your mother here? She can get all of the treatment she needs, and when she's better, she can see Tony; that will cheer her up."

"Yes, yes, that's the plan." Antonio nodded. "It will get her out of this prison cell of a house. Fresh air, a fresh life, family. Yes, that's the plan as soon as possible."

Except…Connie worsened. Her condition deteriorated, and she became sicker. During Stephano's burial, staring down at the ground, she fainted upon seeing his coffin in the hole.

A hole big enough for three.

*****

"Mama, I have to go to town to sort out Papa's paperwork. I'll be back soon. You rest." Antonio sat by his mother's bedside. It was two days after the funeral and she was worse; morose, untalkative, uncaring. Her eyes and soul had died. "And when I get back, we'll get you packed up and to London for treatment so you can get better. You'll be able to see Cynthia and baby Tony." Squeezing her hand, he kissed

165

her cheek and saw no response. He sighed and left for town.

*****

Connie had no recollection of time, no spatial awareness of anything. Her brain was basically shutting down. So was her body. There were still tiny little shreds of memories, voices, images passing through on their journey into nowhere land. She couldn't grasp on to them; couldn't get a grip on the reality that had almost slipped away.

What she did know, felt, was that she couldn't go on anymore. Not for Antonio, not even for baby Tony. Stephano had done more than necessary to drive her out of her mind. And he'd succeeded. STDs... gay disease... Words and voices floated by, and even though she could only remotely register them, they were soon gone as they moved on.

Her body went into automatic mode. It pushed the bed covers back and rolled her out of bed, walked her over to the stairwell that led to the turret in the corner of her and Stephano's master bedroom, and walked her up until she reached the top.

Standing, she didn't move another inch, just stayed there swaying, her mind not thinking, her body not doing, so she had no idea of how long she was there for. Her eyes locked onto the sun setting in the distance and burned as they watched it lower itself to bed for the night. Yes. Bed...that's what she needed. She needed to do what the sunset was doing and follow its lead. Moving towards it, she climbed onto the ledge, stood, and let herself fall.

*****

Antonio didn't arrive home for hours. By then, the sun had set and the light had rapidly dwindled. Driving into the estate, his headlights caught sight of something in the drive near the steps to the house. As he pulled closer, he realised it was his mother. Slamming on the breaks, he pulled the hand brake, leapt from the car, and ran screaming over to her. "Mama, Mama."

Blood was pooled around her mangled, twisted body that lay

splayed on the stone bricks. "Mama." He pulled her into his arms and kept on screaming. "Help, somebody, help. Mama." He cried red hot tears of pain, distress, fear, hell, death.

The maid came running out, saw the scene, and ran back in to call for help.

Antonio didn't notice.

The police, ambulance, doctors, hangers-on, all arrived without him noticing. He was too busy with his grief, too busy screaming and clinging to his mother. Eventually, they had to pry her from his hands to wrap the body and place it on the stretcher.

"Mama," he cried, covered in her blood and his tears. "Mama."

The paramedics rolled her into the coroner's van leaving him in a pool of her blood. The police had called the family lawyers who helped him to his feet and into the house. Eventually, the flashing lights disappeared, the cars and people disappeared, and the caretaker washed the blood away.

Antonio was deaf and blind to all. He heard nothing of what the lawyer said, but shifted into mechanical mode.

The next few days came and went with an autopsy performed, paperwork signed, and another coffin prepared. The burial site was redug, and waited for Connie to take her place beside her husband.

Antonio made the necessary calls, and with the family lawyers as witnesses, he set up the DeLuca estate in his son's name. Any excess property that Stephano hadn't sold off, or had bought, in his final years was quickly sold, assets liquidated, and all was put into the estate. Mechanically, Antonio packed up family photos and albums, his mother's treasures, his father's, and his. Expensive artwork, collections, and paperwork were all stored in the family vault in the upstairs office. It was a cache of potentially hundreds of millions.

One week after his mother's suicide, he received permission to bury her. Speaking to the funeral home, he asked for a coffin to be organised with the initial in gold, paid for it in cash, and left. He'd paid off all debts in full, and organised for the estate to be looked after.

Going home that night before the burial, he set out all paperwork pertaining to what was in the safe, wrote out his will, supplied his parents' wills, and wrote a letter to the family lawyers about what they should do next. He found a large legal size envelope in his father's desk and slid all of the papers into it. Once he was sure he was finished, he drove into town and pushed the envelope through the mail slot of the family's law firm's office.

Sighing, he drove home, went upstairs to the office, locked the door, and sat behind his father's desk. Breathing deeply, and thinking of his family, he squeezed his eyes and hands tightly together, said a small prayer to God to forgive his parents and himself, raised his father's gun to his temple, and pulled the trigger.

*****

The next morning, Mr García, of the DeLuca family lawyers, opened his office and found the envelope. Curious, he sat behind his desk and read over the contents. Understanding what it meant, he leapt from his chair and yelled to his assistant to get the police to the DeLuca estate as he ran through the office. He jumped into his car and sped to the house. The police arrived right behind him, and they tore into the house and up to the office. Finding it locked, they kicked the door in to find Antonio slumped on the desk with a hole in his temple.

García's hand flew to his mouth, and he raced back downstairs to his car, breathing rapidly. Reaching in through the open car window, he pulled the papers out and re-read the letter from Antonio telling him what he was planning and where to find him. All paperwork was legal and gave strict instructions. He sighed at the loss of Spain's most prominent family, and grieved for the fact he would have to fly to London to tell Antonio's widow.

*****

Two days later, Constance Philomena Stephanova Constinopolous DeLuca was buried beside her husband. They slept in the same style black coffins with gold handles and adornments, and big letters. S and C. Right beside Connie's coffin lay Antonio's with a big letter A. He had taken his life as his mother had, torn apart by grief and pain. It was all in the letter; a letter no one besides the lawyer would ever see. He had instructed how to deal with his family, and what to tell Cynthia and Tony. As much as he loved them, the bond he had with his mother was far stronger.

García stared from the letter in his hand to the three coffins in the ground as dirt was thrown into the grave. The instructions were to bury them under the Ficus tree at the dance pavilion, and leave a small brass plaque as the only clue to where they were buried. Stephano had wanted to be buried there, and the plot was big enough for Connie, even though she didn't have a will, so had never stated where she wanted her final resting place to be. Antonio had automatically said *here*. And now García could see why. Turning, he saw the marble tiles being carried away. The whole dance pavilion was being dismantled as per Antonio's instructions. There was to be no clue to their final resting place, and the pavilion was to be dismantled to let nature take its course to bury them even deeper. Not understanding any of it, García walked towards the house before the pathway completely disappeared. With a last backward glance at the grave, he sighed and left the estate.

*****

After flying into London the day after the burial, the DeLuca family lawyer knocked on Cynthia's door.

"Antonio?" She flung it open and stopped. "Oh, I'm sorry. You're not—"

"Your husband?" García's smile was soft, but sad. "No, Mrs DeLuca. I'm his lawyer. I need to talk to you about the DeLuca family. Something has happened."

"Oh," she murmured. "Right, come in." Waving him into the lounge room, she closed the door and settled onto the sofa. "Is Antonio with you? He should have been back by now. I haven't heard from him in nearly two weeks." She lifted a whingeing baby Tony onto her lap.

"Dada?" he asked, staring at the man in his house.

"No, not, Dada." Cynthia kissed his chubby cheek and wrapped her arms around him.

"Naw, no Dada." Baby Tony frowned. He was sick and tired of not having his dada around.

"No. Not him." García's lips set into a line. "I'm afraid he won't be coming home, Mrs DeLuca." Oh, how he hated this shit.

"What do you mean?" She frowned and shook her head, not understanding. "Where's Antonio?"

Breathing deeply, and closing his eyes for a moment to gather his thoughts, he started. "Do you know about your father-in-law?"

"Yes, he died in October, but they weren't able to bury him until a few weeks ago." That cold fist of fear squeezed tight.

"Do you know that he made his wife very ill?"

"Yes, Antonio told me. Is she worse?"

The instructions from Antonio had been very clear. *Do not tell her the truth.* "Yes, Mrs DeLuca. I'm afraid Constance DeLuca passed away last week from her illness."

"Oh, my God." Cynthia's hand flew to her mouth. "Oh, God no, poor Antonio. He must be beside himself with grief. Where is he? Does he need help? Is he coming home? I need to go there."

"No, Mrs DeLuca, no to the last three." He sighed and glanced down, his hands gripping each other like grim death. Oh, God, how he hated this.

"What do you mean, no? Antonio's not coming home?" Her brain wasn't functioning.

"I'm afraid," another sigh, "that during the process of prepping for his mother's funeral, Mr DeLuca," he licked his dry lips, "your husband, passed away in a terrible accident."

Cynthia blinked and stared at García who was staring at the floor, unable to look at her. The cold fist of fear squeezed all the life out of her. "What?"

"I'm *so sorry*, Mrs DeLuca." His face crumpled and he teared up. "I am so, so sorry. But Antonio has passed away too."

"No." Cynthia shook her head. "He's coming…home soon…and bringing Connie with him for treatment…"

"They have both passed away, Mrs DeLuca," García said. "As per his and the family's instructions, they have all been buried together on the DeLuca estate. It was all taken care of yesterday."

"And you didn't call me?" Cynthia was dumbfounded. "Why didn't anyone call? My husband didn't call about his mother, you didn't call about him... I have missed out on the funerals for my parents-in-law, and now you're telling me you've buried my husband. *My* husband without telling me," she snapped. "How dare you!" Tony fussed on her knee from the loud voices.

"I know this is highly unusual, Mrs DeLuca," García pressed on, finally moving his eyes to look at her. "*These circumstances* are highly unusual, but it's the way it turned out." He watched as she gripped Tony tightly, making him squirm and cry. "Your husband changed his will after the death of his mother. The estate will pass to Tony on his twenty-fifth birthday, and you will receive two thousand pounds a month from the estate until then. That's one thousand for you, and one thousand in child support. Once he's twenty-five, you will be cut off, but I'm sure he will take care of you after that. My company and I will look after the estate until then with the upkeep and maintenance. He rolled his trust fund into one for Tony, and this house will be taken care of by it as well. You'll never have to pay for repairs, utility bills, or maintenance. It's all paid for. We'll just need a bank account number to transfer your money into."

"Are you kidding me?" she managed to gasp through her boiling tears. "I'm dealing with the death of my husband, *and* his parents, and all *you're* talking about is the estate. I don't even get to bury him here so I can visit if I want to. He's buried on some Spanish estate I've only been to once and don't want to go to now."

"I know, and I'm sorry, Mrs DeLuca. But we had instructions from Antonio and his father. They were to be buried on the estate. I'm so very sorry." Pulling a large A4 envelope from his briefcase along with a business card, he left them on the coffee table in front of him. "In the envelope are letters for you and your son, and papers with names and numbers on it. When you're ready, call me on my number if you need anything. We are at your disposal." Standing, he let himself out, leaving her to wail and scream in pain with Tony joining in, overcome with his own grief at the situation because that was the hardest thing he ever had to do.

2006

Twenty-seven-year-old Tony Luca grieved the loss of his mother.

She had passed earlier in the year, bizarrely, in January, just like his father, and even though it was May, just like his siblings, he still missed her terribly.

His stepfather, not so much.

The verbal abuse had ramped up after his mother's passing, but, as a DeLuca and firstborn, he took the brunt on his shoulders. And his mother's family could tell.

"Tony, love, why don't you take time off? You've been working yourself ragged these last few months," Aunt Olivia said to him when he visited his family one Sunday. "I have a feeling you've worked hard so you didn't have to think of your mother. Which may not be a good thing." Olivia Rankine set out the table in her mother's house for the usual roast meal. "It's not good to keep it in, love."

"I know, Aunt Liv," he replied and help her with the cutlery and napkins. "But it's the only way I can cope right now. By keeping my mind off it."

"*Have* you dealt with it?" Aunt Veronica asked. "It's been tough on all of us, love, not just you and the kids. We *all* lost Cyn this year."

"I know, Aunt V." Tony gave her a peck on the cheek as he passed her in the dining room. "And I'm coping the best way I know how. By working." He stood back and surveyed his family. Aunts Olivia and Veronica, who looked like replicas of his mother, with pale green eyes and wild red hair greying through, their husbands, Tom and Michael, their kids, and his grandparents. "I'm fine. I'm doing okay. I'm working and out of the house, so I don't have to deal with Brian and the kids and their abuse and demands."

"Has he got worse?" Alice York, his grandmother, asked, serving up plates of roast chicken and veg. She was an older version of her daughters with red hair dusted through to grey and pale green eyes. On the shorter side, she came up to Tony's shoulders. "He called you names before."

"Yeah, it's worse," Tony admitted. "They really ramped it up after Mum died. I think he eggs them on, and I don't know what his actual problem with me is. He never had one until I came out as gay."

"Maybe he hates gay people," Tom Rankine, Olivia's husband, suggested. "Now that your mother's gone, he has no one to tell him he can't do it."

"And we're not always around to tell him that," Olivia added. She'd been a social worker for twenty years, and had been by her sister's side looking after the kids right until the end. She also kept an eye on how they were on a week to week basis. "She knew of Brian's injury, and knew he didn't do much with the upkeep of the family home, and was worried he wouldn't be able to take care of the kids."

"Have you thought of taking a holiday, Tony?" Philip York, his grandfather asked. At six feet, and fully grey, it was easy to tell that Tony had inherited some height from his grandfather as well. They settled at the tables to eat, the kids at one, the adults at another.

"It's nearly summer, Granddad, too busy to take time off." Tony sliced through his succulent chicken breast and the aroma wafted up into his nostrils. His mouth watered. "Besides, I don't think I'd be able to get time off."

"It's not summer yet, so you should be able to," Veronica said. "When was the last time you took a holiday?"

Tony thought about it, but it didn't take long. "I went to Spain in 2003 to see my dad's estate when I inherited. Before that, it was when I was twenty-one."

"You're due for one then," Olivia told him. "Go somewhere to meet boys you can have fun with."

"Aunt Liv." Tony blushed. "I meet boys just fine in the club."

"But have you met *the one* yet?"

"Well...no...otherwise you would have met him by now." Tony stuffed a potato into his mouth and chewed until there was nothing left to chew, just so he didn't have to talk to his family.

"Then it's time you went and had some fun. Take some friends along, go overseas, take them to that fancy Spanish estate of yours—" Olivia was in the middle of saying when her sister interrupted.

"Or Mykonos. Gay people love Mykonos."

Olivia nodded at her sister. "Or Mykonos."

Tony sighed. "Look. I'll think about it, Aunt Liv. In the meantime, can I just finish Grandma's roast?"

Tony thought about it all right. He decided it was a good idea, asked for time off, and asked his three best mates if they'd like to come along, and they said yes.

Like they were going to turn down a free holiday to Mykonos in June...

*****

"Woohoo, I can't believe we're on Mykonos," Robbie Peters cried as he stepped off the plane at the Mykonos International Airport. "*So glad you invited us, bro.*" He threw an arm around Tony's shoulders. "You're awesome."

"Yeah, yeah," Tony said. "You just came coz it was free." He'd had no problem paying for a two-week vacation for him and his best friends.

Will Powers and Travis Pittwater made up the foursome. All four boys had grown up in the same area of London and gone to the same schools. They'd been as thick as thieves then, and continued to catch up most Friday nights, or Saturdays. And fortunately, all three had been able to take time off.

"Who else was I gonna invite, anyway," Tony added as they headed for the bag carousel and their cases. "You can thank Aunts Liv and

Veronica. The holiday was their idea and I went with it."

"Did they suggest it because of your mum?" Travis asked, reaching out to grab the handle of his black suitcase.

"In part," Tony replied, setting his case on the floor and pulling up the handle. "I hadn't gone anywhere since Spain a couple of years ago, and I've been working to keep my mind off Mum's passing. But, here we are, so, let's not talk about it anymore. We're here to have fun and meet men."

"*You're* here to meet men, I'm here to have fun and bang as many chicks as I can," Will piped up. At six feet with curly brown hair and green eyes, he was quite attractive to the opposite sex, and had no problem with Tony coming out a few years earlier.

Robbie had been out since he was eighteen. At five eleven with flaming red hair and green eyes, he'd jumped at the chance to holiday in one of the gay meccas of the world. "I'm with Tony. I'm here to meet men, and the more the merrier. Let's go."

The boys hailed cabs and found their way to *The Windmill Hotel,* perched on a hillside overlooking the town. With a room each, which was Tony's doing in case any of them brought home a conquest, they all had views of the party end of town.

"When are we getting drunk?" Travis asked as he entered Tony's room. At five ten, with jet-black hair and dark eyes like Tony, he was into girls, alcohol, and partying.

"You want to waste your time getting drunk?" Will walked into the room. "When we could be banging all the girls? They don't like drunks, so don't get drunk."

"You boys got your cameras? We need to take lots of photos." Robbie walked in, playing with his five-year-old camera. "I've got plenty of film, and I'm aiming to take pictures of all the pretty conquests I have as a record."

"Seriously?" Will frowned. Regardless of how long he'd known Robbie, his blatant sexuality still surprised him at times. "You'd seriously do that? Take photos of all the men you sleep with?"

"Who said anything about sleep?" Robbie quipped. "I do like to keep a record of all my conquests. Don't you?"

"Ah...no..." Will shook his head. "That's so gross, dude."

"Whether it is, or isn't, let's get this holiday started." Tony pulled some brochures from his carry-on bag. "There's so much to do, so much to go to, so pick something and let's do it." They quickly scoured the travel guides and decided to hit the shopping strips during the day, and party at the bars all night, with some days in between for having fun in the sun down by the beach.

And they did just that. Hit the shops and restaurants during the days, partied the nights away, and everything was going well for all four of them for nearly two weeks until the night they went to a club...

"Whoo, partay." Robbie jumped onto a table and danced with wild abandonment. He fucking loved Mykonos with its free-loving gay lifestyle and was starting to wish he lived there. With a drink in one hand and his camera in the other, he took photos of every man there. Having gone through two dozen rolls in two weeks, he'd taken photos of everything and everyone. The town, the ocean, the people, the places, and most importantly, the men. Whether they were a conquest or not. "Whoo..."

Tony, Will and Travis glanced from Robbie to each other and burst out laughing. They had never seen their friend so wild and free, and had been more than surprised when he'd cut loose on the dance floor in the last week.

"I have never seen him this way before," Will shouted over the loud music. "He's loving himself sick in this place."

Tony nodded. "He is. Maybe we should join in the fun. There's a group of girls over there eyeing you off." He pointed in their direction before adding, "I'm going this way." Flicking a thumb over his shoulder, he headed into a crowd of men dancing on the other side of the club. Letting himself go, he danced freely, throwing back his head and letting the music take him over. Sensing someone beside him, he opened his eyes to see a good-looking Latino man grinding up and down. Smiling at the boy who looked no older than twenty or twenty-one, Tony got into it and let the music take them away. A couple of songs later, the Latino moved on, and Tony turned his interest to a good-looking Caucasian with blond hair and blue eyes.

A few kisses later, and an exotic blend caught Tony's eyes when he waved a finger for Tony to come on over. Tony danced over to him and they got intimate. Hands down pants, tongues in mouths. Tony was turned on and motioned for the man to go outside.

Once out of the club, hands and mouths continued to grope, and they half stumbled into the side alley pulling at each other's clothes.

"Mmm, mmm, just let me get a condom," Tony managed around the man's tongue. He pulled a condom from his pocket, rolled it on, and saw the man was bent over a low brick wall with his pants around his ankles and offering his ass to him. "Okay then." Tony entered and did the job, eliciting groans from the exotic blend of a man. Finishing, Tony backed away, rolled off the condom, and packed himself away.

"So...what was that worth?" Exotic blend asked. "A hundred, two hundred?"

"What?" Tony looked up from his crotch. "What do you mean?"

"I don't fuck for free, sweetheart. I get paid. This ass is *not* free." Exotic blend grabbed at Tony's pockets feeling for cash, or a wallet.

"Hey, get out of it." Tony slapped the man's hands away, but Exotic blend kept going.

"I want my payment, fag fucker. You don't get to fuck this ass and not pay for it."

"You said nothing about payment, otherwise I wouldn't've done it," Tony spat. "I'm not a guy who pays for sex. I don't have any money, and you're not getting any." With both hands, he shoved the man away.

But Exotic blend was light on his feet and whipped out a pocket knife. "Give it up, fag fucker. I want my money."

Having grown up in London, and worked in bars, Tony was more than experienced in dealing with dickheads with knives. He was ready to punch on.

Exotic danced toward him, expertly swinging his knife around, but Tony fought back with a few punches and kicks, and then felt the stinging pain in his left side.

His eyes widened and he looked at the man who had a dark and cruel intention in his eyes. Tilting his head down, he saw the knife in his gut and stumbled backwards, and that was all the time Exotic blend needed.

He grabbed Tony, hauled him over the wall he'd just been fucked over, pulled his pants down, and fucked him up the ass. When he was done, he pulled out and zipped up, watching Tony groggily slump to the ground. Exotic laughed. "Suck it, fag fucker, you've just got the disease…"

Tony watched the man run, his vision blurry with the pain. "Argh…gotta get inside…" Unable to stand, he managed to crawl his way back into the club.

Patrons cried out and stepped aside, but did nothing to help him. They just stopped and stared in horror.

"Tony?" Will called, seeing his friend on the ground. "Tony!" He ran over, Travis close behind, and each got under their friend's arm. "Tony, you okay?"

Robbie stopped dancing on the table long enough to notice, and drunkenly jumped off and stumbled over. "What's wrong with him? He drunk?"

"Argh," Tony groaned as they pulled him up.

"Ah, dude, blood." Robbie pointed to Tony's stomach and promptly turned and vomited all over the floor.

"Jesus Christ," Will yelled. "Let's get them both to the hospital." They half pulled Tony and Robbie out of the club and into the street where they hailed a cab. They made it to the hospital and dragged Tony into emergency. "Help! Our friend's been stabbed. Help us."

Doctors and nurses came running and helped Tony into a room where they examined him. His friends stayed in the waiting room until the doctor came out an hour later.

"I am Doctor Vincenzo Matatta. Your friend will be just fine. The cut was superficial, didn't nick anything of importance, and we've stitched him up. How much longer are you here in Mykonos?"

"Um…" Will glanced at Travis and Robbie who was staring dreamily at the good doctor, and tried to remember how much longer they had. "A couple of days?" The others shrugged. The date of their departure was not the first thing on their mind.

"Then I suggest he stay here for those days to heal before flying home." Vincenzo signed off on the chart in his hand. "We've given him painkillers, anti-inflammatories, and a tetanus shot. You can take him home in a couple of days. Come back then." He left them there wide-eyed and scared, and with nothing else to do, they went back to their hotel.

*****

A couple of days later, they flew home and helped Tony into the loving arms of his family.

"Oh, how I wish I hadn't suggested Mykonos now," Veronica growled. "I feel responsible."

"It's not your fault, Aunt V," Tony mumbled. "It's his. All his fault. I'll be fine. I'll recover and be fine. You can't stop a York. Or a DeLuca."

Or so Tony thought.

Two months later, after a routine doctor's appointment, he was called back into the surgery to get his test results.

He had HIV.

"No, you can't possibly..." Tony shook his head in disbelief. "No. I don't believe you. Run the tests again."

The tests were run again.

The results were exactly the same.

Tony had HIV from the assault in Mykonos.

As if losing his mother wasn't bad enough... The pain and self-torture he put himself through over the next six months were purely of his own making, blaming everyone but himself for the way his life had turned out. The man who gave him HIV, his mother for leaving him, his father and grandmother for dying, his stepfather for being a homophobic arsehole, his siblings for following in their father's footsteps, his boss for firing him, his friends for leaving him, and even the cops who arrested him on Valentine's night and threw him in the clink for being drunk and disorderly. He was angry at everyone and everything, but himself. *He* was not to blame for any of it; not for his family hating him, for the abuse he heaped on his friends, for even hating his aunt for suggesting he take a holiday.

Oh, no, he wasn't angry at himself, but he *was* angry at the judge who sentenced him to six months of intensive therapy.

Standing in the courtroom hearing the verdict, and the gavel come down, Tony wasn't even aware of the fact he hadn't received jail time.

"Well, this is better than jail time," Michael Monroe, QC, told him. "You just need to complete your six months of therapy and you're home and hosed." He gathered his papers and put them in his briefcase. "You'll get my bill next week, Mr Luca. Good luck to you." With a nod, he spun on his heel and left Tony standing there in shock.

"Tony, love." Olivia walked around the low wooden gate and held her nephew. "This is a good thing, Tony. The judge took everything under review. The fact you'd never been in trouble, that your mum died last year, that you were assaulted and contracted HIV last year. We convinced him your life was just a jumbled up mess and you were angry and confused. This is a good thing. Now you can get therapy and finally heal from all of it. You can finally sort through all of your problems and make amends."

"Amends..." Tony finally registered where he was and what she was saying. "I have HIV, Aunt Liv. My parents are both dead, so I'm an orphan. My stepfather threw me out of the house I grew up in. Like their father, my siblings call me a fag fucker. I lost my job, my friends, my life. Everybody left me. Who the hell do I have to make amends to?" Turning, he saw his family standing there. His maternal grandparents, aunt and uncles, but no father, no mother, no paternal grandparents, no siblings. He had no one. Wrenching at his tie, he undid the first few buttons of his shirt. "I can't breathe anymore. I can't think straight anymore. I can't be what everyone else wants me to be anymore because I don't know who the hell *I am* anymore. I grew up as Tony Luca. Found out from my birth certificate that my full name was Antonio DeLuca II. My father died when I was two, my mother died when I was twenty-seven, the same age she and Dad were when they met, and yet here I am. Alone. Without the people I need most and I go and contract HI fucking V." His voice rose to high decibels and spit flew from his mouth. "And now I have court-ordered therapy. How the fuck am I supposed to deal with all of this without the two people I need most? Huh? Tell me how, Aunt Liv, because I just don't know." Fuming, he stormed out of the courtroom and into an even stormier London day.

2008

Antonio DeLuca wafted from the office, down the stairs, and into his son's room to float by the bed. *Oh, Tony, I'm so sorry for not staying. You have grown so much.* Sliding his fingers over his son's face, he noted how much he looked like him. Seeing the photos under the lamp, he touched the one of him and Tony when he was a baby, and moved it across to lay on his son's chest. *I love you, my son.* He cupped Tony's face. *I love you so much, and I am so sorry I did not stay for you.* Glancing over his shoulder, he saw his mother standing in the doorway, a guilt-ridden smile on her face. They had been there for twenty-seven years and had not moved on, but now that Viv had stirred things up and awakened them, they were curious as to what was happening.

Tony stirred and felt the hand on his face. His eyes opened, and for a moment he thought he saw his father staring down at him. "Dad?" he whispered, praying it was true.

Antonio stared down at his son and his lips smiled, even though his heart was breaking. For he had given in to his deep depression over losing his parents instead of fighting to stay alive for his son and wife.

"Dad?" Tony moved to rise and felt the photo on his chest. Picking it up, he saw it was of him and his father. "Dad?" he whispered once more, and saw a retreating shadow float through the door.

"Tony?" Cabot sat up, blinking his eyes against the light Tony turned up. "What's going on?"

"My father." His voice was still low. "My father was here." Staring at the photo in his hand, his tears fell.

"How do you…? Are you sure?" Cabot looked down at the photo and kissed Tony's shoulder.

"Yes," Tony breathed. "My father was here."

*****

The next morning, he told them all about the visit from his father.

"Are you sure?" Viv asked, buttering a piece of toast. "Because I could have sworn I felt Connie."

"I think you stirred them up yesterday, Mrs S," Tony told her. "I put all of the photos on the bedside cupboard, and yet when I was awakened, the one of my father and me was on my chest, and I felt a cool hand on my face, and saw a form move through the door. I *know* it was my father."

Viv sighed and munched on her toast, waiting until she swallowed before saying anything. "Well then, we'd better get talking to them. Get all of your anger and frustration out. Do you know what you'll do when you find them?"

"No, not yet." Tony finished off his coffee. "I'm hoping to get a feel for the place. You don't happen to know if there are photos of the pavilion, do you?"

"There should be in the albums." Viv scooped up the last of her scrambled eggs onto her last piece of toast. "But you wouldn't have recognised it. Whereas I will."

"Can you take a look through the albums for me to see if it's in there?" Tony asked. "The lawyer and agent won't be here until nine-thirty and ten. We have a bit of time."

"Of course. Get the albums ready for me, and I'll look them over after breakfast." She finished off her food, swallowed the last of her juice, and wiped her mouth daintily. "What will you do to find the pavilion?"

"Get gardeners in to clear the path again." Tony shrugged. "If it was there once, it will be again. I'll do it up myself. But first, we must find our way through and look for the burial site."

"Well, I'm finished. So, you get those albums and we'll clear up," Viv said, and started collecting dishes. With help from her sons, the dishes were cleaned, and the leftover food was put away, then Viv sat down to pore over the albums. "This one's all about Stephano," she murmured and put the album aside to pick up another. Flicking through it, she saw it was all about Antonio. "And this one's about your father." A third was all about Connie, and a fourth was parties and celebrations. "Here we go. I'm recognising this place. Oh, there's Connie and me in the pavilion. Oh, God, it was so beautiful."

They clustered around to see page after page of parties. The white marble of the dance floor stood out amongst the summer nights. Fairy lights, marble benches, statues, and railings circled the space.

"Oh, Viv, look at you," Carlos murmured appreciatively. "Beautiful."

She laughed softly. "And I still am, I hope."

"Of course you are, my love," Carlos told her. "You always were and always will be." He left a soft kiss on her cheek and a gentle hand on her back.

"There are no pictures of the statues or floor, no close-ups anyway. I wonder where it all went." Tony was intrigued. It did indeed look like a beautiful place, but if there was nothing left, then where had all the marble gone? And who had dismantled it? The doorbell rang and he went to answer it. "Ah, Mr García, come in."

"Mr Luca, good to see you again." Romondo García walked into the entrance hall and shook hands with Tony.

"It's DeLuca now," Tony told him. "Mum changed it when Dad died and that's how I grew up. But, this year, I've decided to have a fresh start, and go back to my roots and be who I was meant to be. It's officially DeLuca again." Closing the door, he waved the family lawyer through the house. "I have some questions for you. Come, come." Leading him to the back living area, he introduced the family. "Mrs Stephanopoulos knew my grandmother, and Mr Stephanopoulos knew my father." They shook hands and Tony motioned to his future brother-in-law. "They named their son after him. Antonio DeLuca Stephanopoulos."

Antonio shook hands with Mr García.

Tony went on. "And they all know how my family died and have told me. So, how come you have not?" He faced the lawyer square on, determined to get some answers once and for all.

Mr García blushed and stuttered. "Mr Luca, ah, DeLuca, my grandfather was in charge of *your* grandfather's estate. Soon after, he handed it to *his* son, *my* father, and now I'm in charge. Your family's wishes were that you *never* learn how they died. Especially since two of the death's happened here in the house. My family abided by that wish, and followed through on it, just as I did when we met five years ago. It's a very tragic story, Mr DeLuca, and from the letter your father sent us, he didn't want *you* knowing. *Ever.*"

"Did you...bring the paperwork?" Tony asked, his throat momentarily choking. "We've pulled everything out of the vault and gone through it."

"Yes, yes I did." Mr García motioned to his briefcase in his hand.

"Good, we can go over the paperwork here." Tony pointed to the lounge section where everything was still in piles. "We've decided to sell the art and paintings off. But I'm not sure about the coins and stamps." They spoke for the next half hour about the legal papers, selling off the items, and with Tony finally getting to read the letter his father had given the lawyers. "Wow." He teared up. "He really didn't want anyone to find them."

"Not unless you went looking," Mr García said, glancing from Tony to the rest of the family, and wondering why they were actually there, and what they wanted.

"But, my father also assumed I'd be alive to inherit it and want to keep it in the family. More than likely he was assuming I'd have children to pass it down to. I don't, and don't know if I ever will. So, what do I do with it? What if I die and there's no one to pass it to? What was meant to happen then? It gets sold off to someone? Would they be told there are three dead bodies on the grounds? Quite frankly, Mr García, that creeps me out. The fact that there are three dead bodies in coffins somewhere on the grounds. I want to change that."

The doorbell rang. "I'll get it," Carlos called and quickly walked through the house to answer it. "Yes?" he asked the short, stocky man with thick black hair and an even thicker moustache.

"Oh, ah, yes." The man looked startled. "I'm here to see Mr Tony Luca. I am Mr Fernández, the estate agent."

"Of course, come in." Carlos held the door open. "Tony's just talking to the family lawyer. This way." He led him out back and left them to it.

"Ah, Manuel, how are you?" García shook his hand.

"Good, good, Romondo, how are you?"

"Intrigued. Listen up," García said.

They both listened to Tony's plans to reinstate the marble walkway and pavilion. "I have no idea what happened to it, but I want to get the gardeners in to hack through that forest and find it."

"From what I remember it was Martínez Masonry that did the job," Manuel quickly looked through his papers. "Here we are." Reading through them, he noted the name. "Yes, Martínez Masonry removed the marble tiles, statues and benches, and stored them in the old utility building."

"Here?" Tony was surprised. "On the property?"

"Ah, yes," Manuel read. "The one beyond the lawn in the grove."

"So, we can use the original marble to recreate it." The excitement was building inside Tony. "We can recreate a whole new DeLuca home."

"Just the garden, unless you have plans for the house and grounds," Manuel said.

"Oh, yes, yes I do." Tony's eyes narrowed. "I hate this house. It may be where my father grew up, but it's also where he and my grandmother died, and I still feel them here. *Something* is here, but either way, my grandfather will *not* be anymore. I want him gone. I want him out of here. My father and grandmother's deaths are still on his head, and I want him gone. Find a museum interested in all of his stuff, because I don't want it. I want that ugly as hell bull fountain gone from out front. I want all bull statues gone from outside. I even want that inlay gone from the pool. I want this house changed. I want it painted and lightened up. If the wood can be sanded back and lightened, then get it done. I want new furniture, new artwork, new beds. This house is no longer Stephano DeLuca's house. It's *Antonio DeLuca II's* house and it's 2008. I want it updated and cleaned out. And if you can get an exorcist, or priest, or someone in to get rid of the demons in this house, then we'll do that too." He took a breath. "And right now, I'm even considering dismantling that damn bell tower, so no one can go up in it. It's only off their bedroom, the rest of it gets used in each room on each floor. I want it *all* gone. *Everything.* Everything old is out, and everything new comes in. I'm done with what my grandfather did. *It's not me. I'm not him.* We'll overhaul this place this month, and you can get a photographer in to do before and after shots, so you can put it up for rental once more. Tell me, Manuel, what did renters really think of all the bulls?"

Manuel grinned. "Some loved it because it was what they were after, but others wanted the old style villa experience, and with all the bulls they thought it brought an angry tone to the place."

"That wasn't the statues, that was my family's spirits," Tony said. "So, can you get onto any museums that want my grandfather's things? They can take the lot, including the statues. And Manuel, can you get in gardening companies to start on the forest? We'll also need a furniture removalist, but that can wait a few days since we're staying here. And I will need new furniture after that, but for now, it's bull and weed removal time. Can the two of you organise that, please? Today. And we can get started tomorrow."

"Of course," García said. "And I will now leave these papers with you since you are taking over and making changes. Everything will need to be put in writing for our documentation, along with photos to keep note of the changes you are making."

"That's fine," Tony said. "I don't have a problem with that. I will see you back here tomorrow morning with a gardening crew, and someone from a museum."

"And the photographer," Fernández said. "We'll document everything."

"Very well. I'll walk you, gentlemen, out." Five minutes later he was back in the house. "Ready for our trip into the forest?"

"Are you really going to change this house?" Viv asked, astonished by all she'd heard.

"You said yesterday it hadn't changed and was still *all about Stephano DeLuca*," Tony reminded her. "Now, it's about *Antonio DeLuca II* and what *I* want. And *I* want nothing to do with him."

"But your father grew up here. If you change it, it won't be the same," she continued, upset and on the verge of tears at things never being the same again. "This was his house too."

"Yes, yes it was." Tony sobered. "But as you have both pointed out several times in the last few days, it's been twenty-seven years since it happened. It's time to move on. Make this a place *I* would like to come back to every few years, a place people want to stay in over summer. This house isn't it. Not the way it looks. Dark, creepy, smothering. So, Mrs S, since I'm no good with furnishings, can you look in some magazines and figure out what I need?"

"Oh, um…ah yes…I guess," she murmured, worried that she would lose all of the good memories she had of the place.

"Mrs S, are you worried that it will change so much you won't remember anymore?" Tony read her mind.

"Yes, Tony, I guess I am." She blinked back tears. "I had such wonderful times with Connie here. Even though she said the place was overbearing and hated the darkness of it all. But Stephano wouldn't let her change it."

"Antonio hated it too," Carlos added. "Told me how dark and horrible it was."

"Then it's time for a change," Tony said. "The old DeLucas out, the new DeLucas in. It's 2008, it's time to update and bring the place into the new century."

For the rest of the morning they made plans for the house, and after lunch, they changed into sturdy boots and long socks for their foray into the jungle. With small axes, they cut out the path in the grass where the marble pathway would have been, and continued between the trees. The boys cut their way through, going until Viv called for them to stop.

"I think this is it." Staring from the huge green canopy of branches to the circular placement of the trees, she looked at the ground covering of vines and leaves. "I think this is it," she repeated softly, remembering back to all the dances and festivities.

Tony dashed into a frenzy of chopping down small trees, and ripped away vines from the forest floor. "There's no marble. They really did remove it all." He saw Vivian staring past him and turned to see a massive Ficus Alley Alicante tree. Running over and peering at the base, he pulled vines and roots away and found a small plaque attached to it. Leaning in, he read *DeLuca S, C, A, 1981*. "This is it," he yelled, glancing over his shoulder in excitement. "This is where they're buried. The plaque says *DeLuca S, C, A, 1981*. Stephano, Connie, Antonio, 1981." The ground was spongy beneath his feet and he looked down. *I'm standing on them*, he thought. *This is where they're buried. Where they were laid to rest.*

The ground disappeared beneath his feet, and he slid through to his knees. "Oh, my God," he yelled, flailing his arms in panic. "The ground."

"Tony," Cabot yelled, seeing his lover's panicked expression as he fell right through the forest floor. "Tony." Racing over, Cabot was stopped by Antonio and Carlos, and they fell onto the dirt and skidded to a halt.

"The ground might collapse, careful," Carlos warned.

"Tony," Cabot shrieked in hysterics. "Tony, where are you?" Fearful his lover had plummeted to his death, he clawed at the earth around the hole. "Tony."

"I'm okay," Tony called up. "I'm okay. I landed on something. I need some light."

They quickly cleared the dirt and leaves around the hole, making it bigger.

"Tony," Cabot yelled down. "What's down there?"

Tony looked around in the afternoon sunlight lazily filtering down through the trees and into the hole. He was sitting on something hard, his legs stuck between two objects. Blinking to adjust his eyes, he ran his hands over the objects. Long, hard and curved. He felt hard metal handles on the sides, and peering through the dull light, saw he was sitting on a coffin. "Oh, my God," he murmured, his hands sliding over the object in front of him. "Oh, my God." Shoving the coffin aside, he tried freeing his legs while not panicking. But the panic set in any way. "Oh, my God," came out louder. "Oh, my God."

"Tony, what's wrong?" Cabot peered down, but couldn't see much. "Tony?"

"Oh, my God." Tony freed his legs and stumbled onto the coffin, his head barely reaching the top of the hole. "Get me out of here, get me out of here," he shrieked.

Carlos, Cabot and Antonio pulled him out and away from the hole, brushing off the dirt and debris from his jeans and t-shirt as he sat huffing on the ground.

"Oh, my God..." He breathed in great gulps, bending over to lean on his knees. "Oh, my God."

"Tony, what is it? What did you find?" Cabot brushed the dirt from Tony's back.

Slowly, Tony looked up at them. The blood had drained from his face, leaving him whiter than a ghost, and blinking rapidly to clear the dirt from his eyes, he finally looked at Cabot. "Their coffins."

*****

The next afternoon, they stood by while the coffins were completely uncovered. Four gardening companies were tearing through the shrubbery, and the bullfighting museum in Madrid had come for Stephano's belongings. They wanted the fountain out the front as well as all of the posters, paintings, and artwork having anything to do with him in the entertainment room and upstairs office. They quickly packed up what they could and left. The rest of them were outside standing around waiting for the reveal with García and Fernández.

"This is highly unusual," García said, watching as piles of dirt came out.

"No one would want the place knowing there are dead bodies on the property." Tony stood with his arms crossed, his fingers playing with the sleeve of his t-shirt.

"But it just seems a little unfair to be digging up their bodies after so long," García continued. "To have found the place, and be tearing it all up." Looking around, he saw dozens of men working. "And the house. You're taking away everything that was DeLuca."

"That would be *Stephano* DeLuca, *not* my father, and *certainly not me.*" Tony gritted his teeth. "My father may have been born and raised here, but *I* wasn't. *He* chose to die here, all because of Stephano," he spat. "I have a right mind to dump his body somewhere else."

"Tony, you can't," Cabot said under his breath, but loud enough for only his lover to hear as they were standing side by side. "He was your father's father. It would be disrespecting him."

"Like my grandfather disrespected his wife, his marriage, his son?" Tony muttered back. "Stephano can fuck off. I have no need for him and his bullshit."

Carlos heard Tony's words and hid a grin, watching as the last buckets of dirt were lifted out. The workman said something in Spanish and climbed out of the grave.

"He's done," Manuel said and waved the diggers away.

They shuffled closer to the edge and looked down. Three black coffins lay side by side with arched domes, tarnished gold handles, metal inlay, and huge gold initials on top of each. S. C. A.

"Oh." Every ounce of energy left Tony and he sagged to the ground.

"Tony." Cabot kneeled beside him and slid his arms around his shoulders for support.

Staring down at his father's coffin, the pain and anguish came flooding over him. All twenty-seven years' worth that he had endured at never seeing his father again. Not having him, something *of* him, to remember him by. Not having memories. He wept without fear of ridicule and embarrassment, and the others stepped back to give him a moment.

"What's the plan now?" García asked Carlos and Viv as they watched the garden crew remove their hats, cross themselves, and say small prayers.

"I don't know," Viv told him. "Probably cremation, so you can legally say there are no dead bodies on the property. Antonio may have wanted them to remain private, but his son is right. Who's going to want the place with graves on it?"

"True." García resigned himself. "But where will the ashes go?"

"Probably back in the ground," Carlos said, looking over his shoulder at Tony in Cabot's arms. "Ashes are better than bodies. Besides, their souls have more than likely moved on, and Stephano didn't even die here, so it's not as though it matters about him."

"True," Viv murmured. "But we have to do what's right for Connie and Antonio, and that would be to bury them back into the ground all together as a family. It was Antonio who made all the funeral plans. He would have set this up."

"According to Stephano's will, it's where he wanted to be buried," García said. "He wanted to be under that tree."

"So...they would have been digging the hole for his body when Connie..." Carlos swallowed the lump that had arisen in his throat.

"And then Antonio told us the gravesite would be for all of them. He wanted to be buried with his parents...together." García closed his eyes briefly. "And then we got the package from him with a note saying he was going to take his life, and where to find him, and what to do with him. They were very detailed instructions. He had the coffin ready at the funeral parlour. He wanted to be buried next to his parents for eternity."

"And they will be." Tony stopped beside them and sniffled. "Mr García, can you please see to it that they're taken to the morgue and cremated. Please stay with the bodies so they don't go missing, or that their ashes aren't mixed with anyone else's." He wiped his tear-soiled face. "But I want photos first, so Antonio is taking them."

They all looked at the grave to see Antonio taking pictures from every angle.

Tony went on. "I know my father may have wanted this, but considering the situation I'm in, I have no children to hand it down to, so if I want to sell it one day, then they will not be disturbed. Please make sure their ashes are kept together. My father's and grandmother's,

I mean. My grandfather's can stay separate."

"And what will you do with his ashes?" García asked.

"Bury them in the grave, but he can be on his own. He brought shame to my grandmother and father, and quite frankly, he doesn't deserve to be buried here."

"It was his house, and his family. Antonio made the burial plans," Viv reminded him.

"And I bet at the time he didn't think he'd be burying his mother, or himself," Tony said caustically. "He was making plans to bury his father, but he ended up burying the whole damned family, and I have no fucking sympathy for Stephano fucking DeLuca." He stood and watched while the coffins were removed. They had difficulty with Stephano's because a tree root had grown into the coffin. "Right where his cold calculating heart would have been," he muttered, seeing the trouble they had detaching it from the ground.

The workers cut through the root to pull the coffin out, and each was lifted via a small pulley system and placed on the ground. When Antonio's was gently settled, Tony threw himself onto it in sobs. Everyone moved away to give him a moment.

"Oh, Dad." His lip quivered. "How could you? How could you leave me for him?" He was draped over it, running his hand across the large tarnished A on the domed lid. It had a bull monogram under it. "How could you leave me for that bastard? How could you leave Mum to raise me on her own?" All the years of grief made his insides hurt, burn from the clenching anger and hatred for his grandfather. "Why was *he* more important than me? Why was the *shame* more important than me? Why were *they* more important than me? I was just a baby, I was two. From all accounts, Grandma adored me and so did you. You were so happy to know you were going to be a father. Mum always told me how excited you were, and when I was born…you were so happy to have a son to pass your name down to. So, why was I not important enough?"

Tears slid down his face to fall on the coffin, wetting twenty-seven years' worth of dirt with twenty-seven years' worth of pain. "Why did you not love me enough, Dad?" Laying his face on the gold A, he allowed his tears to fall freely and stayed that way until he was done. Not that he would ever be done crying for his father. "I hope you understand what I'm doing, Dad," he whispered, wiping a hand over the muddy lid. "I hope you understand why I'm updating the house and giving *his* stuff away. I don't want it. I don't want a reminder of *him*. He was *your* father, but I cannot forgive him for the impact he had on you and Grandma. I hope you don't mind being cremated. I'll put you back where we got you from and bury you properly, and then I'll mark it by replacing the dancing pavilion. Why should anyone go without such a beautiful place? Besides, by doing the house up, I may have more reasons to come here and see you, otherwise, all I have of you is your jewellery." Resting his right hand on the A, he looked at the ring and bracelet. "I will cherish them because they are yours, *not* because of the DeLuca symbol." Breathing heavily, knowing more tears were welling inside, he quickly added, "I will cherish these forever because they're all I have of you. And…I hope you don't have a problem with my choice of partner. I love Cabot, and the very bizarre fact that I ended up on Mykonos meeting him and finding out his parents knew you and Grandma…I have to wonder if it was all pre-planned. Because without them, I wouldn't have known the truth, and I wouldn't be here now. Maybe *you* planned it. The coincidence is all too much." Kissing the A, he whispered, "I love you, Dad," and slid off to land on his knees beside the coffin. "You can take him now, and be careful with his body." Climbing to his feet, he watched as the morgue attendants carried the coffin down the newly shorn path back to the house. Three hearses were waiting in the driveway to take the coffins away, and the men had already loaded the other two.

Mr García followed and was travelling to the morgue with them.

Tony didn't see the hearses off; he couldn't, so Viv and Carlos did instead.

Once the coffins were gone, the men got back to work clearing the area. Twenty-seven years' worth of tree debris had to be cleared, and wheelbarrow after wheelbarrow had been taken out to the rubbish trucks in the driveway, where a crane and flatbed truck was waiting for the masons to extract the bull statue fountain out the front.

Tony wandered around the garden until he came back to the terrace where he warily sat and stared out over the lake views.

"You okay, Tony?" Cabot sat beside him, having quietly followed him around the garden in case he needed him. He knew his lover had gone through a lot emotionally, and while he hadn't lost a father, or grandparents, he knew he would one day, and that thought killed him inside. So, he could only imagine what Tony was going through.

"I hope they don't hate me," Tony murmured. "I've gone against their wishes, but they didn't really think about the future. *I have to.* I hope they don't hate me for digging them up and cremating them."

"Well," Cabot said slowly. "You'll be putting them back and reburying them, so they'll still be there. And I doubt they could hate you. It's been so long. If their spirits are here, how could they hate you?" He laid a hand on his lover's arm. "I'm sure they loved you very much, Tony, and they won't hate you for what you're doing. It was all left to you, so they must have known you'd freshen the place up one day."

"Yeah, but with what I'm planning, it's going to be huge," Tony said as the rest of the family joined them.

"I've had an idea about that," Viv said as she and Carlos sat on a lounge. "I don't think you should get rid of the furniture. I think you should freshen it up instead. Yes, it's all old and needs work, but you could have a sand back, and some fresh upholstery for the chairs and lounges. The armoires and beds can have a sand as well, and maybe a whitewash to lighten them. New bedding and mattresses and curtains etc, and this place could look a lot different. If you don't need to throw it, keep it and do it up. The style will be in keeping with the house."

Tony nodded. "Yeah, I guess I could. It sounds like a good idea, Mrs S, thanks."

"I'll be glad to pick out colours, material, bedding, and then if it's not done by the time we leave, you can finish up. Are you getting someone in to clear the air?" She casually crossed her legs and dabbed at her forehead with her hanky. It was a very warm spring day. "If there's an interior designer in town, or you can get one in Madrid, they'll be able to do everything for you. And I have an idea." She went on to tell them about doing each room upstairs in a colour associated with Stephano's costumes. "It's more about keeping that touch of finery and richness in colour and materials. Pare that back with lighter floors and furniture, and you have a touch of old Spanish wealth, mixed with updated new century. The fabrics for the upholstery can be rich in colours and prints to add that touch of glamour to the place."

"It all sounds wonderful, Mrs S. Can you organise all of that for me? I'm sure Manuel would know of an interior designer. I want the house to be lightened to cream outside instead of that horrible terracotta. I'm thinking of cream inside to keep it light. I hate the dark wood everywhere, and if it can be sanded back, great. The terracotta tiles are too dark and I want them lightened, and maybe get the electricals updated along with the appliances."

"That's a lot to get done, Tony," Carlos said. "Think you'll get it done in the next couple of weeks?"

"I'm hoping. If we employ all of the businesses in town, and get more in from Madrid, I hope it will only take a few weeks. The rest of May at least. Then I can still rent it out for summer."

"We'd better get to it then," Viv said.

*****

The next day was a flurry of activity. A priest came in to cleanse the air and grounds, the pathway to the pavilion was cleared and flattened for the tiles to go down, all of the tiles, statues, and benches were brought up from the utility shed, and furniture from the main rooms on the ground floor was removed by the detailers who would be sanding, painting and upholstering.

That evening, before the building company was set to come the next day, Tony led the way up to the bell tower. The chill in the space made them shudder, but it didn't stop them from having their private ceremony to commemorate Connie. They read a few bible passages, threw rose petals off the tower, and lit candles. They said a few prayers, and Viv and Carlos came up with more stories. Popping a champagne bottle of Connie's favourite brew, they drank to her.

"Connie, my luv, you are sadly missed." Carlos raised his glass.

"Yes," Viv murmured beside him. "I miss you, my old friend. I miss the times we had, especially here."

"Grandma," Tony said next. "I barely remember you, but I miss you, and will cherish the photos I do have. Take care of Dad, and I hope he's taking care of you."

From her spot on the driveway, Connie looked up at the tower to her grandson and dearest friends, and smiled sadly through her tears.

*****

The second day, new appliances were installed and all electrical outlets inspected and repaired. The pool was emptied and work started on digging up the matador and bull tile mosaic. The ground of the pavilion itself was finally cleared and flattened, and outlines were marked for the marble to be re-laid, and the spots where the statues would be set. The local building company came to remove the top layer of the bell tower under the watchful eye of Manuel, and removed the roof and bricks, knocking it down to the level of the villa's roof, evening it out, and removing the staircase from the inside. They covered the roof to finish it the next day.

*****

On the third day, the interior designer Viv had spoken with at length on the phone, came with samples of material for the curtains and furniture, as well as luxe bedding sets for each room. All was perfect, and the designer would get the fabric to the upholstery company the next day. The roof was finished off with new tiles and gutters, and the rest of it was given a spray down to clean it up. The inside was remodelled with insulation and drywall for the ceiling, and the well where the staircase had been was opened up and turned into a seating area for the master suite.

The pool was prepped for re-tiling, and the dancing pavilion was finally laid. Statues were put in place with benches and railings. Carpenters sanded back the wood floors on the first and second floors along with the staircase, and moved outside to do all of the wood in the entranceway.

*****

On the fourth day, the pool was retiled and finished off, the furniture from all of the bedrooms was removed, except for the three they were using, and was sent to the carpenters. Floors were sanded, bathrooms were updated and renovated, and the bedroom floors were varnished to dry overnight. The terracotta tiles were sanded and sprayed a lighter colour.

*****

On the fifth day, the pool was refilled, and all of the downstairs rooms were painted a light cream that matched the colour of the outside. The bedrooms upstairs were getting a colour update, small things such as kitchenware and towels were brought in, and the back terrace was cleaned over and the barbecue updated. The lawn was given a good feed and water, trees were trimmed, weeds pulled up, the pool and pavilion were complete, and a new statue was installed in the fountain out the front.

*****

On day six, the downstairs furniture was brought back and arranged differently, cushions were laid on couches, and paintings were hung on walls. Curtains went up at all of the windows, and the refurbished four-poster beds and armoires were reset in the bedrooms. New mattresses and bedding were added, and the family moved into three fresh rooms so theirs could be overhauled and cleaned up.

Tony took the carpenters up to the second floor to the office. "I want the walls removed, and if the vault can be removed, do so. I want the whole space opened up for a nice seating area. Rip everything out." He was pointing to the walls either side of the door. "It will open the space up for the two main bedrooms and make a nice sitting area." He left the carpenters to get started on the walls and found the family in the back living room. Falling down beside Cabot on a refreshed lounge, he sighed. "This has been a big undertaking."

"It certainly has," Viv agreed. "But the place is looking great. Very fresh and new."

"You think so?" Tony asked as Cabot curled up beside him.

"Absolutely," Viv said. "It was very dated and dark before. Now, it's light and bright. The furnishings look great with the new colours and fabrics. The knick-knacks and homewares the interior designer found suit the place perfectly."

"And our old bedrooms are being sanded and painted, the furniture will be done in two days, so they'll be complete. After that…" Tony thought about it. "It's just the upstairs office; everything else is done. But that could take a couple of days, so the house should be completed by the time you leave. You'll get to see what it looks like completed."

"We can stay another few days before having to get back, although I can't wait to get back to Adam." Viv smiled happily at the thought of having a grandchild.

"He'll be there when we get back." Carlos grinned. "But from the sound of it, you'll see him in no time. Plus you've been calling every day."

"Once the office is done and the three bedrooms finished off, then it's complete." Tony's smile was sadly melancholic. "Then it can be rented out for the summer."

"Don't you want to rent it out?" Cabot asked.

"I don't know." Tony shook his head slightly. "Now that I've been here and found them, maybe I should spend a little more time here."

"Why don't you?" Viv suggested. "Everything's almost done, but you have a good couple of weeks left of May. Enjoy the place while you have it. But…what about your family's ashes?"

"Yeah," Tony murmured. "The pavilion's done, we just have the flower bed to install once the hole's filled in. But I wanted to wait until the house was done before having that ceremony."

*****

Three days later, with the final bedrooms finished, and the upstairs office now a light, bright sitting room, the house was complete. New wiring, TVs, DVRs, and internet had been added, new light fixtures and homewares, and it looked like a completely different house inside and out. There were no bulls anywhere, no sign of Stephano DeLuca anywhere, and everything was airy. The suffocating darkness it once had was gone. So, with the family, García, Fernández, and the gravediggers in tow, Tony led the way down the newly laid white hall to the beautiful disco ball, and over to the graves for his family. He held two urns of ashes, and had planned a special moment for them. Pausing at the top of the hole, he waited while Manuel set the ladder down. Handing the urn containing his father and grandmother to Carlos, he opened Stephano's urn and dumped the contents where Stephano's coffin had laid. "You deserve nothing else," he muttered, and gave Manuel the empty urn before climbing down into the grave.

Carlos handed down the second urn and watched Tony curiously.

Tony unscrewed the lid and carefully spelt out the letters and shapes 'I heart u' on his father's grave with the ashes. He was also able to create two xs and two os for hugs and kisses on his grandmother's grave, and finished emptying the urn into the heart.

"Oh, Tony," Viv murmured through her tears, her hand on her heart. "That's beautiful."

Tony looked up through his own teary eyes. "Thanks, Mrs S," he barely managed. "Antonio, can you take some photos?" Stepping out of the way, he waited.

Antonio quickly snapped pictures from different angles. "Got them."

"And some of me," Tony added, and carefully sat beside the letters where his father had lain. Antonio took more, and Tony got to his feet. "Hand down buckets of soil. I want to cover them, so they don't blow away when the rest is dumped in."

The men handed down buckets to him, and he carefully spread the soil over the letters so they stayed in place, and kept laying dirt while the men started filling in Stephano's side. Once there was enough soil,

Tony climbed out and helped shovel and wheelbarrow it in. It took several hours to fill up and make sure it would not be washed away again, which was what had caused the soil to disappear in the first place. Once there were only two feet left, the soil was stamped down with flat wood boards that the men stood on and walked back and forth over the grave. It sank a foot, so they kept filling. On the top layer, they added fertilisation for the flowers they were going to plant.

Finally, they stood back, all said small prayers, sprinkled holy water, and had the priest they'd brought back recite a few bible passages. He crossed the air with his gold metal cross and closed his bible. All was calm and peaceful.

"All that's left is to create the garden around the tree, so it's in a ring shape, but we can do that tomorrow," Tony said. "I'm done for the day. Worn out and wiped out."

"Yes, you would be," Viv said. She had dropped roses into the grave before it was filled. This whole trip was her goodbye to Connie, and Carlos's to Antonio.

"And you'll have to do it on your own, I'm afraid," Carlos added. "We need to fly out tomorrow. Mama's birthday is the day after, and their anniversary two days after that. So we won't be back."

"That's okay, Mr S. You've done more than enough to help me." Tony turned from Carlos to Cabot who was red-eyed from silently shed tears. "I hope you can come back and spend some time here with me before we go to England."

"Absolutely." Cabot smiled softly. "I'll be back in a few days."

"Then I say we go and have a bite to eat. The soil needs to settle and become nourished, so there's not a whole lot left to do."

"You've done a wonderful job, Tony. The estate is beautiful," Viv said as they walked back to the house. "I'm glad I got to see it one last time before the changes. Connie would be happy that you've made the place your own. And I think Antonio would, too. At least it will get you back here more often."

"Yes," Tony replied. "I think I'll have a reason to come back every year, it's much more free and beautiful now. Light and airy, and doesn't have Stephano DeLuca's imprint all over it."

"No." Viv smiled. "It has Antonio DeLuca II's imprint on it."

Later that afternoon, after a refreshing swim in the newly blue titled pool, Cabot and Tony wandered hand in hand around the property and down to the lake. There was a pathway and series of built-in stairs leading down, and they sat watching the water lap the shore and locals take advantage of the beautiful spring day.

"Is all of this part of the property?" Cabot asked, scanning his surroundings.

"From what Mr García told me, yes," Tony told him. "It's quite expansive for an estate. Goes on forever in every direction, and down here to the lake. I even think this part of the beach is his, but I can't be sure." Tony glanced from the lake to Cabot and back and thought about asking him. But it didn't feel like the right place, so they wandered back up and found themselves in the pavilion. He knew it there, felt it, that this was the right place even though it wasn't finished. "Cabot?" He tugged gently on his lover's hand to get his attention.

"Mmm?" Cabot's eyes were taking everything in. It all looked so different and pretty and he was imagining himself there with Tony having parties with orchestras as his mother had with Connie, and drinking champagne and dancing long into the night.

"Cabot. I know a lot has happened in the last couple of years, to both of us. My mum, being assaulted, you being assaulted, finding out your parents knew my family. It's all been a bit weird." Drawing breath, he let it out in a sigh and felt empty. "So much has happened to both of us, and it's been bad and horrible, but I feel it's also calming down. With everything I've done here, it's calm and peaceful now." Looking around, he sensed his father nearby. "I feel him, and he's okay."

"You feel your dad?" Cabot moved closer to his lover until he stood right in front of him and grasped both hands. "Do you feel your grandma, too?"

Tony breathed in and his eyelids closed. "Yes. And they're okay, and I'm happy, and that's why…" He opened his eyes and stared into his lover's. "I wanted to ask you to marry me."

Cabot blinked and shook his head. "What?"

Tony smiled and took Cabot's hands to his lips. "I love you, Cabot

Conroy Stephanopoulos, and I want to spend the rest of my life with you. I know we've both been through so much, and we're coming out the other end, and it all finally feels okay. *I* finally feel okay, and I know for a fact that I love you and want to be your husband. I want *you* for my husband."

"Oh… Tony…" Cabot was lost for words. It had only been six months since Tony had told him he loved him, and had only been since Christmas that he'd told Tony he loved him. Christmas had been magical and beautiful, and he knew he loved Tony desperately. But he was still dealing with contracting HIV and finding himself. He didn't know if marriage was what he wanted just yet. Not that he didn't want to be married to Tony, he did, but Jesus, he was only twenty-five, not yet twenty-six, and this was still new. An *actual* relationship was still new. "I," he blinked, "I can't…" Pulling back, he knew the panic was rising and his throat was contracting. "I… Jesus, Tony, I…" Shaking his head, he spun on his heel and raced back to the house.

"Cabot," Tony called. "It's okay if you're not ready. Cabot?" Seeing his lover flee, he deflated, but then felt himself be picked up as if something was lifting his spirits.

You surprised him, give him time, he will be yours, floated through his head and he smiled. "Yes, he will be mine."

That night, as they climbed into bed, Cabot lay as far away from Tony as he could, beet red with embarrassment, and curled up under the covers.

Tony laughed lightly. "Cabot, you don't have to sleep all the way over there. It's okay if you don't want to get married, yet. Silly." He reached out and touched his shoulder. "You don't have to be embarrassed or upset. Come here."

Scared, and freaked out of his mind, Cabot glanced over his shoulder at Tony. He had no idea what to say to him, and had avoided him all day. And now he felt way more than just uncomfortable. "I can't." Diving out of bed, he fled to his brother's room.

"Cabot?" Tony called out in alarm, but ended up smiling instead. "Silly boy." He went to sleep with a smile on his face.

Antonio sensed someone climbing into bed beside him and half woke. "Mmm…Cabot?"

"Tone," Cabot muttered and snuggled down.

"What are you doing in my bed?" Antonio asked, settling back in. "Lovers' spat?"

"No."

"Then what are you doing in my bed?"

"Tony proposed to me today and I'm freaking out, so I can't sleep with him."

Antonio's hand snaked out to flick the light on and he rolled over, now fully awake, to face his brother. "He what? You're kidding?"

Swathed in the fluffy down quilt, with only his eyes peeking out from under it, Cabot eyed him back. "Nope."

"Then what the hell are you doing here, dickface? Go and sleep with your future husband."

*****

Early the next morning, before breakfast, Carlos walked up the marble path to the pavilion, stopped in front of the DeLuca grave and sighed. "Oh, Connie, I'm so sorry. I'm so sorry I didn't tell you. And Antonio, I'm sorry you felt you had to leave your son because of your bloody father." The air left his body and sickness overcame him. Sick with grief, sick with guilt, he said, "If I had only told you, Connie, you could have saved yourself. I should have told you, but I allowed myself to be talked out of it, and I feel so goddamn guilty for it. I could have saved you, and in turn that would have saved Antonio, and he would be here with his son. With your grandson. Instead, both of you had to miss out because of damn Stephano, and the gutlessness of my choice. I should have told you."

"Told them what?"

Carlos spun around to find Tony behind him. He knew it was time for confessions and a clearing of the air and sighed. "Told her about her husband."

"What about him?" Tony stepped closer, knowing something was coming.

Carlos looked away in shame, unable to look at the boy his son had taken to. The boy who looked so much like his father. "That he was sleeping with men."

"You knew that? When?" Tony was surprised.

Blinking back tears, Carlos said, "Early 1980."

"What?" Tony's surprise turned to shock. "How did…? When did…? Why didn't you…?" He was next to Carlos who was staring down at the grave, and trying to get a grip on the tornado of emotions swirling around inside of him.

With a sigh from deep in his gut, and guilt-riddled soul, Carlos went on to explain. "We told you much of it last Thanksgiving. 1980 was a bad year all round. It started off great for us. We'd just spent Christmas and New Year's in Australia with the family, and had come back in time for Valentine's Day at *Studio 69* for our birthdays. But after that, the shit hit the fan and didn't stop." He wrapped his arms around himself and stared shamefaced down at the dirt. "It wasn't called AIDS then. It wasn't even known. The terms that followed were the gay plague, the gay cancer, GRID, the 4 H disease. Over the next two years, it went through many transformative names until they decided on AIDS in 1982. Until then, thousands of people died from the cancer, the pneumonia, fungus, STDs, wasting disease. It was horrible, and no one knew what it was, or why it happened, or how it was passed on." Burying his face in his hands, he breathed in. "Ugh, Tony, I'm so sorry. I'm so sorry I didn't try harder. I'm so sorry I didn't do what I should have done."

"And what was that?"

When Carlos lifted his head, his eyes were red and wet. "I should have called and told her. I should have told her he was gay and had male lovers, but I didn't."

"But how did you know that?" Tony persisted, stepping closer. "How?"

Wiping his face, Carlos took a deep breath and let it out slowly. "After we got back in 1980, people we knew started getting sick and dying, as you know. First, we lost Leon Talley, a co-worker of Pedro and Mike's. He became sick and ended up in the hospital. When Pedro and Mike found him, he only had days, if that, to live. He wanted Pedro to take care of his belongings and contact everyone. Well, Pedro did. He went through Leon's little black book and contacted all of Leon's lovers as he'd asked him to. Many were dead, many were sick, some would be able to attend. Two names on that list were familiar. A Jamal Devron, who was a police officer we knew, and Stephano DeLuca." Carlos blinked back the tears and breathed a ragged breath. "Jamal died a month or two later, your grandfather in October. We've wondered just how expansive the gay web at *69* was because we found out from other friends who died that they'd all been lovers too… In 1980, it wasn't that big of a thing, gay men were getting sick, but no one knew how, or why. I wanted to call Connie and tell her that her husband had been sleeping with men who were sick, or dying, but I was talked out of it."

"Why?" Tony asked, angry and curious and overwhelmed at the same time.

Carlos looked guiltily at Tony. "I was told that other people's marriages were none of my business. And since Connie and Stephano had been separated for five years plus, it really *was* none of my business. Especially since I had taken money for sex from her. She had slept around and so had he. It was none of my business." He sighed wearily. "If we had known about AIDS then I would have. And I know I *should* have, regardless. When I read that letter I felt so goddamn guilty for letting my family talk me out of it, that I've felt the guilt ever since." Staring down at the grave he still felt sick inside.

"Would Grandma have listened to you?" Tony asked.

"I don't know." Carlos shook his head. "I really don't know. And that's been a point people keep bringing up. Even if I *had* told her, what if she didn't listen to me? What if she went ahead and did what she wanted anyway? I just don't know."

"Well…" Tony thought about it and sensed his family coming through. "Grandma would have done what Grandma wanted. He infected her, and she killed herself because of it. But *Dad,* on the other hand, he made a choice, and *he chose them* over me, and we've all suffered for it since."

"Oh, Tony, I'm so sorry," Carlos whispered. "You should not have had to lose your father because of this."

"But I did." Tony glanced from the grave to his future father-in-law. "I lost him because of my arsehole grandfather. Dad made the choice." His lips quivered as he spoke. "He made the choice to leave me and Mum for them."

"If only I could go back and change *my* choice." Carlos stared up at the canopy of trees before closing his eyes. "And I'm sure your father wishes he could too."

"Yeah, he does," Tony muttered. "And Grandma wants you to know she doesn't blame you. There's nothing to forgive, so you need to forgive yourself."

Carlos gazed curiously at Tony. "What?"

"I feel them." Tony smiled. "They're here. I hear them, I feel them, they want you to know it's not your fault, and to forgive yourself. They made their choices, no one made them, or forced them. They alone made their choices."

"Oh, Tony," Carlos whispered. "I'm so sorry." He clasped Tony in a bear hug.

Tony hugged back, glad for some form of a father figure he'd never really had. "I know, Mr S, and you're forgiven. Let it go. It's time to let it go and move on. Both of us."

Pulling back, but still hanging on to Tony's arms, Carlos's smile was full of sadness. "I'll try. But I doubt it."

"Good." Tony smiled in return, thinking about what he had to say next. "Now, about me and Cabot."

Carlos pricked up. "Do you love my son, Tony?"

Tony's smile broadened. "Very much, Mr S, that's why I proposed yesterday. I think I scared him, but he'll come around, and I'm willing to wait forever if I have to."

Carlos remembered back to his own forever with Viv, and his brows rose. "It's *that* serious already?"

"Very," Tony replied. "But I think he's just overwhelmed with everything that's happened to him, and with the six months we've spent together. He needs time to think about everything, and I'm okay with that."

"Promise me something," Carlos said to him.

"Of course, Mr S."

"Besides taking care of my son and loving him, promise me you won't keep things to yourself. If you know something, tell it. Because if you don't and something happens, you'll live with that guilt for the rest of your life. So, promise me you won't keep things in. If you know something, tell the person, don't let them be hurt by the consequences. Please. Because the guilt can kill you." The pain and guilt had not eased with letting his secret be known and spoken out loud.

Tony nodded in all seriousness. "Absolutely, Mr S. I will. And don't you live with the guilt either. It's over now. At the end of the day…" He sadly looked at the grave. "It's neither of our faults they did what they did."

"But we're the ones who have to live with it," Carlos murmured.

"So are they, Mr S. So are they," Tony replied. "We'd better get in for breakfast. You're leaving soon."

They wandered back to the house to find Viv finishing up in the kitchen.

"Breakfast is served," she called and carried two plates to the table.

They ate in relative silence, with only a few murmurings, cleaned up the kitchen, and then finished packing afterwards.

Cabot retrieved his toiletries from the bathroom and placed them in his carry-on bag.

"Cabot?" Tony came into the room.

Cabot blushed and buried himself in the armoire for the last of his clothes.

"Cabot," Tony cajoled and turned Cabot to face him and a grin slowly lit up his face. "It's okay if you're not ready to get married. With everything we've both been through, especially you, and now all of this, I get it. I do. It doesn't mean I love you any less. If anything, I love you even more."

Cabot blushed and looked relieved. "Really?"

"Really," Tony repeated. "I love you. I will wait for you until you're ready."

A sigh escaped Cabot. "I love you, Tony." Kissing passionately, they remained in a clinch until Antonio called out that it was time to go, and fifteen minutes later, Cabot was furiously waving from the back seat of the car as they drove away.

On the plane ride home, Viv noticed her son's strange behaviour. "Cabot, is everything okay with you and Tony? You all but ignored him yesterday."

"And slept in my bed last night." Antonio nudged his brother with his foot.

"I'm fine," Cabot muttered through clenched teeth, and clutched his carry-on bag tighter to his chest as some form of shield. The thought of marrying Tony thrilled him and scared him at the same time, especially after everything that had happened last year.

"Not from the look of it," Viv went on. "Did you have your first fight?"

"No, Mama," Cabot managed, shifting in his seat.

Carlos's grin was ear to ear as he looked at her. "Tony proposed."

"What!" Viv exclaimed, looking at her husband. "When?"

"Yesterday, which is why he's freaked out," Antonio added.

"Ugh," Cabot growled. "I don't want to talk about it." He dashed off for the bedroom and locked himself in.

"Well, what's got him so upset, then?" Viv asked. "I thought he loved Tony."

"Clearly the thought of being married freaked him out." Antonio's grin grew bigger.

*****

They got home early evening and celebrated Jenny's birthday and her and Spiros's fifty-sixth anniversary the next day. She was eighty years old and celebrating with the rest of her family of whom most had already had birthdays. Her boys had turned fifty-one, fifty-three and fifty-five, Viv seventy-one, Angie forty-nine, Roger sixty. Danté was fifteen, Alexis twenty, Dom twenty-five. Those who had birthdays left were Alena and Diana who would be thirty, Spiros who would be eighty-three, and the boys who had their twenty-sixth in July. Everyone was a year older...almost.

During the celebrations, Jenny cast a glance over her family and all the extras that were there. Even though it was only May, a lot had already happened in the family. She saw her sons huddled together in the kitchen, laughing at a joke. Pedro was playfully punching Carlos on the arm, and Tomas was pushing his glasses up the bridge of his nose as they always slid down when he laughed.

Tomas's twinkling eyes caught his mother's and he smiled, raising his glass to her in a celebratory gesture. Carlos and Pedro saw this and followed suit.

Jenny smiled and her gaze moved onto her grandchildren.

Alena was currently back home as Diana and Charles now had the house they'd shared, but since Jenny was in the process of buying more homes for her expanding brood, Alena would soon be getting one of her own. Alena and Diana were also working full-time for *Haus of Stefan*, and had set up *Styled By Stefan*, a sister company to their mother's business, *Styled By Vivian,* that she'd set up back in the '80s. Everyone was at a different point in the process of releasing books through *Prologue Press*, their publishing house, even Tomas, who Jenny had finally cajoled into doing those cookbooks she'd mentioned at the end of last year.

Danté was awaiting surgery on his leg as it wasn't working as well as it could be. She'd looked into plastic surgeons and flown one out from England for an examination, and Danté was booked in for surgery at the beginning of June, with rehab to follow. And Cabot was telling anyone who'd listen that he was going to London with Tony once he flew back, so not to expect him for a while.

All in all, it was just a normal Stephanopoulos celebratory gathering.

*****

The day after, Cabot was lying on his bed in Tomas and Roger's house, staring out the window at the back wall. They had painted a huge mural on it, a seascape, so there was something to look at in the small back courtyard when you looked out the kitchen window. It was eleven, and he heard the door open and close. Hauling himself up and meandering downstairs, he found Tomas in the kitchen with bags of food going through recipes for lunch. "Uncle T, can I talk to you?"

Tomas was leaning over a cookbook on the island bench, but now looked up. "Sure."

Cabot sat on a stool opposite his uncle, but didn't speak.

"Cabot?" Tomas straightened and pushed his glasses up the bridge of his nose. "What's wrong? You've been weird since you got back." Carlos had told the rest of the family all about their trip, including Tony's marriage proposal, and the fact it had freaked Cabot out.

"When did you…?" Cabot started, but blushed and rubbed his hands on his jeans. "When did you…know…you were in love and wanted to get married?" He couldn't look anywhere but down.

Tomas smiled and walked around the island bench to sit beside his nephew. "This is about Tony's proposal?"

Cabot's head shot up in alarm and he blushed harder. "How did you—?"

"Don't worry, your big mouth father told us all about it." Tomas's smile grew larger.

"Oh, for God's sake." Cabot rolled his eyes. "Can't anybody do any bloody thing in this family without everyone finding out?"

"Nope. You should know that by now." Tomas patted Cabot's hand. "What is it? What's going on?"

Cabot took a deep breath and breathed. "When did you…? What did you feel…? Between Luiz and what you felt for him, and Roger and what you felt for him, know, when you were in love and wanted to get married?"

Tomas inhaled. "Ah…" Breathing out, he re-adjusted his glasses and continued. "Luiz and Roger were completely different. Luiz was very passionate and tribal and sexual and over too quickly, so I have no idea what *could* have been, even though I know I *would* have had a relationship with him. I do know it would have been a very passionate one and more than likely one-sided. And being my first, more than likely it wouldn't have lasted. But what I felt for Roger was different. I know I loved Roger the first night we were together. Falling asleep and waking up in his arms was it. I felt it. The love that flowed from my

216

heart and soul. I was his and he was mine. As for marriage, that came later. With everything we all went through, marriage was not even on the horizon. It wasn't legal then as it is now in some countries."

"But you didn't let that stop you," Cabot piped up.

Tomas's smile softened. "*Mama* didn't let it stop her. When we all got to Athens and Carlos and Pedro proposed, we went into a flurry of planning. Mama was in her element, and unbeknownst to me, had planned our wedding as well." He took a moment to reminisce. "When Carlos and Viv were getting married, Pedro and I were the best men, and it hit me like a tonne of bricks. I wanted to get married too. We'd given your father initialled cufflinks for his wedding present, and the next night he and I gave Pedro his. I got all sad and miserable because I was never going to have a chance to get married, a chance to have my brothers give me initialled cufflinks for a wedding present. I felt it at both weddings. The pain of never getting married, never being legal partners in every sense. Not being able to share our joy with my family. But, the next day, Mama pulled a rabbit out of her hat and the family married us. It was the most incredibly beautiful experience of my life. And every year, Roger and I go somewhere private and repeat our vows just for us. To know that thirty years on our love is still strong and alive..." His smile said it all. "I knew at your father's wedding that I wanted to marry Roger and spend the rest of my life with him. Do you love Tony and want to spend the rest of your life with him?"

"Yes, oh, God yes," Cabot cried. "But..." He breathed in and held it.

"But what?"

"But...I..." Cabot stumbled, trying to get a grasp on his feelings and put them into words.

"Breathe," Tomas told him. "Just breathe and relax, and let it out."

Cabot blew his breath out and relaxed. "I love him. I want to be with him. But I don't feel emotionally mature and ready to take, or make, that commitment. With everything that happened to me last year, it's not even a year yet that I was assaulted and contracted HIV. I only met Tony in October. We only got together at Christmas, it's just all too soon. I only admitted to myself last year I was gay and preferred men. Tony's my first relationship. I want to get used to it before settling down."

"Do you see yourself with him *forever*, or is he *just* your first relationship?" Tomas twirled his first anniversary eternity ring on his finger, the one that had *forever* engraved on it. He remembered back to his private ceremony with Roger when they'd exchanged the rings during their European holiday in 1978. Carlos and Viv, and Pedro and Angie had all exchanged them as well.

Cabot took 0.0000 seconds to answer. "He's my forever."

Tomas's smile lit up his face. "Then tell *him* exactly what you just told me. Calmly, maturely. He will understand. And if he loves you too, he will wait for you. If he doesn't and has a problem with that, then he's not the one for you."

"Yeah." Cabot's lips twitched into a small smile. "He did say he'd wait."

"Then what are you worried for?"

"That it's too soon and I'm not ready for it."

"He said he'll wait," Tomas reminded him. "If he's serious, which we all think and see that he is, then he *will* wait."

*****

Two days later, Cabot flew back to Spain and made his way to the DeLuca estate. Rolling his luggage through the front door, he called out. "Tony? Tony? You here?" Receiving no reply, he left his luggage and walked out to the back terrace. "Tony? You here?" Hearing nothing, he wandered up the hall to the disco ball and found Tony pottering in the bright colourful flowerbed that was now his grandparents' grave. "Oh, wow, it's beautiful."

A wide floral ring encircled the massive Ficus tree where the family was buried. The scent was heavenly, the colours mind-blowing, and on the garden bed over the graves was a huge heart made of red roses, surrounded by pink and white ones.

Tony glanced up. "Hey. Didn't hear you come in. You're back." Dusting off his hands, he removed the gloves and dropped them on the ground, and found himself in his lover's arms. "Mmm, I've missed you." He hugged Cabot tightly. "This is the first time we've been apart since Thanksgiving."

"I know, and I hated it. Hated being without you," Cabot murmured before pulling back to gaze into his lover's exotic greeny brown eyes as his hands played with Tony's t-shirt collar. "Tony, I want to marry you, I do, but…I don't feel emotionally ready for it." Remembering his uncle's words, he breathed and tried to stay calm. "I've gone through so much this last year, and you before it, and I'm still learning how to be an independent adult; one who's HIV positive and on drugs for the rest of my life." His eyes widened and the panic rose. "I'm nowhere near mature, or adult, enough to get married, yet. I'm still finding myself and the person I want to be. I'm only twenty-five, and even though Uncle Tomas got married at twenty-two, he didn't have HIV to deal with, and he *was* mature and adult-like. I'm not. I'm still growing and…" He saw Tony's eyes twinkling. "What?"

Tony laughed. "Oh, my darling boy, you are silly. *Of course* I'll wait for you. I love you, I want you to be ready for this, and it's okay if you're not ready now. I'll wait for you until you are. That's all you had to tell me, Cabot. Instead, you got all silly and awkward and ran away from me. That *was* funny."

"Tonee, I was freaking out," Cabot whined. "I wasn't trying to be funny."

"Well, I don't know why you'd freak out when there's so much going on in your family that love and marriage is a normal thing. Your sister got married at Christmas."

"Yeah, I know." Cabot relaxed. "But times are different. This is 2008, not 1977 when Tomas and Roger got married. There's so much more to worry about, and we both have HIV, and I'm still learning to deal with it."

"Did you take your meds this morning?" Tony asked.

"Yes. You?" Cabot replied.

"Of course, and life moves on," Tony said. "I'm not going to let it stop me from loving you, or wanting to marry you. I love you, Cabot Conroy Stephanopoulos."

The dopey Stephanopoulos grin spread across Cabot's face. "Aw, Tonee, I love you, too."

"Good. So, give me a proper welcome home kiss."

Cabot promptly threw his arms around Tony's neck and planted his lips on his future husband's.

They stayed that way for a while, having no concept of time, and just didn't care, pulling apart when they wanted to, and pottering around in the garden some more. Cabot handed Tony small pots of flowers, and Tony planted them, and soon they were done.

"There." Tony dusted himself off. "The garden is finally done. The house, the grounds, all done." He stared down at the grave. The rose heart was blooming already, and the perfumed scent danced around them.

"It's beautiful." Cabot slid his arm around Tony and grasped his hand. "Your parents and grandparents would be so proud. They'll love it here."

"I hope so," Tony murmured. "Although Mum is buried in a cemetery in England. I've wondered the last couple of days if I should have her reburied here, so the two of them can be together."

"That's sweet," Cabot replied, his eyes taking in every detail of the flowerbed and how much work Tony had put into it.

"Yeah, I thought so. But, then I realised they hadn't been together since forever, and Mum had remarried. So, not sure if that would have even been her wish. I never saw a will, never knew what her wishes were when it came to being buried. She's in a family plot of her parents' choosing. My stepfather couldn't have cared less about it. Or her from the looks of things. I always wondered about him."

Cabot looked deeply into Tony's eyes and saw suspicious curiosity. "You don't like him? You haven't really mentioned him except in talking about you letting everyone know your status."

"Yeah..." Tony murmured. "There wasn't much to mention until then. It was all rather boring and normal... My mother met him when I was ten, she hadn't dated, or remarried, or anything after Dad died. But, then she met him and suddenly she was smiling again, and laughing and happy. I hadn't seen her that way in a long time. They married not long after. I thought it was too soon. Didn't like him taking my dad's place, although I hadn't had a dad in seven or eight years. And Mum had never really told me why. Maybe she knew the truth, maybe she didn't. She cried a lot until then. Told me stories of my father and how they'd met. Where they married. Here." He glanced around the pavilion, taking it all in. "It looks the same as it did then. Can you imagine it?" Turning, he imagined his wedding to Cabot the same as his mother's wedding to his father. "They would have had their family and friends here, in this pavilion. On these marble tiles." He looked down at his feet. "We're standing on the same dance floor they married on, and one day," his gaze found Cabot's, "we'll stand here and get married, too. With your family gathered around, and what's left of mine." He noted Cabot's blush and small smile. "Of course, your family will outnumber mine, but my grandparents, aunts and uncles will be here with their kids..." His smile faltered. "Except Mum and Dad won't be here...neither will Grandma..."

"They will be, in spirit." Cabot squeezed his lover's hand encouragingly. "Your grandma and dad are watching you from right here in the garden. And your mum's watching over you from wherever she is."

"Yeah..." Sadness washed over Tony. "I hope so. I've been thinking about that, too." Taking a deep breath, he went on. "I think it's time I find out what really happened. I have vague memories of that man coming to our house when I was two. And Mum being upset after that, and Dad never coming home. But she never told me much. I don't know whether she even knew the story in full, or if she just never told me. And why didn't she tell me I owned the house in London?"

"Maybe she didn't know," Cabot suggested.

"She would have," Tony replied. "Even when I was paid a visit on my twenty-fifth birthday by Mr García, telling me I had inherited the estate, no one mentioned the house in London."

"How did your mum react to that?"

Tony thought back. "She seemed...suspicious...wary...unsure. She kept eyeing him, like she didn't trust him and what he was saying.

And I was in complete shock by it all." His head slowly shook at the memories. "I couldn't believe that it was happening. That I was inheriting my dad's estate. Afterwards…I had so many questions and I was asking her, but she just couldn't answer them."

"Or didn't want to," Cabot said softly. "Maybe it dredged up too many memories for her, and she didn't want to revisit them. Even all those years on."

Tony cocked his head in thought. "Maybe. Or *maybe* she just didn't want to answer my questions in front of my stepfather. He made a big hullaballoo about how I could now repay him for all the years he'd supported me. Mum quietly told him that he hadn't as the trust fund had been paying for us. He didn't like that one bit. Started calling me a fag fucker around the same time. So did his kids. They didn't mind slagging me off on one hand, and expecting handouts on the other." His face screwed up into a scowl.

"They are your half-siblings, though, your mum had them too," Cabot reminded him. "They have her blood running through their veins."

"Yeah," Tony muttered absentmindedly. "But they're also *his* blood and only half mine. I'm a DeLuca, they are not."

Cabot sighed. He knew Tony's family had given him grief over being gay, and then contracting HIV. Tony had shared stories when he felt the need to, but other than that, he didn't discuss them. "Well then, you need to make a choice about what you're going to do when we get to London."

"Yeah." Tony came out of his reverie. "I do. And I've been thinking about that too. I have all of the documents now, I didn't then. I have the paperwork to show I own the house, and my grandparents paid for it as a present to Mum and Dad. And then it reverted to my estate on my birthday. I need to find out what state it's in and then throw him out. He doesn't deserve to live there. He stayed after Mum died because he would have thought he owned it as her husband. From what I read in the papers, it wouldn't matter what the circumstances were, the house was always mine, not theirs. He probably thinks he's living the high life with a nice house that's paid for…bastard!" Fury fled over Tony's face as the memories came back.

"*You're a little fag fucker,*" Brian Smith spat at his stepson who he'd come to hate. "*You fuck boys for fun and think we like it. Well, I hate it.*" He stabbed his fork into his steak and sawed back and forth with his knife. "*You deserve everything you get.*"

Tony watched from across the table, dissatisfaction all over his face. His gut was wrenching at the foul words, and he wanted to fly across the table and stab Brian in the eye with that steak knife. Instead, he turned to his mother. She looked tired and worn out, having a lingering illness that didn't seem to shake itself. "*Mum...I—*"

"*Don't expect your mother to save you,*" Brian told him, shoving another piece of steak into his mouth. Gravy dribbled down his chin and he swiped it away with the back of his hand. "*She won't.*"

"*I don't need to.*" Cynthia tiredly directed her gaze to her husband. "*He doesn't need saving.*" Placing a hand on her son's arm, she added, "*If this is the life you've chosen to partake in, then that's up to you. I love you either way.*"

The relief flooded through Tony. His twenty-fifth birthday was turning out to be quite a big one. Not only had he inherited his father's estate in Spain, but he'd finally come out to his mother, telling her he'd known for a while that he was gay, and he'd finally decided to live his life the way he wanted. "*Thanks, Mum, that means a lot.*"

Still feeling the effects of her illness, Cynthia smiled softly. "*I love you, Tony. I'll support you no matter what.*"

"*Oh, puh-leeze,*" Brian's voice came loudly around the dining table. "*He's a fag. How can you support that? And speaking of support, now that you've inherited your dead daddy's money, you can pay me back for all the years I financially supported you. You're worth a motza, so you owe me a motza.*" He slugged back his beer and burped loudly.

Tony saw his mother wince in embarrassment and squeezed her hand. While he'd had a typical childish dislike for the new man in his mother's life when he was ten, Tony had become accustomed to Brian quite quickly. Brian had gone out of his way to get along with Tony, and acted like a friend instead of a dad. At first. But a few years into the marriage it was evident Brian was in control, and the father figure. With their first child having come into the world, Tony very quickly learned that Brian wanted a firm hand in raising Tony the way he wanted, and it didn't matter if Tony liked it or not. Not that Brian ever took a hand to his stepson, he didn't. But he used a firm hand in dealing with Tony. But, oh, how things had changed in the last fifteen years. Once the man of the house and family, with his own business, an injury at work had set Brian into a downward spiral. He'd sold the business for good money, sat on his backside and done nothing for the last three years, letting his children with Cynthia run amok while Cynthia took over everything. She'd had three more children after marrying, two to three years apart. And with the illness she'd recently acquired, she just didn't have the energy most days to deal with them even though they were all in school.

Cynthia squeezed back and held on tight. "Brian, you never financially supported Tony because his father's estate did that. It's paid for everything, so he owes you nothing. So you will get nothing." So many thoughts raced through her head. There were so many things she had never told Tony, never spoken out loud since she'd received the dreadful news in 1981, and now, with the family lawyer turning up, maybe it was time to get it all out. A sigh left her. So did what little energy she had left.

"What?" Brian's voice rose in decibels. "What do you mean, I haven't paid for him? What was I handing over all that money for?" His fist thumped down onto the table and fire burned in his eyes.

Tony steeled his wits. In the last few years since his injury, Brian's temper could fly out of control at the drop of a hat. Although, why Tony inheriting his father's estate could do that, he didn't know.

"You've been handing over your money for your children and their schooling, for the family holidays, the food we eat, any medicals we need, and anything else that was needed," Cynthia bit back. "The family's estate provided for Tony. You didn't."

The fire burned brighter in Brian's eyes, and Tony couldn't tell what he was thinking. But he knew he had to defend his mother if need be.

Brian, seeing the grip Cynthia had on Tony's hand, and Tony's steely look of determination, calmed down. That little fag fucker's inherited Daddy's estate and I'm not getting a piece of it, *he thought.* Oh, no way in hell. *Changing tack, he said,* "Well, then, Tony. Maybe you can help out around the house then, with bills, eh?"

"I already have been." *Tony eyed his attitude change carefully.* "Since I got my first job at eighteen. I've been paying Mum rent and board. Not that I needed to, apparently." *He glanced at his mother.*

"It helped you learn how to take care of yourself, love. To learn what being an adult was all about. Bills need to be paid; medicals and such. It taught you how to be responsible with money." *Not that she'd told Tony she'd been putting his weekly earnings into a bank account for him so she could give it back to him one day.*

"Yeah, I guess," *Tony murmured. At eighteen, he'd only been able to afford fifty pounds a week, and at twenty-one had doubled that to one hundred. But now at twenty-five, he didn't need to work anymore if he didn't want to. While the lawyer had explained it all to them, he got the sense that only the basics had been covered. The lawyer had kept casting furtive glances at Brian in the other room, and kept telling Tony to read the information in private.* "Okay, I guess I'll continue to contribute while I'm here."

"That would be lovely, Tony." *Cynthia patted his hand and went back to eating. Not that she ate much lately. This illness had taken its toll and her appetite had disappeared. She placed a small piece of potato into her mouth and chewed mechanically. She'd gone to the doctor and been diagnosed with the flu, but had a feeling the illness was much more serious than that. But she hadn't been back. Didn't have the energy to. She glanced at her four children. From twenty-five-year-old Tony, to thirteen-year-old David, eleven-year-old Michelle, and eight-year-old Nathan, she moved her gaze to Brian. Her life had changed a lot in the last twenty-six years, from meeting and marrying Antonio at twenty-seven in 1978, to being widowed two years later, and being a single mother until 1988 when she'd met Brian. He was the first man since her husband that'd she'd been remotely interested in, and they'd met when she'd gone to work as a* receptionist for his company. She'd been a stay at home mother until Tony started school, and had then gained part-time jobs and volunteered to fill in the time while he was being educated. She'd found herself laughing at Brian's corny jokes, and thinking how nice he was, and finally allowed herself to have feelings for another man. And Brian had been a wonderful man for a good ten years, but his injury had made him like a bear with a sore head. And at the end of the day, no one could ever replace her true love, Antonio DeLuca. That was why Tony was more special than her other children. Not that she intended it to be that way.

Tony watched Brian and his mother carefully, his eyes flitting back and forth between the two. He wondered what Brian was up to, and why his mother was so sick all the time. Maybe he could do something to help her out now he had money. He wasn't sure how much, that would probably be in the paperwork from the lawyer, but he would definitely be talking to her in the next few days.

After dinner, while the family watched TV in the lounge room, Tony retreated to his room upstairs. After Nathan had come along, and with Brian's injury, his parents had moved downstairs to the guest room, so the four kids had a room each upstairs. Being the eldest, Tony had moved into the master so he had his own bathroom. He made sure the door was locked before pulling out the paperwork and sitting at his desk by the window to read it.

Under the lamplight, he read every detail twice over from beginning to end. The DeLuca estate consisted of the lavish Spanish home in Manzanares el Real, many family treasures, and a trust fund worth tens of millions of dollars. The letter laid out that his mother had been paid a weekly allowance for herself until he reached twenty-five and inherited. It was now up to him if he wanted to keep supporting her from his fund, in which case, he'd have to set it up. The folder contained pictures of the home, along with a catalogue of work done over the years, and a financial report and bank work on what had been taken out to cover the costs of maintenance. There was a map to show him how to get there, and business details for car rentals and hotels. The letter invited him to visit, so they could decide *how to proceed, whether to keep the house in maintenance mode, or rent it out for the summers.*

Since it was August, Tony decided to pay the family estate a visit. He asked his mother the next morning if she wanted to go with him. Handing over the photos, he watched the expressions flit over her face.

Happiness, joy, sadness, pain, all came hurtling back for Cynthia as she studied the photos. "It's all the same," she whispered. "It's all the same as when I was there."

"When you and Dad got married," Tony replied softly, not wanting to jar any memories for her.

The pain and joy on her face said it all. "It was so beautiful," the whispering voice continued. "So beautiful. We were married in the forest, celebrated on the back terrace, and spent our honeymoon in the family apartment in Madrid. Your father took me to see a bullfight and I hated it. Antonio said he did too, although he'd loved it as a child when he watched his father fight." Her finger slid across the photo and memories poured back. "The house was impressive, but oppressive. Dark wood and terracotta tiles. It was all about your grandfather. All about Stephano DeLuca."

"Will you come with me?" Tony asked. "We can hop a flight over and go and see it. You can show me where you and Dad got married. We can visit Spain. Show me where you went on your honeymoon." He gently touched her arm. "Mum?"

"No." A lone tear slid down her cheek and she shoved the photos into her son's hands. "No. I'm not visiting that place ever again. That was the first and last time I was ever there. It's where your father and grandparents are buried, and I refuse to set foot on those grounds. I won't stop you if you want to go; you have inherited it, after all. But I won't be going with you." She touched a hand to her son's cheek. "I lost your father there. I'm never going back."

"Aw, Mum." Tony took her into his arms and held her while she sobbed.

"Typical. Look what you've done now, made her cry," Brian scolded from the doorway. They were in the kitchen and he'd come

for a beer.

"*Except I didn't,*" Tony replied tartly. "*She's crying over memories.*"

"*Yeah, right. Her life has never been better, being married to me.*" Brian grabbed his beer from the fridge and cranked it open. "*What would she have to cry about?*"

"*My father,*" Tony spat over his shoulder. "*The one and only man she ever truly loved and lost.*"

The red blush crept up Brian's neck to his face. He looked as if he was going to blow.

Cynthia pulled out of Tony's arms and wiped her face. "Now Tony, don't stir your stepfather. Our life was a long time ago, and your father's been gone just as long."

Tony gazed into his mother's green eyes. They were as pale as her British complexion, her once vibrant red hair dulled by time and discolouration as it turned grey. He sighed deep from his gut. "I know, Mum. But it still clearly upsets you. So, you're not coming with me, then?"

"*No, love. You go. Go and see your family's heritage. We'll be here when you get back.*" *She lovingly cupped his cheek. "You go and see what it's like."*

Seeing the pain still bright in her eyes, he nodded and kissed her cheek. Within hours he'd applied for holiday leave from his job, set up his bank account to still pay his mother a weekly allowance, and booked his trip to Spain.

"I came here in 2003, late August. That week-long trip was quite an eye-opener." Tony came back to 2008. "It was exactly like when we came here a few weeks ago. The house was incredibly imposing, very dark, so full of Stephano DeLuca it was smothering. Every wall and shelf and cupboard and table was full of his pictures and photos and memorabilia, just like when we came here. But nothing else. I found all of that in the vault. Mr García took me in there, opened it up, and I walked into a room so dark and deadly it threatened to take my breath away. I didn't stay in it long; just long enough to see boxes and crates and the album sitting on top of it all, as if it was waiting for me. After all those years, it was waiting for me to find it and take it. Which I did, along with some photos. He'd left them there to be taken. I couldn't figure out what to do with it all, and I was so overwhelmed with emotions that I couldn't actually think straight. I never closely inspected it all. But I got the hell out of there. I stayed the whole week in the room we're in now. Wondered what the creaking and groaning was about. Wondered why I always felt a strong pull to the forest, to the upstairs floor and that room, to that place. I knew it was my family's home. My heritage, but I sure as hell didn't know why the pull was so strong. It haunted me. So did the house. It *is* beautiful, yes, impressive, but always, always felt haunted. And now I know why. And now I know why Mum never told me Dad and Grandma killed themselves. Dad didn't want us knowing, and that's why they lied."

"Did the family lawyer mention any more in your conversations?" Cabot asked, heartbroken for his lover.

Tony drifted on aimlessly, not hearing Cabot. "Whether that means Mum never found out, I don't know. I was here five years ago. We had the house done up for renters, freshened up and redecorated. I didn't find my father's things then. The lawyer did give me a very detailed list of everything that was in vault, and I took the album and photos. I went home and told Mum all about it, but by then she was really sick and I got her to the hospital. She'd had the flu for a month or two and it wasn't going away. She was told she had pneumonia and asthma and stayed in the hospital for a month being treated. I made sure she got the best of everything, but while she heard all about Spain, she still didn't tell me anything about Dad's death. She didn't even bring it up. Just listened to me talk."

Sighing, he glanced around the garden. "I wish she could see this now. See how I've restored it to its former glory. I've been looking at the wedding album. It looks the same. I wish she could see it."

"Hopefully she is." Cabot slid an arm around Tony. "Hopefully she's watching you from wherever she is, and she's proud of you." He paused a moment. "I don't know what it's like to lose a dad, or mum, but I do know I'd hate it, and I can't even begin to think what will happen, or how I'll feel, when Grandma and Grandpa go, or even the great Carlos and Vivian. I'll be an orphan."

"Let's hope you don't have to for a long time, yet, Cabot." Tony kissed his cheek. "But for now, I suggest we get this cleaned up." They gathered all of the gardening supplies and walked towards the house. "You know, I get why she didn't want to come." They left the supplies on the back terrace and washed their hands in the sink in the barbecue area. "I do. Way too many heartaches for her. Too much pain. But that just makes me wonder even more if she knew, or figured it out. It was more than just the pain of losing a husband and parents-in-law. It was like she knew *how*...and now that I'm thinking about it, I'm not exactly sure *what* she was told. García said they'd lied to her as per Dad's wishes. But exactly *what* was she told? Outside of the so-called accident..."

"I don't know, Tony, maybe you should talk with García again to see if there's anything else he can tell you. When do you want to go back to London, anyway? Diana and Alena's birthdays are in June, and mine and Antonio's are in July with Grandpa's. I don't want to miss them again."

"Mmm..." Tony finished drying his hands and thought about it. "I was thinking of spending another week here, and having it cleaned out ready for the June renters."

"We could fly back to Mykonos first," Cabot suggested. "Spend a week, or so, then fly to London. What about that?"

Tony wandered over to the terrace railing, reliving more memories. "That was 2003. She was sick. I had a feeling she might even still be heartbroken over Dad. But that was decades ago and she'd moved on to Brian. Part of me wondered if she'd got over Dad. The way she rushed into marriage again. They married within the year and he moved in, but I always wondered if she truly loved him."

Cabot rubbed Tony's back and watched the emotions flicker over his face. "Sometimes, the one true love is the one you never forget. The one you marry first, whether you stay together, or not. Look at my family. My grandparents, my parents, my uncles. All married for decades."

"Yeah." Tony breathed in slowly. "My parents never had that.

Never got to be married for *two* years let alone thirty. Never got to have any more kids, never got to grow old together. My father died when he was thirty. Or should I say, he killed himself when he was thirty. My mother died when she was fifty-six from cancer that I couldn't stop." His brain thought back, drenching up memories. "I'm glad I inherited on my twenty-fifth birthday. It meant I could prolong my mother's life for another two and a bit years."

"Oh, no. She had it that long. You never said," Cabot murmured, linking his arm through Tony's. "I'm so sorry."

"Yeah. That pneumonia she had, and the asthma; when it cleared up the doctor's found cancer growing in her lungs." Tony gasped back sudden tears.

"Oh, no, Tony. Oh, that's so sad."

"Yeah." Tony wiped his face free from tears, but more overflowed. "She had Adenocarcinoma in her lungs, and when we found out, I threw all the money I could at it. I got her treatment and medication, everything I could do, I did. And it helped…for a while. The tumours receded and got smaller, and she could breathe easier, but she never regained her strength, or her vigour. Just wasted away in the final months. It was horrible. I hired carers and nurses to help her at home until the end. She passed in early 2006, just over two years ago. I did everything I could for her. The best care, the best doctors. I even brought in the family lawyers when she asked. Figured it was for her will and to sort out the legals and stuff. But now that I think about it…nothing ever got done." Tony turned around to face the house and leaned on the railing. "I don't think a will was actually read out, but her final wishes were she wanted to be buried at her family's crypt in the cemetery near where her parents lived. They've been there all their life, and will be buried there, too. I wonder if she had a will…" His mind drifted back to her final days. He was there every day, holding her hand, talking to her. Telling her stories, and one day, she had pressed a key into his hand urgently and told him to hide it because it was important.

He came back and gasped. "The key! Oh, my God, I'd completely forgotten about it."

"What key? To where? From who?" Cabot asked, watching Tony

pace the terrace. "You mean your mum?"

"Yes!" Tony exclaimed. "When she was sick at home she was seeing the lawyer. One day, when we were talking, she pressed a key into my hand and told me to hide it somewhere safe and only use it when she was gone."

"Use it for what?" Cabot excitedly paced beside Tony. "What did it belong to?"

"I don't know." Tony stopped. "I...never used it because I'd forgotten all about it. I looked at it lying in my hand." He turned his hand palm side up as if he were actually looking at the key. "It had a small tag on it, but I didn't read it. Mum told me to hide it until she was gone and then use it. It would tell me everything."

"Like what?" Cabot stood before him. "Did you get it after she passed?"

"Uh...no..." Tony frowned in bewilderment. "No, I didn't. I completely forgot after she died because I went to Mykonos and all of that happened. So, it completely slipped my mind until now. My God." He smacked himself on the forehead with his palm. "How could I be so stupid and forget something so important? We have to go and find it. What if it leads me to all the answers I've been looking for? Everything she told me. Because she didn't tell me anything before she died. Just that she was sorry she was leaving and wanted me to look after my siblings..." He stopped. "Oh..."

"What?" Cabot saw the look of dismay.

"Oh, no..." Tony's eyes closed in despair. "I promised Mum I'd look after my siblings and I haven't. Oh, no..." He covered his face with both hands. "How could I be so stupid and selfish. All I've done for the last two years is think about myself. Mum died, and then the assault, and then I went off the rails because of both, and finding out I had HIV... Obviously, 2006 was a fucking shit year, it just went off, and I forgot about them because they'd followed in their father's footsteps of calling me names and treating me like shit. But once I got my money, they expected handouts, oh, my God... I wonder what's happened to them now? Aunt Olivia must be livid."

"Aunt Olivia?"

Tony noticed Cabot in front of him and remembered where they were. "Mum's sister. She's a social worker and promised Mum she and Uncle Tom would look after the kids. Bloody hell. I don't even know if they have been. I haven't been back since early 2007."

"Then clearly, we need to go. Can you call your aunt and find out if they're okay? Call her today."

Tony gazed out over the skyline and saw the sun heading for the horizon. "I guess I could give her a quick call. They're an hour behind us, so she could be at work. How about this... You get us packed, I'll make the call, and then let Manuel know we're leaving tonight and to get the place cleared up for tenants. I need to find that key as soon as possible."

"My cases are still packed and in the hallway, but I'll go up and pack your things while you make the call," Cabot said and hurried inside. He whipped out his phone and dialled the Stephanopoulos jet. "Hey, Pete, Cabot. You left yet?"

"Not yet, sir. Somewhere you want to go?" Pete Simmons, the Stephanopoulos pilot for more than twenty years, knew to always stay in town until he was cleared to leave in case someone needed to fly off somewhere.

"Yes, Pete. London. We'll leave in an hour or two."

"Righto, sir. We'll be ready."

Cabot quickly dashed upstairs to Tony's room and started packing.

"Aunt Olivia?" Tony said down the line to London. "Tony. I can hardly believe I've just remembered my promise to Mum in looking after the kids, and you said you and Uncle Tom would too. How are they?"

"Tony, good to hear from you, love. How are you?" Olivia Rankine replied. As a social worker, she'd helped Tony through his issues following his mother's death and his assault. "The kids aren't doing too well."

"Oh, no. I know we're only half-bloods, and I've been rather selfish just thinking of myself the last two years, and with everything I've been going through I completely blanked it all out. I'm here in Spain at my dad's estate fixing it all up, and all these memories are flooding back, and I found a wedding album of Mum and Dad's things, and now I'm remembering Mum's illness and her death and all the things that happened."

"Take a breath, love." Olivia chuckled. "We wondered if you were off in Spain taking in your dad's side of your heritage, or whether you'd holed up somewhere with some new love interest."

"Both, actually." Tony quickly filled her in on the last year and a half. "Cabot's dad knew my dad, and he told me details no one else knew, and Cabot and I have been together since Christmas and we've been here all month remodelling the house to look more like 2008 and not 1978."

"Sounds like you've had fun, and I'm so glad you've found yourself and sorted things out, love. But I think time is getting critical. I saw your siblings last month. Withdrawn, snarky. Brian wouldn't let me in the house, and the kids told me he let his new girlfriend and her kids move in. So, there seems to be a bit of a problem. I hadn't seen them since Christmas New Year's when they came to stay for a couple of weeks. But from what they told me, it's not good at home anymore."

"Wow, a new girlfriend, already." Tony was only half surprised, figuring Brian would want someone to look after him and the kids since he wasn't around. But it was barely two years since his mother had died. "Look, Aunt Liv, do you think the kids need to get out of there? Live with you and Uncle Tom? Cabot and I are coming to London tonight. I need to go to the house to find some stuff and get the rest of mine, and I have no problems kicking Brian and his new girlfriend out. If you want to take the kids I'll pay for maintenance for them until they're twenty-one. I did promise Mum, and haven't exactly been pulling my weight when it comes to fulfilling that promise."

"You can't kick him out, love. It's his house now."

"No, actually, it's not. Never was. My grandparents bought it for Mum and Dad as a wedding present. It was owned and maintained by the estate that I now own, so it's mine. Didn't you know that?"

"Oh...right, love." Olivia nodded. "I vaguely remember helping your mother sort that out when your dad died. She couldn't deal with the paperwork, so I did. I'd forgotten all about it."

"Exactly. So, if Brian's not living up to his part as a father, then you can take the kids and I'll kick him out. Any chance you can meet us at the house tomorrow morning? We'll try and be there about seven-thirty before the kids go to school."

"David doesn't go to school anymore. He's a layabout, and Michelle is in her second last year, but failing from all accounts. Nathan isn't doing well, either."

"Then we clearly need to step in, and even if they are only my half-bloods and not DeLucas, they still family and I owe it to Mum *and* them." He'd learned a lot from the Stephanopoulos family in the last six months. Regardless of how many people are related, they come together anyway and unite as one family. He'd been at Thanksgiving to meet Alfonso, Angelina Stephanopoulos's half-brother by their father, and heard the story of *their* half-brother, Luiz Manning and met *his* half-brother James Gardo. And then he'd met Simon Dencott, Roger's son, in the days following. There were Mike and Maggie, Angie and Pedro's best friends and honorary family members with their kids, and Dan Ardent and Derek Blaine, the doctors who had saved Cabot's uncles, and Cabot's life too last year. So, yeah, if he could learn a thing or two from the Stephanopoulos family, a family he had now joined, then shouldn't he share it with his own family? Half-bloods, or not.

"I think I can meet you there, love. I'll draw up the paperwork this afternoon and get a colleague to help. We can take photos and put it to the judge to see who's fitter to look after those kids."

"Great. We'll meet you there. But if we turn up first, I'm going in. There's something I need to find, and I'm hoping it hasn't been thrown out."

"Okay, love. See you tomorrow. And I can't wait to meet that boy of yours."

Tony chuckled. "Bye, Aunt Olivia."

"Bye, love."

Tony ended the call and dashed inside to see Cabot setting his luggage in the foyer next to his. "All done? I need to ring the airport for a flight."

"Don't bother. Our plane is standing by in Madrid. We just need to get there."

Tony grinned and gave his lover a kiss. "Did you set that up?"

Cabot blushed. "Figured I'd do something, and the jet always stays a day in case we need it. So, it's here for us to use."

"Fantastic. I just need to call Manuel to get the house cleaned, and then we can go." He quickly made the call about the house, and they ran around locking up. A housekeeper was arranged for the next day to come in and clean up, so it was spick and span for the summer rentals.

After quickly making sandwiches and grabbing bottles of drink, they packed Tony's car and set off for Madrid at sunset. Upon arrival at the airport, they deposited Tony's car at the car rental desk, and jumped in the Stephanopoulos private jet. They left half an hour later and landed in London late that night where they found a nice hotel near Tony's house, and set the alarm for six-thirty a.m.

*****

At seven in the morning, they had a quick bite to eat before heading out to Tony's house. It was in Knightsbridge, a fairly affluent neighbourhood of London that had only gained in popularity in the thirty years since it had been bought by Stephano and Connie. They pulled up out front at twenty past and sat in the two-car driveway.

"Wow, it's so nice, Tony." Cabot gazed out the window at the Georgian style home with cream and white brick façade, dark roof, and colourful front garden. "Really nice."

"Yeah, it is," Tony agreed. "It used to be great inside as well. The estate manages the maintenance for the outside, but I wonder how Brian's managed it for the inside. Let's go in before anyone leaves." He opened his door, alighted, and quietly closed it so as not to draw attention to their arrival.

Cabot did the same. "Aren't we supposed to wait for your aunt?" he asked quietly.

Tony checked his watch. "She should be here by seven-thirty. I told her what time we were going to get here, and that we'd go in without her. I need to find that key. Come on." Flipping through his keyring, he found the front door key and was surprised to find it still worked. "Brian clearly didn't change the locks," he murmured over his shoulder. "Now, remember what I told you. There's only one way to deal with this family, get an attitude and be tough. Don't let them stand in your way. Get a bit of Steele Stefan going if you have to."

Cabot grinned and followed him in.

They stopped in the front entrance hall, shocked at the mess they saw. The staircase in front of them had broken bannister rungs and filthy carpet. There were holes and marks in the hallway walls. To the left, the formal lounge room looked like a rubbish tip, the TV was blaring, and there were strange kids watching it. The door to the right was closed, so Tony opened it. What was once an office and sitting room was now a tip full of towers of junk and boxes piled high with what could only be described as the stench of animal faeces.

"Ugh." Tony closed the door and shook his head. "What the fuck?"

Cabot shut the front door behind him and surveyed the damage. "Oh, Tony. I'm so sorry."

"Are you kids gonna get ready for school, or what?"

Tony's head swivelled to the left to see a bleach-blonde with straggly hair, a cigarette hanging from her mouth, and a face full of make-up, standing in the doorway of the lounge and adjoining dining room, holding up clothes in both hands.

"Oi!" Her eyes grew wide. "Who are you and how'd you get in?" She'd never seen Tony before and didn't recognise Cabot. "Are you breaking in? Brian, Brian, we're being broken into. We have an intruder. Help, call the police," she squawked and ran flapping back into the kitchen.

Tony noticed the curious stares from the kids on the couch, no doubt her sons, and moved for the stairs. "Let's go," he told Cabot, and marched his way up to find the landing to be in the same disrepair as the downstairs. He moved to the master bedroom on the left, and twisting the knob, found it wouldn't open. He knocked. Not that he should be knocking on his own bedroom door. Hearing nothing, and getting no response, he backed up. "Out of the way," he said, "I don't have time for this." With a couple of steps forward, he kicked in the door and strode into the room.

Cabot, stunned to see Tony do such a thing, cautiously followed.

"Hey, what the hell?" The kid in the bed jumped up at the commotion and saw his brother standing at the end of the bed. Brushing his mop of brown hair aside, he stared dolefully at his brother.

"David," Tony greeted the overweight eighteen-year-old layabout. "I never told you you could have my room. Is my stuff still here? Cabot, open the window to let some of this marijuana haze out, will you?" Walking into the closet, he looked left and right for his things but didn't see them. "Cabot, give us a hand."

Cabot hurried from the window into the closet to see Tony climbing up the shelving.

"Give us a hand. I need to get into the roof." Tony shoved a square section of ceiling aside and pulled himself up as Cabot lifted one of Tony's legs and steadied his foot on his shoulder.

"See anything?"

"No. It's all gone. All of my stuff is gone. Let me down." He slid out of the roof with Cabot's help. "It's *all* gone. Everything. And we had boxes of stuff up there."

"What in blazes is going on?" Brian bellowed from the bedroom doorway. "Who kicked in this door? David, was it you?"

"No, Brian." Tony walked out of the closet to face his ex-stepfather. "I did. And I'm absolutely disgusted at the way you've treated my mother's house." He stood before a stunned Brian who was still wearing his blue shorts and coffee stained white tank top he wore to bed. "But, then again, you did let your new girlfriend and her kids move in. Tell me, where are our belongings? The ones that were in the attic." Standing toe to toe with Brian, he saw him shrivel. The girlfriend was off to one side, her kids were hovering on the stairs, excited from all the commotion, and he saw his siblings standing on the other side.

"Tony?" Michelle said cautiously. "That you?"

He finally glanced at her and took in the sight before him. His two younger siblings were completely different from the ones he had two years ago. Michelle had thick black kohl eyeliner and mascara, a pierced nose, and her hair was long multicoloured braids braided together over one shoulder. Nathan looked depressed and withdrawn, sunken, and way too thin for a boy of thirteen. "Yeah, kiddo, it's me, Tony."

"Why are you back?" Michelle asked, curious yet annoyed that he had turned up two years after their mother's death.

"Yes, Tony, why are you here?" Brian blustered, gaining his confidence back now that he saw it was gay boy Tony. "And who's this fag boy you brought with you?" He sneered at Cabot. "Your little cocksucker boyfriend?"

"Pissed off that you're missing out on all the fun?" Steele Stefan reared his head at the insult. "Considering the type of girlfriend you've got, you're probably in need of a good cock."

Tony suppressed a grin at Brian's scowling discomfort.

"Why you little—" Brian made a move for Cabot, but Tony slammed his hand flat against Brian's chest.

"Don't," he warned, seeing Brian look down at his hand on his chest then burn his eyes into Tony's.

"Get your filthy hand off me, you vile little fag fucker. You have AIDS. I don't want you giving it to me. Get out of my house. I've called the police. They'll be here any minute."

"Good." Tony stepped right up to Brian's face. "Then I'll tell them what you've been doing. And by the way, Aunt Olivia will be here any moment for the kids. Now, where are the boxes from the attic, and more specifically, *my* stuff from my room?"

"I threw it out." Brian arrogantly placed his hands on his hips, hoping it would make him look bigger than he was. "I threw it all out."

Tony planted both hands on Brian's chest and shoved him backwards across the hall. "You what?" he yelled.

Brian's arms flailed like a spinning wheel until he landed against the wall with a thud.

"Oh, no," the girlfriend cried out, a hand covering her face in shock, her eyes darting from Brian to Tony. "Get out of this house."

"Tony, no, don't hurt him." Cabot grabbed Tony by the arm, but he was shaken off.

"Where did all of our things go?" Tony growled.

Brian, now fully aware of what Tony could do, didn't want to rankle his ire any more than necessary, but a plan was also forming in his mind.

When Tony didn't get an answer, he turned to his siblings. "Where did all of our stuff in the attic go? Where did all of Mum's things go?"

"Out back in the shed," Michelle said, twirling her braid and wondering what the point of Tony's visit was. A lot had changed in the two years he'd been gone, and she could have done with an older brother to help with all of the shit her dad had dumped on her.

"I've called the police," Brian repeated.

"And Tony called me," Olivia called from downstairs. "I've brought Veronica with me and two fellow social workers to record all the problems. Holy cow." She looked around at the hovel the house had become. "Cynthia *would not* like this. Okay, boys, get to work." She directed her two fellow officers into the lounge and hall.

"Try the sitting room, it's a hovel," Tony called down to his aunts.

Olivia opened the door and promptly shut it. "That's disgusting."

"What you've done to this house since our sister died is disgusting," Veronica added her opinion to the conversation. "And now we're stepping in to fix it."

"Fix what?" Brian huffed and walked down the stairs. "There's nothing wrong with my house."

"It's not your house. It was Cynthia's," Olivia stated.

Tony watched the girlfriend hurry her boys down the stairs then turned to his siblings. Seeing their dishevelment, he sighed. "I'm sorry I haven't been here the last two years, but, as you know, I've had my own shit to deal with. I didn't deal with Mum's death well, and in turn, went and did stupid things to forget, and it's taken me two years to remember the promise I made to her. So, I'm back to offer you the help you need. Aunt Olivia is here to take you with her to live with her and Uncle Tom, and they'll look after you. Brian clearly can't, and his girlfriend's clearly not going to. Nathan." He stared at his youngest sibling. "I'd say that you're being bullied, more than likely by the two new house guests. Your age, aren't they? And Michelle," he turned his attention to his sister. "Rebelling against the establishment. Why? Because Mum died, or because you're sick of being used by your dad? And David..." He laid a hand on his brother's shoulder, surprising him. "You may be eighteen, but that doesn't mean you can be a layabout. Aunt Olivia and I are here to help you get out of this place, and give you a steady home life to live in. She and Uncle Tom will take care of you, and I'll financially support you each until you're twenty-one and your schooling is done. We're giving you an opportunity here, and you are all of an age to make the choice. Even you, Nathan." He laid his right hand on Nathan's shoulder. "I'm sorry I haven't been here. *But* I clearly needed to learn a few lessons in being a man, and a responsible adult before I could come back and take care of you guys. And now I'm here to help. Either way, Aunt Olivia will have you removed from this house and into her care by the end of the day, and I will have your dad and his girlfriend evicted. You don't get to stay here on your own. Since you have aunts and uncles who will take care of you, there's no need for me to legally take responsibility via adoption. But I will take the responsibility of providing you with the rest of your education. That is what we are offering. That is what we hope you take." He saw the desperation, hope, sadness, and every other emotion flick through their eyes. Clearly, life the last couple of years had been tough without their mother. "Take it, it's being offered. And when you're ready, I'll take you to visit my dad's home in Spain, and Cabot's home in Mykonos." He glanced over his shoulder at his boyfriend. "The Stephanopouloses are famous for taking in extra family and bringing them together. We might learn a thing or two. So..." His head swivelled back to his siblings. "We'll holiday in the school break, and you'll work hard to achieve. Schooling's important. It's what we're offering. Now." He stared Michelle straight in the eye. "You said the stuff's in the shed."

She nodded. "He made us clean it all out not long after he kicked you out. All Mum's stuff is in there, too. Well...except for the stuff I sneaked back in. I'm hiding it in my room." She didn't like her dad's new girlfriend, and liked her bratty kids and school even less, but if Tony was offering to pay for her education, she might get into fashion design school, yet. And there was *no way* she wasn't going to recognise Steele Stefan standing in her hallway. *Haus of Stefan, here I come.*

"Okay. I'm going down to the shed, you guys start packing. No school for you today, and Aunts Olivia and Veronica will stay with you until you're done." He hurried downstairs and out the back with Cabot following, and finding the shed locked, he looked around for something to knock the lock off with.

"Will *that* do?" Cabot pointed to the tool leaning against the side wall.

Tony peered around the corner and saw the shovel. "Perfect." With a couple of bangs and a few wrenches, the lock came off. He dumped the shovel and opened the door.

The shed was full to capacity with boxes.

"Oh, no," he groaned. "We'll have to pull it all out."

"Start pulling it out then," Cabot told him. "Let's get to work."

Tony pulled out the first three piles and checked them over. All were marked with his mother's name. Lifting out another pile, he finally found boxes with his name on them. "Here we go. Let's see if it's here." He opened a box and started digging.

"What are you looking for exactly?" Cabot watched Tony dig through, but not find what he was looking for.

"An old Mickey Mouse tin that I kept bits and pieces in." Tony started on a second box, but didn't find it either. He opened a third. "Ah-ha! Here it is." He eagerly lifted it out and pulled the lid up. Pawing through, he found an old toy car. "Just what I was looking for."

Cabot frowned. "An old toy car? I thought you were looking for a key?"

"I am." Tony set the tin down, turned the small toy over, and used both thumbs to slide the bottom off to reveal a small hidey-hole and a key. "Ah-ha! Got it." Holding it up, he grinned. "The key Mum gave me."

"Is that a tag hanging from it? What does it say?" Cabot stepped closer and peered over Tony's shoulder as he read the name.

"Mercantile Mutual. That was a bank, and the number's on it as well." Tony held the key closer to his eyes. "I think they're still around. Okay, let's get this packed up and put back. Once I get the house cleared out, we'll bring it back in and I'll go through it."

"What about sending it to your aunt's?" Cabot repacked a couple of boxes. "It might be better with her for now."

"Good idea. I'll let her know to clear it all out, but we'd better put it back for now, in case Brian or his girlfriend tries something." They quickly repacked the shed and went into the house to find Olivia and her social worker colleagues talking to the police.

"And here's the thief now," Brian's girlfriend exclaimed when she saw Tony. "He broke in and kicked the upstairs bedroom door in."

"Hardly a thief." Tony had pocketed the key when he'd seen the police. "I let myself into *my* house with *my* key." He held up his keyring to show his front door key.

"And this is my eldest nephew, Tony Luca. This house was his mother's," Olivia explained to the police. "We want to take the children out of this filth that Brian has caused and take them with us. And since they're old enough, especially David and Michelle, I don't need Brian's permission."

"But you do for Nathan, and this house is not his." Brian pointed to Tony. "Yes, I married his mother, but when she died the house automatically became mine as the legal spouse. He has no right being here."

"Oh...don't I..." Tony was going to enjoy this so much. His grin grew bigger as he glanced behind him at Cabot, and saw his siblings standing on the stairs with their bags. He nodded and opened his mouth to pounce. Moving two steps closer to Brian, so he was toe to toe, he said, "This house was never legally my mother's. Which means it was never legally yours. Which means you, and especially your girlfriend and her children, are trespassing, and I want you all out of this house by six p.m. tonight, or I will call these fine officers back to escort you out of *my* property."

"Brian, what's he talking about? You said this house was yours." The girlfriend picked at his arm, completely aware of how she must look in front of such good-looking police officers.

"This house *is* mine and he's the one trespassing." Brian pointed his finger at his ex-stepson. "I want this man arrested for trespassing, and breaking and entering, and I want these people," he waved a finger at Olivia, Veronica and the two social workers, "arrested for trespass. They were never invited." His face was cherry tomato red, and he was well aware he was still wearing his shorts and singlet. He called up to his children. "Go and unpack your bags. You're not going anywhere."

"Oh, the hell they're not!" Veronica exclaimed. "Come on, kids, get all of your luggage, and anything else you want downstairs, and we'll get it packed in the van. Make sure you get everything you want."

The kids hurried downstairs and out the door.

"Stop them," Brian demanded of the officers. "She has no right to take them."

"Your sister-in-law is a social worker and has every right. And by the looks of this place," the officer scanned the rooms he could see, "I'd say them being taken is a good thing."

"Well," Brian blustered. "I injured my back a few years ago, and it's hard work to keep up a house." Completely self-conscious now, he smoothed his shorts leg while wiping the sweat from the palm of his hand.

"Now that the kids have decided to go," Tony said, "you can too. The four of you have until six to get out of *my* house, *and* if you're not, then you will be forcibly removed." He eyeballed his former stepfather.

"This isn't your house," Brian yelled. "We're not the ones leaving." He really didn't understand why Tony kept saying they were. It was his house. Not Tony's.

Tony turned to the officers and pulled papers from his denim jacket pocket. "My full name is Antonio Stephano DeLuca II. I'm the son of Antonio DeLuca and Cynthia York, and the only grandchild of world-famous Spanish bullfighter Stephano DeLuca and his wife Constance. When they died the entire DeLuca estate went to my father. When *he* died, the estate was held in trust for me until my twenty-fifth birthday. The estate," Tony handed over the papers for them to read, "and so *I*," he turned to Brian, "*own* this house. It was never my mother's to pass on. It was, and always will be, *DeLuca* owned." He stared Brian down until he finally realised what Tony was saying.

"What?" Brian's brows slid down. "Your mother never… Cynthia never… She never said anything."

"She wouldn't," Olivia told him. "I dealt with all of the paperwork after Antonio's death, she was never interested in what it said." She turned to the officers as they handed the paperwork back. "I met Connie and Stephano multiple times. They bought the property as a wedding present for their son and my sister, but it was always part of the estate. It now belongs to Tony." And with a dark glance at Brian, she added, "*And not you.*"

"Brian, what does this mean?" the girlfriend asked, pulling at his arm.

"Oh, shut up and stop pestering me." Brian slapped her hand away and stared coldly at Tony. "We have nowhere to go." He wasn't about to beg to his former stepson, but wanted him to know he was kicking them out on the street.

"Use the money from the sale of your business," Tony suggested and cast a pointed glance at the girlfriend. "Or go to your girlfriend's house." Kicking his ex-stepfather and his rancid girlfriend out was oh so deliciously sweet.

"I don't have a home. I gave it up when I moved in with Brian," the woman said. "Where will me and the boys live now?"

"Then rely on your family to help you out," Tony told her and slung an arm around his aunt. "Just like I had to a couple of years ago. You've turned this place into a hovel regardless of the fact all the bills were paid for by the estate, *my* estate, my *father's* and *grandfather's* estate. Well, no more. No more taking advantage." He watched his siblings sneak back in and upstairs to collect more items. "The kids are going with Aunt Olivia and *you're* leaving. I'll have skip bins here tomorrow morning to clear out the rubbish, and whatever else filth you've left here, and then I'm doing it up. I'm redoing *my* house in the name it was meant for. *DeLuca.*" He scanned Brian's outfit. "I suggest you go and get dressed. Then pack. Then leave." He turned to his aunt. "Aunt Liv, you here all day?"

"Absolutely, my love. Don't worry, I will see to it that they are gone by six."

"Great." He kissed her cheek. "I'm off to the bank." After shaking the officers' hands, he and Cabot walked out and prepared to leave, but were stopped by Nathan.

"You're not leaving us, are you?" he fretted. Tony had hit the nail on the head, picking out that he'd been bullied by the interlopers. He wasn't sleeping, eating, or doing well at school.

"I'm just going to the bank for a while. I have things to sort out. But we'll be back later." Tony walked back around the car to his brother as David and Michelle came out lugging cases behind them. "Why?"

Timidly, Nathan shrugged. "Just wondering."

"I'm not leaving, not for a while. We're going to stay long enough to get you settled into Aunt Liv's house and in a good school before we go and do anything else. Okay?" After a moment's hesitation, he hugged Nathan and Nathan hugged back.

"Thank you. And I'm sorry."

"For what?"

"For calling you names when you were here. Dad encouraged us."

Tony pulled away to look right into his brother's eyes. "Apology accepted." He noticed David and Michelle come up behind Nathan. "Understand that now," he told them. "The fresh start starts now. No more name calling, no more hate. No more rubbish. Think about what Mum would want. She'd want us to all be happy and get along, and for the three of you to be happy. And by the looks of it, you're not."

They shook their heads.

"Okay, then, new start starts today. Aunt Olivia will be here all day, so make sure you have everything, and I will try and be back later. I have lots of things to organise, like a skip bin for tomorrow. So, get inside and get your stuff."

All three nodded and spun around to go inside, but turned back and enveloped Tony in a hug. He hugged back and watched them run inside. Wiping away his tears, he ran around the car and got in.

Cabot slid into the passenger side. "Naw, Tony." Watching his lover wipe away tears for a moment, he changed tack to get Tony back on track. "Do you know where the bank is?"

Shocked that he'd forgotten, Tony pulled the key from his pocket and rattled off the number. "I don't know where it is exactly. I'd better call." Pulling out his phone, he dialled and was connected instantly.

"Mercantile Mutual, how may I direct your call?"

"Yes, hello. I need to know what your address is." Tony wrote it down on a notepad and thanked the girl. "It's in town, let's go."

They managed to find the bank, and a parking spot out the front, and went inside. It was busy and every teller was helping a customer.

"Can I help you, sir?"

Tony spun around and saw it was he being spoken to. "Ah, yes..." He pulled the key from his pocket and held it up. "I need to get into my mother's safety deposit box."

"Do you have permission from your mother?" the attendant asked, noticing Cabot and recognising one half of the great Stefans.

"No. But since she's dead, I guess I'd better speak to the manager."

The attendant turned his attention back to Tony. "Right this way, sir." He led them down a hallway and motioned to a small waiting area. "Wait here." Walking through a door, which he closed behind him, a few moments later he returned with the bank manager. "Mr Monolo will see you now." He left with a backward glance at Cabot.

"Yes, hello, how may I...Antonio?" Monolo stared in shock at the young man before him, and how long it had taken for him to come in.

"Mr Monolo, good to see you again." Tony eagerly shook hands with the manager.

"Oh, my boy, I've been waiting for you to come in. I did try calling a few times, but was told by your stepfather that you weren't there."

"Yeah, I got into some trouble and had to fix myself. It's taken a while," Tony told him and then spoke to Cabot. "Mr Monolo came to the house when Mum was sick and helped with her affairs. I didn't realise he was from this bank."

"Yes, yes," Monolo said. "In conjunction with your family's law firm, I set up all of the DeLuca accounts here in London. I've been with the bank thirty-five years now, and dealt with your family's estate since 1978."

Cabot raised his brows in surprise. "So, you knew Tony's grandparents?"

"Ah, not quite," Monolo muttered. "Met them once, but dealt with the family lawyers, and then your aunt, and then your mother mainly. I was so sorry that she passed away and was waiting for you to come in. Do you have the key?"

Tony held it up. "Can you believe I only remembered yesterday that I had it? We flew in yesterday and booked into a hotel last night. We were only down in Spain at the family's estate."

"Is that still being taken care of?" Monolo asked as he led them down another hallway. "We only ever dealt with anything here in London."

"Yes. I finally went back and remodelled the old place. Found where my dad and grandparents were buried."

Monolo stopped at the vault door. "Oh, Tony. I'm so sorry about all of that. Your mother told me some things during my visits, but obviously, I wasn't privy to all of it." He unlocked the gate and they went into the vault. "I'll just get your mother's box. I need to explain some things to you." He pulled box 1319 from its slot in the wall, and placed it on the table in the centre of the room. "Your key?" He held his hand out for the key and inserted Tony's, and his, into the two slots. He turned both at the same time and unlocked it. Lifting the lid, he moved it closer to Tony. "You will have questions. I should be able to answer them."

Staring at the box in trepidation, Tony swallowed the dry lump in his throat, licked his lips, and reached into the box. The first article was a large A4 business style envelope which contained a pile of letters. Second, was the same size envelope containing piles of photos. Third was an envelope containing his mother's personal items. Fourth was a white photo album. "Oh, I know…" Memories flooded back as he lifted it and opened the cover. "Their wedding album. I knew I remembered her looking at it and crying after Dad died. But after a few years, I never saw it again." He lovingly turned the pages to see similar photos to the album he'd found in the DeLuca vault. "Oh, Mum."

"There's your dad, Tony," Cabot murmured and gently rubbed his lover's back to comfort him. "That photo wasn't in the other one."

The photo was a candid snap of Antonio and Cynthia dancing in each other's arms, not even noticing that their picture was being taken.

"Oh, Mum…Dad…" Tony whispered, his finger tracing their faces.

"Your mum knew that not every album would fit into the deposit box, so she removed all of your photos from the albums and placed them in the envelope," Monolo explained.

"Why didn't she just give the albums to my aunts for safe keeping?" Tony asked, placing the album on the table.

"She wanted everything to be legally yours so Brian couldn't take them. That's why I dealt with the family lawyers. To make sure it all went to you." Monolo picked up the envelope containing the personal items and carefully emptied it onto the table. Her wedding rings from Antonio, his ring, the jewellery he'd given her, the jewellery from Stephano and Connie, and jewellery from her own family were there. So was a bank book. He picked it up and presented it to Tony. "We've made the account electronic as they all are these days. All of the money she was given went into it."

"What? What money?" Surprised, Tony accepted the book and opened it. His eyes widened. "Why is my name on it?"

"It's all the money you paid her in rent and board. She opened the account after your eighteenth birthday. What money she had left from the DeLuca estate payments was also transferred into it, from all the years she received funds, and in the last few years that she received them from you via the estate."

Cabot leaned closer to Tony and read the amount. "Tony, that's over $150,000 dollars."

"Yeah," came out in a whoosh. "Rent and board from when I was eighteen, the DeLuca money all those years, the money I continued when I turned twenty-five, plus all the interest it would have accrued. Wow, that's a lot."

"She knew it was yours and belonged to you," Monolo said softly. "It's all in your name."

Breathing calmly, Tony closed the book. "And now I need to decide what to do with it." Emotions were overwhelming him, hitting him left, right and centre. But he knew that while it was technically his money, it had another job to do. Placing the book on the table, he picked up her rings and held them in his hand, weeping softly.

"Oh, Tony." Cabot wrapped his arms around him and held on tight. "It's okay, it's okay. He watched Tony pick up his father's wedding band and slide it onto his right middle finger. It fitted perfectly next to his father's DeLuca family ring.

"And that's where it will stay for eternity," Tony whispered. After a moment, he slipped everything else back into the envelope and picked up the one containing the letters. There was a pile of opened letters tied together, and three long cream envelopes, all unopened. One was addressed to him in his mother's writing. The other two were addressed to him and to his mother in handwriting he didn't know.

"They are letters from your mother to you," Monolo said. "Your father to your mother, and your father to you. Your mother never opened them."

"Ever?" Tony was bewildered. If his father had written to his mother, then why wouldn't she read it?

"Not the ones that are unopened. That's the last one from him, that the family lawyer delivered when he went to your home to tell your mother the bad news." He watched Tony solemnly. "The pile is what your mother and father sent each other during their relationship. Those three," he pointed to the cream envelopes, "are from their deaths. And I suggest you're somewhere private when you read them." He checked his watch. "Why don't you take everything now? You don't need to be in this dreary hole any longer. You must have things to do?"

Sighing, Tony felt a burden he hadn't in a long time. "Yes, I do. Thank you for all of this. I wish I had've been in sooner."

Monolo extended his hand. "Your mother was a big believer in everything happening for a reason, and you only remembering that key now, when you're at your family's estate in Spain, is not a coincidence."

Tony shook his hand. "No. Maybe you're right. But either way, I have a lot to do. You wouldn't know of a skip bin company, by chance?"

Monolo did, in fact, know of one, and got them the details while Tony picked up his mother's belongings. Once back in the car, they called the company and ordered their largest bin for the next day. "Ready to dump some rubbish?" he asked Cabot after the call.

"Sure. Gotta burn off all those calories I gained back home." Cabot's grin was brief before he got serious. "What will you do now?"

Tony deflated as he thought about it, and absentmindedly played with the letters from his parents. "Go back home and help my aunts for now. Get the kids moved into their new home. Clean out *my* home. Think your mother would want to come over and decorate?"

Cabot's laugh was light. "Probably not. She's completely besotted with Adam, but you could ring her for ideas. Skype her, even."

"Yeah." Tony breathed deeply to clear the cobwebs. "I'll try and remember some of the tips she gave me in Spain."

"But this is London," Cabot reminded him. "This is *your* home, make it about *you* and *your* life here, make it something your parents would have lived in. Decorate *for you.*"

Tony glanced over at him and locked hands with his. "No. I'll make it something *for us.*"

Smiling, they headed home and asked Aunts Olivia and Veronica if they knew of any house cleaning companies and got a few ideas. After making calls, they hired two companies to come the next day. Tony helped his siblings finish with their belongings, and then ordered pizza for everyone. They watched as Brian and his girlfriend lugged their bags out to their car, and they were indeed gone by six p.m. when Tony finally shut and locked the door.

"I hired a security company to watch the place for the night," he told his aunts. "I don't want Brian coming back for anything, or the house being trashed or burnt down."

"Do you have everything set for tomorrow, love?" Olivia asked as they walked to their cars. She was taking the kids home with her while her colleagues filed the injunction papers.

"I do. Skip bin is here at eight, cleaning crews at eight-thirty. Oh, did you get all of Mum's stuff from the shed? Cabot and I emptied it, but aren't sure if you got it all."

"Made the kids load up the van." Veronica had brought her florist's van with her and had been loading all day.

"Good." Tony heaved a sigh of relief. "Tomorrow we start cleaning this place up."

"Did you let the lawyers know that the house needed to be cleaned out?" Cabot asked. "The estate's paying for maintenance, so they'll need to know."

"I did. Put in a call this afternoon and they'll send someone around tomorrow to pick up the paperwork for bills and survey the damage."

"Then it sounds as though you're all set, love." Olivia studied her nephew and Cabot. "Why don't you two head back to your hotel and get some rest? I'll take the kids and get them settled in, and we can all come back tomorrow and help."

"I need to stay until the security car comes, but we'll leave after that, so see you tomorrow, Aunt Olivia. Veronica." Tony hugged them both together. "I'm sorry I haven't been here for the last two years or so. I guess I just needed to find my inner strength to deal with it."

"It's okay, love," Olivia said. "We've been doing our best, and your timing couldn't be more perfect."

He let them go and opened their car doors. "I'll see you tomorrow."

"Thanks, love. Kids, time to go." Olivia beckoned the three siblings over, but instead of getting in the van, they hugged Tony.

"Hey." He held them for a few moments. "It's okay. Things will be better now." He ruffled Nathan's hair. "So, go home, have a good feed, a hot shower, and a good sleep. I'll see you tomorrow if you want to come."

"How long are you here for?" Michelle asked, still a little wary at having her eldest brother back in town, but also excited and grateful at the help being given.

"A month or two," Tony told her. "I need to get the house sorted and redone, I'll get you kids set up at Aunt Olivia's, and sort out your education and finances. Plus, I probably have some legals to wade through."

"Can you stay through summer?" Nathan asked, excited that he might be getting a big brother back in his life when the one he had, David, was all rather useless.

"Maybe." Tony smiled softly and tweaked his ear. "Or, maybe I'll take you all on a holiday and you can see Spain and Greece."

"Sounds cool," David murmured, impressed by his elder half-brother, but tried not to show it. If he could get free holidays out of him, all the better.

"In the meantime, you need to go and get some food and rest. I'll see you tomorrow if you come back." He gave them a quick hug each and ushered them into the van. Sliding the door shut, he leaned in the passenger side window. "You here tomorrow, Aunt Liv?"

"Of course, love. I want to see this house restored as much as you do. But for now, *you* need to go and get some sleep. I'll see you tomorrow." She slowly backed out of the drive. Veronica followed and he waved them off. With a sigh, he looked back at his house. His grandparents had bought it for his parents and he'd grown up in it. But now, just as with the estate in Spain, the time had come to make it his and bring it into the here and now.

"You okay, Tony?"

A soft smile lit up Tony's lips and he thought about it. "Yeah, Cabot, I am."

The security company arrived at that moment, and Tony introduced himself and gave them their orders for the night. He'd see them at eight in the morning.

Tony and Cabot left, had a quick bite to eat at a local restaurant where Cabot was recognised and posed for photos and autographs, then headed back to their hotel. It had been a long day, an even longer month, and an even longer two years for Tony. His whole life seemed to be one big lie, and it wasn't sitting well with him. He hoped that his mother's and father's letters would explain the final piece of the puzzle.

After a hot relaxing shower together, they curled up on the bed with all of Tony's new belongings around them. The photo album, his mother's jewellery, the letters and photos.

"We'll have to get an album or three," Cabot said, picking up a photo of Tony and flipping it over to see if anything was written on it. "August 18, 1988, Tony, ten years old. Hey, it's your birthday." Studying it closely, Cabot took in every detail of a ten-year-old Tony.

Tony peered at it and smiled. "Yeah, that's me. Mum had met Brian by then. Worked for him, anyway. We had a big party at Grandma's house." He picked up a photo of him and his mother. "I think I was five in this one. Look at how sad she was still was." His heart melted at his mother's depressed expression and he could feel the sadness come through the photo. "She's still so sad."

Cabot glanced at the picture. "Naw, poor Tony. Your mum was missing your dad still. But you look happy."

Tony saw his own smiling face and twinkling eyes in the photos. "Yeah, I looked it, but for the life of me, I can't remember if I was." Sighing, he put it down and picked up another. "My first day of school. She's still not happy." They were standing side by side with Cynthia's hand on Tony's shoulder. He had his uniform on, and his bag strapped to his back.

"Is this high school?" Cabot held up a similar style photo of the two of them standing side by side.

Tony held his photo beside the one Cabot was holding and compared them. "Yeah, first day of primary, first day of high. She'd had David by then." His mother was smiling in the second photo and the before and after showed a big difference. A sad depressed Cynthia in the first photo, a smiling happy Cynthia in the second. "What a difference six or seven years makes." He continued through the photos. "We're going to have to get some order to these. And how many albums should we get?"

"Don't know. Maybe Mama and Grandma could sort through them for you," Cabot suggested as he saw Tonies of all sizes throughout the years.

"I think maybe Grandma and Aunts Olivia and Veronica should do it. They were here for most of it, so they'll know how to set them all up. Let's put them back in the envelope and I'll hand them over tomorrow with some money for albums." They gathered the photos into the envelope and sealed it up. Then they did the same with his mother's jewellery.

"Have you figured out what you're doing with the money your mother saved?" Cabot asked, watching Tony open the bank book.

"Yes." Tony stared at his name typed neatly on the inside. "I'm going to set up three bank accounts for my siblings, divide the money, and then add to it. I'm going to look after them like I promised Mum."

"Aw, Tony. That's so sweet." Cabot beamed with pride at him. "Your mum would be so proud of you. Coming through everything you've been through, and growing up into the man you have. She'd be so proud."

Tony's grin was soft. "Yeah, I think so." He set the book on the side cupboard and picked up the envelope with all of the letters. Emptying it onto the bed, he set aside the three letters not yet read and picked up the pile that had been. Untying the old red ribbon, he began reading from the top. "Dad's on Mykonos, still working. He misses her…hopes she's enjoying her job back at the record company." He picked up the next. "More of the same, mentions his dad and catching up, made mention of your dad and his disappearance, misses Mum." He picked up a third. "Missing her terribly and wishes he could see her, but he's busy working." And a fourth. "Dated October, he's finishing up work at the end of the month and then he'll be in London to see her." He gazed at the letters. "Only four, all dated the first of each month. July, August, September, and October 1977. I wonder why he only wrote four?" He flicked through the rest and sorted them into order.

"Maybe he called the rest of the month," Cabot said.

"Yeah," Tony murmured, still holding the four letters in his hand. "And these others are all Mum's replies. She saved them all. I think Aunts Liv and Veronica sorted Dad's stuff out when he passed. But Mum must have kept these herself and tied them all together." He set them all in order and read his mother's replies to his father's letters, and the story unfolded.

"Mum's madly in love with Dad, Dad loves her too, can't wait to see each other. Mum wrote four times as many letters as Dad, so…she was writing one every week and it looks like," Tony checked the dates, "he replied once a month." They fell from his hands and he glanced at

Cabot. "Wow, I just realised…this is their love story. This is the origins of their love story. The passion, the fire, the letters to and fro. This is where *they* began. Where the courtship began. With these letters, after they met." He read through a few more. "Mum's recounting their meeting, their holiday. Yes, that was how they met. These letters were their courtship, and then once Dad got here to London, I was conceived in 1977. November 1977. They married in May 1978, I was born August 1978." The air escaped from his lungs. "That…*this*…is the DeLuca origin story." Slumping against the pillows, he stared at the letters before him, the meaning of all of it overwhelming him.

"And you are the result of that love, and now you're here," Cabot soothed him.

A huff came from Tony. "Yeah, I am. But without my parents."

"Then maybe it's time for you to read those other letters and get the answers you need to close that chapter."

"I don't know if I can. I don't know if I'm ready." The air whooshed out of Tony. "What if it's too upsetting? What if it leaves more questions? What if I never get my answers?"

"What if, what if, what if," Cabot repeated. "You won't know until you read them."

"But I don't know if I want to read them. I only just found out about them today." Tony gestured to everything on the bed. "I only just found out about *all of this* today. I just booted my ex-stepfather out of my house today. Saw my half-siblings for the first time in nearly two years, today. Saw my aunts again since last year. This is all so much." Getting off the bed, he stood by the open window and breathed in the cool London air. Fortunately, it wasn't smoggy, and the late spring weather was pleasantly drifting over his skin.

"Aw, Tony." Cabot moved to his side. "Do you want to wait?" His fingers slid into Tony's hand and entwined. "That's okay, you know."

"Yeah." Tony's hand closed around Cabot's. "Yeah. I think I need to let it all sink in, deal with my siblings, the house, all of the legals and financials here in London, and then I can sit down and read them. Because I just don't think I'll be able to do anything else once I do. I have a feeling I'll fall apart and stay that way for quite some time while

I deal with whatever's in them."

"Okay. That's okay. There's nothing wrong with that," Cabot said. "So, let's pack it all up and maybe watch some TV to get our minds off it. We have a big day tomorrow." He led Tony over to the bed, they tidied up, and watched TV for the next few hours.

*****

The next day, they were up and at the house by eight when the skip bin arrived. The cleaning crews arrived a half hour later, and Tony directed them through the house to start cleaning. Olivia and Veronica turned up with the kids, and so did Cynthia's parents.

"Grandma, Grandpa." Tony hugged them both together. "It's so good to see you."

"Good to see you, my darling. Where have you been? We've heard nothing from you," Alice York said as she hugged her grandson. "Where have you been?"

"Mykonos, mainly, for the last seven months." Tony introduced Cabot. "I went there in search of answers, trying to find out more about my father, and to see if I could find the man who assaulted me and gave me HIV. Which we did. We found him in America and had him arrested and charged. He did the same to Cabot, and dozens of other men."

"Well, it's good that you caught him, then," Philip York told him. "At least he can't hurt anyone else. Now, young man..." He pointed at Cabot. "Why do I know you?"

Tony grinned at the blush creeping over Cabot's face. "He and his brother are world-famous models. So's their sister and mother. His father's a world-famous film director and producer. And his cousins are world-famous singers and DJs. His whole family's pretty famous."

Cabot's blush reached his hairline and he brushed away a lock of hair away in embarrassment. "Mmm, apparently we are."

"Oh, I think I've read about you in magazines," Alice said. "Because it's not as if Tony's written to us about you."

It was Tony's turn to blush. "Sorry, Grandma. Dealing with a lot of things this last year or two. We found our attacker. I found out how my dad's side really died, we've been doing up the estate in Spain, and I've been falling in love with and spending time with this guy here." He put his arm around Cabot's shoulders and pulled him close, getting a nervous giggle out of Cabot. "See, isn't he adorable."

"Tonee." Cabot blushed harder and became fidgety. "God, how embarrassing."

"See, he *is* adorable." Tony chuckled.

"He certainly is, and you clearly love him, so I'm glad you've finally found someone to be stable for, *and* with," Alice told him. "Now, what are you doing with your mother's house?"

Tony led them through the pandemonium. The cleaning crews, his aunts and siblings were all carting boxes of rubbish out the door, and dumping them in the skip bin, and with help from Alice and Philip, all of Brian's leftover possessions were removed, his girlfriend's junk was taken from the sitting room, and the upstairs bedrooms were emptied of objects by lunchtime.

After a break of pizzas and sodas, everyone spent the afternoon removing all of the furniture that wasn't bolted to the walls. What was salvageable went to the local op shop, what wasn't, was chucked in the skip. By the end of the day, the house had been emptied of every object.

"Wow, it's so bare," Tony muttered as his family stood in the empty lounge room.

"And it reeks to high heaven." Cabot held his nose until he needed to breathe.

"We've had the windows open all day," Olivia said. "But it's clearly in the carpets."

"Hello. I'm after Mr Tony DeLuca."

The family turned to see a man standing in the doorway and Tony hurried over to introduce himself. "I'm Tony DeLuca."

"Ah, Mr DeLuca. I'm Frederique Von Baylo from *First Rate International* here to walk through the house with you to see what needs doing." In his fifties, Von Baylo was used to dealing with insurances and family estates. And as he didn't have to deal with the DeLuca estate often, he had been surprised when he'd got the call.

"Of course. We've just finished emptying it out, and were about to do a walk through ourselves. Come." Tony led him through the house and Von Baylo stopped to take periodical notes and photos. At the end of the tour, he shook his head. "This place will definitely need a lot of work. It's a pity it was allowed to go to rack and ruin. We upkeep the outside, but knew nothing of the inside."

"Neither did I until yesterday," Tony replied, ashamed of how Brian had up kept his mother's house. "I'm quite shocked that my ex-stepfather allowed it to happen. So," he crossed his arms and homed in, "How do we do this?"

"Every time you get a bill, bring it into the office, or, have the companies automatically charge it to the DeLuca estate. We get the bill and get it paid. And then we send copies with a detailed report back to the family law firm, so they know what's happening. It's how we've done it since 1980."

Tony nodded. "Looks like it's something I'm going to have to educate myself on, so I know the ins and outs of my family's estate. I'd like to be more proficient in running a family empire, and the DeLuca empire is still alive. I just need to figure out what I'm going to do with it."

"You don't have to think about that now, love," Olivia told him. "Let's get this house sorted first, and *then* you can build your empire."

Tony grinned at her words and escorted Von Baylo to his car. When he came back, he suggested everyone head home for a rest as there was still work to do.

"Do you need us to come back?" Veronica asked as they locked up for the night. "I've taken two days off work now."

"No, no. You guys don't need to come. It's just carpets being ripped up, and the house will be inspected for mould, rats, infestations, etc. That's just going to be boring." Tony escorted them all to their cars.

"Why don't you come round for Sunday dinner?" Alice suggested as she settled into her car. "I'm making a roast, so we'll have more than enough for you to bring your young man with you." She pointed at Cabot and Tony shut her door. Winding down the window, she added, "I make lots of veggies, too."

Cabot grinned. "You sound like my grandma. She's Australian, and makes her famous roast chicken every Sunday."

"Well, then, your grandma and I should talk. We could exchange new recipe ideas, and talk about our grandsons dating. Bye," she called as Philip backed down the driveway.

Cabot's grin didn't stop. "She's *just* like my grandma."

Tony's laughter bubbled away from his grandmother's comment. "Yeah, and I'm so glad I have her." He hugged Cabot. "And I'm so glad you have your grandma, too. Where would we be without them?"

"Dead!" Cabot said, knowing full well he was right.

*****

The following day, the carpets were ripped up and the house inspected. The shed out the back was torn down, and the garage cleaned out.

Over the weekend, Tony and Cabot spent time with Tony's grandparents and aunts going over all of the details for his siblings' living arrangements, and how he would be setting up their financials. After a chat to the kids about what they wanted to do, a plan was drawn up ready to go. So was a plan for the house. With everyone's help, Tony found a list of companies he needed and made a bunch of calls on Monday morning.

*****

It took over a week for the interior of the house to be repaired before carpets were laid and the painting was finished. Electricals were updated along with the wiring, and broadband was added. Light fixtures, curtains, and finally, furniture were added; all brand new and picked out by Tony and Cabot. Simple, sleek, but homey *and* homely. By the first week of June, it was complete, and they stood in the lounge room once more.

"I think your mum would love it," Alice said as they looked at the way it had turned out. "It's simple, beautiful, and is very you." She hugged her grandson and he rested his chin on the top of her head.

"Can we come and stay?" Nathan asked, hoping he could come back to the home he'd grown up in.

"When I'm in town, sure. You can come and stay. Just as members of Cabot's family can come and stay when they're here." He glanced from his brother to his lover. "Think Mr and Mrs S would like it?"

"They'd love it. Just don't expect Mama to be here any time soon. She's still in baby mode with Adam," Cabot replied, worn out from the last couple of weeks.

"We'll have to ask her when we get back." Tony let go of his grandmother. "How many days do we have left?"

"Three. And then it's on for young and old." Cabot grinned, excited at the festivities to come.

"Cabot's sister and cousin are both turning thirty," Tony explained to his family. "We're going back for a couple of days to celebrate."

"Do you have to go?" Michelle asked, secretly hoping to go along since she knew all about the Stefan family and was a huge lover of the girls' label, *Haus of Stefan*.

"Well, I *don't* have to, but it would be rude of me not to since I'm Cabot's partner. But don't worry, I'll be back within a week and we'll spend some time together. And when you have holidays, I might take you to Mykonos to meet Cabot's family."

"Why do we need to meet them?" David's sneer didn't last long, especially when his aunts and grandmother glared at him.

"Because they could teach us a thing or two about families and uniting broken ones," Tony told him. "We could learn something."

David stubbed his toe into the carpet and had the decency to look contrite.

"So…we can't move back in then?" Nathan had been doing better in the last week. Getting decent sleep and good meals, he was almost back to normal.

Tony moved over to him and enveloped him in his arms. "The best place for the three of you is with Mum's family. Aunt Olivia and Uncle Tom can take care of you, feed you, clothe you, and get you to school on time. It's better that you live with them in a warm, loving environment. I'm going to be on Mykonos a lot, but it's only a plane ride away, so I can come back every couple of months, and you can come and see me in the holidays. But in between, you need emotional and physical stability, and Aunt Liv can give you that. Okay?" He looked into Nathan's pale green eyes and got an unsure nod. "Okay. You're going to live with Aunt Liv and are going to a new school. Michelle's finishing off school and doing fashion college part-time. And David's doing what?" He turned to his brother. "Have you figured it out yet?"

David shrugged. "I kinda thought music, or gaming. I know how to do stuff on the computer, so maybe I could design games, or something." He flicked his hair out of his eyes, but kept his gaze down.

"Okay, well, we'll have to see if there's some sort of class for that." Tony glanced at his aunt and got a surprised expression in return. "Until then, I suggest we go home and just hang out for the next few days. What do you say? Burgers on me."

*****

Two days later, they flew home to Mykonos, enjoyed thirtieth birthday celebrations, and told the family everything that had happened. Tony showed his future parents-in-law the love letters from his parents, and spoke at length about them, trying to sort out everything in his head. He explained about the money his mother had saved, and the things she'd left behind, including his father's wedding ring which he proudly showed off, and the three letters which he was yet to read. He discussed them with Carlos and Viv, as well as Jenny and Spiros to get their viewpoint on them, and all were in consensus. It was totally up to him, and he should take time out to deal with whatever aftermath came with it if he did. Jenny even suggested a trip to Athens to see Xanthe Metlos if Tony needed counselling afterwards. He declined the offer, but kept it in mind. They also talked about setting up their own house on the island, and asked what the family thought of it.

Jenny offered one of her recent purchases, one of the four homes either side of the six they had. When the boys looked it over, they agreed it was perfect and accepted it. And that meant Antonio and Dom could share the house below Pedro and Angelina. Alena had been given one for her thirtieth birthday, and Simon, Roger's son, and his wife and children got one as well. The fourth went to Dan Ardent and Derek Blaine for all of their help through the years. It also meant Jenny was well on her way to owning an entire street full of houses for her family.

*****

When the week was over, Tony and Cabot flew back to London and entered their home.

Tony breathed in, his eyes closing as he remembered. "It still feels like home. Is that weird?"

"Not really." Cabot closed the door behind them. "You did grow up here."

"Yeah, I know. But things are different now. Brian's gone. The kids are gone. Mum's gone. And Dad's been long gone. It's just…"

"What?" Cabot asked after a few moments of silence. "It's just what?" He watched Tony slowly move into the lounge room and look around.

"You know, I don't know if I told you this, but I placed all of the furniture in the same place as we had it when I was little, for some reason…" His fingers trailed across the back of the sofa chair. "I just felt the need to do it." Settling into the chair, he sighed.

"And that's okay," Cabot told him, sitting on the chair arm and running his hand through Tony's wild and woolly black hair. "And that's okay."

Tony turned his face up to Cabot. "Is it? Yeah…I think it is."

Cabot smiled, kissed Tony on the forehead, and slid onto his lap.

*****

"We've done the albums for you, love," Olivia told her nephew when he and Cabot turned up at his grandparents' home for Sunday lunch. "We managed to buy some nice ones for all of those photos and put them in order."

263

"Thanks, Aunt Liv." Tony kissed her cheek, hugged his grandma and Veronica, then strolled into the lounge room to hug his siblings and cousins. "How you kids doin'?" He ruffled Nathan's hair and sat on his chair arm to watch TV.

"Good. We saw Dad yesterday," Nathan replied. "He wants us to come live with him, and reckons he'll sue you and Aunt Liv for custody." His teenage brow was puckered with worry. He'd enjoyed staying with his aunt and uncle, and felt safe where he was. He didn't want to live with his dad, and his girlfriend and her bratty sons who'd picked on him and bullied him. It had been a horrible experience the last year or so, having to deal with her coming into the family and their home. And while he still loved his dad, he also knew that his dad had loved the luxury of living in a nice house with no bills to pay for. They'd just been left to fend for themselves. And the girlfriend certainly didn't care. Her kids were treated better than they were.

"And how is your dad?" Tony asked cautiously, not wanting to cause a problem.

"Fine," Michelle replied, lazing on the sofa with her latest *Haus of Stefan* look book that their online customers received with purchase. She still couldn't believe that her brother was dating Steele Stefan, brother of Diana, cousin of Alena. And she studied Cabot as he stood beside Tony. "When are you going back to modelling, Steele? I see you and Phoenix are in the latest catalogue." She held it up for all to see.

Cabot blushed and thanked her for buying their products. "Antonio and I have already done a couple of photo shoots this year. We average one or two a month at this point, and *always* model for *Haus of Stefan*. You'll see us in every catalogue. Thanks for being a fan."

"Your sister and cousins are gorgeous and I'd love to meet them, and have a tour of *Haus of Stefan's* head office. I'll be going to fashion school, so would love to see a real fashion house firsthand." Michelle was a little nervous being so bold, but she knew if she didn't take a chance, it wasn't going to happen. Her eyes flitted from Cabot's proud smiling face to Tony's grinning one. He knew what she was up to.

"I'll let D and A know that you're a fan, and when you come to Mykonos we'll organise a tour," Cabot told her, proud of the fact his sister and cousins were so world-wide known. Even his future sister-in-law was a fan. Who knew?

"Cool, can't wait. I love the current summer collection, and the autumn collection that's coming looks awesome. I love Alexis in this dress." She held up the book and pointed to Alexis standing, hands on hips, legs apart, looking straight into the camera wearing a black leather bustier dress with a crisp white shirt underneath, and chunky black thigh high patent leather boots. "She looks edgy and sexy and H.O.T. hot. Can I meet her, too? I love her hair short like that."

"Sure. You'll get to meet the whole family when you come over." Cabot was chuffed that his potential sister-in-law already loved his family, but was also wary of his family being used by Michelle to get ahead in fashion. "There's more of us now. Diana's married with baby Adam, Alexis is dating a hot doctor, Antonio and Dom are still single, but busy. You've got my parents, uncles, grandparents. We're all there most of the time."

"Cool. Are Summer and Melody there too?" she continued, looking at a two-page spread of the twins showing off brightly coloured wool dresses and jumpsuits.

"They live down the road with their brother Nick, who's Danté's best friend. All of us kids model for *H.O.S.* except for Dom. He's not into fashion, just his music."

"Cool music too," David finally piped up from the other easy chair closest to the TV. He'd been googling the family like his brother and sister, and if he went into music, he knew he could learn a lot from Dom and Danté. "It'd be cool to see them in person. He really knows how to make music."

"He does." Cabot was proud of his cousins and siblings for all they had achieved and had told them over New Year's. As part of his therapy, he'd decided to be more open about his love for his family, telling them often how he felt, and he was proud of all their achievements. "Learned from Uncle Pedro and Aunt Angie. She's Juilliard trained and Uncle P's been a DJ since he was eighteen. Runs in the family, it's in the blood. Just like modelling and acting is in mine, Antonio's and Diana's."

"And you're all a very good-looking family, love." Olivia walked up behind him and put a hand on his shoulder. "We've read up on your family to see who Tony's been hanging out with, and you've got quite a large ensemble going for you. We know our Tony's going to be safe in their hands."

"Aw, thank you." Cabot's blush raced up his neck. "That means a lot. I know they won't mind having you all over for a holiday if you have the time. You can meet everyone, and spend a week or two enjoying the Mykonos lifestyle. It's quite laid back and relaxing during the day. And the weather's beautiful. I don't give it enough credit." He wistfully thought back over the years he was growing up there.

"It *is* very beautiful," Tony added, sliding an arm around Cabot's waist and pulling him close. "So are the people."

"Aw, Tony." The blush hit Cabot's hairline and he went giggly.

"And you seem very happy for being there." Olivia smiled. "But lunch is ready, so let's go."

They gathered in the dining room and ate Alice's roast beef and dumplings, and had Spotted Dick for dessert. Afterwards, the kids settled back in the lounge room to watch more TV, and the adults went into the adjoining sitting room where Olivia presented Tony with the five photo albums. "Here you go, love."

"Thanks, Aunt Liv." Tony set four of them on the coffee table in front of him and flipped through the first. "Ah... Dad..." The pages were full of his parents. His mother pregnant with him, his dad rubbing her bulging belly, and then to his parents holding him while he slept in their arms. Pictures of his first and second birthdays, Christmases, Mother's and Father's Days. "Oh..."

Cabot was beside him on the couch, sitting so close their thighs were touching at their full length. His arm was around Tony's shoulder. "Aw, Tony. Your parents looked so happy."

"They were," Alice commented, wistfully remembering back. "Cynthia was so happy. I'd never seen her happier. She definitely met her soulmate in your father, Tony. She couldn't stop gushing about him when she came back from her holiday. Showed everyone all of the photos she'd taken, gushed about his phone calls, him, their future life together. She was so happy. And then we finally met him, and he was such a polite young man. So in love with our Cynthia." She brushed her tears away. "She became pregnant before marrying, as you know." Smiling at her grandson, she added, "Your mother was so happy when you came along. Her little family was complete."

"Were they thinking of having more kids?" Tony gazed sadly from his grandmother to the photos. "The house is big enough."

"Kids were definitely on the cards," Veronica said from the couch opposite. She and her husband, Michael, relaxed while watching the events unfold. "She just wanted to enjoy a couple of years with you first."

Tony came to the end of the first album and sadly closed it on the past. A sigh escaped him, and the overwhelming burden of not having both parents weighed heavily on his shoulders. He quietly explained to them all that he'd found out from Carlos and Vivian, and then what they had unearthed in Spain, especially the letter his father had left the lawyers, telling them to lie to Cynthia about his and his mother's deaths. "I was even wondering if I should have Mum reburied there to be with Dad, but then...she didn't die there with him. She died twenty-five years later in another country. There would be no point in digging her up. Their souls are in two different places."

"That was a sweet thought," Alice told him. "But you're right. Your mum had moved on, and she hated that estate when your dad died. We only ever went there for the wedding, and she never went back. Only your dad did when he left to deal with his father's burial, and then his mother's..." she trailed off.

"Yeah," came out softly. Tony flicked through the second and third albums, remembering birthdays, school days, plays and sport. "Mum was still so depressed." He picked up the fourth and flipped through from start to finish. "Now she's happy."

"Because of Brian," Veronica muttered. "He actually gave a damn in the beginning. He was wonderful to your mother, wonderful to you—"

"And then he had his accident, and I inherited a fortune and came out, and then he became mean and intolerant," Tony interrupted.

"Yes, unfortunately," Olivia said. She glanced over at all of the kids in the lounge room to make sure none was listening. Her four were there, along with Veronica's three.

Tony picked up the fifth album of his eighteenth, his twenty-first and twenty-fifth birthdays with a few extra pictures dotted in between, and only a couple of photos after. He closed the book and remembered back to when he'd returned from Spain after his twenty-fifth. He was so happy to show his mother the photos of the place and tell her all he'd done and what he'd found, but she just burst into tears and didn't stop crying for four days. He'd held her while she cried, but she wouldn't tell him why. And he'd known for years that Christmas and New Years were particularly hard times for his mother. She'd gone without his father at Christmas and New Year's 1980, only to lose him a few weeks later. January was always a hard time in the DeLuca Smith household. "Did Brian know?"

"About your dad?" Olivia asked.

"About all of it? Any of it?" Tony sighed. "He clearly didn't know about the house, but did he ever know the full extent of what happened?"

"I think Cynthia glossed over the details." Veronica drained her wine and placed the glass on the coffee table then sat back and crossed her legs. "Just told him what the lawyer had told her. That he'd died in an accident. But then, she didn't know any better."

"And she clearly never read the letter he left her." Tony pulled the unopened letters out of his satchel and laid them on his lap. "Didn't she want to know what he had written?"

"I think she was too devastated," Alice replied, remembering how her daughter had fallen apart after being told. "Your mum was in a comatose state for nearly a year, passing through life, but not seeing, or hearing. The first anniversary was horrible. She cried for days."

"I remember. She always looked at the white album and cried. On the same day every year." Tony stared down at the envelopes, wondering if it was time.

"They won't open themselves, Tony," Olivia said softly, watching the multitude of expressions flit over his face. "If you want some privacy, you can pop out to the pergola, or use the spare room."

"Oh, I don't know if I ever want to read them. I have one that Mum left me when she died. She gave all four of us letters telling us how much she loved us. But why would she write another one just for me? And why did she never read Dad's letter to her, or Dad's letter to me? Why didn't I get that when I turned twenty-one?" He glanced at each of his aunts and grandmother and saw they had no more answers than he did. "When I went to Spain five years ago and found the vault, there was so much paperwork, and so much to deal with, that I left it for the family lawyers. I didn't find my dad's things there, and was only told about Dad's letter to me. But I didn't get it. He said it had gone to Mum. When I got back and asked her, she said she didn't know anything about it."

"She more than likely forgot," Olivia said. "I dealt with all of the paperwork at the time, calling the family lawyer, setting up all of the accounts so she had money to live on and you and the house were taken care of. Your mother was in too much shock to realise anything. And I can't remember where I put those letters, whether I put them in the wedding album, or gave them to the lawyers to deal with. But, she clearly got them back, or still had them if she put them with the rest of her belongings in the bank."

"She set up the bank account when I was eighteen. That was twelve years ago. She kept it up until I turned twenty-five, and then added all of the money I gave her to live on when I changed the rules of the estate. The estate paid for her funeral. It's paid for the house, it's paid for everything."

"And now, from the kindness of your heart, it's paying for your siblings' futures and care." Veronica smiled sadly at her nephew. "Your mum would want you to pursue your heritage, would want you to finish caring for your siblings."

"Yeah, she told me just days before she died when she gave me the key to the deposit box." Tony remembered back…

"You've always been a good boy, Tony." Cynthia weakly grasped his hand. "Your father and grandparents would be so proud of you. I'm proud of you," she rasped through a coughing fit and wiped her

mouth free from blood. "Just promise me you'll take care of your brothers and sister. I don't think Brian will do much of a job once I'm gone. You'll need to step up." The cancer on her lungs had taken its toll, and she knew her time was coming any day. Looking into Tony's eyes, she smiled sadly, noting how much he was growing into his father. "You have his looks," she whispered. "You look just like him now. Except you have my eyes, and your hair's a little redder. You've always been a good boy, Tony, and I know the last couple of years have been tough on the family. You in particular. You lost your dad when you were two, and now you're losing me. I'm so sorry, Tony."

"Oh, Mum, you have nothing to apologise for. You haven't done anything. You were the best mum you could be." He held her hand to his lips and kissed it. "I love you, Mum. I don't want you to die."

"I don't want to die either, my darling. Just like I didn't want your dad, or your grandparents to die. But we all do." Her baby boy had missed out on so much, and so had she. She'd missed out on her husband, the love of her life, the father of her child. And even though she had money to live on, and raise her son on, it didn't make up for not having her husband. Glancing around the room, she thought back to all the times Connie had stayed with them when Tony was a baby. She had doted on her grandson every time she'd come. If only she had hung on longer and willed herself to live. And Antonio. The accident was clearly a freak sign from God that he wanted all three DeLucas in a short amount of time. God works in mysterious ways, she thought. And I've never forgiven him for taking my Antonio. "My darling." She gently pulled Tony's hand to her mouth to kiss. "There's something I need to give you. Can you get me the small tin, just here under the mattress." She pointed to the side of the bed. "Up near the top, here."

He dug between the mattresses and pulled out a small tin. "Here. What's in it?"

"Open it for me. I'm too weak." She watched him open it and hold it out for her. Pulling back the material inside, she lifted out a small brass key belonging to a safety deposit box. Furtively, she pressed it into his hand. "You need to hide this. It's important. It contains all of the secrets *of your past. Keep it safe. Keep it secure. And only use it when I'm gone."*

He looked at the key. A small brass tag hung from it. *"What's it for?"*

"Answers." She wrapped his hand around it. *"Don't show anyone. Don't tell anyone. Say nothing to anyone. Promise me, Tony."*

He noted the pain and fear in her pale green eyes and his heart went out to her. *"Okay, Mum. I promise."*

"I can't believe I completely forgot all about it until we were in Spain, two years later." A sigh flew out of Tony. "Glad Brian only chucked my stuff in the shed and not the dump."

"So are we, considering we didn't even know she'd set it up," Alice murmured.

"But, Mr Monolo from the bank knew, so I'm surprised he didn't get in contact," Tony said. "We met when he came to the house. He knew where I lived, so he could have come by."

"Either way, it's over and done," Olivia replied. "Do you feel ready for those letters now?"

"No." He fingered the three cream envelopes. "I never will be. What could my father have to say in a letter that meant more than staying alive for me? He killed himself. He took his own life over his mother and left me, *his son*, behind. What could he possibly have to say to me?"

"You won't know until you read it," Alice told him. Her heart ached for her grandson; losing one parent was bad enough, but losing two would have been horrendously emotional for a young man. But then, Tony had dealt with a lot over the last couple of years.

My son, Antonio DeLuca II was written across one envelope. *My darling wife Cynthia* was written on a second. And *My Darling Tony* was written on the third. "I know I'm going to cry, that's why I thought it would be better to do it here with all of you…" His head shook lightly. "Just looking at the writing on the envelopes is making me emotional. I'm not sure I'll ever be ready for what's in these letters."

"Then don't read them today," Philip said. "Read them when you get home. Take a break from the family, read them in the place you grew up. Where your parents first lived. Where your mum passed away. Read them in the place that means the most."

Heaving a ragged breath, Tony slowly let it go. "Yes, yes, I'll do that. I'll wait until we're home, and then take the week to emotionally deal with it. Good idea, Grandpa. I just can't do it now." Sliding the letters back into his satchel, he checked his watch. "What's for tea?"

*****

They arrived home around eight-thirty, and after a hot shower, settled onto the sofa in the lounge room to watch some TV.

"Are you going to read the letters?" Cabot asked, munching on a red licorice stick. It was the only flavour he could tolerate.

"I don't know," Tony murmured, his eyes not leaving the screen. "I know I said I would…but I don't know."

"There's no rush, you know." Cabot entwined his fingers with Tony's. "You don't actually need to read them if you don't want to. You didn't know about them your entire life. No need to worry about them now."

"I know." Tony's left arm was flung sideways over his head as he lay slouched on the sofa. A part of him didn't want to know. A part of him did. Except he knew he wasn't ready for what was in them. "What if they leave me with more questions than answers?"

"Won't know until you read them." Cabot pulled another stick of licorice from the bag and studied his fingernails. They needed a good manicure and a soak in Vaseline for moisture. Cleaning out a house had a toll, and busted nails was it. He also had a photo shoot with Antonio coming up, and needed to look his best. Long gone were the days of black nail polish and blue-black eyeliner that he used to wear when he went out partying as Steele Stefan. The year 2008 was a fresh start on many levels. Personal, business, emotional and psychological levels, as well as on a health level. Everything had changed in 2007, and this year was getting better with every day.

The energy drained from Tony. "What if I don't want the answers? What if it will just make things worse?"

"Won't know till you read them."

"What if I just end up a bawling mess?"

"Why would that be a bad thing?" Cabot looked at his lover. "Considering how you fell apart last November when you found out about your family, I'd say you still have a hell of a lot of emotions inside you. Maybe it's time they come out. Unless you want them to stay inside."

"I don't know," Tony mumbled. His eyes were glassy and blurred. "I just…don't want to be pushed into reading them." He abruptly sat up and pulled his hand from Cabot's. "I just…want to read them when *I'm* ready."

Startled, Cabot stopped munching. "We didn't say you couldn't, just that you won't have any answers *unless* you read them. When you do, is up to you. We're not forcing you."

"I know, I know." Tony ran his hands over his face and through his hair. "Maybe it's being back in this place." His eyes glanced over the room. There were photos on the wall of him and his mother, and framed pictures on desks and tables. "It was nice of my aunts and grandmother to get all of these photos done. But by God, it's making the memories slush around in my head. I'm so overwhelmed, I feel drunk, or something. Unable to comprehend, or think straight. The memories are fogging me up, and I don't know if I want to read them, or not." Pushing up from the couch, Tony stormed through the dining and kitchen and out the back door. He strode down the back stairs and into the middle of the yard where he stood looking up to the sky, breathing heavily. The back yard had been tidied and cleaned up as well during the process, and smelt of freshly watered grass.

"Tony?" Cabot quietly moved to his lover's side. "No one's pressuring you. If you're not ready to read those letters, then don't. If you want to wait until we go back to Mykonos and stop on the way to see Xanthe to talk it through like last year, then we'll do that. No one said you had to read them yet. It's up to you. *But,* they're clearly affecting you."

A sigh from deep in Tony's gut came up through his windpipe and expelled itself into the night. "I know. I'm just so overwhelmed with memories of Mum, and Dad, and why she left all of that stuff in the bank and didn't tell me. And why Dad told the lawyers to lie about how he died. Argh." He grabbed two handfuls of hair on his scalp. "*Why, why* did they do this? Why me, why them, why us?"

"Aw, Tony." Cabot rubbed his back to soothe him. "I'm so sorry you lost your dad and then your mum. I don't know what it's like, but I feel so bad for you. I sense your pain and it hurts." After being counselled by Xanthe for so long he'd learned to tune into his empathy and feel for others and their pain. And he was feeling Tony's.

"Ah...thanks Cabot...that's sweet. And true. I am in pain." Tony glanced at his lover and smiled softly. "I'll decide when I read them. Okay?"

"Of course." Cabot nodded his consent and looked up at the night sky. "It always looks so different in another country, or city. New York, Mykonos, Australia, now London. The night sky is always the same, but it just looks so different."

"Yeah." Tony's gaze wandered over the black velvet sky with its billion fairy lights all shining brightly. "Even in Spain it looked different. Even as a little kid it looked different. Now, as an adult, it still looks different. *Everything* is different." He tried to breathe through the overwhelming suffocation that suddenly arose. "My dad's gone, his death, my grandparents' deaths, Mum's death, me contracting HIV after an assault. Throwing Brian out of my house, taking the kids and being responsible for them financially. Everything is different and I can't breathe." His body bent at a right angle, he rested his hands on his knees to keep himself up, and he sucked in great gulps of air.

"It's okay, just breathe slowly, Tony." Cabot continued the back rub. "Just breathe slowly. In...and out...and in...and out..."

After a few moments, Tony straightened. "I'm okay...just...wow...I can't believe how suffocating memories can be."

"They can be if you let them and don't put them into perspective. Maybe that's what you need to do. Put your feelings about your grandparents into one box, your feelings about your dad into another, your feelings about your mum into a third, and anything else you've got can go into a fourth box. And then, when you're clear-headed, and the weight has left your shoulders, you can tackle one box at a time. But…" He stared at Tony until he got his attention. "I don't think you can fully do that until you've read those letters. Maybe it's time to clear house…"

Tony's smile was grim at Cabot's choice of words. "Maybe it is."

They walked back inside and watched night-time TV until well after midnight when they retired to bed. Tony's bed. Upstairs in the master suite. The room that was originally his parents', and became his when his mother and Brian had moved downstairs after Brian's injury.

Lying in bed, sleep was anything but peaceful. Visions, dreams, nightmares. They haunted Tony and made him toss and turn until he woke with a shuddering jerk into a sitting position.

Gasping, he took a moment to calm himself and breathed in the cool London air that drifted through the open window. Waiting for his heart to slow back to normal, he recalled that night in Manzanares at the family estate when he'd felt his father's presence. He'd *sensed* him, *seen* him. How that photo that he'd placed on the bedside cupboard had suddenly been on his chest, and who or *what* could have put it there. He knew it was his father. Who else would place a photo of Antonio holding baby Tony on *his* chest? Both his grandmother and father were sensed there. And he wasn't the only one to sense them. Viv, having known Connie for years, had sensed her friend, too.

Sighing until depletion, Tony glanced at Cabot and saw he was still asleep, curled into a little ball with his hands under his chin. Smiling, he turned his head to look at his travel clock on the bedside cupboard. Not seeing the usual glow of it, he carefully clicked on the lamp and saw the letters sitting in front of the clock, blocking the view of it. "What the hell…?" he muttered. *I didn't put them there. They were in my satchel… How the hell…?* His head moved, turning in each direction to see if anyone was in the room. But except for him and Cabot, there was no one. *How the hell…?* Casting another glance at Cabot, he picked up the envelopes, turned off the light, and quietly left the room.

"Okay," he whispered. "If this is your way of getting me to read these letters, Mum, you got my attention." He quickly descended the stairs and walked into the sitting room-come-office, shut the door, and turned on the light. The room was cold and uninviting, and he knew it. He sensed it. That it wasn't the place to read those letters. Quickly, he left the room and moved into the lounge, but that didn't feel right either. Wondering where he needed to go, he found himself moving toward the back of the house and into the guest bedroom.

"It's you, Mum," he whispered. "Who else would have brought me here?" After closing the door, he found his way over to the bed and managed to turn on the bedside light. It illuminated the soft blue walls, and pink and peach covers and accents. Curling up on the bed, he thought back to the final days of his mother. The moments they'd shared, the topics they'd discussed, and how much she'd told him she loved him. And even as she was leaving, she told him she hoped to see his father to escort her to the other side before she finally left. She wanted to see him one last time.

"Oh, Mum. I hope you got your wish." He stared at the letters in his hands, and, settling into the pile of pillows, he kept the one from her and laid the other two on the bed beside him. Compelled, he carefully opened the seal and pulled out the letter, and with trembling hands, he unfolded it and began to read…

To my darling Tony, my son.

I am so proud of you and how you turned out. Even though you didn't have your father growing up, and Brian was only a substitute, I clearly did a good enough job to have a handsome young man to call my son. I know I already left you a letter. I left all four of my children one, but this letter delves a little deeper into your history that I didn't want anyone else knowing about, or seeing.

I've done some things, Tony, as you would have seen by now since you're reading this letter. First, I saved all of the rent and board money you gave me into an account in your name. You had no reason to pay it as your father's estate paid for you anyway. So, I saved it, along with my leftover money from the estate, so that you could have it back to do whatever with. And when you turned twenty-five, that money went in too. Thank you so much for saving me, my baby boy.

Following in your father's footsteps by having me be taken care of by the estate. Your father did all of that before he died. And that's what I want to tell you about.

In the deposit box, you would have found our wedding album, still intact, plus all of your pictures that I pulled out of the albums so Brian didn't throw them away after my death. They are yours, so they go to you.

Second, my and your father's wedding rings, plus all of my jewellery he and his parents gave me are in an envelope. Your father's ring was returned to me after his death by the family lawyers who visited soon after your father passed. Life was tough after that night. That visit. I mourned and grieved for your father so much, that still, come January every year, I still grieve for him.

Antonio is the love of my life. I met him in 1977 in Mykonos at a beach bar. It was June, and I had saved up for three years to go on holiday with my friends. I met him a couple of days after arriving and fell, not only into bed with him that night, but madly in love as well. We spent the next twelve days together, and I begged him to come to London with me, but he had his work commitments. I admired that about your father, along with so many other things. That once he committed to something, he stuck by it and saw it through.

Once he came to London in November we were inseparable, and I quickly became pregnant with you. As you know, by the wedding album, we married in May 1978, and I had you in August. We wed on the family estate in Spain, and spent two weeks in Madrid for our honeymoon. They were the best weeks of my life. The whole time I had your father was the best time of my life, and I have never forgotten it, or him.

What happened to your grandmother was shocking. Your grandfather died in October 1980, and from what your father found out, he had been sleeping with men and contracted many diseases, even dying in the arms of one of his lovers. But that's a different story I hope never has anything to do with you. Over the years I've thought about it and figured one of those was probably HIV/AIDS, to which I say, I am so sorry, Tony. And, I hope, now that you've come out as gay as well, that you do everything you can to be careful and not contract it, or any other disease from being gay. Your father flew out to Spain to be with his mother. She loved you so much and stayed here often, as you may remember. She became violently ill, and your father not only had his father to deal with, but his mother as well. The morgue dragged out Stephano's autopsy and they didn't get his body back for burial until December. That's when your grandmother became seriously ill and your dad was calling every day. I told him time and time again that I'd pack up and come down there to see him for Christmas and New Year, so none of us spent it alone. But your dad insisted that we stay home to be safe in case we caught your grandmother's diseases.

After your grandfather's funeral, your father and I had discussed bringing your grandmother here to London for treatment, but it was too late, and wasn't meant to be. Your grandmother passed away, and I didn't see, or hear from your father again. The lawyer came about a week later and told me your father had died in an accident while making burial plans. I automatically went into a comatose state and didn't comprehend anything else he said. But from the paperwork your aunt sorted out, that he had left that night, the family lawyers buried your father next to his parents at the estate in Spain. I not only missed out on my parents'-in-law's funerals, but my own husband's. I hadn't seen Antonio since October. Three months I went without my husband. You went without your father. I never got to see him, kiss him, be with him again. And you missed out on him forever.

I am so sorry, my darling boy. I'm so sorry that you had to go through that. I didn't know what was in the envelope, but I definitely remembered it when I was told I was dying. I knew I had to make sure it went to you, and found out from your aunt which bank had dealt with it all. She told me she put everything in a vault for safe keeping. I asked Mr Monolo to bring it, and that's when I saw your father's wedding ring had been in the parcel, along with the two letters. One to me, and one to you, both from your father. Mr Monolo told me the family lawyers had been in touch to sort it all out in 1981, and that the rest of the paperwork was with them in Spain. But then, you visited *after inheriting your trust fund, so you know that anyway. That surprised me, that did. I had completely forgotten about it until the lawyer turned up. Oh, God, how it made memories come racing back.*

Your father was the love of my life, Tony, and I have never forgotten him. I see him every day when I look at you, my baby boy. You are so much like your father, not just in name and looks. Your manners and demeanour. You take after him in every way. Except for being gay. You take after your grandfather that way. I want you to continue as you are, and take pride in your Spanish Colombian heritage. Whether you ever visit the family home again is up to you, but remember, there are good and bad memories there, and many I wish I didn't have. I hope you can forgive me for never giving you your father's letter, or his ring. I'd completely forgotten about those things until now. I've added the love letters we sent each other to the package, so you can see how much we loved each other. I just don't know why he didn't love me enough to come home earlier. But it's too late now.

As I finish up, know this, I love you. Yes, more than David, Michelle and Nathan. And I love your father more than I could ever love Brian. He was a good man that made me laugh and smile again, and I knew he could take care of us and provide what we were missing. A father for you, and a husband for me. I'm sorry he's been such a bully these last few years. That wasn't fair to you and not right on his part. I saw that the injury made him angry and abusive, and he took it out on you, and sometimes me. I also saw how much he expected from you after you inherited and that wasn't fair either.

I've had talks with the kids about their behaviour toward you and asked, for my sake, that they stop and accept you regardless of what their father tells them. Until the last few years, we'd been a family unit, but Brian looks set to destroy that, and I'm sorry.

There's not much left to tell you, so I'll sign off now. Never forget how much I love you and your father. Never forget how much your heritage means to you and meant to him. Never forget how much he loved us, as did your grandparents, regardless of what happened, and how much you end up finding out. And if you're wondering why I haven't read your father's letter to me, I just couldn't. Even if what he had written made all the pain in the world go away, I just couldn't read it. I hope you do, and find some semblance of peace after I'm gone with whatever demons you have over this whole thing. Your dad didn't mean to leave us, it was a horrendous mistimed accident that took him away, and he wasn't to blame. I hope, if you feel angry, that you can forgive him for it, and me, for not remembering that letter sooner.

I love you, my baby boy, my Antonio Stephano DeLuca II. I always have, and I always will. I'll see you again one day soon. I love you.

Mum.

"Aw, Mum," Tony stuttered through his tears. The letter fell from his hands. "If only you knew the truth about Dad. He didn't die in an accident, he killed himself to be with his mother. Ah, Jesus..." He grabbed a pillow and smothered his cries as his heart poured out in pain. He had no idea how long he lay curled up, but when he pulled the pillow away daylight was filtering around the curtains. Sniffing, he wiped his face and re-read the letter, then carefully folded it, and placed it back in the envelope before sitting it on the bedside cupboard. Next, he picked up his father's letter to his mother and carefully opened it.

My darling Cynthia,

I'm writing you this letter to tell you how much I love you. With my father's passing, and you not being here, my love for you has grown exponentially. I miss you so much. When I first saw you at the beach bar you were eyeing off Carlos, but soon, your eyes found their way to me and stayed there. I'm not sure if you fully comprehend just how much I love you. You are my life, my love, my soulmate. I love you with everything I have and all of the man that I am. I thank God every day that I have you and baby Tony in my life, and that you have stood by me all these months, understanding why you couldn't come here, and why I couldn't come home yet.

It's New Year's Day, baby Tony's third, and the first that I haven't been here. I am absolutely gutted that I was not there to see him open his presents this year, so I hope you've taken lots of photos and video footage of him. I'm hoping for all of this to be over soon, and I'll be back in the loving arms of my wife, the beautiful Cynthia. You are my beloved, my one and only. I love you. I'll see you soon.

Antonio xxoo New Year's Day, 1980.

Air escaped Tony's lungs. "Oh, Dad. If you loved Mum so much why did you bloody kill yourself not even a week later?" He put the letter down and considered it. *Clearly dated New Years, clearly written before Grandma died. Clearly didn't know she was going to kill herself, and clearly before you thought of killing yourself. So, it wasn't a letter about killing yourself. Well, it's a pity Mum didn't read the letter after all. But then, she would have only been reading what she already knew. That you loved her.*

Folding the one-page letter back into the envelope, he picked up the last.

My son, Antonio Stephano DeLuca II

And now I'm wondering if I'm ready to read this…

Taking a deep breath and letting it out slowly, he slid his finger under the flap and carefully opened it. Pulling out the letter, he unfolded the paper and started from the beginning.

To my son, Antonio II,

I am so proud of you, here on your twenty-first birthday, at the family estate here in Spain, celebrating it with all of your family and friends just as I did many a decade ago. I have kept this letter for many years, having written it at New Year's 1980. Currently, your grandfather has passed away and your grandmother is very ill, so I'm not there with you and your mother in London. With the death of the great Spanish bullfighter, your grandfather, Stephano DeLuca, it has made me very aware of how short life can be. You are only two and a bit and celebrating your third Christmas and New Year as of this writing. But I hope to be back with you soon, and have celebrated every year since into the one to mark the year you are now twenty-one.

It's now 1999 that you are reading this, and I hope to be alive and still married to your mother when we see out firstborn son celebrate his manhood. By now, I have given you the same tokens that I received for my birthdays. For my sixteenth, I received a white gold ID bracelet with my name on it. For my eighteenth, a white gold bull pendant necklace, and for my twenty-first, a white gold signet ring with the bullhead insignia with emerald for eyes. You see that even today I wear all of those pieces with the white gold Cartier watch I received for my twenty-fifth.

And so, today, on your twenty-first, when you finally become a man, I have presented you with your own bull insignia ring to show off your heritage. I hope you will wear all of your pieces with pride as a DeLuca. But I will understand if they are not for you, and you choose not to wear them.

I want you to be your own independent man, just as I was, who goes out into the world and makes his own mark on it. We have raised you to be the exceptional man that you are, and I hope you continue being. You have made me so proud. So proud that I have an exceptional son like you. Your mother and I have done a wonderful job of raising you, and I am so proud of how you've turned out. Now, go out into the world and make your mark in it, my son, and know that I will always be here for you. Your mother and I will always be here for you if you ever need us in any way. But with the hard-working exceptional man you've become, I know that you won't. Go out and make your mark, and make us prouder than we already are. I love you, you are my son, my namesake, Antonio Stephano DeLuca II.

Love, your father,

Antonio Stephano DeLuca I. New Year's Day, 1980.

"Oh, Dad…" whispered out of Tony's mouth and he glanced up to see Cabot standing in the doorway, red-eyed and crying. He opened his arms to envelop his lover, and sobbed from the bowels of his soul.

*****

In the months following the lack of revelations in his parents' letters, Tony held heartfelt discussions with both his family, future in-laws, and Xanthe Metlos to try and sort out what was going on in his head. In the end, he decided to try and set the past aside and move on with the future. And that meant fulfilling his mother's promise to look after his siblings.

In the July school holidays, he took his entire family to Madrid for a week, and then a week at the DeLuca family property in Manzanares in between summer rentals. He showed his siblings his family history, where their mother had married his father, and showed them pictures of the wedding.

In August, he took them all to Mykonos for two weeks and introduced them to the Stephanopoulos family, where they spent time learning how to get along as a family. Michelle got her tour of *Haus of Stefan* in Athens and got to hang out with Diana, Alena and Alexis, as well as Summer and Melody. David and Nathan got a tour of *SB3* and *Sync*, and hung out with Dom, Danté and Nick. They went sailing on the family yacht, and enjoyed Jenny's Sunday roast chicken, and Tomas and Roger's lamb and salad recipes. And Alice finally had those conversations with Jenny over their grandsons dating.

Then it was back to London for new schools in September when he tracked down his three best friends, Will, Robbie and Travis, and had heartfelt discussions with them, apologising, and catching them up on everything that had happened in the last few years. The HIV, the arrest of the attacker, meeting Cabot and his family, and everything he'd learned about his own family. They accepted his apologies, and commiserated over his mother and the HIV. Robbie came clean and admitted he'd recently contracted HIV too, after much screwing around, so he could hardly hold anything against Tony, now, could he. They all promised to catch up like old times, while making new times, at the same time.

It all started coming together and mending itself to the best of everyone's abilities.

New schools, new courses, renewed friendships, a new life, and a new path for this broken man and his family to walk down together.

2012

May fourteenth, 2012, was beautiful and warm. The flowers were in full bloom, the aroma was heaven sent, and the white marble pavilion was full of loved ones, family, and friends, the people they wanted to share their private moment with. The house was full, as were the local inns, the grounds were blanketed with spring leaves, and everything was perfect for such a monumentous month.

Today, four years after Tony had proposed to Cabot in the white marble dance pavilion on the DeLuca property, they were both there again to make it happen. The fact that gay marriage still wasn't legal didn't stop them, for the family had once again come through. And just like thirty-five years earlier when Jenny had made it happen for Tomas and Roger, Carlos and Viv made it happen for their son and future son-in-law.

The family stood in a semi-circle around Cabot and Tony as they stood holding hands. Dressed in back wedding suits, they looked mature, and madly in love. Beyond their smiling faces, Stephano, Connie and Antonio stood over their graves watching their baby get married with tears in their eyes and smiles on their faces.

"Do you, Antonio Stephano DeLuca II, take Cabot Conroy Stephanopoulos to be your wedded husband? To have and to hold, for richer or poorer, in sickness and in health, till death do you part?" Carlos asked, bible in hand. They were standing at a portable altar in front of the boys, and facing the tree the family was buried under.

"I do." Tony's smile was whiter than the marble they were standing on, and he stared excitedly into his lover's bright blue eyes.

"And do you, Cabot Conroy Stephanopoulos, take Antonio Stephano DeLuca II to be your wedded husband? To have and to hold, for richer or poorer, in sickness and in health, till death do you part?" Carlos asked his beaming son.

Cabot's grin matched Tony's as he stared at his lover of nearly five years, and his knees threatened to buckle out from under him. "I do. Oh, God, I do."

"Then, by the power vested in me as your father and father-in-law, I now pronounce you, husband and husband. You may kiss the bri- husband," Carlos stumbled, but laughed in recovery.

With matching grins, Tony and Cabot gazed lovingly into each other's eyes, cupped each other's stunned face, and kissed.

Connie's hands flew to her mouth as tears poured down her face. Her only grandbaby was getting married, and she wasn't there to hug and hold him and welcome her best friend Vivian's son into her family. Oh, how she'd love to sit and chat to Viv again. But she couldn't. Because she was dead. By her own hand.

Antonio tried holding back his tears, mentally kicking himself that he wasn't there in physical form to celebrate with his son. At least he got to sit and watch as they slept in his old room. But it wasn't the same. It never had been, and never would be, all because of his stupid selfish choice at taking his own life. And he'd searched high and low for Cynthia, unable to contain his excitement at seeing her again, to take in her beauty and remember when they got married there in the disco ball pavilion. He'd hoped to sit by her bed and marvel at her beauty. But she wasn't there. Which meant she had moved on into her own realm. And that meant he would never see her again. His heart dropped into the pitiful bowels of hell. All by his own hand.

Stephano, well, he stood there beaming proudly that his one and only grandchild had turned out just like him. But he was pissed that he'd changed the house to his own liking. The house was no longer his. His life was no longer his. History was no longer his. And he hated it.

The family crowded around, hugging, kissing, and slapping on the back as Cabot and Tony made their way through receiving congratulations from everyone.

Diana hugged her brother. "I love you, Cab, congratulations, you've finally grown up."

"Aw, thanks, D." He squeezed back then let go to hug Charles who held their one-year-old daughter Jaqueline in one arm, and had a hold of five-year-old Adam with the other. "Hey, kiddos, Charles." He moved on to Alena and her husband of one year, the gorgeous Italian American singer-musician, Luca Saint. Alexis, who was fresh out of her five-year relationship with Lorenzo, was single and ready to mingle, and Dom and Danté were still single as well. Mike and Maggie Gatos were there with their kids Summer, Melody, and Nick. All three were on the lookout for hot Spanish men and women. Doctors Dan Ardent and Derek Blaine were as proud as punch of their boys and all they had achieved, and Xanthe Metlos was there as well. Simon and Deidre Dencott were there with their kids, Stella and Liam, as well as varying friends of Cabot's, along with Tony's grandparents, aunts, uncles, cousins, his siblings, and three best friends.

Yes, May was going to be a monumental month indeed, as it also would have been Antonio and Cynthia's thirty-fourth wedding anniversary if they had still been alive and married. That's why Tony had chosen this date to marry, so it was the same as his parents. Same time, in the same place.

Tomorrow, they would be celebrating his brother-in-law Antonio's wedding to Maria Van Star, the beautiful French Italian model he'd met and fallen madly in love with three months earlier. And in a week's time, they would be celebrating Jenny's 84th birthday and 60th wedding anniversary with Spiros.

Yes, it was just another wedding in the Stephanopoulos family, and there was another to celebrate tomorrow, but until then, they would celebrate all night under the twinkling lights in the dancing pavilion, for the first time in thirty-four years.

About the Author

L.J. has been writing since 2006, when her first of many novels, *The Road To Vegas,* was born. In 2016 she created the *Porn Star Brothers* series about three sizzlingly hot Australian born Greek Island raised brothers who became the hottest porn stars in '70s America.

L.J. lives in Australia, loves '80s music, disaster movies, and collecting Jackie Collins books as Jackie is her inspiration and mentor.

L.J. Diva is the adult pen name for author Tiara King. You can find more about Tiara on her website; follow her on social media, or visit her publishing house, Royal Star Publishing.

Socials

tiaraking.com.au/ljdiva

royalstarpublishing.com.au

Sign up for *Tiara's* Newsletter...

Make sure you're always in the know and never miss free exclusives, the latest news, book updates, and so much more with newsletters from...

tiaraking.com.au

Have you read these?

THE PORN STAR BROTHERS SERIES

Carlos: Book 1
Pedro: Book 2
Tomas: Book 3
Retribution: Book 4
Porn Star Brothers
Forever
Love Never Dies
Stefan: The New Generation
DeLuca
Spiros & Jenny
And Always

THE ILLICIT THINGS SERIES

Her
Him
Madam X

A NOVEL INVESTIGATIONS SERIES

Designs in Crime
A Killer Plot
Murder on the Set
A Novel Investigation (omnibus)

Or these?

NOVELS

Burning Desires
Anything for You
Falling for London
The Road To Vegas
Hollywood Dreams
The Billionaire's Dirty Little Secret

SHORT STORIES

The Body
The Perfect Plot
The Star of Your Own Crime Scene